The Photograph

PENELOPE LIVELY

LARGE PRINT
Oxford

First published in Great Britain 2003
by the Penguin Group

Published in Large Print 2003 by ISIS Publishing Ltd,
7 Centremead, Osney Mead, Oxford OX2 0ES
by arrangement with Penguin Books Ltd.

British Library Cataloging in Publication Data
Lively, Penelope, 1933–
 The photograph.–Large print ed.
 1. Married people – Fiction
 2. Psychological fiction
 3. Large type books
 I. Title
 823.9'14 [F]

20020252

ISBN 0–7531–6901–0 (hb)
ISBN 0–7531–6902–9 (pb)

Printed and bound by Antony Rowe, Chippenham, England

Contents

Glyn

Kath.

Kath steps from the landing cupboard, where she should not be.

The landing cupboard is stacked high with what Glyn calls low-use material: conference papers and student references and offprints, including, he hopes, an offprint that he needs right now for the article on which he is working. The strata in here go back to his postgraduate days, in no convenient sequential order but all jumbled up and juxtaposed. A crisp column of *Past and Present* is wedged against a heap of tattered files spewing forth their contents. Forgotten students drift to his feet as he rummages, and lie reproachful on the floor: "Susan Cochrane's contributions to my seminar have been perfunctory ..." Labelled boxes of photographs — *Aerial, Bishops Munby 1976, Leeds 1985* — are squeezed against a further row of files. To remove one will bring the lot crashing down, like an ill-judged move in that game involving a tower of balanced blocks. But he has glimpsed behind them a further cache which may well include offprints.

On the shelf above he spots the gold-lettered spine of his own doctoral thesis, its green cloth blotched brown with age; on top of it sits a 1980s run of the *Yorkshire*

1

Archaeological Journal. Come to think of it, the contents of the landing cupboard are a nice reflection of his own trade — it is a landscape in which everything co-exists, requiring expert deconstruction. But he does not dwell on that, intent instead upon this increasingly irritating search.

He tugs at a file to improve his view of what lies beyond and, sure enough, there is a landslide. Exasperated, he gets down on hands and knees to shovel up this mess, and suddenly there is Kath.

A brown foolscap-size wallet file, with her loopy scrawl across the flap: *Keep!*

She smiles at him; he sees her skimpy dark fringe, her eyes, that smile.

What is she doing here, in the middle of all this stuff that has nothing to do with her? He picks up the file, stares. He cannot think how it got here. Everything of hers was cleared out. Back then. When she. When.

Hang on, though. Here underneath it are a couple of folders, also with her handwriting: *Recipes.* Since when did Kath go in for serious cooking, for heaven's sake? He opens the folder, flicks through the contents. Indeed, yes — cuttings from newspapers and magazines in the late 1980s, but petering out fairly rapidly, which signifies. He investigates the second folder, which contains receipted bills, many of them red-flagged second demands, which signifies also, and an incomplete series of bank statements, indicating a mounting overdraft.

It would seem that this assortment of her things got pushed in with his papers by mistake during the big clearing-out operation. The hurried, distracted clearing-out operation. Elaine had volunteered to sort out and dispose of Kath's possessions. She missed this lot. And here they have lain ever since, festering.

Well no, not exactly festering, but turning a little brown at the edges, doggedly degrading away as is everything else in here, doing what inanimate objects do as time passes, preparing to give pause for thought to those whose business is the interpretation of vanished landscapes.

The wallet file is brown anyway, so degradation is not much apparent. He dumps the folders on the floor and goes to sit on the top step of the stairs, holding the file.

He opens it.

Not much inside. Various documents, and a sealed brown envelope containing something stiff. Glyn sets this aside and goes through the rest.

A jeweller's valuation for a two-strand pearl necklace and a pair of drop pearl earrings. Originally her mother's, he seems to remember. Kath wore the earrings a lot.

Her medical card. And her birth certificate. Aha! So this is where that was, the absence of which caused considerable nuisance back then, necessitating a visit to Somerset House. No marriage certificate, one notes. That too had gone missing, making difficulties. And is still lost, it would seem. Not that that is, now, a problem.

Her O-level certificate. Seven subjects. A grades in all but one. Glyn scans this with some surprise. Well, well. Who'd have thought it?

The injunction on the file's flap was presumably to herself. This was the repository for items she knew that she must hang on to, but — knowing herself — that she knew she was only too likely to lose. He experiences a stir of fondness, which disconcerts him. And he has been entirely diverted from the hunt for that offprint, which is a matter of some urgency. Fondness is overtaken by annoyance; Kath is getting in the way of his work, which was not allowed, as she well understood.

There is also a National Savings Certificate for £5, bearing a date in the mid 1950s. When she was about eight, for heaven's sake. And some chequebook stubs and a Post Office savings book showing a balance of £14.58, and a clutch of letters, at which he glances. The letters are from Kath's mother, the mother who died when she was sixteen. Glyn sees no reason to be interested in these and pushes them back into the file unread.

He is left with a semi-opaque folder which turns out to hold a sequence of studio portraits of Kath. She is looking at him in glossy black and white, now made entirely manifest. Young Kath. A backlit Kath with bare shoulders, head turned this way or that, eyes to camera or demurely lowered, provocative smile, contemplative sideways gaze. These would date from the aspiring actress days, long before he knew her. Very young Kath.

Glyn studies these photos for quite a while.

Kath.

He returns everything to the file. There is now just this brown envelope. He notices for the first time that something is written on it. In her hand. Lightly pencilled.

DON'T OPEN — DESTROY.

And for whom is this second instruction intended?

He opens the envelope. Within are a photograph and a folded sheet of paper. He looks first at the photograph. A group of five people; grass beneath their feet, a backdrop of trees. Two members of the group, a man and a woman, have their backs to the photographer. Of the other three, Elaine can be identified at once, visible between the two whose faces cannot be seen. Near to her stand another man and woman, whom Glyn does not recognize.

One of the back-turned pair is Kath — he would know that outline anywhere, that stance. The someone else, the man, is at first a bit of a teaser. Familiar, surely — the rather long dark hair, the height, a good head taller than Kath. A slightly hunched way of standing.

Glyn brings the photo closer to his face for more minute inspection. And then he sees. He sees the hands. He sees that Kath and this someone, this man, have their hands closely entwined, locked together, pushed behind them so that as they stand side by side in this moment of private intimacy, this interlocking of hands would be invisible to the rest of the group.

Except to the photographer, who may or may not have been aware of what had been immortalized — the freeze-frame revelation.

And now Glyn recognizes the someone, the man. It is Nick.

He turns to the folded piece of paper that accompanied the photograph. He feels as though gripped by the onset of some incapacitating disease, but this paper requires attention.

Handwriting. A brief message. "I can't resist sending you this. Negative destroyed, I'm told. Blessings, my love."

No signature. None needed. Neither for Kath then, nor, now, for Glyn. Though confirmation is needed. Somewhere he will have an instance of Nick's handwriting. A signature. A letter from way back when he was a consultant, or some such nonsense, on that landscape history series Nick published and about which he endlessly and ignorantly enthused, as Nick always did.

The disease now has him by the throat. The throat, the gut, the balls. What he feels is . . . well, what he experiences is the most appalling stomach-churning, head-spinning cauldron of emotion. Rage is the top-note — beneath that a seethe of jealousy and humiliation, the whole primed with some kind of furious drive and energy. Where? When? Who? Who took this photograph? Who presumably passed it on to Nick and destroyed the negative?

The telephone rings, down in his study. Such is Glyn's powered state, his consuming purpose, that he is at once on his feet and halfway down the stairs to pick it up and snap: "I am not available. Sorry."

I cannot be doing with you right now because I have just learned that the woman who was once my wife apparently had an affair with her sister's husband — at some time yet to be identified. I am evidently a dupe, a cuckold. My understanding of the past has been savagely undermined. You will appreciate that for the foreseeable future this requires all my attention.

The phone stops. Of course. The answerphone is on.

Glyn returns to the top of the stairs. He sits holding the photo and the sheet of paper, looking from one to the other. Kath is everywhere now, the landing is full of her, and the staircase, and the big brimming treacherous cupboard; there are dozens of her, from different times and at different places, all talking at once, it seems. She curls up against him in bed, chattering about some film she has just seen. She puts her head round the door of his study, sunnily smiling, offering coffee. She skids ahead of him down a Cumbrian hillside, a small brilliant figure in a red jacket.

Questions are pouring through his head. When and where and who? But also — who else? Who else knew about this? Did Elaine know? Did Elaine connive? Was this matter common knowledge? Was he the innocent, the fool? Did people mutter to one another, throw him patronizing glances?

And for whom did she pencil that scribble on the envelope:

DON'T OPEN — DESTROY.

For herself?

For me?

Did she plan this, step by step? Did she plan this moment? That she would fall from the landing cupboard, set me ablaze?

Well, no. Because Kath was not like that. Kath never planned. Kath never looked beyond tomorrow. Kath seized the days as they came and discarded them when done.

No, she came across that file one day, into which she had shoved various items. She flicked through them — looking for something, maybe — and saw that envelope. Took out the photo and the sheet of paper, thought "Oops!", scribbled on the envelope, shoved everything back.

But why not just kill the photo, there and then?

Because she might want to look at it again. Because it meant something to her. Something? A great deal? Everything?

This file was a safe deposit in which she stowed away things that she needed to keep for reasons of expediency or convenience or . . . sentiment.

Why not segregate the categories? One file for documents, another for matters of the heart.

Because Kath never operated like that — in a careful, considered, rational way. She simply pushed these things into the same file because she wanted or needed to hang on to them. And on the occasion when she wrote these words on that envelope perhaps the phone rang while she was riffling through the contents. She put everything back, then had a sudden thought. She pulled out the envelope, quickly scribbled on it, returned it to the file, put the file in the drawer or the cupboard or wherever she kept it at the time, and forgot about it. She picked up the phone, cried out, "Oh, *hello* . . . How lovely to hear you, I'm so glad you've rung. I was going to . . . Listen, what are you doing today? I've got this sudden yen to go to —" And off she spun into another spontaneous activity, some more uncalculated hours.

But in writing these words — in thinking of writing them — she had some subliminal notion of a person who might at some point be going through her things, might come upon the envelope, might open it.

Me.

So she tells me not to open it.

And does she expect me to comply? Or does she assume — with a little curve of her mouth, a tiny shrug, a roll of the eyes — that I will open it?

Be it upon his head, she thinks. I *told* him not to.

All in a matter of seconds. As the phone rings. As she picks up a pencil.

Glyn has been sitting on the stairs now for so long that his backside is beginning to ache. He gets up, returns to the cupboard. He picks up from the floor the landslide of files and puts them in a pile on the windowsill. Kath's file he lays to one side, along with that envelope and its contents. He sets about a search of the area behind the files, which is silted up with miscellaneous papers alongside which, finally, there do appear to be some offprints.

That initial incandescent shock and rage have given way now to a sense of consuming purpose. He knows what he is going to do — but first things first. He is still raking over what he has seen and all that that implies, but at the same time he will grimly keep to its appointed course this day which has turned out to be a day apart. He will find that bloody offprint.

He burrows through the detritus of thirty-five years. Paper, paper, paper. Entire forests that have died for him. Oak, ash and thorn have perished to sustain his career — well, no, Scandinavian pine, more likely. In this heightened state he finds himself able to think in complex ways. Thoughts hurtle in parallel; thoughts shunt one another aside. He homes in on the photograph: when? who? He spots a box of slides, remembers a lecture he has to give, pulls them out. *Where* was the photo taken? Where are they standing, the pair of them? No offprint, so far. He returns the stack of files to their place and moves up to the next shelf. Newspaper cuttings, bulging boxes; another forest has been felled. He imagines the axes — no, chainsaws, it would have to be. There were trees in the background of that photograph, he remembers. What kind of tree? A clue; check later.

He takes down a box, opens it. Notes — reams of handwritten library notes from the days before photocopying facilities. Work. His own laborious hours of work. Heaven knows how many hundreds of thousands of hours of work the contents of this cupboard represent; his work, the work of others. And his work is in its turn the reflection of the work of countless nameless dead. "A landscape historian deconstructs the physical evidence of work done by generations of nameless people. The daily application of a faceless horde, century after century — labouring away hour after hour, year after year, hot, cold, wet, hungry, with aching limbs. Digging and shovelling and hauling. Fetching and carrying. Hacking and chopping. Loading, stacking, lifting. Herding animals, tending animals, butchering animals. Felling trees, quarrying stone. Turning wood and rock into houses and barns and churches and cathedrals. Heaving stone and glass up into the sky. And all this manipulation of the physical world carried out by scurrying, driven people, set only upon survival, upon working in order to eat, in order to live from one day to the next, in order to feel the sun and the rain and the wind, get a bellyful of food, catch a few hours' sleep, wake to see another day."

When did I write that? he wonders. Not bad, eh? He seems to remember saying it to camera, when they did the first television series. That heady time. Those were the days. Being whisked around with that attendant entourage — the pretty feisty girls with clipboards, and the director and the camera people and the sound people — and himself always at the hub of it all. Holding forth on hillsides and halfway up cathedrals and realizing that he loved every minute of it. Being recognized by strangers once the programmes had gone out: that sideways glance in the street or on a railway platform. Snide remarks from colleagues, for which he didn't give a damn. Jealous, weren't they? Oh, it was a helter-skelter, full-pelt time, that was.

But work, all of it. Well, there's work and work. And I've been wet and cold too, thinks Glyn, and I've done a spot of digging, though I pass on shovelling and hauling, and hungry hasn't much come into it. But there's not a day of my life in which I haven't worked.

And here Kath comes in, dead on cue.

It is her voice that is clearest. What is said. Why is it that words hang in the mind for ever? A sentence that is spoken over and over again. In his head, Kath is words quite as much as she is flesh and blood.

"You're not going to come with me?" The tone shoots up — a high emphatic note: ". . . *with* me?" And now he sees as well as hears. She is sitting at the other end of the table in the kitchen in Ealing, a letter in her hand. It must be summertime; her skin is very brown against her white shirt. That gold chain is round her neck. Her hair is damp from the shower, flattened against her neck.

"You're not coming with me to Devon for a lovely weekend with the Barrons?" Now she gives him that teasing look — never pleading, oh, never that, just a take it or leave it quirky glance. "Plenty of landscape in Devon."

And he explains — no doubt for the second or third time — that there is this conference.

"Never mind," she says. "Too bad. Toast?"

Kath did not work. Kath was not fettered by obligation, by responsibility, by having to be in a certain place at a particular time, by having to do things she might not especially wish to do. In the mind's eye, Kath is forever breezing down the street, smiling, travelling light, while all around her is perforce and necessity: the postman dealing out mail, door to door, the van driver heaving cartons into the corner shop, the patrolling traffic warden, the gang busy with hydraulic drills and JCB, the estate agents displayed at their desks, the driver of the taxi panting at the lights. All except Kath, who is bound for some destination of her choice, to do something she prefers to do.

And even when Kath did work she did not appear to be doing so. When she had a job — in those interludes when she was employed, gainfully or otherwise — it was because she had elected to do so. It had seemed suddenly interesting or entertaining to help out in an art gallery or a craft centre, to get involved in a music festival, to do picture research for a publisher. And when the interest and entertainment faded, somehow Kath was no longer there. She had simply melted away, from one day to the next — perhaps with a vague apologetic smile, perhaps not.

Glyn knew these episodes, because he was sometimes on the receiving end of the enquiring phone calls, which could range from perplexity to indignation.

How did she do it? Well, thinks Glyn, she managed nicely for ten years because she was married to me. I paid the bills. I fed her and housed her and clothed her, pretty well. But before that? After all, Kath was a fully-fledged adult by the time she came into my hands. She was thirty-six, she had been on the loose for twenty years, given that the home more or less broke up when the mother died. The girls each had a bit from her, of course, but not enough to live on. Well, not quite, but enough to scrape by, perhaps, in a hand-to-mouth sort of way. With the occasional top-up from somewhere or someone. I suppose that is the answer. And Elaine, being Elaine, set to and learned a trade and worked for the next forty years — very lucratively, these days, one understands — while Kath, being Kath, did not.

Glyn is still ferreting away in the cupboard, but if the offprint comes his way he is in danger of missing it entirely, so dense are his thoughts. He is finding that these thoughts are nothing new, but that everything is somehow skewed by what has just happened. This illness that he now has — this fever — has given everything a twist. Kath is both what she ever was, and she is also someone else. He is looking differently at her — he is looking differently for her.

She toiled not, neither did she spin. She did her own thing. In that sense she was in tune with the spirit of the day. But in other ways she was not. She didn't care a jot for achievement or status — neither for herself nor in others. She laughed at pretension. The hedonistic climate of the times suited her well, but the confrontations of the day were of no interest. I don't remember Kath ever getting exercised about the international situation or how she should vote. Feminism passed her by. Women's rights meant nothing to her because she had them anyway. Nothing had ever been denied to her because she was a woman. Being a woman enabled her to sail through life, setting her own course, following mood and fancy.

But not every woman can do that, thinks Glyn. Oh dear me, no. And why could Kath do it?

Because.

And at this point consideration gives way to imagery. He no longer thinks about Kath but sees her, experiences her. He sees her breasts. Small, neat breasts — little cones tipped with those surprising chocolate brown nipples. He could not take his eyes off them, once, and they surge again, full frontal, at this moment. That bush — a rich, silky pelt exactly matching her hair. Those legs. Her slim feet. And her face. Oh, yes — her face.

Kath could do it because she was a startlingly attractive woman. Not a conventional beauty, but with looks that were maverick and mesmerizing. The small face with those delicate features — the set of her nose, green eyes that seemed to catch the light, mouth tilted when she smiled. If she was present, you noted that everyone's glance strayed towards her. Men, women. Even children. Kath had an affinity with children. They drifted her way, and she to them. Perhaps if . . .

God, no. Kath as a mother? She with the attention span of a butterfly. Just as well it was never on the cards. And, anyway, I never wanted children.

He has reached the top shelf of the cupboard now. More files; more boxes of this and that. *Oxfordshire Drove Roads — 1984*. He opens the box: maps, photographs, and Kath once more. Not as such, not standing somewhere sometime holding someone's hand, twisting the past, but lightly laid across that time, staking a claim.

"Why are we here?" she says. "It's getting terribly muddy."

She has climbed on to a five-barred gate and sits there, squinting into the sun. She is wearing jeans and a T-shirt with no bra. Glyn can see the shape of her nipples through the thin material; this sight distracts him from the matter in hand, which is close inspection of the Ordnance Survey map. If there were a nearby haystack he would take her into it and be done with it. But when did you last see a haystack? He does not yet know this woman very well, but soon will, if things go according to plan.

They have been following a track between fields, the grassy surface of which has now given way to rutted mud and puddles. Glyn is interested in the width of the track. He considers this, resolutely ignoring Kath's nipples. One thing at a time. "We're here," he says, "because I think this track may be an early drove road. I need to check it out. I did mention this when we set off."

"So you did. I keep forgetting you're *working*." She laughs. That laugh. Like no other. "It feels like a country walk. But, actually, would you mind if I stay put here while you check out the rest of it? I'm going to sunbathe behind the hedge."

And she is over the gate, into the field, and is sprawled with her back on the grass, T-shirt off, bare-breasted to the sky.

16

He shoves the box back on to the shelf, and as he does so he spots a cache of papers behind. Offprints — aha! And, yes, here at last is the quarry: "Basic Patterns of Settlement Distribution in Northern England", *Advancement of Science, 1961*.

Had he started at the top, that file would never have come to light. Or not on this particular day. The day would have proceeded as it should; he would now be at his desk downstairs, getting on with the work in hand.

Glyn sweeps up all that he needs, closes the cupboard and goes down to his study. There he sets the offprint to one side. He will get back to work in due course, dammit.

He takes out the photograph.

Look again. I may have missed something first time round. Kath is wearing a full skirt, and some sort of black top that shows a lot of her neck and back. I think I remember that top. She has dangly earrings. Those too I remember.

Nick wears dark trousers and a short-sleeved check shirt. Neither item strikes a chord but I remember well that characteristic somewhat too long hair and the way it flopped across his forehead. Here, it obscures his face, which is turned to one side, looking not at Kath but towards someone else. Towards Elaine, it seems.

Elaine faces the camera. She is speaking, perhaps — her mouth is slightly open. Maybe she is speaking to *them*. She wears trousers and a casual sort of sweater thing, a bag slung over one shoulder, a denim hat.

The other two I do not recognize. A tall thin man. A shortish woman with dark curly hair. Also dressed in light, casual clothes which tells me only that this is summer, and that the occasion is distinctly informal.

Quite a little party. And then there is the photographer, of course. Him; her.

Where am I? Well, patently I am not there. I was absent, elsewhere, about other business.

And where are they all? The background is anonymous. A belt of trees. Grass on which they stand. Sky — blue, the odd white cloud.

An outing. A little excursion. "Listen, let's go to . . . Drop everything, why don't you! It's a heavenly day. Elaine's coming, and Nick of course . . ."

When? Judging by Elaine's youngish face we are looking back into the 1980s. Thereabouts.

But one would like to know precisely when. No — one would not *like* to know, but one feels driven to know. I am driven to extract from this vital piece of evidence all that it can tell about how things were back then, since it appears that they were not as they seemed to be at the time, nor as I have believed them to have been ever since.

When was this photograph taken?

And who was the photographer? The person who collected a wallet of developed film, idly inspected the contents, looked more closely at this print, did some quick thinking, cut the negative from the strip, passed on the print to *him*.

Tacit collusion. By whom?

The person who can tell me, of course, is Elaine. Who may or may not have been in collusion herself — and that I need to know — but who will certainly be aware of the identity of all members of the party on that interesting little outing.

And now it is Elaine who fills the room. He sees and hears her, in various incarnations. He has known Elaine for a long time, in different ways. Crucially, she is Kath's sister, and it is as such that he now examines her.

Well, they weren't all that close, of course. Elaine the elder by far, and the two of them poles apart — in looks, inclinations, personality, everything. But there was something going on between them — that odd mix of tension and commitment between siblings. Elaine sniping away about Kath being Kath, which she never apparently came to terms with — but then coming over all protective. Kath suddenly nipping off to see Elaine for no good reason, ringing her up late at night.

None of my business, anyway, thinks Glyn. It was up to them. But now suddenly it is his business. Where does Elaine stand over this matter? Does she know? Did she know?

He scrutinizes Elaine — Elaine of that time, successful garden designer, burgeoning business-woman, Nick's wife. Long-time associate of his own — he and Elaine go way back, after all. But Elaine is tiresomely inscrutable. She speaks and looks and does as she always has: no clues. Perhaps she was ever thus — quite a cool customer, Elaine.

She was in this room, once. Back then. When. After. "Will you go on living here?" she asks.

And when he replies she makes no comment. She offers to see to Kath's things. Which she did, though not, evidently, achieving a clean sweep.

As if he needed a house move, on top of it all. Yes, of course there would be . . . resonances. But there would be resonances anyway. One would have to learn to live with them.

He dismisses Elaine. She has nothing to offer, or at least not in this form. He pulls his notes towards him, switches on the computer: it is mid-afternoon and enough of the day has been dissipated.

That photograph smoulders in its envelope, and in his head.

Dispassionate appraisal is Glyn's working method. Appraisal of evidence, consideration of the available facts. A system which has produced several books, many articles, a torrent of lectures and papers and reviews. Opinion comes into it as well, of course, and Glyn is known for forceful opinion and vigorous defence of his position. But detachment and the balanced view are paramount.

A dispassionate view of Glyn himself, at this moment, would show a man of around sixty staring at a computer screen, a shock of dark hair, flecked with grey. A square, rugged face that has evidently seen a good deal of fresh air — the reddened, weathered look of a farmer. Large brown eyes, chunky brows. Mouth pulled down at the corners, indicating perhaps embattled concentration. He thumps the keyboard, making a lot of errors: a two-fingered typist. Once in a while he reaches for a paper from the pile beside him, scowls sideways at it, bangs away again.

The room is a workshop, that is clear enough. It is lined with bookcases, crammed from top to bottom: books vertical, books horizontal. Tables and chairs piled with papers. Filing cabinets. There is little that is decorative or non-functional: a pair of Staffordshire dogs on the mantelpiece, a lustre jug on the windowsill, a worn Persian rug on the floor. A framed Ordnance Survey map of a patch of Yorkshire from the mid-nineteenth century. Some aerial photographs of green sections of landscape. A colour photograph of Glyn himself, a couple of decades younger, handsome on a wind-blown hillside, with scrawled signatures beneath his feet: "Greetings from us all: *Changes in the Land* team 1980."

Pull back further — take a more distanced view — and the room is subsumed within a house that stands in a tree-lined street of detached homes with small gardens: a 1930s development, the pre-war extension of the southern English city that can now be seen — pull back further yet, up into the ultimate dispassionate eye, the sky itself. And there is the city, there is the accretion of stone, brick, wood, glass and metal. There is the cathedral, riding high amid the central jumble. There are the ravines of roads, the encircling discipline of chimneyed terraces, a belt of parkland, the white cliffs of office blocks, and on the outskirts the neat geometry of the university at which Glyn is employed.

No people here; the insect-crawl of cars. Glyn's house is lost now, digested into the urban mass, a tiny box in a row of similar boxes. And the mass itself, the inscrutable complex muddle, bleeds away at its edges, getting sparser and sparser until it is lapped entirely by space. Or rather, by spaces — squares and triangles and rectangles and oblongs and distorted versions of such shapes, edged sometimes with dark ridges. Dark spongy masses, long pale lines slicing away into the distance. Here and there a miniature version of the city density, a little concentration of energy at the confluence of lines. And then eventually space gives way — there is spillage, seepage, a burgeoning unrest that condenses once more into city format: the enigmatic fusion of now and then, everything happening at once.

If you know what you are looking at, that is. If you are Glyn Peters, who has got up now from his computer and is pulling out the wide shallow drawers of a cabinet. He finds what he wants — a map and a large aerial photograph. He spreads the two on top, side by side, pores over the aerial spread, seeing not space and shape but an assemblage of time. He sees centuries juxtaposed, superimposed, carving each other up, pushing one another out of the way. He sees the labour of medieval peasants etched beneath the rigorous lines of eighteenth-century enclosure; he sees a motorway slammed across a Roman road; he sees the green mound of a Norman castle thrusting up from the clutter of a city centre.

He sees himself, staking out private territorial claims. Been there, did that. There is Bishops Munby, where he spent the summer of 1976, supervising the excavation of a lost medieval village. He can see that field still, with

22

its eloquent lumps and bumps and declivities, its record of the little buildings that had been here, the village street, the string of fish ponds. Days of sun, days of rain, the wandering inquisitive cattle, the makeshift canteen in a tent. The evenings in the local pub, the jolly student labour force. He sees the girl from Durham, Hannah someone, young lecturer, with whom there had been a mutually satisfactory arrangement over that time: frayed denim shorts and long brown legs, glinting a conspiratorial smile as she trowels away at a wall.

He is down there ten years later, amidst that industrial conurbation, matching street patterns against the early survey maps. Solitary work, the place eddying around him, people casting a glance at the man with his clipboard and knapsack who prowls to and fro. A time of furious application, with his big book in the pipeline, his head buzzing with projects. And Kath's voice comes in here, rising off the glossy surface at which he is staring, which is overlaid now by that rank-smelling hotel in which he used to stay, Kath's voice on the phone: "I'm off to France for a couple of weeks with some people, since you don't seem to be around this summer." A pause. "Do you love me?" she says. He is writing up his notes in his hotel room: and there is Kath, a hundred and fifty miles away. She is reverberating still. But he hears only her; he himself is extinguished. What did he say to her? Goodness knows.

He looks up from the spread photograph and stares out of the window, struck by this. Odd. All that swilling speech in the head comes from others, never from

23

oneself. It is they who say things: you do not reply. There is no exchange; vital evidence is missing. And I've never been what you might call lost for words, thinks Glyn.

Interesting. The operation of memory would seem to be largely receptive: what is seen, what is heard. We are the centre of the action, but somehow blot ourselves out of the picture. Glyn rakes around some more and finds that he cannot much hear his own voice. Just occasionally, in delivery of some lecture, or holding forth to camera, but that will be because the lines have been committed to paper and so are familiar. But in all those scenes with others, he is silent — he who seldom was.

It occurs to him that there is perhaps a telling analogy to be made here with the silence of the dead. The myriad dead with whose lives he is concerned, whose affairs he tries to reconstruct from what they have left behind — brick and stone and the disturbance of the landscape and a blizzard of paper in a thousand archives. That great mute mass, who perpetrated everything but cannot tell you how it was for them, whose voices can only be heard at second hand, filtered, diluted, distorted. Yes, a pungent paragraph in some article. Make a note of it. The idea is not watertight — what about diaries, letters? — but it is worth playing with.

He continues to stare into the unkempt rectangle of his garden, in which a pigeon patrols the shaggy lawn and a squirrel pours down the trunk of the cherry tree in one fluid movement. He seldom steps into the garden, nowadays, and the house itself is simply bed and workstation. When in need of company he lines someone up for a bite in a pub — colleagues, one of his research students. For more extended solace there is Myra, who works in the University Registry. A discreet relationship; Myra has long accepted that a permanent commitment is not on the cards and that what is between them must remain a private concern. Myra cooks a mean Sunday roast, her bed is deep and soft; he keeps shaving kit and a toothbrush in her bathroom cabinet.

Glyn is now watching the squirrel, mindlessly. The squirrel loops about on the grass; from time to time it freezes, quite motionless, tail curved. Then it shoots into a bush and is gone.

Glyn surfaces, angry with himself: he is not a man who gazes out of the window at squirrels while working. This is the inertia of emotional strain, he decides. And it will not do.

He drives himself back to the computer. The aerial photograph remains spread out on the top of the cabinet; it has served its purpose, and other purposes which he had not intended. He jabs away once more at the keyboard; text piles up on the screen. And eventually honour is satisfied; the substance of his article is there. Final grooming can be left until tomorrow. Right now, he needs to get back to what has happened. He needs to get things into perspective, order his own responses, consider a strategy.

It is evening now — a long, light evening of early summer. Glyn goes into the kitchen, opens the back door. He has been cooped up inside all day; maybe fresh air will do something to alleviate his state of mind. He takes the old basket chair out on to the small paved terrace. He fixes a plate of bread and cheese, with a dollop of pickle, an apple. He opens a bottle of red wine.

He settles down out there, in the benign light of this fine evening. All around the suburb is noisily appreciative: lawnmowers, children playing. Glyn is impervious to this; he is not here at all, not here and now, but grimly focused on an elsewhere.

He is at the scene of that photograph. He does not need the thing itself, he knows what he saw, just as the words of the accompanying note are printed in his mind.

Right, let's be objective about this. What is there to see? Two people holding hands, in a way that would appear furtive. To hold hands suggests, well, familiarity at the least, but not necessarily a carnal relationship. The language of the note is intimate — "my love". It is also conspiratorial. The implications of the way in which the photograph was passed on by whoever took it further compound the suggestion that something was going on that had to be kept under wraps. In other words, they were fucking.

Since when? For how long? And does this raise further questions? Was this part of a pattern? Did Kath skip merrily from one lover to another? And did everyone know this except for me?

Evidence, he thinks, I need evidence. Well, I can look for evidence. But first things first. What do I know that is certain?

He scrutinizes his marriage.

He considers the bald narrative, which would run something like this. On Saturday, 25 August 1984 Katharine Targett and Glyn Peters were married at Welborne Register Office. They took up residence at 14 Marlesdon Way, Ealing. In 1986 they moved to 29 St Mary's Road, Melchester by reason of Glyn Peters' appointment to a professorial post at the University of Melchester. They continued to live at this address for the duration of their married life.

There should perhaps be a preamble to this: Glyn Peters met Katharine Targett at the house of her sister Elaine, whom he had known for a short while. A brief courtship ensued.

The facts. And Glyn is of course a facts man, par excellence. But he looks at these facts with fair contempt. They tell him little. They tell him only what he knows, and it is what he does not know that matters now.

It is the sub-texts that signify, the alternative stories that lurk beyond the narrative. The fragmented versions of those years; his and hers. His own version has different facets. There is his life with Kath and his life without her. The times when they were together — eyeball-to-eyeball across the breakfast table, limb to limb in bed, out and about as a conventional couple — and the times when they were apart, when he was just himself, as he ever had been. Walking, talking, working, living a life of which she knew little, now that he comes to think about it. The sealed life of professional commitment.

And what about Kath's sub-text? For, of course, she too led this dual existence. And he knows nothing, now, of either, it seems. And her evidence is irretrievable, wiped, lost.

While his own is now fatally distorted. There is what he knows, and there is the lethal spin imposed by the photograph and that scribbled note.

When was this going on — her and him?

Glyn lays those years out for inspection.

He places them in order. There were the immediate post-marriage years in London, before he got his Chair. The house in Ealing. The daily termtime tube trek to the college; teaching; snatched hours in the library. The vacation escapes — field trips, conferences, extended library time. And what was Kath doing? He remembers a spell helping out in a gallery, a period when she got involved with some festival and would vanish for days on end, a brief flare of enthusiasm as a tyro jewellery designer in someone's studio. But what about the rest of that time? Tracts of it. He samples his own returns from the college, of an evening, or from some excursion elsewhere. Is Kath waiting with a drink in her hand and something fragrant in the oven? Well, no — but that was never Kath's style. If she was there, then often others were there also — that network of her chums, who now merge into one another, in recollection. And if she is not, there was no knowing where she might be. A note on the kitchen table, perhaps: "Back later. Kisses. K."

The move to Melchester, to this house. To a life of intensified activity, for him. And now Kath is more elusive yet. She discovers a talent for interior decoration; she stencils, she stipples, she rag-rolls. The walls of this house are a legacy from Kath. Glyn sees her up a stepladder, in jeans and a baggy shirt, her hair caught back in a cotton kerchief: "Hey," she calls, "get this! How's this for a designer home!"

The house is full of her. Coming in through the front door — "Hi! You're here — great!"; in the bath, scented, foam-flecked, humming to herself — and he is deflected by desire; burrowed beside him in sleep — waking with a little grunt of protest as he reaches for her. He has lived with these ghosts for years, they were tamed, under control, but now things have shifted; he summons her up in anger and frustration. There she is, as ever, but unreachable in a different way.

He sees her at some gathering in the university, being the professorial wife, which is not Kath's scene at all. He sees the attentive glances of his colleagues, and tracks her progress through the room with complacent pleasure; she is herself, as always, but here she is also his — an asset, an accolade. Other men's wives are dimmed in Kath's wake.

And she has no idea. Afterwards, she says, "Sorry — I disgraced you. They were all in party frocks and I wore my denim skirt. It's probably grounds for divorce."

He examines those years. And everywhere there are perforations. There are holes through which Kath slips away. That year he was in the States for a month. Where was Kath? He has no idea. Was she alone here, perfecting her domestic skills? Unlikely. And if not, who was she with?

For suspicion smokes, now. Who else may there have been?

When first he knew Kath there were a couple of other blokes sniffing around, who had to be seen off. He cannot remember experiencing jealousy, merely a brisk and businesslike intention. Once he had seen her, he had known that he had to have her, and not just for weeks or months but for good. Marriage, this time. The absolute certainty of this surprised him — the onslaught of need. So those others had to be cut out, and the best way of doing that was by establishing possession as swiftly and as indisputably as possible. He assumed success.

That brief time is now compacted into an impressionistic blur of things said, things done. He is on the phone to her, hour by hour, talking, talking, but he cannot hear a word of his own, now — just her. She laughs — that laugh with an odd little catch to it: "Glyn, *honestly* . . ." she says. "Oh . . . it's you," she says. That breathless, urgent note. "I *am* listening," she says. "I'm listening fit to bust." And they are in his car, he is whisking her here, there and everywhere, because he doesn't want to let her out of his sight; he has her in the corner of his eye, her profile, the dark fronds of her hair against her skin. He takes her hither and thither — his siege of Kath is woven into the pattern of his working life. Kath climbs Iron-age hill forts, she tours industrial sites, she attends lectures. "We're going *where*?" she says — incredulous, laughing. She is not always pliable. Sometimes she has slid away; the phone does not answer, she's terribly sorry but she can't make it. But evasion serves only to fortify Glyn's persistence. "I'm doing things I've never done in my *life*," says Kath. "I don't know what's come over me." But she does know, she must know; Glyn has come over her. He is an unstoppable force; he has taken himself by surprise, as well as her. Who would have thought that he could be in this driven state about a woman?

Elaine stands by the mantelpiece. They are alone. Kath is out of the room; Nick is — heaven knows where.

"So it's you and my sister, is it?" she says.

He spreads his hands — propitiating, placating. He has nothing to say, for once.

And the matter is never raised again. Kath announces that they are getting married. Elaine is at once brisk with plans — the reception in our house, leave the nitty-gritty to me, do you want a buffet or sit-down affair? She goes into cheerful overdrive, marshals lists, caterers, cars. "It's too much," Kath protests. "We could have a get-together at that pub by the river, just a few of us." "You're only getting married once," says Elaine. "At least I trust and hope that you are."

When they come out of the register office, Elaine is on the pavement with a camera. "Stop!" she calls. "Right there. Like that. Big smiles, please. Kath — give your skirt a tweak, it's crooked."

Glyn has by now consumed the bread and cheese, pickle, the apple and two glasses of red wine, without noticing. The light has started to drain from the garden; all around the neighbourly sounds are subsiding — lawnmowers docked, children summoned within. Glyn has never had much truck with his neighbours; a student of communal life and activity, he is himself oblivious to community. So what next-door does or does not do is of no interest, and anyway he is off now on to the next level of churning thought.

He has reviewed the years with Kath, and has found small comfort. Now, he turns to Elaine.

He is going to show the photograph to Elaine. And the note.

She does not have to know. She does not need to know. She is better off not knowing. But I know, and I cannot bear to know alone. I need some community of outrage, or grief, or retrospective jealousy, or whatever it is that I am feeling. So I am going to show her.

Most of all, I need to know if she knew. Back then. If she has known since.

It is a while since he saw Elaine. Quite a while — a couple of years, perhaps more. So there is every reason to call her up, suggest lunch, a drink . . . Such is the imperative of his condition that he is minded to get in the car next day and drive right over to her place — only sixty miles, after all. But that would not do. Nick might well be there.

He will have to be patient. A phone call. An arrangement.

Elaine

Kath.

Kath always swims into view just here, as Elaine waits for the traffic lights to change, with the Town Hall in Welborne High Street plumb opposite. Kath comes down the steps, again and again and again, with her hand on Glyn's arm. Kath — a married woman, for heaven's sake. Elaine sees her today quite clearly, just as she saw her back then, through the lens of the camera, having nipped out ahead to take the opportune photo: the competent elder sister who has masterminded the day. Kath is laughing. Someone has thrown confetti and there are bits in her hair; she comes down the steps laughing, for ever and always.

Actually, just so long as I'm around, thinks Elaine. The lights change, the car moves off, Kath disappears. Kath is biddable now, docile, as she never was in those days. She comes and goes, and sometimes she comes when she is not wanted, but she is under control.

Elaine is in any case preoccupied. She is driving on autopilot now, nose towards home, and in her head she is back at the site she has recently left, where there is a garden to be designed. Elaine thinks laburnum alleys. She wipes out the laburnum and substitutes wisteria on wrought iron hoops, underplanted with alliums. She thinks water features and woodland walks and walled vegetable areas. The wife wants a potager. Well, she shall have a potager. The husband, from the sound and the look of him, would rather be at the golf club, but he is very rich and has just spent a lot of money on a mansion in Surrey which must perforce be appropriately decked out.

The wife wants decking too. She has been watching television gardening programmes and knows what's what in garden fashion, or thinks she does.

The wife will not get her decking, if Elaine has anything to do with the matter. She will have to put it across to the wife that what is all very well for a semi in Birmingham will not do for a 1910 Surrey stockbroker hold-out with Lutyens-style features and two acres of grounds. The grounds are a mess, but they have interesting bones. Elaine spotted the archaeological remains of what must once have been a Gertrude Jekyll-inspired sunken garden, complete with rill and fountain. She will have that restored.

Definitely no decking.

"You're *so* judgemental," says Kath. "Don't be so disapproving. Be *nice* to me." She has come rooting back, superimposing herself on the Surrey garden. She is just a face and a voice, like the Cheshire cat. She does this. She has said precisely that, many times before, head slightly tilted, fiddling with an earring.

Elaine sends her away.

No decking, and the water feature will be the restored Jekyll-style rill. None of your excavated pits lined with heavy-duty polystyrene. The wife will not have heard of Gertrude Jekyll but Elaine will blind her with science, and since this couple are paying rather a lot of money for Elaine's name and know-how, and because she is not some fly-by-night television presenter but a highly esteemed doyenne garden designer with major projects to her credit, along with various glossy publications, they will probably feel outflanked and start to doubt their own desires. In a few years' time, they will be displaying the sunken garden, the woodland walk and the wisteria pergola, and dropping Elaine's name to the husband's business associates, who won't have heard of it but know a class job when they see one.

Elaine does not usually much care for her clients. She prefers them when they are the faceless apparatchiks of large corporations. The gardens of Appleton Hall, acquired by one of the big banks as a staff training and conference centre, were one of her most satisfactory commissions. No opinionated but unknowledgeable pair breathing down your neck and squabbling with each other about what they really wanted — just a business-like brief, a budget, and get on with it. She is proud of the gardens of Appleton Hall — the parterre with the box hedging, the blue and silver border, the jewel-like glimpses of surrounding landscape framed at the end of grass walks.

Elaine does not design gardens for suburban semis. The owners of suburban semis would not be able to afford her fees; there is a host, a multitude, of outfits around now which attend to the likes of them. Over her working life Elaine has seen garden design go from a rarefied activity catering only for the wealthy few, to a cottage industry available to anyone with a bit to spend on property embellishment. Gardening is a mania now, it seems. Time was, the nation's gardeners were either obsessive specialists growing prize sweet peas in back gardens, or patrician experts presiding over bosky acreages. Nowadays, every houseproud couple knows their ceanothus from their viburnum.

Elaine is amused by this phenomenon. Her trade is now fashionable, instead of being either fuddy-duddy or elitist, depending on the perception. This is good for business, though she is well aware of bustling competition. But at sixty she is starting to wind down; she is being more choosy about commissions, she is capable of saying no when the job looks too problematic or too boring.

Once, she took everything she could get; that was when she was starting out, fresh from the years of learning plantsmanship, fresh from the time working for derisory wages in famous gardens to learn how it was done. She would design anything, back then: landscaping for a hotel forecourt, plantings for a new housing estate. She had to, as the most junior apprentice and general dogsbody for a slick little firm operating in one of the leafier parts of outer London.

Those years have been expediently glossed over in the CV that she supplies to prospective clients. Since then there have been bigger fish to fry, and her brochure lays them out for inspection. The brochure has had to be frequently updated. The first one of all was a fresh and innocent affair by comparison with the designer product of today. It was compiled with Nick's help, tricked out with little decorative floral motifs done by a girl illustrator he knew, and printed by the people he used when he first set up the publishing house. Back in those heady early years of marriage, and of work: her work, his work.

Elaine is now on the last stretch of the drive home. She passes the junction with the road that leads to their old place, the house in which family life was carried on cheek by jowl with a small publishing business and an embryonic garden-design venture. The busy, cluttered place in which every room housed filing cabinets, someone sitting at a desk, stacks of books. The kitchen where Polly was enthroned in her high chair or crawled about on the floor while people made out invoices and answered the phone.

The old house sends out signals, an unquenchable Morse code that is always to be heard around here. She is not thinking of the house, but nevertheless fragments of that time tumble haphazardly in her head, mixed with consideration of planting schemes for the Surrey mansion. A bog garden? Species roses for that long bank? *Hydrangea paniculata* against the walls? And, alongside, the thought that she must do a major supermarket shop tomorrow. Now, as the fragments tumble, Nick swings into focus, perhaps because she is approaching that pub that they used to go to of a Sunday lunchtime, way back. There he is still, sitting at one of those tables with fixed benches, on a summer morning, wearing a dark-green short-sleeved shirt, hair flopping, holding a pint mug which he waves around, in full flow about this new project.

"Roads," he says. "Lost roads. Prehistoric, Roman, cattle roads. An entire series. Canals and railways have been done to death. The Lost Roads of Britain — how about that!"

Oliver is present. The other half of the firm — friend, crony, partner. He is silent, in this clip from that time. He sits there, also with beer mug in hand, in quizzical silence. Not surprising — Nick in full enthusiastic spate was not to be stemmed. Sensible, pragmatic Oliver, who looks at the bottom line and deals with the nuts and bolts of the business, leaving editorial flair to Nick. Good old Oliver. Dear Oliver, Elaine sometimes felt, when Nick was being especially wayward or perverse, when he was in obsessive pursuit of some probably unviable plan. For Oliver was there then to provide reassurance and solace and to suggest that it will all blow over, like as not, and if it doesn't, well, we'll get it sorted out. Sometimes the shifty thought used to come that she might be better off married to Oliver, and, occasionally, when being counselled by Oliver, she was distinctly stirred. But Oliver would never betray his friend, not by thought, word or deed. And in the last resort, Elaine loved Nick, didn't she?

"You're not listening, sweetie," he is saying, still waving the beer mug, looking directly at her. "You're thinking about some blessed garden. I want you to think about roads."

She is past that pub now and the Nick of then is effaced by the Nick of today, who may or may not be at home, and if he is, she thinks irritably, you can take it as read that it will not have occurred to him that he might check the fridge and make a trip to the supermarket. Not a bit of it. He will have spent the day swanning around — reading the papers, playing with the internet, conceivably writing a few words of a review or one of his hack travel pieces, that is if he has any work to hand at the moment, which he probably has not. While Elaine has driven a hundred miles and spent four hours acting with constraint and civility in the face of a couple of morons.

She goes through the village. She turns off on to the side road. The old house had neighbours. The new house — well, the new house of the last ten years — is elegantly isolated, folded into a particularly appealing valley, complete with stream and woodland. They had eyed it for years, she and Nick: a little Georgian building with several acres of grounds that Elaine itched to get her hands on. And then it came up for sale. She had commissions pouring in, she was buzzing with schemes; the time was ripe to take a risk.

In ten years, a garden matures. Those covetable grounds are now Elaine's most prized creation. It is young, as yet; the pleached lime walk is a mere stripling, the ginkgos have to grow, there is infilling to be done and mistakes to be rectified. And she would make no majestic claims for it; this is not Hadspen or Tintinhull or Barrington Court. But it is a statement of her taste and talent, it bears her signature, it is her showcase.

Past six, now swinging into the circular driveway in front of the house, she sees that everyone has gone home. Only Nick's Golf is parked there. During the day, there is quite a line-up of cars. Sonia, Elaine's personal assistant, drives from her home ten miles away. Three times a week there is Liz, who deals with the paperwork Sonia hasn't time for. The red pick-up belongs to Jim, who does the heavy garden work. And then there are the relays of horticultural students serving their apprenticeship in the workshop of a master, just as Elaine herself once did. The current apprentice is Pam, who is a little northern butterball, sturdy as an ox, and exuberantly sociable, which makes her good front-of-house material on Saturdays when the garden is open to the public. Then, all hands are needed to patrol the grounds and to man the sales area, where plants are on offer, along with a judicious selection of garden implements, seeds, gift-shop paraphernalia and books — not least a complete display of Elaine's own publications. On those days, the paddock next to the driveway becomes the visitors' car park. Sometimes Elaine herself is on hand in the garden to be graciously responsive to queries and compliments. Initially, she found this stimulating and good for the ego. Nowadays, she gets rather tired of being asked if this or that is an annual or a perennial, and how to prune a rose. She tends to retreat to the house and leave customer relations to the students, who enjoy it.

When she first started opening the garden three years ago, the idea was that Nick would come into his own. Nick, after all, is nothing if not sociable and enthusiastic. The enthusiasm could surely be channelled into visitor reception and salesmanship, or at the very least, car park duties. And indeed to begin with

Nick was all compliance. He hung about the terraces, treating middle-aged women to dollops of boyish charm, he swept little parties off to the stream garden to display the primulas, he manned the till in the shop and added everything up wrong but nobody minded because he was so patently a beguiling amateur. Jim took over the car park after Nick directed a BMW into the boggy bit at the bottom, where it stuck fast. And in due course Nick's commitment to Saturdays withered and died. Elaine remonstrated, tight-lipped. "Sweetie, they keep asking me what this is called or whether that will grow on acid soil, and I haven't got the foggiest idea. The girls do it much better. And we all know I can't do money, don't we?"

Oh yes, she knows that. You cannot successfully keep a small publishing house afloat without a degree of business acumen. You must be able to gauge what will sell and what will not; you need to balance risk and costs and profit margins. You require a certain facility with figures, an aspect of the activity that Nick found distinctly tiresome. He tended to avert his eyes, for the most part. When Hammond & Watson eventually crashed, despite Oliver's best efforts, the warehouse was full of unsold stock, authors and suppliers were owed, and what had started out as an enterprising small imprint with a name for topographical and travel writing had become a liability.

It took a year to sort out the mess. Nick was chastened but buoyant. Never mind. It was good while it lasted. And he had plenty of useful contacts now, lots he could do in travel journalism, stuff for the Sundays, maybe guidebooks, that sort of thing: "Listen, Oliver, what if we —"

"No," said Oliver. "Count me out, this time round. No hard feelings. We had a run for our money."

To Elaine, Oliver said, "Sorry. I should have been able to keep things under control. I feel I've let you down."

Since when, she had thought, has anyone kept Nick under control? I too should have seen the red light. From now on, there will be changes. She had felt older, harder, and, in some odd way, exhilarated.

She collects her papers and clipboard from the back of the car. She goes into the house.

Windows open to the summer evening. Music filtering from somewhere. Nick is in the conservatory with a drink in his hand and something emollient on the stereo. After his taxing day.

Elaine goes into the office. Sonia has left a pile of letters for her to sign. There is another tray of letters and faxes that she must read. She gathers these up. She puts her notes from today into the appropriate file.

In the kitchen, Pam and Jim have both left scrawled messages on the blackboard. Pam has finished tidying up the long border, but needs instructions about the box hedging and those fuchsia cuttings. Jim says the tractor mower has packed up again, he's called in the mechanic and let's hope he comes in time to get the grass done by Saturday.

Elaine walks through into the conservatory, where the plumbago is a sight to behold. Beyond, the garden is glorious in the evening sunshine. Elaine is able to pay only token respect; her head is jangling from her day and her focus is on Nick, positioned precisely as she had anticipated. He has not heard her enter, but catches sight of her as she sits down.

"Hi! You're back. I didn't realize."

"Naturally not. Do you think you could turn the music down a notch?" She starts to go through the mail.

Nick does so. He gets up to refill his glass, then has a sudden thought. "Drink?"

She nods.

"We're out of that nice Australian white you got. Let's get some more."

"Thank you for reminding me," says Elaine.

The touch of frost in the air is apparent to Nick. He gives her a wary glance. "Poll rang. Says she'll call back."

"Mmn."

Nick is now cheerfully concerned. "Don't do all that wretched paperwork now, sweetie. Relax. Enjoy this gorgeous evening. Tell you what, why don't I knock us up an omelette and a salad later on and then you needn't bother cooking?"

"Yes, why don't you . . ." says Elaine. She returns to her letters.

Nick's concern hovers in silence for a while. He gives her a furtive glance. "Pesky clients?" he asks, with professional solicitude.

"Many clients are pesky, as you put it. If I let that bother me I'd soon go out of business."

Nick changes tack. There is an element of self-preservation here.

"I've had someone called a fact-checker on my back today. Nit-picking away about could I verify this, and give a reference for that. Remember that piece I did for the *New York Times* travel magazine?"

"And could you?"

"Well, here and there I could," says Nick. "But, I mean — what a sweat! On and on she went — 'Now can we look at paragraph two on galley three —'"

"An appalling imposition." Elaine's tone is level, inscrutable. She picks up another letter from the pile.

Nick's strategy is not working out quite as intended: the establishment of his own demanding agenda.

"And of course I was wanting to get to the library. I need stuff on Isambard Kingdom Brunel. I'm really excited about this book project."

Elaine perceives that Nick will probably not be invited to contribute to the *New York Times* travel magazine again. His relationships with commissioning editors are frequently short-lived: he finds deadlines offensive and briefings tiresome. The book project will remain a gleam in his eye, which is no doubt just as well, since it is unlikely to thrill publishers, there being certainly a swathe of works already on Isambard Kingdom Brunel far superior to any contribution Nick might make.

Occasionally, over the years, she has asked herself if she should feel sorry for Nick. But Nick does not invite sympathy, because clearly he does not feel that there is any problem. When one area of activity sputters to extinction, he is blithely accepting: "Actually, it was a bit of a bore anyway, and I've got a rather good idea . . ." Enthusiasm becomes itself an occupation. "What one should be getting into nowadays is desktop publishing . . . I've got this marvellous scheme for up-market canal boat holidays for rich Americans . . . the really interesting thing would be to set up a travellers' consultation service . . ." Once in a while, such schemes get beyond the stage of exuberant speculation, and Nick goes in tentative search of the necessary funding. But potential backers are irritatingly uncompliant. They start asking for something called a Business Plan, which has Nick running for cover. The project in question ceases to be a preoccupation, it melts into obscurity, he retreats into writing the occasional letter soliciting a book review. He becomes immersed in transitory interests. His comings and goings are unpredictable; there is always some pressing need, some undefined engagement. But he appears to be a man at ease with himself and with the world. This is hardly a case for sympathy.

Elaine has been married to Nick for thirty-two years. When she looks at Polly, their daughter's firm assertive presence seems to be the expression of that expanse of time. She cannot now conceive of a world in which there was not Polly, and she cannot well remember a life without Nick. But these days it is Polly who is the most inevitable development. Polly is ineluctable; Polly of today — capable, positive, employed. Polly is a web designer — "a here and now sort of job", as she herself describes it — and seems to Elaine to have been ever thus: brisk, busy, slim, trim, an adult who has somehow entirely absorbed all her former selves. Elaine has to search for the baby, the child, the adolescent. Nick on the other hand, Nick who has not much changed, who is simply a weathered version of his younger self — Nick sometimes appears to Elaine to be oddly fortuitous.

From time to time she wonders how she came by Nick. Why is she with Nick rather than with someone quite other? Well — because we pair off with the person we come across when the time is right. The young are like dogs on heat. In your twenties, when the hormones are roaring, it could be pretty well anyone. That someone else who is also currently available, not otherwise committed, ready to pair bond. Oh, love comes into it — but love is an opportunist. Love can be expedient.

There was Nick, when Elaine was twenty-six. There he was, always the animated centre of any group, always good-humoured, always game for any proposition, gleaming with good health and well-being. In other species, choice of a mate concentrates upon physical attributes — the indicators of good genes. Nick signalled good genes, if you went by surface appearances. And Polly does have his height, his good facial bones, his teeth that do not decay. But Polly, thanks be, does not have his lack of application, his idleness, his capacity for diversion. Polly is focused, in the language of her day and of her trade.

A question of timely collision. The two of you being in the same place at the same moment. The intersection of trajectories. The conjunction of Nick and Elaine took place during the 1960s, a good time in which to be young, according to legend. It now seems to Elaine that Nick was more resolutely young than ever she was. Even at the time, she felt herself to be on the margins of progressive action, reading about it in magazines, observing posses of contemporaries who had clearly got it right. And, when first she met Nick, he was a member of just such a posse; the centre of attention at some party where she was a more tentative bystander. But he had noticed her, he had sought her out — this appealing entertaining personable man, two years younger than she was but never mind. "Maybe he likes mother figures," a friend had joked, causing offence. Elaine had been cautious; for months their association had been spasmodic, undefined. And then something habitual had crept into it, and an unstated assumption that this was probably permanent. Over a pub lunch one day he said, "You know, honestly, we should get married, we really should." Thus had she come by Nick.

Nick has not matured well. Sometimes Elaine feels that he has not matured at all. Behaviour that is engaging in someone of twenty-five becomes less so at forty, let alone at fifty-eight. Where once she was beguiled, she has for many years been exasperated, though exasperated in the tempered, low-key way of long-standing acceptance. It could be worse, she has thought: he could be a drunk, or a crook, or a philanderer. He is merely feckless, and short on judgement.

He is on the sidelines of her life, in a crucial sense. She shares a bed with him at night, she eats a certain number of meals in his company, but he is excluded from the onward rush of things. He is not part of the faxes and phone calls, the consultations with Sonia, with Jim, with the gardening apprentices, the juggling of time and energy. He knows little of her cross-country journeys to client meetings or the production process of a book. "You're going where?" he says. "Warwick? You should look at the canal near there. Longest flight of locks in the country — amazing!" He steers clear of the books after an unwise surge of interest a few years ago: "You know, we could do these ourselves. *I* could. Desktop publishing. Cut out the middle man. Simple . . . OK, OK . . . it was just an idea . . . forget it."

Oh no, she had thought. No way. I've been there once. Not again. And this is my operation — books and all.

The sun is going down. The evening light has intensified over the garden. Elaine spares a moment for an appreciative look. Next year, some late tulips down by the yew hedge would be a good idea, to light up that dark corner. She returns to the letters. Nearly done now, sorted into two piles — one for Sonia to deal with and another with those to which she must draft a personal reply. An invitation to speak at a literary festival; yes to that — books will be sold and it is useful publicity. Would she attend the end of year prize-giving at a horticultural college as principal guest? Probably — for similar reasons. Could she please visit the garden of a couple in Shropshire (". . . a bit out of your way, we realize, but we'd love to put you up for the night . . .") who have written four pages about their tedious planting theories and probably have no conception of her consultation fee, or indeed that such a thing is appropriate: over to Sonia. Faxes from clients; faxes from contractors; a blizzard of promotional material that must be glanced through at the very least, in case there is something she should know about.

Nick has refilled their glasses. He is about to sit down again.

"How about that omelette?"

"Omelette?" Nick sounds surprised. "Ah. Yes. Omelette and salad. Right, then. Shall do."

"Good," says Elaine. She picks up some stuff about a new brand of fertilizer, skims through it, throws it in the wastepaper basket. Nick is still standing there. "What's wrong?"

"Nothing. For a peculiar moment you looked like Kath. OK — supper coming up." He goes.

This is profoundly irritating, for reasons that she cannot or perhaps does not wish to define. She does not look like Kath, and never did, which is why Nick has called the moment peculiar. They both know that she and Kath were about as unlike as sisters can be. Nevertheless, she knows what he means. She has seen it herself, in the mirror. Something about the mouth. A particular expression. Some genetic quirk — an arrangement of lip. When, otherwise, it always seemed as though she and Kath shared no genes whatsoever.

How odd, that Kath should survive thus — in the twist of someone else's lip. What would she have to say about that? She'd make some throwaway remark — one of those oddball witticisms.

She'd laugh — that wry little laugh. Hanging on like this in the shape of my lip, thinks Elaine. And in my mind. And in Glyn's and I dare say in Nick's and I suppose in Polly's and in those of a great many others. Many different Kaths. Personal Kaths. She is fragmented now. The dead don't go; they just slip into other people's heads.

It occurs to her that there is an eerie connection between Kath's presence in her mind nowadays and the way things were in their childhood, when Kath was a permanent, peripheral feature of the domestic landscape. Back then, when she was relegated simply by that matter of age, the wedge of years that sat between them, prescribing and directing. A twelve-year-old does not play with a six-year-old, or that particular twelve-year-old did not. A person of sixteen is not much interested in someone of ten. Elaine remembers the closed door of her own room, the edgy contrived accommodation of family holidays. That time consisted of the long years when Kath was merely a tiresome feature, an occasional source of jealousy, a local climatic effect to be ignored or irritably tolerated. She got more than her fair share of parental attention: "Do remember she's only five . . . seven . . . nine . . ." Her existence meant that there was always this unstable element within the household, generating concern, requiring other people's energies and help.

And then that time came to an end. Quite suddenly, it now seems. Kath grew up. One day she was no longer that annoying appendage but a person. She had fledged, grown wings — or rather, she had metamorphosed. This girl had appeared. From the child chrysalis there had emerged this sprite-like creature — elfin, gamine, all the well-honed terms applied. There she was, slim and quick, with long legs and small perfect body and that pointed face with the thin, neat nose and those lake-green eyes and the high curving brows and the brown-black crop of hair — the ensemble that had everyone looking, and then looking again, homing in on her when she came into a room. You saw people glance, and then keep glancing back, with surprised interest, attention, pleasure. And she had no idea. No more idea than has a bunch of flowers, a picture on the wall, a jewel — anything that seizes the eye, that gives a momentary uplift.

"You're *so* unalike," they began to say. "No one would realize you're sisters." This by then would, perhaps, have been better thought than spoken.

Nick is now in the kitchen. Elaine can hear his inexpert clattering with pans and plates. She is still here in the conservatory sifting the final tranche of paperwork, which does not require much attention, so that she is also elsewhere, in another time and place, despatched there by Nick's provocative remark. He did not of course intend to provoke. Nick never does. That is one of the things about Nick — something that is in itself an aggravation.

She hears her mother's voice. This is unusual; her mother is not much with her these days, nor has been for many a year.

"Our ugly duckling is turning into a swan," says their mother. "Look at her!"

And Elaine, home from college for the vacation, takes a look and sees that this is so.

"People have said she ought to think of going to stage school," their mother continues.

Elaine is consumed with annoyance. Typical! she thinks. Typical Mum. Typical people. "Why?" she snaps.

Their mother blunders on. She has come to be mildly afraid of Elaine, but has never learned how to step cautiously.

"Well, because she's so pretty, I suppose."

"And can Kath act?"

Their mother refers to a supporting role in a school nativity play, some while back. She speculates that after all you go to stage school to be taught how to act, don't you?

Kath did go to stage school, in the fullness of time, perhaps because of their mother, perhaps because of these anonymous people with their unconsidered opinions, and much good it did her. But by then their mother was dead.

The trouble with Mum, thinks Elaine, was that she took everything at face value. Literally, in that instance. Her views were simplistic, if one is being entirely honest. Not her fault. A restricted education; a life centred upon family and home. And Dad, not exactly stimulating, was he? I don't remember any kind of discussion ever taking place, except about what colour to paint the kitchen, or where to go for the summer holiday. They were comfortable and unambitious. Mum looked after Kath and me, put food on the table and saw that everything was in prime *Good Housekeeping* condition; Dad went to his office, brought home a salary, piled up a pension. They were entirely satisfied.

No, I'm not being patronizing — I'm being objective. I'm seeing them as they were, which doesn't mean I wasn't fond of them. And yes, I know that they lived as the vast majority of the population lives, and what's wrong with that? All I'm doing is taking the detached view. Mum was fine, but she had her limitations.

And she died. At forty-three. They hadn't reckoned on that. Well, who would?

I remember Kath phoning me: "Mum's got something horrible wrong with her." That was the first I knew. It was months only, after that — four, six? I went home as often as I possibly could, but it was a hectic time, my first job — even at weekends I had work to catch up with. And Kath was there.

Yes, I *know* she was only sixteen. But she'd always been closer to Mum than I was. She'd been agitating about leaving school anyway, even before Mum got ill. Well, she could have gone to sixth-form college or something later, couldn't she? But she wouldn't, would she?

I saw to the funeral, didn't I? It's all a bit hazy now, but there are moments that float to the surface. Dad sitting there blank-faced, helpless — this was right outside his remit. Me saying, "It's all right, I'll sort it out, don't worry." Phoning priests and undertakers. Twenty-two-year-olds don't have much experience with such people, but I managed. I remember feeling quietly pleased with myself — thinking, if I can deal with this I'll be able to deal with other things.

Kath seemed to be in a kind of trance, over all that time. She hardly spoke. And her looks went. It was as though she'd been blown out, like a candle. She became this ordinary teenager — peaky, with a little monkey face. She was like that for a year or so, and then gradually it all came back, and people were glancing again, and there began to be boys by the shoal, of course. She ran wild rather, I suppose. Dad was like an automaton, just doing what had to be done, day by day. And then he took up with Jenny Peterson down the road, or rather she took up with him, and they got married.

Kath says, "I can't go on living there. Jenny doesn't like me." She has been saying this over and over, down the years. She says it very precisely — she sounds distant, calm. But that is all she says. Listen as she may, Elaine can now hear no more.

What did I say?

Look, there was no way I could have had her move in with me. I was in that bedsit in Chiswick, saving up every penny for a mortgage deposit. She was going on nineteen by then. We were poles apart — not just the age thing any more, but tastes, inclinations, everything. We'd have driven each other mad. And it wasn't as though she didn't have friends. Kath always had friends — droves of them.

I kept in touch, didn't I? Not that it was easy, the way she flitted around. You could never be sure where she was or what she was up to from one week to the next. That was the drama-school time. Which didn't last long. One minute she was all wide-eyed about it, and the next thing you knew it was all off: "That? Oh, wasn't working out. Some people I know have asked me to come and live in their squat in Brighton."

It was the 1960s. Kath suited the sixties — the sixties suited her. Letting it all hang out, doing your own thing. It was the right climate for her — she was young at the appropriate time. Whereas I wasn't. To be industrious and achieving was to be out of step. And gardening had no cachet at all, back then. It meant old men with allotments, or middle-aged ladies in Gloucestershire. Kath waltzed about the place — to be honest I don't even know what she was doing, half the time — while I knew just what I wanted to do and what I wanted to be.

Of course I was concerned about her. Of course. But she was a consenting adult by then, wasn't she? It wasn't for me to tell her what to do and what not to do. Even if there was no one else, Dad having opted out altogether. And if you did say something, she had this way of side-stepping.

"You're *so* judgemental," says Kath. "I come all this way to see you and you tell me I need a haircut. Be *nice* to me. Listen, I'm learning to drive — how about that!"

The money Mum left me went towards the deposit on the flat. I told Kath she should do the same with hers, but she didn't. Naturally not. She lived hither and thither, wherever she happened to fetch up. A room in someone else's house, flatshares, a friend's sofa . . . Goodness knows what happened to the money. I suppose she just nibbled away at it, over time. Not that she was extravagant. At least, only in odd ways.

Kath is on the doorstep. At least, on the doorstep there is this great sheaf of flowers, a cornucopia of lilies and through it peers Kath, smiling, sparkling: "Surprise! When I woke up this morning I knew the one thing I wanted was to come and see you!" And all Elaine can think of is that there must be twenty pounds' worth of florist's goods there, which will die within days.

Of course I didn't *say* it. Not outright. I suppose I may have hinted — I mean, she was always skint, jobless more often than not. Possibly I murmured something.

When Kath is full and strong in the head, there is frequently this sense of a mute subversive presence, of someone playing devil's advocate. Elaine knows perfectly well how things were, what happened, who did what, but there is often now this interference, that distorts and confuses. As though one were not in control of the facts.

Nick is shouting from the kitchen. The omelette will be on the table in a couple of minutes.

Elaine gets up, puts the paperwork back in the office, visits the downstairs loo. There she takes a quick look in the mirror for signs of Kath, and can see none at all. Her mouth is her own once more. Moreover she is not displeased by what she sees: a face that has improved with age, settled into something more arresting than ever it was in youth. What was never pretty has now become handsome. Shapely nose and jaw, wide-set eyes, discernible cheekbones. Thick brown hair; not much grey as yet. Wearing nicely, thinks Elaine — that's what comes of a rewarding occupation, not to mention a lifetime of fresh air and moderate physical labour. Reinvigorated, she goes to join Nick in the kitchen.

The omelette is leathery and the salad indifferent. Nick has never bothered with the acquisition of domestic skills. Nevertheless, he presents this meal as though he were a gracious and benevolent host: "There! And I've opened a bottle of red. Now relax!"

They eat. Nick talks about Isambard Kingdom Brunel, and about the engineering complexity of the *Great Britain*, which reminds him to remind her that his car has to go into the garage tomorrow to have a new exhaust — any chance of borrowing hers? He leaps from thence to reflection on an idea he has for a series of handbooks on geological walks: "Region by region . . . Follow the Blue Lias from Yorkshire to Dorset, go Cambrian in Wales . . . you'd need a team of researchers, of course."

Elaine hears all this but her attention is upon her own concerns. She roves between contemplation of today's commission, notes for further action and various flotsam that sneaks unsought into the crevices. Regale lilies with a backdrop of dry-stone walling become entwined with the rehearsal of a stroppy phone call to a recalcitrant compost supplier; a vision of *Sorbus vilmorinii* is swept aside by an unquenchable memory of walking with Polly along the Cobb at Lyme Regis, prompted by a glance at the flowered dish on the dresser, bought back then. Polly is eternally eight and a half, wearing pink shorts and T-shirt. "Can I have a choc bar?" she says. Elaine is pondering whether or not to splurge on this piece of Victoriana by which she is tempted. "*Can* I?" Where is Nick? Why is he not involved in the dish and the choc bar? But Nick is not there, and the moment is finite; at some point she must have returned to the antique shop and bought the dish, but that she cannot remember, and she no longer knows if Polly got her choc bar. Probably, being Polly.

And now this incarnation of Polly is replaced by another — prompted by nothing in particular, it would seem, just part of a chain of imagery. This Polly has shrunk by a few years. She is four, or thereabouts. She is dancing. She is dancing with Kath, in the living room at the old house. There is music — a tape, the radio? Elaine can hear the music: "Here we go round the mulberry bush, the mulberry bush, the mulberry bush . . ." Melodic, compelling. Polly and Kath face each other, holding hands — small Polly, grown-up Kath — and they whirl about the room. "Here we go round the mulberry bush . . ." Their faces are rapt, smiling, intent. Polly gazes up at Kath, and they whirl on and on. For ever, apparently.

Definitely a wisteria walk for the Surrey mansion, but would alliums be right for the underplanting? Tomorrow she must get to work on the new book proposal, must have a session with Pam, must talk to the accountants. She looks across at Nick, who is still in full flow, and these considerations are eclipsed by the sight of his left ear, which prompts the resurrection of their wedding night, or rather the morning after their wedding night, when she awoke to find herself staring in surprise into a pink whorl on the pillow alongside her. She had never studied an ear with such intimacy and intensity before; so this is marriage, she had thought.

Now, she finds herself wondering if she could pick out Nick's ear from any other. Would she recognize it, unattached? If, say, it were sent to her in an envelope, as kidnappers are said to do.

"Of course there are guides galore to good walks," Nick is saying. "But a thematic line would be something new. One could go on to botanical, historical, you name it —" He breaks off. "Why are you looking at me like that?"

Elaine abandons the thoughts provoked by the ear, challenging as they are. "Will you undertake these walks yourself?"

"One hasn't really got the time. A team of volunteers is what I'm thinking of. I'm wondering if the garden girls —"

"No."

"There could be an expense allowance, of course."

"The garden girls, as you call them, are horticultural trainees, not freelance ramblers." Elaine gets up. "Do you want coffee?"

"OK, if you're making it. I may do a bit of preliminary scouting around tomorrow. Locally. Just to get ideas. So all right if I take your car?"

"No. I have to go to the supermarket. Unless you'd care to do that."

Nick pursues this line no further, as was to be anticipated. He changes tack. "Not to worry. I'll do it when mine has been fixed. Actually, we're going to have to think about replacing mine — there's too much going wrong."

"And what will we replace it with?"

"I thought one of those new Renaults might be fun," says Nick eagerly. "Like in the ads, you know? Red. I've always wanted a red car."

"I wasn't talking about the replacement car. I was asking what money we would be using."

This is bad manners. There is a tacit agreement that the fact that it is Elaine who pays the bills is not openly contemplated. At least, it is a tacit agreement so far as Nick is concerned.

He pulls a face. He shrugs. He gives her what she thinks of as his beaten puppy look. It is a look that used to disarm her twenty years ago, but has somehow lost its potency in recent times.

Elaine makes coffee. There is silence now in the kitchen, which also serves as a workplace, with reminders on all sides of what goes on there: the blackboard on the wall with its chalked messages from the labour force, the publishers' posters of Elaine's books, the windowsill dense with a propagating frame, pots of this and that, the copper jug crammed with *Iris sibirica*. For Elaine, the silence is barely apparent, her preoccupations still loud. The blackboard reminds her that it is probably the tractor mower that requires replacing rather than Nick's wretched car; the irises provoke concern about an overdue bulb order. But

60

these thoughts float above more insistent background noise which is not to do with things that have happened and things that have not happened and the way things are. She is feeling irritated, burdened, and a touch belligerent. She puts a mug of coffee in front of Nick, with unspoken comments. You are complacent, she tells him. You have always been complacent about me, above all. A mistake. I have not always been as I have perhaps seemed. There have been times when I have been a long way away from you. One time in particular, I suppose. Take note.

The phone rings. "I'll get it," says Elaine crisply.

Polly. "Hi, where have you *been*, I tried you earlier . . ." Polly is at once in full flow. Elaine pictures her, feet up on the sofa in that small Highbury flat ("the mortgage payments are wicked, but it's *so* nice, and it's two minutes from the tube station"). Polly has had a punishing day, she is wiped out, no one would *believe* the trouble there's been with these new clients, she's just off to chill out with some friends over a meal. She'll call again before the weekend, maybe she'll shoot down for lunch on Sunday, depending how things are — anyway, this is just to check in, this week has been crazy, take care, see you.

Polly's voice invades the kitchen like a message from another planet, which in a sense it is. Elaine knows plenty about her daughter's life: the feverish mix of work and play, the determined application to everything she does. Polly is a thirty-year-old web designer. By the time she is a thirty-four-year-old web designer she intends to be running her own business and will be thinking of a baby. As yet, the putative baby has no putative father, but all in good time. Elaine finds herself admiring Polly's strategic approach to life. Months and years are mapped out, a matter of target achievements; new carpeting for the flat when I get my salary increase, a job move next spring, split up with Dan by Christmas if things don't seem to be going anywhere. It is an approach mirrored by the question apparently asked by potential employers: "What do you expect to be doing in five years' time?" Or perhaps the question has conditioned the outlook of a generation. Elaine herself, at thirty, would not have cared to hazard a guess about what she might be doing in five years' time. Or rather, she would have felt that to do so would be tempting providence. Certainly, she could not have given the confident and ambitious reply that is evidently de rigueur. She admires this combination of pragmatism and positive intent; this is a climate that would have suited her too. As it is, her own success has been achieved by hard work and a degree of opportunism rather than any calculated ascent.

"Poll hard at it?" says Nick. He chuckles. "I was filled in earlier on. A job for some big outfit, apparently. It's all go, isn't it?"

For Nick, Polly remains a source of benign amusement, just as when she was six or sixteen. Polly, over the years, came to treat her father with impatient tolerance, like some wayward older brother. She bustled around him: "Dad, your desk is a shambles, I'm going to do something about it." She would contemplate him, her mouth knotted with disapproval:

"You *cannot* wear that tie with that shirt." There was affection here; when Polly did not care for people she did not bother to sort them out. And Nick, congenitally disposed to delegate anything that did not appeal to him, made no objection. Nowadays Polly deals with his income tax for him, such as it is. She prescribed Chinese herbal medicine for his hay fever and has chivvied him into membership of a health club. That undertow of irritation has been replaced by a sort of protectiveness, as though he were some flawed but valued institution. Elaine finds this attitude both annoying and perverse.

The thing about coming home, says Polly, when she dashes down for a night, or a meal, is that everything's always got to be exactly the same. Don't you see? I mean, you can have some new curtains occasionally, if you like, within reason, but basically it's got to stay put. I've got to be able to touch base. Totally self-centred, I know, but you don't *mind*, do you? The occasional innovation I will allow, actually a makeover of the bathroom would be no bad thing, but basics have to stay the same, right? No blue rinses, Mum, OK? And if Dad ever goes in for grey flannels and a tweed jacket I'll slaughter him.

Whenever Elaine hears this mantra, she is both touched and slightly mutinous. All right, all right, she thinks. I take your point. But you've got nothing to worry about, have you? Oh dear me, no. Any radical steps taken around here are to do with planting schemes or office equipment, with which presumably you would be in sympathy.

Nick has finished his coffee. He is now leafing through the newspaper in search of the television programmes. Elaine picks up her address book and pulls the phone towards her. She must call a client who is only available in the evenings. Nick glances across the table.

"That reminds me. Glyn rang. Said he'd try you again tomorrow."

"Glyn?" she says. "Oh . . . Glyn."

Elaine and Glyn

Why this restaurant? Why not come to the house? Why, anyway?

Elaine drives into the car park behind the Swan, finds a space. She tidies her hair, checks her face. It is a long while since she saw Glyn; longer still since she ate a meal alone with him.

The Swan is apparently a halfway point, as near as makes no odds. Thirty miles for each of them to drive: Glyn, brisk and practical — "So, thanks for your kind offer, but if you don't mind . . . It'll be good to see you." And the phone is put down without further explanation.

So here she is. And as she walks into the Swan's dining room — dark panelling, red-checked tablecloths, limited clientele on this weekday lunchtime — she sees that here too is Glyn. He rises to greet her: the polite kiss. "You're looking well, Elaine."

Glyn is surprised. Elaine must be sixtyish, for heaven's sake, but she does not look it. Any more than one does oneself, come to that.

She sits down, making a crisply critical comment about the hotel's garden, which is visible beyond the window. He takes note of her; becoming haircut, clothes that are casual but smart. There was always a compelling vigour about Elaine; she still has it. Fellow eaters glance at them. If things were otherwise, he could be enjoying this occasion — a pleasant get-together with a woman he has known for many years. But this is no indulgent arrangement. There is an agenda; it is smouldering in his pocket, distracting him as the waiter proffers menus, as Elaine asks some question.

So what is this lunch about? Elaine knows at once that Glyn is in a heightened state. Mind, you need close experience of Glyn to be aware of that — not a man who was ever less than charged. But there is something up today. She can sense it; an absence of concentration, a restlessness. It is apparently an effort for him to give a run-down of his latest project, a reticence which is unusual. So what is afoot? Maybe he is about to remarry and considers it proper to tell a former sister-in-law in a formal manner? Perhaps he has been elevated to the peerage — well, he is a prominent academic, occasionally outspoken on public issues. Possibly — here Elaine's interest is sparked — possibly he has some professional scheme requiring garden-history expertise as he did . . . back then. If that were so, one might well find oneself available. All the rage, these days — lost gardens. Prime-time television and all that. No bad thing to become involved.

The waiter returns. Choices are made, the meal ordered. "Nick sends greetings," says Elaine.

Glyn becomes busy with his napkin. He butters a roll. "And how's business, Elaine? Lots of work?"

"All I want."

"Good, good. You're a fortunate woman. You embellish the landscape and get paid for it. As opposed to those of us who fritter away a lifetime asking questions about it."

"You too get paid," says Elaine.

"True." He reaches across the table, pats her hand. "I'm glad things are going well. You deserve it. You're a worker, always were."

Glyn is a physical contact man. An arm-round-the-shoulders man, a hand-on-your-elbow man. The pat reminds her of that; his mode of emphasis.

"I'm certainly not complaining. Only when it comes to the more perverse clients."

"Ah, that's a hazard of the trade. Capability Brown had plenty to say about his. Repton too. Dealing with patronizing eighteenth-century aristocrats. Bear in mind that it is they who will vanish without trace. Your creations will outlast the merchant bankers or whoever they are that plague you."

He continues along these lines as the first course arrives. He talks of some stately home magnate who had a lake dug and then didn't care for the effect and had the lot filled in again. He moves on to cite instances of vast expenditure on historic garden creation. Elaine had forgotten his compendious resources, that capacity to conjure up facts, figures, anecdotes. Compelling enough, in its way, but there is the hint, just now, of a routine.

Glyn is treading water. He would like to get on with the matter in hand, his mind is on that and on nothing else, but good manners would seem to insist that the niceties are observed. A period of general chat. A decent interval of white noise.

"Fascinating," says Elaine. "What a mine of information you are, Glyn — I'd forgotten. I'm flattered at being lumped in with Repton and Brown. Can't say I've dug any lakes lately, but perhaps my day will come."

Glyn ploughs on. This is conversation, of a kind: comments are made, opinions exchanged, occasionally there is glancing reference to some past shared experience. Plates are taken away; more food arrives. Now, thinks Glyn. In two minutes, when she's finished eating.

Elaine is talking of Polly. Glyn stares at her, trying to focus. The daughter. That's right, the daughter. "— web designer," Elaine is saying. Glyn inclines his head, all interest.

"Do you know what a web designer is?"

Glyn spreads his hands, defeated.

Elaine puts her knife and fork together, dabs her mouth with her napkin. "Actually," she says, "I don't think you heard a word of that, did you?" She gives him a long, speculative look. "Come on, unload. I've got a feeling we're not here just to chat, are we?"

"Ah . . ." Glyn pushes his plate to one side. Right, here goes. Suddenly, he feels once more in control, back on course. Some questions will be answered. He reaches into his pocket. "Actually, you're right, Elaine."

Elaine sees and hears that this is something of another order. This is not marriage, or ennoblement, or garden history. She feels a creep of disquiet.

Glyn is holding something out to her. She takes the photograph. She takes that scribbled note. She looks first at the photograph. She looks at it for quite a while. Then she reads the note.

She says nothing. She holds them, one in each hand, looking, not speaking. Then she looks across the table at Glyn.

"In a file in the cupboard," he says. "Must have been there since she — Since then. They were in this." He pushes across the table towards her that envelope. DON'T OPEN — DESTROY, Elaine reads.

"So . . ." says Glyn. "So here's a turn-up for the books." He watches her.

Elaine looks back at the photograph. Something strange is happening — to her, to the figures that she sees. She sees people who are familiar, but now all of a sudden quite unfamiliar. It is as though both Kath and Nick have undergone some hideous metamorphosis. A stone has been cast into the reliable, immutable pond of the past, and as the ripples subside everything appears different. The reflections are quite other; everything has swung and shattered, it is all beyond recovery. What was, is now something else.

"Or perhaps you knew?" says Glyn.

"No, I didn't know. Assuming that there was indeed something to know."

"Well, what does it look like?"

Elaine has seen enough. The hands. The handwriting, the language. She picks up the photograph and the scribbled note and puts them in the envelope.

"I suppose it looks like — what it looks like. And, no, I didn't know."

"Then I'm sorry. This is as much a shock to you as it was to me. I'd begun to think I was the only one in the dark."

Elaine makes no comment. The ripples are widening; the reflections become clearer. But, at the same time, they are not clear at all; they are ugly, distorted, deceptive.

"When was it? Where were you all?"

"It must have been in the late 1980s-87 or 88. We'd gone to the Roman Villa at Chedworth. I forget quite why. Mary Packard was there, and the man she was with then. Do you remember her?" Elaine speaks dully. She would prefer not to speak at all.

Glyn shakes his head. He is not interested in Mary Packard.

"Who else was there? Who took the photograph? And passed it on to Nick?"

Elaine is silent. At last she says, "Oliver."

Oliver. Even as she speaks, Oliver falls apart and is reassembled — in a nanosecond, in a single destructive instant. He too becomes someone else. The Oliver who has been in her head these last ten or fifteen years disintegrates and is replaced by a new and different Oliver, one whom she does not know. Did not know.

"I see. Him. Nice, reliable old Oliver. In collusion, apparently."

The waiter is hovering, menus in hand, proposing dessert. Elaine feels now as though she had fallen from a great height and were picking herself up, gingerly testing limbs. "Nothing else," she says. "Just coffee."

Never mind Oliver, thinks Glyn. I'll get to him in due course. The point is that there are now two of us in this. He looks guardedly at Elaine; she has been rocked all right, he saw that in her face, but there is no sign of collapse. Well, Elaine is not the type to run weeping from the room.

"I'm sorry," he says. "It's a slap in the face, isn't it? I've had a few days to digest. Not that I find that makes a great deal of difference."

"Difference to what?" This is not so much a question as a prompt. Talk, thinks Elaine. Just talk and let me consider. Let me do some steady breathing and take stock. I seem to be intact, more intact than I would have expected.

"— point is the suggestion that nothing was what it seemed to be," Glyn is saying. "That what one has been carrying around in the head is apparently fallacious. That one was, that we were, unaware of a significant fact, namely, that your sister — my wife — at one time had an evidently intimate relationship with your husband, to put it baldly. Suddenly everything has to be looked at in a different light."

"Some might prefer not to look," says Elaine.

"Unfortunately I don't find that possible. Do you?"

A pause. "Probably not."

"I can't tolerate a misconception. Everything is thrown into doubt. At least that is what I'm finding. Everything." He stops abruptly. He is finding also that he does not wish to pursue this line. Personal breast-beating was never on the agenda. There was an entirely practical motive for this meeting, and that has now been satisfied. He knows what he needs to know. Or rather, he has begun to know what he needs to know. He is side-tracked now by a new line of thought.

"Professional conditioning, to some extent, I suppose. We don't like the status quo to be upset. Some new and vital piece of information comes along and the whole historical edifice is undermined. Take Carbon 14 dating. They've got everything nicely worked out — what is contemporary with what, a chronology set in tablets of stone — and then along comes dendrochronology and the whole thing is shot to pieces. Stonehenge is earlier than the Pyramids, the Neolithic isn't when they thought it was. Throw it all out. Think again." He gives Elaine an interrogatory glance. "You know about Carbon 14 dating?"

"As much as I need to know at this moment."

"Recent history is less vulnerable. More a question of constant raking over of the ashes. Reinterpreting. Arguing. The sudden reversal is less likely. It's the early stuff that is the shifting sand. Let alone when you get back to palaeontology. A minefield. That said, nothing's sacrosanct. There's always the possibility of startling new evidence that moves the goal posts. The drought summer of 1975 made possible aerial photographs that showed up a whole range of early settlements on the southern gravel terraces that were completely unsuspected. Prehistoric population estimates had to be entirely revised. You follow me?"

"I take your point. Your personal goal posts have been moved, right now."

Glyn stares across the table at her. "Is that not how it seems from your perspective?"

Coffee has arrived. And with it, for both of them, a further presence. Kath is around. Or rather, several Kaths have arrived. For Glyn, she is for no apparent reason sitting on the roof of a narrow boat, somewhere in a Northamptonshire reach of the Grand Union Canal. Her arms are wrapped round her legs, she wears rope-soled canvas shoes, her tattered straw hat has a bright-blue scarf tied around the crown. And what was he doing? Steering the boat, presumably, which Kath never learned to do, and if the other couple he hazily remembers to have been there on that weekend outing are present, they are not evident in this slide. Kath sits alone, and she is gazing at a couple of children running along the towpath. Quite small children — oddly he still sees them also. Kath gazes, and presumably he, Glyn, was yanking away at that wheel and anticipating the next lock, while Kath's mind is patently on something quite other.

Elaine is experiencing several Kaths, who tumble in her head. Kath is not under control, she will not be dismissed. She is a continuous effect, as she was in childhood, a glimmering presence, flickering away there on the perimeter. She cannot be disregarded. "Here I am," she says. "Here I was. Look at me."

And Elaine looks. She sees a new Kath, who is coloured by what Elaine now knows. She is angry with this Kath: angry, resentful, frustrated. But she is also

baffled and a touch incredulous. Why? Why Nick? Kath
hardly noticed Nick. Or so one thought. Nick was
simply a person who was around, as far as Kath was
concerned. Familiar, and inevitable — my husband.
But apparently all the time . . . or some of the time.

Elaine summons up that day, the day of this
photograph. In a snatch of time — as she stirs her
coffee, sets down the spoon, lifts the cup to her lips,
drinks, returns it to the saucer — she recovers those
hours. But there is not much to recover — tracts of it
have gone down the sluice, it seems. She sees neatly
restored ruins, a mosaic pavement, a glassed and
labelled fragment of Roman cement on which is the
paw-print of a Roman dog. She sees a grassy bank, the
surrounding woodland. She sees Kath walking towards
them in a car park, Mary Packard and her companion
behind: evidently they all met up at this place. The
arrangement, and its reason, are gone. But can be
surmised: Kath's phone call — "Listen, Mary and I
have this plan . . . yes, yes, tomorrow as ever is . . . *of
course* you can drop everything, both of you, bring
Oliver too . . ." And now a picnic comes floating up:
Nick is rummaging in the coolbag, he looks up at her,
he says, "Is there any fruit, sweetie?" Mary Packard and
Kath lean over the railing that surrounds the mosaic,
laughing at something. Mary Packard's man is so
irretrievably consigned to the sluice that Elaine cannot
supply him with features or a name; he is just a lurking
presence. But Mary Packard is loud and clear; Kath's
longtime friend, the crony, the soulmate, the abiding
element amidst the ebb and flow of Kath's associates.

Short curly hair, emphatic manner, a potter by occupation.

Glyn is trying to sort out the years, but to no great effect. He could do with pen and paper, but that would hardly be appropriate just now. What was he doing in 87 or 88? Which was the year he was up in the north for much of the summer — did this take place then? More accurate dating will be necessary. And there is a sense in which Elaine has failed him. She did not know, which removes the biting thought that he was the sole innocent, that all around were wise to what was up, and tacitly pitying, or jeering. She did not know, but others may have done. Oliver, patently. He will see to Oliver all in good time. For now, first things first.

"You think 87 or 88?"

Elaine puts down her coffee cup. She is silent, staring at the table. She is considering the query, it would seem.

But no. "Does it matter?" she says.

"It does to me."

She shrugs. "Sometime then."

"Can't you be more precise?"

"No."

"Oh, for God's sake, Elaine —"

"And don't snap at me."

He is contrite. "I'm sorry. Sorry, sorry. Look, I'm not snapping at you, I'm snapping at . . . at what apparently happened."

"Retrospective snapping will get you nowhere," says Elaine. And furthermore, she thinks, let's be clear about this — we don't have a common cause, you and

75

I. All right, we've both been wrong-footed, we're both outraged, but that is the beginning and the end of it. Whatever comes next is a personal matter, for each of us."

"Why Nick, one asks?" The contrition has evaporated; this is speculation with a note of insistence.

"Why indeed?"

"And if Nick, who else?"

"Is this wise?" says Elaine.

"Is what wise?"

"Questions."

"Possibly not. But what else can I do?"

She meets his eye. "Nothing?"

"I am not a do-nothing man. I am conditioned to ask questions. Will you do nothing?"

She inclines her head. No answer.

"I'm sorry you had to know this," says Glyn.

"I didn't have to know it, strictly speaking."

This takes effect. There is compunction, but also defiance. "Right. OK. You've got a point there. But you might well have done the same."

"And you had to know if I knew."

Does this mean he is exonerated? No way of telling. He is evasive, now. "Whatever . . . Here we are. There it is."

"There it was," says Elaine.

"A fine distinction, to my mind. If a distinction at all."

She considers, apparently concedes the point. "Perhaps. But asking questions won't change that. Could even make it more so."

"So be it," says Glyn.

Determination, or perversity? There is a pause; both of them possibly weighing this up.

Elaine steps in. "I suppose there is one question that springs to mind."

Glyn waits, wary; something in her tone has him on his guard.

"Did Kath ever know?"

"Know . . . what?" Glyn is prevaricating. Both of them are well aware of this.

Elaine gives a tiny shrug, a steely glance.

"Well, there wasn't so much to know, was there?" He shoots up his eyebrows, that Glyn expression of deprecation, surprise — whatever is appropriate.

"Maybe not," says Elaine. "But did she?"

"No. She had no idea."

Elaine reflects, and decides that this is probably true. There is silence between them. Something has been let loose; she has broken a taboo.

"Long time ago . . ." says Glyn. He avoids her eye. Is this necessary, for heaven's sake? An aberration, after all, surely that has long been understood?

Yes, indeed — time out of mind ago. But not entirely out of mind, and that is what is at issue. We were both there, after all, thinks Elaine; nothing can change that. We are the same people. Up to a point. She watches Glyn; it is astonishing to her that, once, she burned for this man.

Glyn is experiencing something of the same sensation. Before them both there hangs that time of the Bellbrook garden project. Both shed eighteen years, and see one another again for the first time.

Elaine sees a muddy wasteland, girdled with Portakabins, littered with bulldozers, piles of bricks and planks. She sees the aerial photograph of the same site before this invasion, that has been handed to her, with its provocative patterning of lines and depressions. She sees the television team that is here to record the shadowy presence of the gardens of a vanished Jacobean mansion discovered on the building site of a new housing estate. And especially she notes the talkative personable presenter of this programme in the making. A landscape historian, she has been told — the first time she had heard of such a trade.

Glyn sees the inviting potential of this unusual site. He assesses the contractors' crane, from which it is proposed that he should make the opening commentary, with the camera panning away to a bird's-eye view of the garden's outlines disappearing beneath the geometry of suburban streets and crescents. And he turns from consideration of subsequent shots to inspection of this expert on garden history and design who has been called in to elucidate the visible evidence. "This is definitely a parterre," she is saying. "And it looks to me as though the vista runs along that axis . . ." He steps across, hand outstretched: "Glyn Peters. Great to have you with us. Now. Tell me —"

She tells. She gets out pencil and paper and sketches a possible design for this extinguished landscape. "Assuming that this pattern is complemented by an identical layout on the other side of the central path, which it must have been, you've got the whole thing extending — oh, a couple of hundred yards or more, most of it built over already. I do feel that some sort of central basin and fountain is implied . . ." Glyn eyes her. He rather likes what he sees. Something in her eyes, and the curve of her mouth. He feels a distinct flare of interest. He is all exuberance and enthusiasm. He lays a hand on her arm: "Wonderful! Thank goodness they brought you in. Listen — let's take off to the pub while they set up the cameras and then we can really talk."

He talks. He is an exhilarating and refreshing companion. They are noticed in the Crown and Cushion of some unmemorable high street. He recounts entertaining anecdotes of filming experience, he is compelling about field-systems and drove roads, or so it seemed at the time. Elaine remembers thinking with approval that this is enthusiasm bolstered with the authority of knowledge. This is a man who knows what he is doing. She likes that Welsh intonation, too.

And thus by the time they return to the site there is a definite rapport, an alignment firmer than that required by this transitory professional association. Glyn wonders if he might pick her brains at some point about early park plantings; Elaine finds that she would have no objection at all to this. Addresses are exchanged. "Are you married?" Glyn enquires. "Of course," comes her brisk reply. "Aren't we all?" He laughs: "In my case, no, as it happens."

The filming takes place. Glyn holds forth from the contractors' crane; at ground level he strides around this scene of devastation, conjuring up the elegant formality of another century. He describes clipped topiary, fountains, gravelled paths. In between takes, he rejoins Elaine: "You're a magician! I'm reinventing the text as I go, thanks to you." Elaine observes with amusement and fascination. This beats client meetings any day, she thinks.

In due course, a week or so later, she sees Glyn again. He is anxious to show her the grounds of a derelict mansion in Northamptonshire that he has come across. She drives many miles to this assignation, which for some reason she describes to Nick, dismissively, as a consultation with turf suppliers. Glyn and Elaine trespass the grounds of the mansion by way of a crumbling wall and a thicket of brambles, with much laughter and exclamation. When Glyn puts both hands on her waist to jump her down from the wall she realizes that, should the question arise, she is likely to commit an infidelity for the first time in her married life.

All the signals were there. No doubt about that. It was not a question of if, but when — when this undeclared interest would tip over into an admission. She had thought that Glyn did not seem a man to hold back. And she had known that, when the time came, she would not either. She is astonished by this now. She feels as though it were some other woman who was caught up in that flurry of sexual interest. Which is made more mysterious by the fact that in all the subsequent years of their association, she never saw

Glyn in that way again. It was as though his allure withered the moment he was with Kath.

There had been other meetings. Two? Three? Not many more than that. All are hitched to the lingering background of some significant place. Maiden Castle: they climb the grassy ramparts, he takes her hand to help her up the steep slope, meets her eye, the tension sings between them. They are on an ancient stone bridge over a little river, leaning on the parapet while Glyn talks. She no longer hears a word of this, but sees his face still as he turns to her, stops talking, puts his hands on her shoulders, kisses her on the mouth. She feels the flick of his tongue.

But he had come to the house, also. Had he not . . . Well, had he not we would not be here today on this freighted occasion, thinks Elaine.

Glyn visits Elaine at home. He wants to see a book Elaine has mentioned that has early photographs of the grounds of Blenheim Palace. When the suggestion is made Elaine notes that he could quite well consult this book at some library. On the day that Glyn comes to the house Nick is out, by coincidence, and Polly is of course at school. Glyn and Elaine spend hours together — eating lunch, talking, looking over those convenient photographs. The tension is there again — enhanced, wrung tight. The air crackles with what might be, what may be.

And somehow Glyn does not leave but stays on into the evening. Polly returns, and so does Nick, who easily digests an unanticipated visitor, as always. Elaine is just putting together a meal for everyone when the door bursts open and here is Kath, on one of those unheralded surprise visits.

The evening is prolonged and convivial. Nick is in high spirits. Glyn scintillates. He turns frequently to Kath. And when at last he leaves, Kath leaves with him. He has offered her a lift to the station.

Elaine stands at the window, watching the retreating lights of Glyn's car. She thinks, so that's that. He had only to set eyes on her. Wouldn't you know?

Glyn's voice jolts her back to the restaurant table and the matter in hand. "*That* has nothing to do with this," he is saying emphatically.

She looks at him.

"If you are suggesting that Kath took up with your husband because briefly, long ago, you and I . . . eyed one another . . . then I'm telling you that she had no idea. No idea at all. Not from me." His return look is a challenge.

"Nor from me," says Elaine. "All right, she didn't know. I'm merely noting a symmetry."

For Christ's sake! thinks Glyn. What did she have to drag this up for? Irrelevant. And symmetry be blowed. I hardly laid a finger on her, as I recall. All that was wrapped up when I married Kath. Never referred to again. Why revive it now? Surely there's no question . . . He shoots her a glance, but it seems to him that Elaine's expression is one of controlled dislike rather than latent interest.

In fact, Elaine's somewhat wooden look is the product of distraction rather than dislike. She is assessing her own condition. Within the last hour her perception of the past has been questioned, her understanding of three people has been shown to be faulty; yet she is surprised to find that, far from feeling diminished, she is filled with a sense of grim purpose. Glyn is rapidly becoming superfluous.

"My dear Elaine," he is now saying, "that really is water under the bridge —" a propitiating smile — "We both know that. Not that I haven't always had a great affection for you. But it has no bearing on . . . this other thing." He changes tack. "This would seem to be . . . well, the evidence suggests a great deal. But there is only one person now who can tell us exactly what."

"Are you planning to have a word with Nick then?" Elaine is icy.

"Perish the thought. That is your prerogative, if you so wish."

Quite, thinks Elaine. But you're not going to leave it alone, are you?

"Nick is your concern," he continues, dismissively.

"He is indeed. And what is yours?"

Glyn stares at her. He has the intense and concentrated look that she remembers from those times when he would be expounding some new theory, holding forth on a current investigation. He does not reply.

Nick is oddly insignificant, Glyn is finding. He is puzzled himself by this. An initial urge to seek him out and punch him on the nose has given way to a kind of indifference. His business is with Kath, not Nick.

The restaurant has emptied. At the edge of the room, staff loiter.

Elaine folds her napkin, puts it on the table. Glyn cocks an eyebrow in the direction of a watchful waiter. The bill arrives.

"Well," she says, "thank you for the lunch."

He grimaces. "I wish the circumstances could have been different."

"It seems that they were decided a long time ago."

Except, of course, that they were not. The photograph might have lain unrevealed in Glyn's landing cupboard; Glyn might have found it but chosen to remain silent. Alternative scenarios flicker in their minds — significant but, now, irrelevant. I know, thinks Elaine, and that's that. Now for what is to come.

"Just one last thing," says Glyn. "Can you let me have Oliver's present address?"

Oliver

Glyn?

Oliver has not set eyes on Glyn in years. He seldom thinks of him, except in a subliminal way in which past acquaintances can sweep briefly into the mind, and as rapidly evaporate.

But now here is Glyn, fair and square in the office, sprung by Sandra's terse remark: "Someone called Glyn Peters rang — left a number. Please call back."

"Right," says Oliver. He sees Glyn now: that square face, the thick brown crop of hair. He hears the voice, with its tinge of Welsh. Assertive, confident, but always rather compelling. The man addressing you as though you were a seminar, but you listened.

Something in Oliver's voice has evidently alerted Sandra. "Who is Glyn Peters?"

"Glyn?" says Oliver casually. "Oh, Glyn was Elaine's brother-in-law. You know . . . Elaine, wife of Nick, my erstwhile partner. Can't imagine what he wants."

And, indeed, he cannot.

Sandra has picked up on a point here; the professional eye for detail. "Was?"

"Kath . . . died," Oliver explains. He gets busy at his screen. "We need to have a talk about the new layout for *Phoenix*."

"OK," says Sandra crisply. "Right away, if you like." He has got her back on course; she is now applying herself to the design problems of the alumni magazine of an Oxford college.

Precision is the name of our game, thinks Oliver. He thinks this with pride. Accuracy. Every comma and full stop in the right place, each paragraph correctly indented. Footnotes, indexes, contents pages. Not a letter out of place. The discovery of a typo in one of his publications can give him a sleepless night. He is more satisfied than ever in his life. Desktop publishing was made for him. No tricky editorial input, no headaches about marketing and distribution. Just take the commission from the client and set about creating the immaculate product. He loves the screen on which he can conjure this precision: the compliant technology, the wonder of being able to twitch lines and letters this way and that. He is always reluctant to delegate; he surreptitiously checks and rechecks the work of even their most reliable operators. Even, it must be said, that of Sandra herself, who is a bird of his own feather. When they are alone together in the office they sit before their screens in companionable absorption, and Oliver knows that Sandra is experiencing a pleasure complementary to his own — creating text, marshalling text, positioning headings and notes. They are both getting the same buzz. It is almost like sex, he thinks.

Which is perhaps how their alliance came about, the reason that a business relationship shifted into something more, so that here they are now together by night as well as by day, in amiable conjunction, an agreeable conjugality. Oliver thinks of Sandra as friend rather than lover. Best friend. Friend with whom he makes friendly love, in the king-size bed in the first house that he has ever owned. No more seedy flats. No more fridges in which lurk nothing but a wedge of mouldy cheese and a pint of sour milk. Clean shirts to hand. Spare light bulbs and loo paper.

Oliver is still astonished to find himself one half of a couple, at this relatively late point. After the long bachelor years, the occasional forays in half-hearted pursuit of someone, the withdrawals into not especially discontented solitude. Sex on tap is indeed a luxury, though, truth to tell, both of them are somewhat less inclined these days. The cheerful roistering of their early time together is pretty well a thing of the past. But, in any case, lust was never really the driving force where his gathering interest in Sandra was concerned. More affection, appreciation — and along with these the realization that, yes, it would be rather good to go to bed with her.

And thus it was that one day he put a finger on Sandra's knee — a nylon-clad knee from which her skirt had ridden up as she sat bolt upright in her desk chair. "I've been wondering . . ." he said.

And Sandra did not slap his face, or his hand, or rush from the room. She made a correction on her screen, turned to look at him. A long, steady look. "As it happens," she said, "so have I."

Sandra is nothing like the girls he used to run after, time was. She does not have long blonde hair or legs to her armpits. She has full breasts and quite muscular calves. Her face is rather flat, all on one plane, it seems; large grey eyes, the mouth a trifle thin. Her neat cap of brown hair is streaked with grey — becoming silver glints. She is quick and calm and cool. Oliver has never seen her truly fazed, that he can recall. An essential quality in a business partner and also, he now finds, one conducive to a tranquil home life. The fridge is always stocked, the bills are paid, the insurance policies are in order.

Actually, Sandra is nothing like the people he used to know. She is nothing like Nick. As business associates, Sandra and Nick might as well be from different planets. She is nothing like Elaine.

She is nothing like Kath. Above all, she is nothing like Kath.

As if, thinks Oliver.

Oliver used to know all sorts of people. Quite a few of these were women in whom he was currently interested, but usually not sufficiently interested to make a great issue of it. He took them out from time to time, and then, usually, they went off with someone more pressing. The rest were people with whom he had a drink or a meal every now and then. Some of these were fall-out from the days with Nick. Nick and Elaine. The business generated a vibrant social life; there were always people turning up at the house, those whom Nick thought potential contributors to some series and had invited along with a gust of enthusiasm — picture researchers, photographers, freelance designers. Temporary assistants came and went, hired by Nick and then gently fired by Oliver when it was realized that resources couldn't run to this. Oliver had his own office in the converted barn that adjoined the house, and a scruffy flat in the nearby market town. In his office he dealt with what Nick called the boring part of publishing: the negotiations with printers, with distributors, with accountants. Over in the house, the fun went on. Nick seldom came to the barn, though Oliver was frequently in the house, summoned to meet this brilliant photographer, this amazing writer. He spent many hours at that kitchen table, while ideas were bandied about over glasses of red plonk. Often Elaine was there. Polly was a baby in a high-chair, then a toddler, eventually a schoolgirl.

Sometimes Kath came.

Oliver did not contribute much to those fervent creative sessions around the table. He would come up with quickly calculated figures when appropriate; occasionally, when the level of unreality was getting high, he would be quietly insistent about costings and projections. But not too insistent; he had learned that it was better to have a chat with Nick at some later point, by which time he might have gone off the whole idea anyway. Besides, Oliver enjoyed those occasions. He enjoyed the heady to and fro of ideas, Nick's flights of fancy, the provocative range of people. He liked the fetching girls with portfolios of artwork — and tried his luck with these, every now and then. He was properly impressed by the erudite experts on this and that, who might or might not be just the author they were looking for. He was well aware of his own role and image: the sweet voice of reason, sensible Oliver who'll sort out the paperwork and get this off the ground. But it seemed as though he had taken on a degree of protective colouring; he too was caught up in the creative process. He was a modest but essential adjunct to all this excited planning. He contributed by his very presence, and thus became a part of the fluctuating society around Elaine's kitchen table. He stepped out for a while with a girl Nick brought in to do design. He struck up a friendship with a man who knew all there was to know about windmills. He became someone people invited along to Sunday lunch gatherings, he was a useful extra car driver for spontaneous excursions. That was a breezy time; there was always some new venture in the pipeline, other projects charging ahead, fresh people conjured up by Nick. Thus it was perhaps that Oliver's natural pragmatism was set aside, that he failed to be alert to the warning signs until it was too late. Then there were the unnerving weeks when he went over the figures again and again, looking for some lifeline, and could find none.

"I feel I've let you down." It was to Elaine that he had said this, not Nick. And he remembers being surprised by her calmness in the face of what was happening. Her husband was about to go out of business, but she seemed quietly buoyant. "We'll be all right," she had said. "I've got some plans. What will you do, Oliver?"

He too had had a strategy in mind. He had seen what he could do, even as Hammond & Watson was laid to rest. He had taken happily to computers. That was the way to go. Word processing, printing on demand. He had side-stepped Nick's bustling ideas for future collaboration and slid away. Sometimes he thinks of those years with a touch of nostalgia; mostly he relishes his present certainty and control. Satisfaction lies in an impeccable page, and healthy accounts.

Sandra knows little of Nick, or of Elaine. Least of all, does she know anything of Kath. She is aware that Oliver's previous business venture had to do with mainstream publishing, and that his partner was the inspirational and creative member of the team and ended up if anything a mite too inspirational and creative, which was why the thing folded.

Both Sandra and Oliver are reticent about other times. Sandra is divorced, but Oliver knows little of why or when. "'Nuff said," says Sandra crisply. "Over and done with." Equally, she does not press Oliver for information. There is tacit agreement between them that both have lived other lives and that a mutual respect for privacy is appropriate in a late liaison such as theirs. Oliver finds that he is distinctly incurious about Sandra's past. This fact has occasionally given pause for thought; it seems to indicate a detachment that is perhaps not quite right. He reminds himself of Sandra's qualities and of the reasons why life with her is so compatible — her unruffled efficiency, her household management. Her compact, nubile body — nicely sexy when you wanted to see it that way but not a daily disturbing provocation. Her panache behind the wheel; he has come to dislike driving. Her *bœuf en daube.*

Given all that, an obsessive concern with Sandra's previous life seems superfluous, and indeed childish. Leave that to young lovers.

And Sandra too steers clear of enquiry. Though just occasionally an edge creeps into her voice which perhaps indicates suppressed attention. She comes across an inscription in one of Oliver's books: "Happy birthday — tons of love, Nell."

"One of your ladies, I suppose." Crisp, but a statement, not a question. The matter is not pursued.

Where Nick and Elaine are concerned, she is apparently uninterested. The business was wound up; Oliver went his own way. That will do, it seems, for Sandra.

Nowadays, Oliver does not know nearly so many people. He has lost touch with pretty well all of those acquired during the Hammond & Watson years. His clients of today do not move on to a more intimate plane; many of them he never meets — they remain a voice on the phone, a sender of faxes and emails. Occasionally he and Sandra entertain another couple for supper. He has moved into that closed society of coupledom, he realizes, on the fringes of which he hung round for so many years. A member of a couple always has someone with whom to go to the cinema, to take a walk. The unattached are flotsam, eddying about the solid purposeful mass of the coupled. From time to time, he does give a wistful thought to life as flotsam: it had its compensations.

"Kath?" says Sandra.

She speaks so abruptly that Oliver is jolted to attention. He has been cruising happily, fingers tapping out a routine task, thoughts quite elsewhere. He stops tapping, and returns to the office.

"The sister. What did she look like?" Sandra is wearing that intent look that he knows so well, like a dog pointing. This can be applied equally to the choice of a cut of meat or consideration of a page layout.

What did Kath look like? Oliver is stymied. How did you begin to describe Kath? "She was . . ." he begins. "Well, she . . . She had dark hair. Not very tall."

"There's a photo I saw once in that envelope you've got in your desk at home. I noticed it when you were trying to find an old photo of yourself to show me. A girl sitting beside a pond. Is that her?"

Sandra's observational talent. He knows at once the picture she means. Kath is sitting cross-legged on the grass in front of the garden pond at Nick and Elaine's house. Her eyes are screwed up in the sunlight, she has bare arms and legs, and a radiant smile, beaming straight at the camera: she is entrancing. Yes, Sandra would have noticed that photo.

"That's her," he says. "Yup."

"I see." Sandra looks reflectively at him. "She was extremely attractive, then?"

"Yes," says Oliver. "She was. Yes, you could say that."

"I'd taken it that the photo was of some girlfriend."

Oliver is almost shocked. "Oh, dear me, no. No, no."

Sandra gives him a little smile. She turns back to her screen. Kath has been dealt with, so far as she is concerned.

It still seems incredible to Oliver that Kath will not suddenly walk into the room. Never again. That is what she did, back then. No one was expecting her, Elaine didn't know where she was, what she was doing, and then there she would be — smiling, laughing: "Are you all terribly busy? Can I come to lunch?"

He sees her arriving thus with a great tray of peaches in her arms. She has bought up the entire stock of some greengrocer. "Here . . ." she says. "I couldn't resist. Let's gorge." And Elaine has pursed lips. Oliver can read her thoughts: extravagant, exaggerated, they'll go bad before they can all be eaten.

Elaine was strange where Kath was concerned. You could feel that she was unsettled when Kath was around, there was that sense of concealed tension. She watched Kath a lot — but then, everyone did that. And she chivvied her. Criticized. Elder sister stuff — but there was a compulsive edge to it. Though it all seemed to roll off Kath; she would smile, deflect. "All right, I'll reform, I promise . . . Listen, I want to tell you about this amazing place I've found —"

Kath. What a shame it was, thinks Oliver. What a crying shame. When Kath comes into his mind, it is always like a sudden shaft of light. She is talking about a place she's been to, a person she's met, she is all zest and animation, a group springs to life when she is there. There was nobody, Oliver thinks, but nobody, less likely to be . . . dead.

He sometimes wonders why he did not fall in love with her. Plenty did, after all. But no. Kath always seemed out of bounds. Sacrosanct, in some curious way. Not for him. She was never less than warm, friendly, welcoming. But then she was like that with everyone. Almost everyone. If Kath didn't care for a person she simply moved away; you never saw dislike, disapproval, but she would have created a space, turned aside. What a talent, thinks Oliver. But that was how she seemed to run her life. When things no longer suited her, she moved on, moved off. Or so one understood. He remembers Elaine's terse enquiries: "You mean you're not working at that gallery any more?" and Kath's light responses: "Things weren't going quite so well. And I've met this nice man who wants me to help with a festival he's running."

Occasionally, when Kath turned up, there was a man with her. Hardly surprising. Oliver can barely remember these men. One cast an eye over them, of course. Envious? Well no, not that — but with a kind of proprietorial concern. Was this fellow worthy? And since the same man seldom came a second time, and more often than not she was alone, there was no reason to get exercised about the matter. It seemed remarkable that no one had snapped her up on a permanent basis, but clearly she had this talent for evasion.

Which made Glyn Peters all the more surprising. Oliver remembers well the advent of Glyn Peters. One became aware of an intensity about Elaine, a tautness. And then one day there was Kath and she had this bloke with her, very much at home apparently, knees under Elaine's kitchen table as though he had a right there, one eye on Kath all the time, holding forth. Oliver had been wary at first, hackles raised: gradually he had found himself intrigued, even slightly mesmerized. The man had a way with him, no doubt about that. Not surprising he'd been a hit on the telly, apparently. He had that knack of talking whereby he seemed to be addressing you personally, as though you were especially equipped to appreciate all this intriguing information. Oliver can hear him now, giving them all a breakdown on medieval crop rotation systems, on how to date a hedge; he would glance in your direction, and you felt flattered, singled out, recognized as a connoisseur.

Was that what Kath had felt? Elaine put her head round his office door one morning — brisk and to the point: "A date for your diary, Oliver. Kath's getting married. We'll have a bit of a party. You met Glyn a few weeks ago — remember?" And that was it. Well, well. Lucky Glyn Peters. How had he done it? Oliver remembers Kath at one of those kitchen gatherings, the table awash with food and drink, Nick talking, Glyn talking most of all, and Kath sitting slightly apart, on the window-seat, her legs curled under her, Polly alongside. Polly was always wherever Kath was. Kath is plaiting Polly's hair — Polly's long schoolgirl hair. She combs the hair and looks towards Glyn, a speculative look, as though she is asking him something, asking herself something. They are shortly to be married. Oliver inspects Kath for indications of consuming passion; but there is just this querying gaze. Puzzled, almost.

You could not but be absorbed by Kath, even if you did not fall in love with her. There was what she looked like, and there was what she was. She was . . . What was she? thinks Oliver. She was an entirely nice person. Nice? What does that mean? A non-word. You couldn't imagine Kath doing anything mean, or malevolent, or despicable. She was nice to people — hang on, that word again — she was friendly, and interested, and kind. And a provocative thought arises: was she able to be that way because of what she looked like? Because the world smiles upon the physically attractive and they can smile back? But the world is also well stocked with malign beauties, and ever has been, from Snow White's stepmother onwards. A ravishing woman can also have a vile temperament. So that theory won't wash.

When Oliver remembers Kath, that luminous quality predominates. The way your spirits lifted a notch, just because she was there: the day seemed more promising, the adrenalin ran stronger. And really, Oliver thinks, that is distinctly odd. Perverse, even. Kath had gaiety and verve, but she was not especially wise, nor clever, nor well-informed. If one is being realistic, one would have to say that her contribution to society was nil. She did nothing useful, had no sustained employment, was neither creative nor industrious. She had no children, if children are to be seen as fulfilment of a social purpose. She simply was — as a flower is, or a bird. People are meant to be more than that, are they not?

Oh, come on, thinks Oliver, this is getting heavy. It's enough that she was a startlingly appealing person, in every way.

She could surprise you, take you unawares. Once, he was with her in the courtyard between the house and his office in the barn. They were sitting on the bench there, waiting it seems for someone or something — the framework of the moment is gone now. And she turned to him and said, "Are you happy, Oliver?"

He had clenched in alarm. He had wanted to protest that he wasn't the sort of person who answers that sort of question, or to whom that sort of question is put. He had gazed at her beseechingly: was he supposed to say, "Are you, Kath?"

She had gazed back, thoughtful, expectant, really wanting to know, it seemed, as though his reply might solve some problem. And when he went on saying nothing she smiled — that smile, that great smile that always made you smile back, willy-nilly: "I bet you are. You've got more sense than to be unhappy."

When he realized that there was something going on between her and Nick, he had been disturbed. More than that — incredulous, alarmed, offended. How could this be?

The first intimation had been a look, quite simply. Nick watching Kath in the way that others watched her, those coming across her for the first time, people who hadn't known her for years, as Nick had. Elaine had not been present; Oliver had been uneasily glad of that.

After that, small disconcerting signals. Nick covertly attentive when Elaine was on the phone to Kath, pretending to read the newspaper. Kath visiting less, rather than more. Elaine saying one day, "Ages since Kath showed up — where's she got to now?"; Nick's furtive look, his apparent casual lack of interest.

And then one day Oliver had gone to the Blue Boar in Welborne to meet a man for a drink — a piece of fellow flotsam from that footloose uncoupled time — and there at a table across the room were Nick and Kath. Quite evidently intent upon one another. Oliver had been all of a dither. What to do? March up to them, jolly and unconcerned: "Hi there — what a coincidence! Tom's with me — you know, Tom Willows — we'll join you." And then he had hesitated, headed in one direction and then another, and they had looked up and the expression on their faces was not one of cheery innocent welcome but of dismay. Oliver had flapped a hand, mouthed some dismissive greeting, bolted for an alcove as far from them as possible. "Isn't that your partner?" said Tom Willows, puzzled. "No," said Oliver. "I mean, yes. Business meeting — no need to get involved. Pint?"

Later that day Nick came across to the barn. "Just to have a word about print runs for the new series, and to ask what you think about this jacket artwork — fantastic, isn't it?" The usual Nick, all lit up with plans and ideas. "I think we should really go for broke on this one, don't you —?" And, at the end of it, turning to go, he had shot Oliver a look — a wary, propitiating look: "Oh . . . and, Olly, incidentally, you didn't see me this morning, OK?"

I don't want this, Oliver had thought. I don't want any part of this. This is nothing to do with me.

But it was, now.

No one else must know: that was paramount. He knew, who had no wish to, but there must be no others.

Above all, not Elaine. Above all, not Glyn Peters — a man who struck Oliver as being quite likely to come charging in with a horsewhip.

The matter was never raised again between him and Nick. Except that once, tacitly. The business with the photograph. That had been his warning shot. Nothing said. Just that silent indication: watch it, stop it. And, eventually, he assumed, that was just what had come about. It ended, as these things do.

Oh well . . . long out of the way, all that, thinks Oliver. Laid to rest, thanks be. No harm done, in the end.

"I'm off out," says Sandra. "I've got to go to the bank. Mind the shop for half an hour, will you?"

And she is gone. Oliver makes himself a cup of coffee. He yawns. He is drifting rather this morning — he will need to go over those pages carefully. He stares out of the window for a moment, remembers that call. He picks up the phone.

"Oh — Glyn? Oliver Watson here, returning your call."

Elaine and Nick

Nick goes to a health club these days. This is on account of his paunch, which has been causing him disquiet. He is also disturbed about his bald patch, and while he is aware that visits to the health club will not do much for that, he feels that all the same there may be some general knock-on effect. Nick cannot understand how he has come to be fifty-eight. This is ridiculous, frankly. Time has been stalking him, but the thing to do was to give it the cold shoulder, pay no attention. And now suddenly it has reached out and clobbered him. He does not care for what he sees in the mirror; he is pained and affronted.

At the health club, Nick jogs and cycles and pumps. He ploughs up and down the gold-dappled blue waters of the pool. He is bored to desperation while doing this and the jogging and pumping make him ache, but he is satisfied with his own strength of mind. He weighs himself frequently, finds that he can definitely chalk up the loss of two and a half pounds, and buys a new pair of jeans to celebrate the fact. Elaine has made it plain that she thinks men of his age should not be wearing jeans, which is unkind, he feels; why should he give up the habit of a lifetime?

The boredom of the health club is somewhat tempered by idle observation of those around him.

Most are much younger — in their twenties or thirties. Many of the girls are tattooed — a butterfly on the shoulder, a spray of leaves on the thigh, a star on the ankle. To pass the time, Nick makes a mental inventory of these tattoos, which means he needs to look quite closely at the girls, though he is careful to do so discreetly, knowing how easy it is for men to be misconstrued these days. He has listed clover leaves, and ivy and daisies, and a single rose. He got a fleeting glimpse once of a dragon round the midriff, which needs a confirmatory sighting. The girls themselves are of course pleasing, though that is about as far as it goes. He can honestly say that while there is the odd *frisson* of sexual interest, he is not tempted. Occasionally, he exchanges a few words with one of them in the cafeteria — could I take that paper if you've done with it? were you wanting this chair? — and the girl will be polite enough, though not what you might call encouraging. In transitory glum moments, Nick wonders if he is emasculated by the paunch and the bald patch.

But Nick is not constitutionally glum, never has been.

All his life, he has woken up each day with a renewed surge of interest. When he looks back — which in fact he does not much do — he has this gratifying sense of busyness, of teeming schemes and projects, of some unquenchable source of stimulation. Admittedly plenty of schemes and projects never came to fruition, and indeed he has forgotten now what most of them were, but it is the general effect that counts. He has never been bored — or, if he has, he has quickly side-stepped.

Which is why he is proud of his tenacity at the health club.

And he has plenty still to do. He has two or three ideas on the go that just need some more research. A gazetteer of eighteenth-century follies; the definitive series on hill walking; a photographic survey of World War II pillboxes. Truth to tell, it is a blessing that with Elaine doing so well for years now the pressure is off, he can take his time, play around with any new inspiration and look really carefully at what might be involved. And there's no need to do too much hack stuff, where the money, to be honest, is neither here nor there. Quite a good idea to keep one's hand in with the odd piece of journalism, but no point in becoming a slave to it.

"There is something we have got to talk about," says Elaine.

Her tone of voice sets an alarm bell ringing, but only a muted one. This matter of upgrading his car? Probably. Nothing that can't be sorted, if he goes about it in the right way.

It may be that the demise of Hammond & Watson was all for the best, in the long term. Of course it was tremendous fun, at the time — that non-stop activity, new books brewing, those heady moments when the first bound copies arrived, the pursuit of likely authors, all the comings and goings. But there had been also the endless niggling tiresome background irritations of accountants and suppliers, and all those bloody figures which apparently forbade one to do this or that. Admittedly, Oliver took much off one's back, but they were always there, like some po-faced inappropriate guest at a party, clouding things.

No, he doesn't regret those days so very much. The time since has been something of a liberation, Nick now realizes. He has been able to give proper consideration to a project, drop it if it seems likely to become a bore in the end, instead of being obliged to plunge ahead because a publishing house must publish, after all. And then sometimes one got tired of the book or the series in mid-stream. No, he can take things as they come — do background work on some idea when he feels inspired, and accept fallow periods when nothing much springs to mind, but that's not so bad because there are always plenty of agreeable ways of passing the time. He is aware that Elaine gets a bit uptight about this way of doing things, but it is so shortsighted of her. As he has tried to explain — but she never quite seems to get the point — you are actually much more productive if you pace yourself. He had never realized that was the case, back in the Hammond & Watson days, when he used to be scurrying around like some demented ant — day in, day out. Of course Elaine's own style is one of relentless work. He's always telling her she should let up a bit, take a few days off. But no — if it's not client meetings and site visits, it's paperwork with Sonia or sussing out some new supplier. And when she's not doing any of that she's out in the garden, fossicking away.

★   ★   ★

"Oh . . . right," he says. "Over supper, OK? I was just going to the health club."

"*Now*. I'm away tonight."

Mind, he'd be the first to agree that Elaine's industry is remarkable, and that her success is a great blessing. All credit to her — he would never have believed that the outfit she's got now could have arisen from those small beginnings. He got a bit of a shock the other day when he heard her discussing last year's turnover with Sonia. And incidentally, given that, it really is a bit stiff to be getting all flaky about replacing the car.

Just occasionally, Nick looks at Elaine and is disconcerted. He gets this odd feeling that she is someone else, a person he doesn't know all that well. Which is absurd, she is the woman with whom he has been getting into bed every night — well, most nights, admittedly Elaine is elsewhere rather more often nowadays — for God knows how many years. How long have they been married? He'd need to work that one out. And of course this is nonsense — Elaine is as she ever was, just older. But sometimes this stranger glances across the table at him.

She's in the top league now, it seems, in her trade. There's talk of a lecture tour in the States, and she's designing a garden for next year's Chelsea Flower Show. She's busy. Which means that she is not always as attentive to what Nick may be saying or doing as she once was. Maybe that accounts for the sense of alienation. But it's not a problem.

Nick has always given problems a wide berth. Problems should not be what life is about. When running a business, you hire someone else to deal with nuts and bolts, as good old Oliver did. Nick is always saying to Elaine that she should pass on much more to Sonia than she does, or bring in some troubleshooter. And, above all, you never allow yourself to get rattled if things aren't working out the way they should. Just move on. Cut your losses and forget about it.

This is the best policy for personal life also, Nick reckons. The snag is that other people tend to ambush you, from time to time. They create difficulties. They misunderstand, they misinterpret. It has to be said that Elaine has a tendency in that direction. Some small thing can be absurdly inflated, an obstacle found where there need be none. Such as this nonsense about the car.

"In the conservatory," says Elaine. "Sonia will be here in a minute."

He follows her. Really, this is getting a bit out of hand.

How long *have* they been married? He must remember to check that out with her, though obviously now is not the moment. Nick is well attuned to Elaine's state of mind, and it is clear that this morning is a bad patch, for some reason. The strategy will be, as ever, to be nicely propitiating, lower the temperature, change the subject and, with any luck, whatever is riling her can be laid to rest.

Nick is definitely fond of Elaine. Absolutely no question about that. He cannot imagine being married to anyone else. Time was — and he is prepared to admit this — he used to look around a bit, once in a while. But everyone does that when they're younger, don't they? There's nothing of that kind now, hasn't been for many a year. Elaine suits him nicely. Their sex life has rather gone off the boil, but presumably that's true of anyone of their age. Though Elaine of course is a touch older than he is, not that he's ever made anything of that.

Nick can't quite remember how he and Elaine came to get married. No wonder he's not certain how long ago it was anyway. An awful lot of years, that's for sure. He's never gone in for mulling over the past. What's done is done. You can't change what's happened, so why keep hauling it out and looking at it? And he has never wished himself not married to Elaine; just occasionally it has been therapeutic to . . . look outside a bit. Back when he met her there was such a crowd of people about, melded now into an impressionistic blur. Lots of girls. Somehow it was Elaine he married rather than someone else, and he is inclined to feel that that has been nothing but a blessing. All right, she can be edgy at times, such as right now, but one can handle that. And she has always kept things running — he is absolutely prepared to hand it to her there, if it weren't for the way she has got her own business off the ground they might well be in a bit of a pickle at this point. No, Elaine deserves all credit, no question. If she gets rather fraught on occasion, well, that's understandable. She's under a fair bit of pressure, and the thing is to be understanding and accommodating.

"Actually," he says, "I've given it a bit of thought — this car question — and I reckon we don't need to go for brand new. A year or two old would do me fine."

"We're not talking about your car."

It has to be said that Elaine can be just a mite governessy. Ever has been — and getting more so, Nick fears. One is going to have to be tolerant. It was never a good idea to make a stand when she got ratty about something quite trivial — best just to back off and, with any luck, it would blow over. In the past, he could always placate her, talk her down, be especially friendly and helpful and all that. Lately, this approach somehow doesn't seem to cut so much ice. The best thing is just to keep his head down, go his own way, which is, after all, what he has always done, and take care not to get into antagonistic situations. Elaine likes to run a tight ship, she likes to know what's going on around her, but nowadays she is pretty well taken up with the business and frankly there's no need for her to be bothered about Nick's day-to-day arrangements. Actually, it would be a lot more sensible if there was some more fluid system over cash flow, and then he wouldn't need to involve her when something crops up like this matter of the car. He's suggested this more than once, but Elaine can be funny when it comes to money. Distinctly shirty.

★ ★ ★

"Oh . . . right." He gives her a questioning look. An open, sunny, at-your-service sort of look.

Damn. That means the car matter has simply been put on hold, stashed away in one of Elaine's mental "pending" files, and he will have to allow a judicious interval before he brings it up again. Which is a blasted nuisance. The Golf has over eighty thousand on the clock, one thing after another is going wrong, and he wouldn't really want to do a long trip in it. Which means that he has got to get it replaced before he can go up to Northumberland and have a few days pottering around Lindisfarne and Alnwick and places like that, which he feels might be inspirational.

Elaine is silent. Nick waits. Back in the house, the phone rings, stops. Sonia has picked it up. Outside, Jim rides the tractor mower to and fro, to and fro.
"So the mower's running OK now . . ." says Nick.

Which is all to the good. Bad news if it was packing in. God knows what those things cost. Not as much as a car, though, surely? But of course it's not the car we're here about, apparently. There's something else.
When Elaine comes on all heavy like this the thing is to play it down. Nick does not like rows. In fact, he never has rows — not with anyone. If a row situation threatens, he somehow just is not there any more. This technique has worked with Elaine, up to a point. It is difficult for anyone to get satisfactorily confrontational

with someone who will not confront back. Nick is aware that he is rather skilful at marital peacekeeping, at the avoidance of overt hostility, at the adroit use of diplomatic initiatives. On occasion, he has wondered if he ought not to be exploiting this experience, this facility. When lifestyle publications became a boom industry, he thought of stepping in with a really definitive book on married life from the man's point of view. With a pushy title — *How to Stay Married*, that sort of thing. A combination of wry humour with practicality. And a literary slant as well — cite some famous abiding marriages and look at the ups and downs. D. H. Lawrence and what's-her-name. Tennyson was married for donkey's years, wasn't he? Dickens — no, that went off the rails. One would have to get it all up, but that could be quite amusing. In fact, the thing was definitely a promising idea, but somehow it was a project he had never felt able to run past Elaine. Normally he gave her a progress report on any scheme he was working on — not that there was ever very much of a comeback, not much constructive input from her, put it that way. Sometimes you could even feel that she wasn't giving the sort of attention that she should be. Anyway, he'd somehow had this sense that she wouldn't really get the point of the marriage book idea, so it was never mentioned and eventually he'd abandoned it. It was something one could always pick up again, if there was nothing much else in mind.

But Nick knows that he is sensitive to the coded language of married life. He can negotiate. And so he is not going to allow whatever is at issue just now to get out of hand. Easy does it.

"Kath," says Elaine.

It is curious how her name instantly summons her. She is right there, for an instant, looking at him. And he feels . . . well, there is a pleasant sense of well-being, a little lift of the spirits. Kath could always do that. A whole troop of Kaths flit about him, stemming from different times and places. She is dancing with Polly — a child Polly. She has just married Glyn, and stands hand in hand with him, beaming. She sits cross-legged in the garden here, making a daisy chain. She . . . And then again she . . .

"Kath?" he says.

They seldom talk about Kath. At least not deliberately, as it were. She crops up, often enough. Naturally. Some casual mention. "Wasn't Kath there when . . .?" "Didn't Kath use to go to such-and-such . . .?" Polly talks about her quite a lot. She and Polly were always thick as thieves.

So why, all of a sudden . . . ?

"You and Kath," says Elaine.

There is this heave of the gut. The room seems to swing a little. The troop of Kaths is quite gone. It is just him and Elaine, sitting there in the conservatory, with the

111

tractor mower going up and down outside, a bee buzzing in the blue plumbago. Everything is quite real and precise, unfortunately. It is Tuesday morning, about half-past ten. He should be on his way to the health club. Instead, he is here, with a sick feeling in his stomach.

What is going on? Not . . . Surely she can't have . . . How could . . . ?

"I've seen a photograph," says Elaine. "And a note from you that was with it."

Oh God. It comes rushing into his head as she speaks. That photograph. Of course. He can see it. He remembers laughing when first he saw it. And he couldn't resist sending it to Kath. She didn't keep it? The silly girl didn't go and hang on to it?

"I see you know what I'm talking about," she says.

Jesus Christ. But . . . Hang on, how did . . .? Oliver. It was Oliver who handed over the photo. And one — well, one sort of squared Oliver. And he said he'd binned the negative. So has bloody Oliver . . .? Otherwise it has to be that it has somehow turned up. Where?

"Glyn found it," says Elaine.

Now the whole place whirls. The floor rocks. That bee makes a shrill, insistent din, like a dentist's drill. This shouldn't be happening. But it is.

Get a grip. Take control. This is bad, but it is nothing that cannot be contained, like everything else. Naturally Elaine is upset; she has had a shock. It will take a while for her to digest this; he is going to need all his resources.

"Ah . . . Glyn," he says.

Now it is Glyn's turn to come surging in. Nick can see him plain, and he is looking like thunder. Nick cannot hear what he is saying, which is probably just as well. Glyn — a nasty complication there. But first things first.

"Look, love," he says. "What we have to do is get this thing into perspective. OK — I'm not going to defend myself or tell lies. I wish it didn't have to be like this, but now that it is . . . well, I'm just going to be entirely honest. Yes, Kath and I once, just for a while, we —"

"I don't want to know," says Elaine. "I don't want to know when, or where, or for how long. It's enough that it was."

"Listen," he says. "It was a flash in the pan. A silly, idiotic, passing thing. It was all over, long ago. Long before she —"

"No doubt."

"It makes absolutely no difference to *us*," he says. "Neither then nor now. It was a stupid mistake. Kath herself would say that. Believe me. I know she would."

"Very likely."

★ ★ ★

This isn't going right. He has struck the wrong note, somehow. And Elaine is unnerving him. She just sits there, quite calm, staring him down. Right now he feels more strongly than ever that there is a stranger there, not her.

The bee is silent. Jim and the tractor mower have gone. The ground is steady, the room no longer rocks, but it feels alien. Everything is just the same, but not the same at all.

"What can I do?" he says. Very quiet voice. Careful, sorrowful.

"I want you to go," says Elaine.

He gazes in total disbelief. "Go where?"

"That is entirely up to you. Away from here. Away from this house."

He is about to say, "But this is my house," when he remembers that it is not. It is Elaine's house. Elaine put down the deposit, Elaine pays the mortgage.

"So long as you are here," says Elaine, "I shall be reminded of this every time I look at you. I shall have all the feelings that I am having at the moment. And I don't propose to remain in this condition for the foreseeable future. I have better things to do."

"But I live here," says Nick.

"At the moment."

Scuttling thoughts. No, not thoughts — panicky explosions in the head. But she can't! Yes, she can. What will I . . .? Where can I . . .? This is so unfair.

Years ago. I haven't committed a *crime*. I mean lots of people . . .

Stay cool, that's the thing. Sweet reason. Elaine is a reasonable woman. She must see that this is . . . exaggerated. Of course it's shaken her up, of course she's angry. She has every right.

Quiet voice, still. Gentle, persuasive. "Listen, I absolutely understand how you must be feeling. And I'm with you. I'm wiped out by this myself. But we can manage. We can't let it spoil everything. In time, we'll be able to live with it."

"You apparently have been doing so for years, quite comfortably," says Elaine. "Personally, I don't feel so confident about that."

Back in the house the phone rings again. It stops. Nick sees Elaine shoot a glance at her watch.

"Honestly, sweetie," he says. "This is all a bit over the top. What we need to do is wind down, sleep on it, and have a little talk in a few days' time."

Elaine gets up. "In a few days' time you won't be here," she says. "I'm off shortly. I'll be back late tomorrow afternoon, and I expect to find you gone. Money is being paid into your account, and will be each month. Enough to rent a place and meet modest living expenses. Take your car. And your books. We can sort out what else belongs to you at some later point."

And she goes. Outside, Jim is back with the tractor mower. The bee is joined by a friend. The day marches on.

Glyn and Oliver

Bloody hell! What a mess. After all this time. Just because of a wretched photograph.

Oliver feels trapped. Here he is in his own familiar pub along the road from the office, and nothing is as it should be. Instead of a pint and a quiet half hour with the newspaper he is eyeball-to-eyeball with Glyn Peters. The pint is there, but he is not enjoying it. Glyn is a heavy presence, grilling him. He leans insistently across the low shiny round table, moving beer mats with one finger. He fixes Oliver with those glittery dark-brown eyes.

"What I need to know —" he says.

You'd be a damn sight better off not knowing, thinks Oliver. Just leave it alone. Nothing to be done about it now. All over with. And, no, I don't know how long it went on for and I don't want to know and nor should you. It's nothing to do with me, never was. Anyone would think I was some sort of accessory to the crime.

"Why did you photograph them?" demands Glyn.

For heaven's sake! "Look, I didn't see until after I got the prints. I just snapped the whole group, standing there chatting to each other. I hadn't noticed that Kath and Nick were —" He shrugs.

And when you did, thinks Glyn, you got into a right old panic, didn't you? Your business chum and his sister-in-law. And you all matey with everyone — always in and out of the house . . .

Years since he set eyes on Oliver Watson. The man much the same as ever — that slightly apologetic manner, self-deprecation tinged with complacency. Running some sort of small printing outfit these days, it seems. Little office with computers. Lady who appears to be rather more than an assistant, taking a distinct interest in one's arrival. Oliver rather keen to get them both off the premises sharpish: "Glyn Peters — Sandra Chalcott. Sandra's my partner. We'll push off to the local, shall we, and have a chat there?"

"How did you find me?" Oliver enquires. "Given that we've rather lost touch?"

"Elaine."

"You've told Elaine!"

"I needed to establish certain facts. There was no alternative." Glyn is impatient rather than defensive.

"Nick?" says Oliver, after a moment.

"That's up to Elaine. I am frankly not much interested in Nick."

Oliver takes a swig of beer, which does nothing for him. He wishes he were back in the office. He wishes Glyn were anywhere but here. He is irritated, and also faintly apprehensive. There is something evangelical about Glyn's approach to this, the sinister evangelism of the obsessed.

Glyn hammers on. "You must have seen a good deal of Kath, over the years?"

"Well . . . yes. She was often around." What is this leading up to? Good grief . . . is he going to accuse me of having it off with her too?

Glyn leans back in his chair. He places his fingers tip to tip, rests his chin on them, becomes reflective and confidential. "Let me tell you, this revelation has stopped me in my tracks. You must understand that. I am confronted with . . . an unreliability about my own past. My past with Kath. I am not interested in recriminations. My concern is purely forensic. Do you follow me?"

"Not really," says Oliver.

"I want to know if Kath was in the habit of infidelity. I want to know about her."

Oliver is shocked. But you were married to her, for Christ's sake, he wants to say. It's a bit late in the day to start talking like this.

Glyn finishes his beer, rises, gestures at Oliver. "Drink up."

"Actually, I won't have another," says Oliver. "I've got an afternoon's work to do." But Glyn has ignored him, and is already heading for the bar.

When he returns he is in full flow before he has sat down. "I have to look at this as I would at any other major piece of research. Every clue must be followed up . . . I have to take a detached view, lay everything out for inspection, pay attention to even the most marginal pieces of information —" Isolated phrases reach over, rising above the background buzz of the pub; Oliver wears an attentive expression, and allows himself to drift. What's with the man? Was he always like this?

Well, yes — somewhat. And the voice — great delivery. Generations of Welsh preachers behind that. "Method, patience. You start out with an open mind, prepared for whatever may turn up. Which doesn't mean that you don't follow a hunch, do you see? Now, seeking you out may take me nowhere, but it was worth doing. Kath is now my area of study —"

"But she's not an area," Oliver interrupts, goaded. "She's a woman. Was."

Glyn jolts to a halt. He stares. Annoyed, it would seem. But the mood switches. "Point taken," he says. "That's the whole trouble, isn't it?"

Oliver looks down into his unwelcome second pint. No answer to that one.

"So tell me, then. Was she known for this kind of thing?"

"Not to my knowledge."

"Before she married me she had . . . admirers. Par for the course."

"Quite," Oliver agrees.

"I'm concerned with a subsequent pattern of behaviour."

Oliver is finding it hard to believe that this conversation is taking place. He surveys the room. He eyes other pairs of men, presumably having a comfortable post-mortem on some business assignment, or talking politics or sport or last night's television. While he is landed with the manic concerns of a bloke he thought he no longer knew.

"You must have had a general impression about her, as a person."

No comment required, it would seem.

"Did you know her friends?"

Enough, thinks Oliver. "Look," he says. "Kath is . . . dead. Not here. Can't put up any sort of defence or explanation. Is this fair?"

Glyn spreads his hands. "But that is the whole point about the dead. Precisely. They are unaffected. Untouchable. Beyond reach. The rest of us are still flailing around trying to make sense of things. Addicts like myself choose to do so as a way of life."

"Well," says Oliver. "That's your view. Not mine, I have to say."

Glyn takes stock. This is not going anywhere. Impossible to get one's point across. Stonewalling — that's what the man is at. Why? What's his agenda? Is there something he knows? If so, he's been pretty quick on his feet. Had no idea what I wanted to see him about until half an hour ago. Whatever . . . no point in spinning this out.

He smiles — genial, equable. "And I respect your position. But I'm sure you appreciate that I've been somewhat thrown by this."

Actually, Oliver does. At least, at this moment he does. It must indeed have been a slap in the face. He manages a wan reciprocating grin.

Glyn downs his beer. "Well — good to have met up again after all this time. Pity it had to be about this."

Oliver mumbles some similar sentiment.

They get up and move towards the door. Outside, Glyn pauses. "The other couple — on that occasion.

Woman called Mary Packard, I believe. Friend of yours?"

Oliver shakes his head, wanting to make a bolt for the office.

"Artist of some kind, is that right?"

"Potter," says Oliver desperately. "Lived in Winchcombe." Oh, treachery. But what is Mary Packard to him? Anything to have done with this. "Have to dash," he says. "Client due shortly. Good to see you."

Polly

Kath! I can't believe all this is about *Kath*.

I mean, basically she was just such an amazingly nice person. I adored her. So possibly I'm prejudiced, but that's how she was for me. I thought she was wonderful. Of course, that rather went down like a lead balloon with Mum. She and Mum . . . Oh well, old history now. Except that apparently nothing is. But it was all more on Mum's side, you know. Always Mum being uptight and critical and Kath going her own sweet way. I suppose that was the problem — Kath just carried on regardless and other people were left to look on, and they didn't always look kindly. Though what business it was of theirs, frankly. I mean, Kath just lived life to the full and what's wrong with that, say I?

She was *so* attractive. That face. And the way she moved and sat and stood — you always found yourself watching her. Not that she was the slightest bit vain, never bothered about clothes or hair — well, she didn't need to, but the point is she never realized she didn't need to. Just didn't much care. Of course you can only be like that if you *are* that compelling, so I suppose in a way she did know, kind of unconsciously — it comes full circle.

But she wasn't full of self-confidence — not a bit. It was more that she was . . . well, she had some kind of glow. And dash — always off somewhere, meeting someone, jumping in the car. She didn't hang around. Almost as though she didn't dare to, when one thinks about it. As though if she stopped, something would catch up with her. Anyway, self-confident isn't the term — definitely not. But she must have *known* the effect she had. Men, after all . . . It was more as though that just didn't have any effect on *her*. Or any sort of ego-boosting effect. She didn't really seem to have an ego, come to think of it. Self-centred she was not, if that's compatible with always doing pretty much what you want. Hmm . . . more complicated than one reckons.

I remember when my first boyfriend dumped me, when I was at college. What? Oh yes, definitely he was a rat. Hey — are you having a go at me? Well, good, then. Anyway, it was Kath's shoulder I wept on, of course, rather than Mum's. Kath said, "That's what they do." And sort of shrugged, with that little odd smile. And I remember I said, "I bet no one's ever dumped *you*." And she thought for a moment and she said: "Not as such, I suppose, but there's other ways of going about it." I can still hear her saying that. I didn't know what she meant, and I don't now. Women dump too? Well, of course. Too right they do. I'm not talking general theory, I'm talking Kath, do you mind? And then she took me out shopping and we bought me a crazy ridiculous dress I'd never have bought on my own and had an extravagant lunch in an Italian place. That was Kath all over — turn your back on life's glitches, go out, go away, ring up a friend.

Sort of thing that made Mum go all tight-lipped. Not Mum's style, you see. There was something tortoise and hare about Mum and Kath. Oh, but it's the tortoise that wins, isn't it? Hmm . . . food for thought there. Not that it was a race, or even the usual sort of sisterly rivalry stuff. Frankly, they never even seemed like sisters. But there was some kind of eerie connection. Umbilical cord — no, that's not right, but you know what I mean. I suppose it's always like that, with siblings. I wouldn't know, not having any.

When I was little, Kath was where the fun was at, whenever she came to our house, always unexpected, out of the blue. Bringing lovely silly presents that I've never forgotten — paper flowers that opened in water, and a kite like a dragon, and a ginger kitten that just about had Mum hitting the roof. She made up games that we played and she read me stories and she did my hair in funky styles and she discovered face-painting for kids before everyone else was doing it. When she walked in the door it was suddenly like it was Christmas, or a birthday.

It's funny she never had children of her own. She and Glyn. Mind, I can't imagine Glyn with children. Doubt if he wanted any. It wasn't something she ever talked about. I wonder . . . well, whatever reason she didn't, she didn't.

You can imagine not wanting children? Oh, you can, can you? I see.

Thinking about Kath, I suppose one thing that sticks out is that she never worked. Not properly, that is. I mean, for most people — for practically everyone —

work is what you are, in a sense. What you have to do, day in, day out, decides everything else. How much money you've got and therefore how you can live. And it either builds you up or grinds you down, doesn't it? Personally, I consider myself pretty lucky, work-wise. I like it. I get paid not too badly for doing something I don't at all mind doing. And I get an odd sort of kick out of knowing that what I'm doing is absolutely a here-and-now sort of thing. A today kind of job. I mean, if you'd said to someone twenty years ago, she's a web designer, they'd have gone: eh? They'd have been thinking crochet work. It's like operating the Spinning Jenny at the beginning of the Industrial Revolution — or stoking the first steam engine or whatever. Nobody's done this before, I say to myself. Nobody's spent their days sitting in front of a box with a glowing window, flicking images around. What I'm doing is precisely where the human race is at, today.

OK, laugh. I knew it was pretentious when I said it. Oh — funny — right.

No, you're not. Excuse me, but no way is estate agent cutting-edge stuff. Estate agents have been around since the Ark. There'd have been an estate agent on Mount Ararat, telling Noah this was a prime development site. Sorry, Dan.

Don't worry, you'll always make lots more money than I do. But I wouldn't want to be doing anything else. It beats stoking engines any day — if this is the new technical revolution then we slave workers have certainly got it easier this time round. In fact, the slave workers are somewhere else now, aren't they?

They're out there mending the roads and carting rubbish and heaving bricks, like they always were. Of course, it helps to have had an education a cut above the average. Three years at college and all that. I was never going to end up on the checkout at Tesco, whatever.

Kath. I've got right away from Kath. Her not working. Or not working in any serious sense. Just stuff she'd do for a few weeks or months and then pack it in — temping with a publisher, front-of-house girl in an art gallery. God knows how she managed, income-wise. But she never went in for mortgages or rent either. She just seemed to perch — here, there and everywhere. Mum was always fussing because she didn't know her address.

No, actually some guy was *not* paying the bills. You're quite wrong there. Not that there weren't plenty who'd have been glad to. There was always someone hanging around. But Kath wasn't one for commitment, or at least not for a long time. Frankly, I think she had a problem.

Excuse me, Dan, but you are so wrong. Of course a person has a problem if they apparently can't commit themselves to a relationship by the time they're thirty-five.

And there was no question of career motivation in Kath's case. Way back, when she was very young, she was going to be an actress. Why, oh why, is it that for any girl with definitely above average looks it becomes inevitable that she's going to be an actress? Nowadays it would be modelling, wouldn't it? Kath would be talent-spotted in Oxford Street. Back then, people must have kept saying, "Honestly, with your looks, you just have to go for acting . . ." Until it became what she had to do.

I mean, that's so stupid. The idea that what a person looks like decides what they ought to do. You might as well say that red-haired people should drive London buses. And it happens to women more than men. Above all it happens to ultra-decorative women. A good-looking guy can ride it out. He can end up as prime minister, or governor of the Bank of England, or whatever you like. I'm not saying that they do, but you get the point. If a girl is very, very pretty then that's going to put a particular spin on everything that happens to her. She's privileged, but there's a sense in which it's a curse as well. She's directed by her looks. In Kath's case the actress stint meant that there was no college, no learning how to do anything, just muddling along until that becomes a way of life.

All right, I dare say a nice-looking girl *does* get on well in the property business. Which doesn't prove much, if I may say so.

And then she met Glyn. Do you know, I've no idea why she up and married him. I mean, he was an academic — not really her scene at all. Mum knew him first, apparently — I've never known quite how. Not that he was your straightforward scholarly type, Glyn. He was on the telly a lot, back then — climbing around Roman forts and stuff, holding forth. Actually when I was a teenager he made quite an impression. All that talk — and a whiff of Richard Burton about him. Richard Burton meets Heathcliff. And apparently he made a dead set at Kath, soon as he saw her. But she'd had that happen before, often enough, for heaven's sake. Anyway, this time she gave in. Commitment, finally.

And it stuck. Until she — until that awful time. I've told you. They got married and stayed married. It seemed to work. Mind, it was a very coming and going sort of marriage — Glyn off doing what he did and her hanging out with friends like she always had and getting involved with this and that. Kath wasn't going to sit at home doing the devoted housewife bit. She never talked about him much. Just little throwaway remarks — "Glyn's off conferencing somewhere, so I'm on the loose. Hey, let's go up to town . . ." And she'd sweep me off on some spree. You always had such *fun* with Kath. And do you know, even in the middle of all this, I can't feel any differently about her. I mean, because of her there's this almighty fuss — well, because of her and Dad, let's get things into perspective. And for me she's still the same person. Kath. I can't somehow relate this to her.

All right, we'll talk tomorrow. Actually it's not *that* late, but never mind. I'm really, really worried about my parents, that's all. And now I'm wondering how far you're there for me on this, Dan.

Elaine takes the phone through into the conservatory, where Sonia cannot hear. Sonia's polite constraint is becoming a mild irritation — her determined pretence that everything is as usual. The instrument bleats on as Elaine walks, as she sits down, as she looks out towards the pergola and sees that the wisteria is starting to show colour. Polly's agitation seeps into her ear, creating jagged unrest on that side of her head.

"— and it's all so long ago!" wails Polly, grinding to a halt.

"Up to a point," says Elaine. In fact, it is not so long ago. It was fifteen years ago, or thereabouts, which in the context of her life is a mere trifle. Odd things happen to time, as you get older. Time compacts. Where once it was elastic, and ten years seemed an eternity, it has become shrunken, wizened — nothing is all that long ago. But for Polly fifteen years is an age.

Polly is off again. "— and I know it's a shock and it's hard to come to terms with, but does it have to matter *so* much? I mean, you and Dad are still the same people."

"I'm finding that we are not," says Elaine.

"Mum, I can't believe this is happening."

Elaine notes that the grass is patchy under the crab apple — some reseeding needed there. Pondering the sight-line down through the pergola, she wonders about the crucial focal point beyond: that acer is not earning its keep.

"I don't *understand*," cries Polly. "Well, of course I do understand, I understand entirely how you feel, Mum, *of course* I do, but . . . does it have to be like this? Couldn't you —"

"No," says Elaine. "I can't. I've explained. Just as I've explained to your father."

"But one cannot imagine how he . . . I mean, how's he to *manage*?"

Elaine abandons consideration of the acer and that sight-line. It is not that she is seeking distraction, or is impervious to Polly's distress. Rather, she is interested to find that normal preoccupations continue alongside the current clamour. This is surely a healthy sign. And, today, Kath is nowhere in evidence. She does not come swimming up; she is silent. Contrite? Defensive?

"I've made an arrangement with the bank," says Elaine.

"Oh, I know, I know. Dad said. I don't mean money. I mean how's he to sort himself out? Do you know where he is?"

Silence.

"Here," says Polly. "He's here, in the flat. Until he can fix himself up with somewhere else. Or at least that's the idea. On my sofa. The new one from Habitat."

"Ah. I see." Elaine's composure is now ruffled. "I see," she says again. "Your sofa."

"He's gone out to buy some socks. At nine o'clock in the evening. He forgot to bring any. He seems to think he can buy socks at an all-night petrol station."

Elaine is groping now. She has no comment. The socks are a blow below the belt.

"I'll have to go," says Polly. "He's back."

For Polly, it seems as though a virus is at work. Order and expectation have been violated. Nothing is as it should be. Alien data have flashed up on the screen — uninvited, unwelcome — and they cannot be dismissed. People are not behaving as they should; moreover, it appears that they never did. Polly has always believed in forward planning, which requires a reliable infrastructure. Now there are faultlines all over the place. Her mother has apparently flipped; her father is camping on her sofa, with no spare socks, and his shaving kit is all over her bathroom. She does not know if she should rush home this weekend and exhort her mother further, face to face; she will have to put on hold the planned supper party for friends, so long as her father is invading her space. She dotes on them both, of course she does, but they should not be doing this. They have broken the rules. They have ceased to be the essential backdrop, the calm, still centre; they have become a further perverse element, impeding smooth progress.

People split up. Naturally people split up. All around, relationships are in a state of fission — that is to be expected. But not these people, that relationship. And not because of a distant transgression, a mishap long ago, something packed away into the past, over and done with. What has got into them? Why can't they be grown up about it?

She scolds Kath. What were you thinking of? she says to Kath. How could you? Now look what you've done!

But Kath is impervious. In Polly's head, Kath does what she always did: she flies the dragon kite; she plucks a dress from a rail and cries, "This one!"; she laughs across a restaurant table. She is beyond the uproar of the present, except in blame. And Polly cannot be angry with her. The scolding is a ritual gesture. Why? she says to Kath, just once. And still Kath is unreachable. But Polly glimpses something in

Kath's eyes that perhaps she never saw before. Someone else looks out of them, someone sad. But Kath was never sad — not Kath.

Polly fumes and fusses. She rehearses further appeals to her mother. She yanks the Habitat sofa into its bed mode, which means that her sitting room is barely navigable. She knows that she will sleep badly tonight, and be fouled up for work tomorrow.

And another thing. Dan is not coming out of this well. Probably she needs to stop seeing Dan sooner rather than later.

Glyn and Kath

Glyn is concerned with time. He is also worried about the time: it is twelve forty-five, he is sitting on the side of a Dorset hill, and at two o'clock he has a seminar in the university, which is well over an hour's drive away. He should be getting a move on, instead of which he is sitting here brooding about time.

Time is his most essential professional tool, he reflects. Without it he would be faced with a chaotic and incomprehensible medley of evidence, much like the confusing juxtapositions of the landscape itself. Time is the necessary connection between events. Time is the device that prevents everything from happening at once. Pioneering archaeology went all out for the establishment of chronology, and no wonder.

A kestrel hangs in the wind, level with his line of vision. Beyond it, in the distance, the green complexity of field patterns is interrupted by a large, long building with tall chimneys which he knows to have once been a nineteenth-century mill, today a development of luxury apartments. Just below him the hillside ripples away in a series of ledges; these he recognizes as the eroded ramparts of an Iron-age hill fort, which is why he is here at this moment. He is working on an article for which this hill, which he has not visited for some while, can provide some useful references.

The kestrel evokes Kath. He came here with her once: another kestrel performed similarly, and Kath remarked on it. "It stays still," she had said. "The wind is rushing past it, and it stays still. How?" He sees today that other bird, and Kath's hair blown across her face, and feels her hand on his arm. "Look!" she is saying. "Look!"

Glyn is now diverted from his reflections on the functions of time; he notes that his flow of observation — unconsidered, uncontrived — is a nice instance of the tumultuous, spontaneous operation of the mind. He knows enough of the theories of long-term memory to identify his recognition of the mill and the hill fort as the practice of semantic memory — the retention of facts, language, knowledge, without reference to the context of their acquisition. He simply knows these things, along with everything else he knows that makes him a fully operational being — a being considerably more operational than most, in his view. Whereas the vision of Kath sparked by the kestrel is due to episodic memory, which is autobiographical and essential to a person's knowledge of their own identity. Without it we are untethered, we are souls in purgatory. Those glimmering episodes connect us with ourselves; they confirm our passage through life. They tell us who we are.

Glyn stands up, impelled by his own circadian clock, which is muttering away about that seminar. The kestrel swings suddenly sideways and down. Glyn heads for his car, which he will recognize thanks to a further spurt of semantic memory and which he will be able to drive because procedural memory keeps all such skills alive. Without that, we would fall over, be struck dumb, stare bemused at the driving wheel.

Precarious, he thinks, as he plunges surefooted down the steep hillside. The precarious fusion of automatic processes, all of them necessary for daily functioning, all of them operating at the same time. And indeed even as he thinks this he is also taking note of various things about this site, carrying out the purpose of his visit. He assesses the alignment of the ramparts, and the trace of a possible entrance. He relates this place to other known Celtic sites. But these thoughts are permeated with something else — not so much a thought process as a condition of the mind, a climate: all the while, that episodic memory mode is in operation, reminding him that he and Kath paused just about here to eat sandwiches, that she found an orchid, that she called out, "Come! Something amazing!", that a shower of rain sent them running for the car.

And when was this? Neither semantic, episodic or procedural memory can help here. Clearly the mind rejects the concept of chronology. It is an unnatural idea, fostered by perverse chroniclers ever since the Old Testament.

And what else was going on then for Kath? Glyn gets into the car, starts the engine. Now that he knows what he knows, the Kath that he sees is infused with something dark and unwelcome. Was she betraying him at that very time? Was she thinking of Nick, as she watched the kestrel, as she caught sight of the orchid?

It is several weeks since his discovery of the photograph, the event that has come to seem a defining moment. There was before the photograph, a time of innocence and tranquillity, in so far as such a state exists. Now it is after the photograph, when everything must be seen with the cold eye of disillusion.

Well, not everything. His marriage, simply. Which is quite a lot. He is calmer. The initial consuming fire has banked down to a steady smouldering purpose. He must reconstruct his years with Kath, scrutinize them, search for further enlightenment. He must discover if this was an isolated incident. If it was, that is bad enough; if it reveals an entire lifestyle unknown to him, then he is discredited. He is proved to be without powers of observation or perception. Worst of all, everything that he remembers of that time is shown to be faulty.

He is in the process of creating a retrospective diary of the period. Where he was, when, and for how long. And so, by extension, where Kath was and what she was doing — as far as this is possible, which largely it is not. His own files are the reference source for his activities, but piecing things together is a laborious process taking up far too much time. Kath's part is more elusive, and requires input from others.

Oliver Watson proved pretty useless. Perhaps not altogether so, because this woman Mary Packard would have to be sought out at some point, and might be more productive. But generally speaking the meeting with Watson had been futile, like a cross-country trek to some archive in pursuit of a document that turns out to be unrewarding.

The purpose of the exercise is to identify and interrogate key figures with whom Kath was involved: friends who may be persuaded to bear witness, men who may have been lovers. Of course he is not going to come out with it, just like that. He is not going to say, "Do you happen to know if my wife was promiscuous? Did you by any chance sleep with my wife at any point?" He is going to probe. He is going to be devious, circumspect. He will go in with some pretext, put out feelers. He will know, the instant he is on to something. He will know by the inflexion of a voice, by an intonation, a hesitation, an evasive reply. He is, after all, trained to home in on significant omissions. He knows when absence of data is suggestive. He can recognize the implications of a gap in the record.

Right. Now for the list of witnesses. He will need a swathe of material: diaries, telephone directories, newspaper libraries, compliant contributors. He will need the name of the woman who ran that gallery in Camden, and information about craft centres and arts festivals — all those erstwhile haunts of Kath's. He will need patience, and his own professional skills. He is stimulated rather than daunted. This is after all his *métier*: the pursuit of information is what he does best.

But first of all he must interrogate himself. His prime resource is the leaky vessel of his own memory. At times he views it thus, quite literally — as some old pail with holes and rusted seams. Alternatively, he imagines an extensive manuscript of which there survive only a handful of charred fragments; it is like trying to piece together the Gospels from the Dead Sea Scrolls.

He makes lists. He rummages through files and old engagement diaries, and so discovers where he was and when during those ten years of marriage. This is where the leaky vessel comes in, the charred fragments. He remembers that during the summer of 1986, when he was working on early population densities and spending a great deal of time in the British Library, Kath was helping out with a music festival, or so she said. She came and went. There was a man who used to ring up a lot, one of the organizers. Glyn picks up an echo of his voice: "I wonder if Kath is around? Peter here, from the Wessex Festival . . . If you could just tell her I called."

That festival is entered on Glyn's chart, fleshing out 1986. This Peter is entered also, underlined.

The project occupies Glyn's every spare moment, along with many moments that are not strictly speaking spare at all. He examines old files when he should be reading departmental papers, or going over a lecture. His thoughts drift in that direction during meetings. Now, in the car heading towards the university and that seminar, he is in full undistracted contemplation of the matter. All right, this is obsessive behaviour, and he is perfectly aware of that. But that is par for the course; Glyn does obsession, always has; a five-star capacity for obsession is what makes him a painstaking researcher; obsession has produced seminal books and articles.

He reaches the university, dumps the car, hurries to his office where a posse of students is camped outside his door. He switches to charm mode, apologizes for being late, apologizes for his muddy shoes (see, I have been out on the job), sweeps them into the room. He must now apply himself to agrarian change in the sixteenth century; later on, back to the matters in hand.

There is a further task which is ancillary to the fact-finding process and the pursuit of witnesses. You could call it the examination of motive, Glyn supposes. Several motives. Why did he marry Kath? Why (to be fair) did Kath marry him? Above all, why did Kath cheat on him with Nick? And with others, if others there were.

Why? Why? Why? Motive is all. Motive is clarification. Motive explains. Motive soothes, perhaps.

He is good at nailing motives. The landscape heaves with hidden motives, coded motives. It looks the way it does because people chopped trees down to build ships, because they overran the place with sheep when wool was in high demand. It is scarred with the effects of cupidity: shafts sunk because this man wanted to get rich, villages swept away because another man needed to improve his view. Motive is Glyn's speciality.

"Can you help?" says Glyn. "I'm wondering if that is Peter Claverdon?"

He is in a dispiriting public library in a small market town. He has arrived here after consulting back issues of newspapers, the internet, and by way of five phone calls to total strangers. But here he is on a Friday evening, having driven sixty miles, about to attend a poetry reading.

His most recent informant had said that, no, there shouldn't be any problem about getting a ticket. And, no, there is not. The library is well furnished with computers, and rather more lightly equipped with books. Uncomfortable chairs are arranged in a semi-circle, confronted by three further chairs in a row. Eleven people are seated in the semi-circle. A man has emerged from a back room and looks around, apparently checking the arrangements. Glyn has already deduced that this must be his quarry, but he consults the librarian who sold him a ticket. Yes, that is Peter Claverdon.

Glyn inspects. He now knows something about this fellow — long-term arts administrator, something of a jack-of-various-trades, peripatetic and evidently versatile, hired to mastermind arts events from musical extravaganzas to this evening's contribution to a weekend of poetic commitment. Lean build, casual dress, late fifties. And undoubtedly the guy from those remembered phone calls. Glyn experiences a stir of hostility, which will have to be kept well under control.

He chooses a seat at the back. Three more people trickle in, plumping the audience out to fourteen, which looks less amid the empty chairs. The poets arrive, shepherded by Peter Claverdon. They do their stuff. Glyn pays token attention, watching the quarry and considering tactics.

The reading concludes. Two members of the audience buy copies of the poets' works. The poets chat among themselves.

Glyn picks his moment, and advances. He introduces himself. "The name should ring a bell with you. You knew my wife."

The man looks blank, and then there is a gleam — a definite gleam of something. "Oh — *Kath*. Good heavens — Kath." Now there is compunction, concern. "What a tragedy. I was so sorry —"

Glyn's expression indicates stoicism, grief suppressed. He gestures gracious acceptance of sympathy. He allows a moment of tribute. Then he proceeds. He explains. He appeals. He has this notion to write a brief private memoir of Kath, for circulation amongst relatives and friends. There are some areas of her life about which he needs to know more. Periods when she had commitments away from home. People who knew her then. Such, I understand, as yourself. Wondered if I could take up a little of your time. A chance to colour in some of the blank spaces . . .

Glyn observes the man keenly as he speaks. What is he seeing? The man is responding, definitely. But what is the response? Something flickers in his eyes. Passion recalled? Guilt? Embarrassment? Glyn is alert; he scents involvement.

When Claverdon replies, he is all compliance — he seems enthusiastic. Yes, he saw quite a bit of Kath back then. What a lovely person she was. Used to ferry performers around for us, that sort of thing. See them into their hotels, get them to the venues on time. An entire Hungarian string quartet fell in love with her.

A red herring? Glyn registers benign interest.

The audience is ebbing away. The poets are packing up. "I've got some photos, come to think of it," says Claverdon. "Why don't you come round to my place? — I live five minutes from here. The poets may want to get drunk, but I'm sure they can manage on their own. I'll just point them in the direction of the White Hart, and we can be on our way."

This helpfulness is disconcerting. Glyn feels wrong-footed. What is going on? It is clear that the man did indeed know Kath. His tone, and that betraying movement of the eye, suggest that he knew her well. Just how well? Is this willing invitation some crafty smokescreen?

Peter Claverdon disposes of the poets. He leads Glyn through the market square and down a side street, talking about these photos: definitely one of Kath escorting a well-known conductor, if he can lay his hands on it. "She did some office filling-in for us a year or so later — you remember?" He shoots a quick look at Glyn, who expediently remembers. "She was a person we liked to call on — very popular girl, Kath."

They reach a terraced cottage. Claverdon unlocks the door, calling out, "Hello!"

No reply. "Ah," he says. "My partner should be back any minute. Coffee? Drink?"

A partner. Was she around then? Was she aware of Kath? Is the smokescreen for her benefit also? Glyn accepts a glass of wine, his attention now in overdrive.

There is something about this guy, something he cannot quite nail. And there is a note of comfortable intimacy when he speaks of Kath.

The photographs are found, after some rummaging in drawers. And, sure enough, there is Kath. There is Kath beside the prominent conductor, who had taken rather a shine to her, says Claverdon. And here is Kath in a jolly line-up of the festival staff. Kath is next to Claverdon; Glyn finds himself scrutinizing them very closely. He cannot see their hands. Kath is beaming. She looks happy, relaxed. She is radiant. Glyn has an odd feeling of exclusion; he knew nothing of that day, of these people.

It strikes Glyn that it would be appropriate to establish himself. He is a mere cipher at the moment, where Claverdon is concerned. He swings the conversation round, and makes clear who he is and how he stands. But Claverdon knows, it seems. He nods — a neutral sort of nod, with perhaps not quite enough recognition of status. Yes, Kath said. Said you were always very busy. Said landscape history took up all your time.

She did, did she? This is provocative. Suggestive. There is the smack of intimate exchanges here. Glyn is bristling, but must keep his cool. He turns back to the matter of Kath and the summer of that festival. He mentions that he cannot remember where she used to stay. Hotel, was it? He is trained on Claverdon, watching for some giveaway.

There is the sound of the front door opening. "My partner," says Claverdon.

And into the room comes a man. A man slung about with supermarket carrier bags, a domestic and slightly out of breath man, who dumps the bags, aims a kindly smile at Glyn, says to Claverdon, "I thought I'd better do a Sainsbury before the weekend."

Claverdon explains Glyn. "You remember Kath Peters? Who was one of the Wessex Festival team? You and Kath were great mates. Poor Kath —"

The man is all interest. Of course he remembers Kath. Who wouldn't? He makes a face of regret, of sympathy. He starts at once on some anecdote involving Kath.

Glyn is barely listening. He feels like some kind of dupe. Partner. How was he to know the guy was gay? His time has been wasted. No point in hanging on here. He finishes his glass, waiting for the moment when he can get up and leave.

The two men are recalling some occasion when Kath apparently saved the day with an emergency sprint to Heathrow to collect a replacement performer. Glyn shifts a hand and notices his watch with exaggerated surprise. "Heavens! That late . . . I must be off."

Claverdon's partner has poured himself a drink and is settled on the sofa, talking the while. "Game for anything, wasn't she? And she was on such a high that summer. What a shame it all went wrong. She was so upset — you could see."

Glyn does not hear this; he will hear it later, much later. He is on his feet now, pleading time, distance, fatigue. "*Many* thanks," he is saying. "Good to see those pictures —" His hosts also rise; Claverdon looks rebuffed, as well he may. The partner hovers. When Glyn is outside the door, heading for his car, the image returns — the pair of them, staring at him. Well, one could hardly have set to and explained, could one?

All right, then. So why did he marry Kath? He married her because she was the most desirable woman he had ever met: he had to have her, he had to go on having her, he had to make sure that no one else had her, ever more.

So you loved her?

Of course.

Did you say so?

Probably. Surely. Anyway, that is immaterial. I never went in for those statutory exchanges.

He married Kath because it was an imperative.

"Clara Mayhew?"

"Speaking."

"Ah. You don't know me — Glyn Peters. But I believe you used to run the Hannay Gallery, and would have known my wife, Kath."

Pause. "I did. She worked for us from time to time." Further pause. "I was told she —"

"Yes. Yes, I'm afraid so. Please forgive me for bothering you, but I wondered if possibly —" Glyn floats the idea of a memoir once more. He is getting adept at the memoir; he convinces himself, the work takes shape in his mind.

"You've gone to a lot of trouble to find me," says Clara Mayhew, after a moment.

This is not quite what she is supposed to say, but no matter. Glyn agrees with her — he has indeed. He does not mention the systematic programme of enquiry, and merely says that he is relieved to have struck lucky. "I believe you knew her fairly well?"

"Did I?"

This is unanswerable, which is presumably the intention. Glyn is now backing away from the idea of a meeting. Perhaps Clara Mayhew is another dead end. All the same, Kath spent many weeks and months at that gallery. He tries a shot in the dark. "I think she had a particular friend amongst the artists who used to show there, but I cannot remember the name. I just wondered if you might be able to help."

"Help?"

"Help with the name of this . . . this person. This artist."

A sigh. "I seem to recall that Kath had a lot of friends. Always in and out of the gallery."

"I just have this feeling that there may have been —"

"There was the portrait, I suppose. Did it ever get done?"

"Portrait?" Glyn leaps to attention.

"Ben Hapgood. Wanted to paint her. Mad keen. No doubt he did, I wouldn't know."

It occurs to Glyn that this Clara is bored rather than obstructive. Not a particular mate of Kath's then. But productive — oh, distinctly productive. He becomes brisk. "Hapgood? That'll be the chap. The name certainly rings a bell. Do you by any chance have an address?"

But Clara's patience has run out. No, she does not have an address. All she knows is that the man lived in Suffolk, back then. And she's afraid she really has to go, so if he will excuse her . . .

Gracefully, Glyn does so. Ben Hapgood. Right.

Why did Kath marry him?

She married him because she found him charismatic, charming, because he made it clear that he was entirely focused upon her. She married him because he offered a different kind of life, because he wasn't like the others, because he was a blast of energy.

Sex?

Of course.

You were handsome.

I was. Kath was outstandingly attractive. I was a good-looking man. There's usually some symmetry about these things, one notes.

All the same.

All the same what?

You weren't the first, not by a long chalk. So why you? Why indeed?

She married him because he insisted that she should.

This woman Clara has dropped the name Ben Hapgood into Glyn's mind. There it lies, fermenting. Glyn works away. He checks directories, he consults websites, he locates lists of artists, and before long he has the fellow, who does indeed still live in Suffolk. Which will mean a long cross-country drive, but what is that to a man with a mission?

But the fermentation has had further effect. Something has come bubbling up from the vaults of memory — a lost moment, a vanished moment, a moment in which Kath is sitting in the garden on that red-striped deckchair. She wears skimpy clothes and dark glasses, her head is tilted back in the sunshine. She is talking. "Ben Hapgood," she says. "He is *such* a good painter. And he's just won this important prize. I'm so pleased . . . you're not listening, are you?" she says. And the rest is drowned out by that: "You're not listening, are you?", the dark glasses turned towards him now, and a little exasperated smile. So what was he, Glyn, doing? Reading? Thinking? Also talking? Not listening, no. But now he is listening. He is listening hard.

He listens day after day, but there is no more. Kath has gone silent. He listens all the way to Suffolk, picking his way through the hierarchy of the road system, from motorways to dual carriageways and eventually on to minor roads that have him reaching again and again for the map. Ben Hapgood is not expecting him. Ben Hapgood is expecting a person who is interested in his work, who happens to be visiting the area, wondered if he might call in . . . a person who did not give a name because, when Hapgood asked, the line unfortunately went dead. Cut off. What a pity.

So Ben Hapgood will not be concerned, apprehensive, suspicious. Glyn is already visualizing Ben Hapgood; this man who was so keen to paint Kath's portrait, so infatuated maybe, so involved. Glyn sees a man who complements Kath's dark looks, as he does himself, he sees an ur-Glyn, more *louche*, touched with artistic glamour. He sees this man in his studio with Kath. It takes time to paint a portrait, does it not? Many sittings. Many cloistered hours together.

Did these hours of intimacy take place here? Did Kath too pick her way down these winding side-roads? It would seem so. And suddenly Glyn has a vision of Kath in that little Renault, off somewhere, going places, one hand out of the window, waving goodbye: "See you soon . . ." And he feels a spasm of pain; he is clutched by an unfamiliar sensation. These glimpses of Kath do not provoke anything much, in the normal sense of things. He lives with them; they are a part of an interior landscape, they are simply there, and that is all there is to it. This is disconcerting. "See you soon . . ." But she will not. Never again.

He jams a foot on the brake. This is it. This is where Ben Hapgood lives. This is the white cottage with a picket fence, on the right of the lane after you have forked left.

Two cottages knocked into one more precisely, plus a rambling range of outbuildings in which, presumably, is the imagined studio. Glyn drives up on to the grass verge (did Kath too make this same manoeuvre?) and gets out. He stands for a moment, gathering himself, before he moves forward and lifts the latch on the gate. Precisely as he does so, the front door opens and out steps, presumably, Ben Hapgood. Who is short, ginger-haired, smiling cheerily and behind whom hovers a woman. Both look to be in their mid fifties.

Greetings all round. "Glenda, my wife. And you are . . .? I'm afraid I didn't catch —"

Of course you didn't, thinks Glyn. "Peters — Glyn Peters." He watches intently for recognition, but none comes. Fair enough — a not uncommon name, after all.

They move into a farmhouse kitchen. Tea is made. More chat. Have you come far? Hope my directions worked all right. That sort of thing. A friendly couple, unexceptional, untouched on the face of it by artistic glamour. Kath liked artists, thinks Glyn. She had a bit of a thing about artists, she was by way of being a camp follower, I suppose. He considers Ben Hapgood who is swigging tea and talking about his vegetable plot, visible out of the window. Glyn notes the wife also, and wonders how long she has been around.

Ben Hapgood supposes that Glyn would like to have a look at the studio. Glyn agrees that he would like to do so. The three of them move to one of the outbuildings. Classic studio stuff: smell of paint and linseed, canvases stacked up, others on the walls, clobber all over tables and shelves. Big easel with work in progress. Couple of old deal chairs, basket chair with grubby cushions. No chaise-longue, no bed. At least, not today.

Now is the moment. He will have to come clean, blow his cover.

He does so, at length. He is charming, apologetic, a touch rueful. When he comes to the point, when he mentions the portrait, he is intent upon Ben Hapgood, with half an eye on this Glenda. He wants a reaction. He has already had a response to Kath's name — the response with which he is becoming familiar: both

150

register pleasure, affection, regret . . . Glyn is by now experiencing doubts. But what about the portrait? What about that, eh?

"Oh, *yes* . . ." says Glenda. "She was such a marvellous subject. And Ben did her proud. One of his best — I can say that, he can't." She laughs, lays an uxorious hand on the artist's arm. The artist smiles fondly.

So. Glyn eyes them. Either they are putting up a show, these two, or *she* has not known what *he* was getting up to, or he, Glyn, is once again wrong-footed.

"She came here?" he enquires.

Yes, certainly, she came here, it seems. She stayed here a couple of times. She was such a lovely person to have around, they had a lot of fun, the children were teenagers then and Kath was so brilliant with kids, she'd suggest these crazy games, they still remember her . . .

When?

There is consultation. Late 1980s, they think — summer of 1988? Yes, definitely, because the show at which the portrait was sold was 1989. Snapped up.

Snapped up?

Apparently. This bloke came to the opening view and just homed in on it. Or so it was said. Spoken for within the first ten minutes.

Really? *Really?*

Glyn moves quickly. He revises his position, in a split second. He sees where to go. He explains that of course all along what he had so very much hoped was to be able to acquire the portrait. He had of course been aware of it ("You're not listening, are you . . ."), but Kath had been vague as to what happened to it — only recently had he begun to wonder if perhaps by some miracle it might still be around . . .

Who was this man? The man who bought the picture outright, as though he had been waiting for it, as though perhaps he already knew about it, as though he knew Kath, as though he knew Kath so well that he must get his hands on her picture before anyone else did?

". . . obviously it was too much to hope that you might still have it. But someone has. Is there any chance you'd know who that purchaser was?"

And, yes, Ben Hapgood keeps a record of where his work has gone. He fishes a file from a drawer and starts hunting through it. Glenda is talking about Kath. She talks about that summer when, it seems, Glyn was away a lot, involved with his work: "I'm sorry, I don't remember exactly what you do, Kath did say . . . so she was rather on her own, I think she was quite glad to come here, once she took the girls off camping on the coast for a couple of days. What a shame it was she never . . . not that she ever said anything, but one always sensed —"

Glyn is concentrated upon Ben Hapgood, who cannot lay hands on the stuff from that gallery — damn, did it get chucked out? — no, hang on, here we go. A Mr Saul Clements — and here's the address and phone number. London. Sounds an expensive address. Laughter.

He has him. He has this man. This is the real quarry. Ben Hapgood was a distraction, but who was to know that? Ben Hapgood was simply the unwitting facilitator. He painted Kath's portrait, had indeed been mad keen to paint Kath's portrait, but for entirely painterly reasons, and who wouldn't? But as soon as the portrait is put on exhibition, is offered for sale, it is pounced on. By whom? By someone waiting for it? Someone Kath had been talking to about it? Someone Kath was seeing that summer?

All that remains is to disentangle himself from the Hapgoods. Who remain remarkably good-humoured and hospitable given it is now clear that Glyn's interest in the artist's work is entirely self-serving. In an attempt to improve his record, he pays belated attention to the works by which he is surrounded, asking questions, offering the occasional deferential comment. Hapgood is a figurative artist, and so presumably right outside the contemporary swim, judging from what is to be picked up from the Sunday newspapers. This deduction allows Glyn to line himself up on the side of the angels, with some disparaging remarks about unmade beds and pickled animals, which seem to go down satisfactorily.

Hapgood is now distracted from discussion of contemporary art by a sudden thought. It has occurred to him that he will have a slide of that painting of Kath, should have, if he can find it. Let's see now . . . He plunges once again into drawers and files. Glyn finds himself mesmerized; somehow he had not reckoned with the actuality of the thing, in this form or any other. Kath. Here, now. Ben Hapgood shuffles through folders and albums; Glenda is saying something about Kath — she is saying that it was a problem for Kath, looking the way she did. Problem? Glyn notices this Glenda, briefly — she is dumpy, fresh-faced, wholesome-looking, she reminds one of a small brown loaf, she is the antithesis of Kath. Problem? But now her spouse is saying, ah, here we go, he has opened an envelope and is holding slides up to the light. Should be here, he says, this is the lot from that exhibition. And then — "Yes!" He passes a slide to Glyn.

Here is a tiny, jewel-like Kath, glowing in the light from the window. The slide is too small to make out detail, but there is no mistaking that stance, the way she is sitting with her legs curled beneath her, head turned aside, chin on her hand, elbow on the arm of the chair. Glyn peers into this crystallized moment, this time when Hapgood saw Kath sitting thus, when Kath spent so many hours thus arranged, perhaps in that chair there, looking probably out of that window. He feels oddly excluded. There she was; there he was not. And now he is here, and she is not, and this fact is suddenly chilling.

Hapgood talks about the painting. It was not so much her beauty, he says, one doesn't necessarily want to paint someone because they are handsome — it was the way she composed herself. The way she stood, sat, moved. Arresting. And so absolutely natural. Like some elegant animal. He had agonized over the pose — had thought of having her sit, stand, be this way or the other — and then one day had noticed her settle herself like that in a chair and had thought, yes, that's it.

Glyn scarcely hears him. He is intent upon the little translucent shape in his hand, this Kath preserved in amber light. He finds that he does not want to give it up. He searches for Kath's features, but the scale is too small. Eventually he hands the slide back to Ben Hapgood. "Thank you," he says.

Glyn drives home in a trance. He pays scant attention to anything; the landscape whips past unobserved. He makes none of the usual mental notes about place names, about a road arrangement to be checked out later, about buildings, about field structures. He can think only about that slide, about the lost and unknown Kath that he held for a few moments in his hand. Kath is interfering with his work again, but he does not notice.

She came this way. Not once, but several times. She went to that house, talked and laughed with those people, played with their children, was welcomed. She sat in the basket chair in Ben Hapgood's studio, for many hours, gazing out of the window. Thinking about what?

He had never been jealous of her friends, had never resented that shifting pack who drifted in and out of the house, who kept her forever on the phone. They did not much interest him, truth to tell. Lovers would have been one thing; friends were neither here nor there. He is in pursuit of lovers right now, but it is these others who are unsettling his life, stirring up these unaccustomed feelings of . . . of what?

Feelings of exclusion, of ignorance, of deprivation. He is glimpsing a Kath whom apparently he did not know, a Kath known to these others who are themselves mysterious, so far as he is concerned. Strangers, who were nevertheless entirely familiar to the person with whom he lived in that ultimate intimacy.

You knew that at the time. You knew she had friends.

Of course.

So why is this now causing difficulties?

How should I know? How the hell would I know? Glyn sweeps onwards round the M25. Counties wheel past to one side; London lurks out there on the other. He sees none of it. Faces are streaming through his mind, the alien faces of the Hapgoods, of Peter Claverdon, faces that are underpinned by words, the continuous repetitive refrain that plays unprompted — from just now, from long ago: "What a shame it all went wrong . . ." "It was a problem for her, looking like that . . ." "You're not listening, are you?"

He steps from the lift of this block of mansion flats. The place is hushed and carpeted and proposes solid wealth. The voice of Saul Clements on the entry phone has told him to come up, and Glyn is preparing himself for this man. He knows better now than to second-guess; he has no image in his head, but he is on guard, he is in his corner, waiting for the bell. This is where he is going to need all his perceptiveness, all his powers of deduction, for the man who so urgently bought Kath's portrait.

The door to the flat is already open. And there stands the ugliest man Glyn has ever seen. This man is a toad, a gnome, a troglodyte. He is as squat as a barrel, his nose is bulbous, his mouth is a letterbox. He is seventy-five years old at least. This man was never Kath's lover?

The troglodyte leads Glyn into a room whose furnishings are deep and rich and darkly gleaming. The world beyond has been turned into exterior décor — a glimpse of the London skyline framed in thick glowing brocade curtains, the faintest purr of traffic sound. There are velvety sofas and chairs, desk and tables of museum quality, all the wonders of the orient underfoot. Oh, there is the smell of money here. And the walls are covered with paintings, each softly and precisely lit. This is perhaps a William Nicholson, and that one maybe an Ivon Hitchens, and over there is possibly a Lucian Freud. This man likes art, it seems. He likes it a lot. He has splashed out, over the years.

It is impossible to imagine Kath in this room. Except that there she is, there in that corner, suspended above a delicate little eighteenth-century davenport. Spot-lit Kath. Kath framed about two foot by three, wearing a plain green dress, arms bare, legs tucked under her, sitting on the basket chair that Glyn saw in Ben Hapgood's studio, her face in semi-profile, turned to the light of the window, the light of another time, a time of which Glyn knew nothing.

The man who cannot have been Kath's lover steers him over to the painting. He is speaking. His voice is firm, patrician, modulated — as elegant as his appearance is uncouth. Glyn finds himself silenced. He feels suddenly chastened. He feels like the guest who has committed a solecism, he feels like some hapless schoolboy. He wants out, but he is here now, he got himself into this, he has only himself to blame.

Glyn gazes at Kath. He sees her face — pensive, abstracted. Oh, he knows that sideways look, that partial removal of herself, that retreat into reflection. He stares at Kath, at this vanished Kath, who lives on in this man's gilded cage, who has lived here for years, locked into another time, other days, sealed within a frame by Ben Hapgood. He wonders about those hours. What did they talk about, she and Ben, and Glenda who perhaps wandered in and out with cups of coffee, or a summons to a meal? He strains to hear Kath's voice. In the most bewildering way, he wants, he needs that voice — here in this alien place, amid the man's great sofas and his groomed antique furniture.

The man is talking. He says that when he bought the painting Ben Hapgood's work was not familiar to him, but that as soon as he saw this painting in the exhibition he was at once struck by it. He was entranced: "A quick and easy decision. One rather welcomes those — the knowledge that one must have this picture and that is all there is to it." He smiles at Glyn, a collusive look as though to a fellow collector. He draws Glyn's attention to the modelling of the face. He indicates the use of light, the way that it falls upon the arm, upon the protruding corner of a yellow cushion.

158

He is all courtesy, this man. His letter was all courtesy, in which he replied to Glyn's enquiry — Glyn's ever-so-carefully phrased enquiry as to the whereabouts of the portrait of his late wife, which he has been given to understand Mr Clements purchased back in 1989, and which he would so very much like to see and photograph. Glyn's camera is in his pocket.

And now the man asks a startling question. He asks what Kath's name was. He has never known, it seems; the portrait was sold to him as that of a friend of the artist, unspecified. When he is told, he looks long and hard at the painting.

"Kath," he says. "So. Kath. I have always thought of her simply as — she. Respectfully, you understand — but she has always been anonymous. Now, it will be oddly different. Kath. And knowing that she is no longer alive."

Glyn files away Mr Saul Clements, who was never Kath's lover, who did not know Kath, but now lives with her in a strange daily intimacy. He files away Peter Claverdon and Ben Hapgood, who also were not Kath's lovers, but who was to know? He has been up several blind alleys, but that is always the case with a research project. Glyn is well used to the sense of frustration, the need for patience and tenacity. But he is not accustomed to the feelings generated by this particular project. He is unnerved, unsettled, he is not in control of his own reactions. Instead of a calm commitment to the objective — which is to establish whether or not Kath was in the habit of infidelity — he finds himself waylaid and distracted. He should be able to discard these various unfruitful areas, now that they are investigated and seen to be unpromising, instead of which he broods upon them. He thinks constantly of that studio in which Kath sat, and talked, and laughed. He sees the spot-lit portrait. He wonders about the summer of that festival, when Kath was so radiant in the group photograph. He wants to go back there and ask her questions — questions he never asked at the time. Where are you going? Why? What is it like there?

Nick

Nick is in a daze. He doesn't feel very well. He loses track of time, of the day of the week. He wanders about London, because it is worse to sit in Polly's flat, but he cannot think of anything he wants to do. A jaunt to London used to be an indulgence; now he feels as though he has been despatched to Siberia. When he is hungry, he must find food, because Polly is out all day and most evenings, and her fridge is not like the richly furnished fridge at home. Home? But he no longer has a home, apparently. Goaded by Polly, he goes into estate agents' offices and asks about rentals. But he barely hears what they say, and the lists that they give him lie about unread.

This cannot be. This is all some absurd mistake. He telephones Elaine, but she is never available. Either Sonia answers, and is evasive and diplomatic, or the answerphone is on. He leaves messages — appeals that are initially dignified, but which soon degenerate to petulant cries and abject supplication. Elaine does not respond.

Polly goes to see her mother, and returns cross and flustered. "You'll have to give it time, Dad," she says. "And, look, have you been to see the place in Clerkenwell? I thought that sounded just the sort of thing you want."

But Nick does not want a stunning loft conversion in EC1. He wants to go home, not after time, but now. He wants this nightmare over, stashed away in the past where mistakes should be, out of sight and out of mind. Which is where the whole Kath thing belongs, and where it safely was until this . . . this ludicrous accident, this insane intervention by bloody Glyn.

It was over and done with. All right, it shouldn't have happened, but no harm was done, only *now* is harm being done, and that is so unnecessary. Nick cannot believe that something long since laid to rest can thus come bubbling up and wreck his life. He is affronted, run ragged; no wonder he has these headaches, this heaving gut. He and Elaine should be working this out together, quiet and calm, as he is sure they could if only she would give him the chance.

Instead of which, here he is pacing horrible London, occasionally meeting up for a drink with some old acquaintance. But such arrangements have lost their kick. Furthermore, he no longer wants to go and potter around Northumberland for a few days, and the various projects he was considering are not of the slightest interest to him. Can Elaine seriously think that he is able to work under these circumstances? He can barely focus for long enough to buy himself a newspaper. He sits on park benches with a beer in his hand, like some wino, staring at the ground.

And staring also at what happened back then, which should not have happened, which should not be roaring up to clobber him like this.

★ ★ ★

He looked at Kath one day and saw that she was *so* pretty. Had he never realized this before? Well, yes — but in a casual, take-it-or-leave-it sort of way. Now suddenly her prettiness was of another order: it was relevant, it related to him, it made him feel he needed to do something about it.

He wanted to go to bed with her. As soon as he recognized this he was shocked. Look here — this is Elaine's sister. Elaine's *sister*, for Christ's sake, whom you've known for years.

And it made no difference. None whatsoever. So? said some still, small voice. So she's Elaine's sister? Things like this happen, don't they? Nothing anyone can do about it. It's not your fault or hers.

He remembers that onslaught of . . . well, lust. He remembers looking and looking at Kath, astonished that he should be looking so differently, that Kath's familiar presence was suddenly something quite other. Astonished but also quietly thrilled. He remembers how the days took colour, how he brimmed with energy.

He remembers all that. He remembers less about the sequence of that time. How long did it go on? Six months? A year? How many times did they make love? Not that many. In his head, the whole thing is now compacted into a handful of vibrant moments: Kath's face, her body, her voice.

She rolls away from him. "Why are we doing this?" she asks. She stares at him — he sees that look still, an intent gaze, that has something of resignation about it.

It is a look that bothers him, and he should not be bothered at this particular moment. *"You're* doing it for the reasons that men do —" she corrects herself — "that people do. But why am *I* doing it?"

He tries to hush her. At least he supposes that he did. When he listens to her now, it seems to him that there are things he should have said, but apparently he did not.

"You're Elaine's husband. Is that why I'm doing it? Is it *because* you're Elaine's husband?"

He remembers the day of the photograph. That bloody photograph, but for which he would not be here now, sitting on a bench with crisp packets swirling round his feet, alongside an old fellow reading the *Sun.* I can't go on living like this, he thinks, I can't.

Why did they go to that place? Was it Kath's idea? But Kath was never into Roman villas. It seems to Nick that maybe he himself proposed that excursion, tenuously linked perhaps to some project. But in reality it was an excuse to see Kath, because at that point it was essential to be with her, even if it was in the company of others. So there they all were — Elaine and himself, and Kath, and that woman Mary Packard with some man, and Oliver. Fateful Oliver, who went and brought his camera along.

He remembers a picnic. All of them sprawled around on the grass, and him intensely conscious of Kath — being careful not to pay her significant attention, assiduously behaving normally, treating Kath just as he always had, for years. He remembers her wandering off with Mary Packard, the two of them looking at some mosaic, laughing together. He had wondered if Mary Packard knew; Kath's great friend, she was. How much did Kath confide in her? He half wanted to think that Mary Packard knew.

He remembers that they were standing around, and he found himself beside Kath. Found himself? Positioned himself, probably. And he had not been able to resist reaching for her hand — had reached for it and clasped her fingers and pushed their two hands back behind them, out of sight, hidden by her billowing skirt. The secret intimacy had given him a thrill, intensified perhaps by the fact that Elaine was there talking to them: he had felt guilt and euphoria all in one. For seconds only they had been like that, and then Kath's hand slipped away. But Oliver had chosen that snatch of time in which to raise his camera to the eye and commemorate the outing. Unwittingly — that Nick is quite prepared to believe — but fatally.

It is so *unfair*. Elaine is being so unreasonable. He has been given no opportunity to persuade her that, in time, this thing could be seen in perspective. He is being quite disproportionately punished.

You should have considered this outcome back then, says another sultry voice. Did he? Did they? Well, yes, sort of . . . if guilt and the occasional bout of nerves amount to consideration.

One was so swept up in it, there was an inevitability about everything, it was unstoppable. Of course one was worried, of course one agonized, from time to time. But there was always this feeling that it would be all right, it would work out . . .

And Kath? What about her?

Nick finds that Kath is inscrutable. He can see her and hear her still, but he has no idea what she is thinking or feeling — correction: what she thought or felt. He is annoyed with her; look, there are two of us in this, it was you too, and you kept that wretched photo and that note.

Why? This thought introduces a further level of disquiet. Were they kept because she was careless, or because they meant something to her? This notion makes Nick profoundly uncomfortable: he does not want to think that there was a dimension to their involvement of which he knows nothing. It was a temporary madness, that was all, something quite irresistible, and eventually quenched, as such passions are.

Indeed, the memory of passion makes him uncomfortable. There is recollection not with tranquillity, or yearning, but a sort of incomprehension. Had one really felt like that? Well, evidently. But he tunes in now as though to some alien persona. He hears himself with a certain incredulity. He hears himself saying to her: "I want you — God, how much I want you."

She stares at him — considering. Those marvellous eyes. "Want . . ." she says. "Want . . ." And the look is not right, he needs responding fervour, not that querying gaze. He seems to have fallen short in some way. What is he supposed to be saying?

He can't really remember what they used to talk about. Well, probably he did most of the talking: Nick is the first to admit that he does tend to go on a bit. He was up to his ears in publishing enthusiasms, back then, there was always something absorbing on the boil, he would have assumed that she'd like to be involved. And there seems to be an impression of a listening Kath, of a Kath who sits across the table from him in some pub, smiling, apparently intent. Yes . . . and Oliver turns up there, which is a bit of a problem, and Nick has to deal with that later, have a quiet word.

"Is it *because* you're Elaine's husband?" Nick does not care for that. He would prefer not to have that still in his head — Kath going in for amateur psychology, which does no one any good, and anyway it wasn't very flattering, was it? And he hears her again: "When I was younger I wanted to *be* Elaine. More than anything I wanted to be like her — to be organized and sensible and confident." A little laugh, a rueful sort of laugh. "She won't ever have realized that, I imagine.

"Maybe I'm doing this because I still want to be Elaine," she says. "What do you think?" She stares at him; she sits on the other side of a table in that pub, that quirky look on her face. But he does not think anything, not then nor now.

He feels a touch resentful towards Kath. She should be with him on this; she should be in it with him. Instead of which she is this impervious presence in his head, re-enacting frozen moments. Saying the same things again and again. And it seems to him that there was something unreachable about her even then, even when she was flesh and blood beside him, beneath his hand. You never really knew where you were with Kath; she listened and she looked and she talked — oh, she talked, but she never told you much. Just inconsequential stuff, about where she'd been and what she'd done. And she was always slipping away; she was that suddenly vacated chair, the phone that rang and rang with no one answering, the car disappearing round the corner.

And, eventually, of course, she went altogether. Nick does not care to think about that, even now.

Kath is no help, whatsoever, and Elaine has turned into someone else. She has become this implacable stranger, who has pronounced judgement against which there is apparently no appeal. Nick has had to tread warily for some while now, for the last few years she has been getting ratty for no good reason at all, but this is of another order. He sees her stony face in the conservatory that morning: "I want you to go."

It is *so* unfair. He is too old to be treated like this. Old? And as the word comes swarming in, Nick's distress is notched up higher still. Yes, he is getting old. Oh, *shit*.

Elaine and Kath

Elaine is full of vigour. She feels calm and purposeful. She has done the right thing, of that she is certain. She has done the only thing that rang true, under the circumstances. To have continued to live with Nick as though nothing had happened would have been impossible; the thing would have stared her in the face every day, each time she looked at him, each time he spoke. As it is, she will be able to give herself entirely to work, and that will enable her, in time, to digest this business. She is revising her decision to wind down, to do less; on the contrary, she will do more. She will firm up that American lecture tour, plan a new book, make a determined pitch for a space at the Hampton Court Show next year.

Today she is judging a garden competition in a prosperous London suburb. This is an exacting process — not so much on account of the footwork, the relentless progress from garden to garden, but because of the diplomatic neutrality of manner that is required. She must remain polite but noncommittal; her reactions must be tempered — all right to indulge in the occasional indication of approval, but aversion must be contained. The garden owners are hovering, smiles glued to their faces, laser eyes trained on her. They would dearly like to get a look at the notes she makes on her clipboard. The organizers move around with her, a protective cohort. The atmosphere is foetid; the whole area steams with rivalrous emotion. A charity is involved here — most of these gardens are open in aid of something this weekend — but charity is not much in evidence right now.

Elaine walks amid roses. She notes the blackspot on "Madame Alfred Carrière", assesses "Paul's Himalayan Musk", suppresses a shudder at "Peace" and "Piccadilly", communes with "Cardinal de Richelieu". She winces before a blaze of pelargoniums, appreciates some *Dicentra eximia* and *Polemonium carneum*, deplores a ghastly magenta *Lavatera*, takes attentive note of an unfamiliar *Corydalis*. It is impossible to sideline personal taste, but she tries to give proper credit to the demonstration of gardening skill and commitment, even when the products of these are a tortuously constructed rockery or a rash of carpet bedding. The nation gardens according to whim, and there is whim on show today by the spadeful, though the dictatorial hand of television is also much apparent. Water is being moved around on the scale of the Hanging Gardens of Babylon: rills, channels, miniature rapids, fountains, ponds. Contemporary gardening is a question of engineering quite as much as of plantsmanship. The furnishings are diverse and elaborate; some gardens are ankle-deep in gravel, others have absorbed a lorry-load of beach pebbles, one has a fifteen-foot plastic totem pole, in another a Roman bust rears from a shrubbery. Occasionally Elaine finds herself in a time-warp space of rectangular lawn surrounded by a border of annuals;

the accompanying organizers glance nervously at her, wearing deprecating smiles. They hurry her along the street, where a wild garden is on show, a tangle of poppies, scabious, ox-eye daisies and meadowsweet tucked into the end of a fifty-foot plot.

She is looking for structure, for imaginative use of plants, for interesting colour combinations, for evidence of horticultural prowess along with individuality. She seldom finds all of these together. Too often the gardening skills have been applied to some disastrous concept, or a promising design is betrayed by unfortunate plantings. Take this long narrow back garden, for instance: its length and narrowness have been quite cleverly disguised, the space broken up by bold groupings of shrubs, a wandering path to one side leading away to a focal point at the end. But the focus is a clump of pampas grass, that old stalwart of the suburban front garden, which sits there harsh and uncompromising amid the bosky setting. What went wrong here? Elaine frowns at the pampas grass, and makes a note on her clipboard. At the same moment, Kath floats into her head, along with another garden.

Kath says, "Can I do it too?"

"No," says Elaine. Kath is four; she is ten. And she is making a garden. The base of the garden is an old tin tray. She has lined it with soil and she is now intent upon the design and the planting. The lawn is made of moss; there are little clumps of hairy bittercress, some forget-me-not, a tussock of sedum from the garage roof — Elaine knew the names of things, even back then.

The tray garden is clear in her head, to this day. She can see it. Maybe that is how it all began for her, on that spring morning when she was ten. But now as she fetches it up, sees the sprig of catkins that was a weeping willow, she becomes aware also of Kath, lurking on the periphery.

"Shall I find more of that stuff?" says Kath, pointing to the moss. She has crept closer — a small, insignificant figure. Pleading.

Elaine ignores her. Kath is a local disruption on the fringes of her vision. Elaine is pondering what might serve as a tree, just there, and how to do a pond. Of course! A mirror! How is she to get hold of a tiny mirror, like the one her mother has in her purse? Is it conceivable that her mother would let her have it?

Kath is there again. "I've got this." She is holding out a pansy — a great, fat, blowsy pansy. It is her offering, for the garden.

Elaine frowns. "You shouldn't have picked that," she says. "You know you're not allowed to pick things." And can't she see it would ruin the whole garden? It is wrong in every way — size, shape, colour.

A kind older sister would have taken the pansy, thinks Elaine. Incorporated it, adjusted, accommodated. She stares at the discordant pampas grass in this London garden, and wonders if someone arrived triumphant with it as an unsolicited gift — spouse, mother-in-law, friend.

Her view of this garden is now skewed. She can no longer judge dispassionately. She cannot give it a gold medal, or indeed a silver, but finds herself awarding a bronze, despite the pampas grass, or perhaps because of it. Kath has intervened, again.

The tour of inspection completed, Elaine is taken to the house of one of the organizers for rest and refreshment, and to pronounce judgement. She is treated with great deference and solicitude, which is rather good for the ego, and she has of course given her services free: good public relations, and you never know what may spring from such an appearance. Book sales, naturally, but possibly some interesting commission. So she remains resolutely polite and cooperative, over and beyond the call of duty, even to the extent of a supernumerary visit to the deplorable garden of the chairman, to advise on a problem with a recalcitrant pittosporum. She is allowed a period on her own with a cup of tea and her notes, for the judging process — a welcome interlude, since it is now five o'clock, she left home at seven, and still has to fight her way back through the South London traffic. She allocates the gold, silver and bronze medals — a decision which will no doubt further fuel the animosities in this Arcadian suburb. And then at last it is time to be extensively thanked, to smile and smile again, and to get gratefully into the car.

A working day. And a relatively lenient one, in the general scheme of things. I could have been stacking supermarket shelves, thinks Elaine, or pushing millions around on a screen in the City. Instead of which I come and go as I please, and have done so for many a year —

subject, of course, to commitments made, and to the overriding need to earn a living.

She cannot now detach herself from what she does. Her work identifies her, both for herself and, presumably, for others. She cannot imagine a life that was not dominated by the requirements of the occupation. If it were removed, if it had never been there, she would not be the person that she is. She sees herself as shored up by alley and arbour and knot garden, by pergola and parterre, by vista and axis and drift and focus. She is activated by emphasis, harmony, contrast. She flourishes on the rich compost of all that she knows — a library of botanical knowledge into which she can dip at will, bolstered by pruning lore and growth habits and species attributes and a thousand plants that she can conjure up in the mind.

Elaine finds herself considering this as she picks her way out of London and on to the familiar route home. Her current state of heightened purpose is owed entirely to the fact that she is fortunate enough to have something to be purposeful about, she supposes. Without clients and engagements and plans and schemes and the trainees and the Saturday garden openings she would be at the mercy of what has happened. She would spend all her time in resentment and bitterness. Instead of which she is able to sideline the whole business, put it away out of sight and out of mind.

Except that that is not quite what is happening.

Right now, as she pulls out to overtake a Golf, she is reminded that Nick's car is still sitting outside the house. Does he propose to remove it at some point, or not? If not, she must get rid of it. But in order to find out his intentions she would have to speak to him, and she is not yet ready thus to expose herself.

And then there is Kath. Kath seems to be with her all the time, these days. Sometimes she is in the wings, as it were, but ready to invade at any moment — a constant preoccupation. At other times she steps centre-stage, as she did today, aged four, or twelve, or in some adult incarnation. And these last versions of Kath give Elaine trouble, these adult versions: was this before the day of the photograph, or after? Was this when she and Nick were having their affair, if that was what it was, or not? There is now an innocent Kath, and one who behaved inexplicably. Why? Why *Nick*?

There were so many men, over the years. Before Glyn. When Kath turned up, there was frequently some suitor in tow: "Oh . . . this is James." Or Bruce, or Harry, or whoever. And suitor is somehow the word that springs to mind. Not lover. They were always supplicants, these men, on probation. Did she sleep with them? Not always, Elaine feels. Perhaps not that often. They were followers — that old below-stairs term is neat — and when they followed too assiduously Kath disengaged herself. Next time she came, there would be no man, or a different one. And in all that time, she never looked twice at Nick, Elaine is sure of that. She treated him with casual familiarity; he was just someone who was always around — brother-in-law, Polly's father.

She came for Polly, as much as for anyone, thinks Elaine. And suddenly she sees Kath approaching along the maternity ward, the day Polly was born. Kath is carrying a cornucopia of blue sweet peas, she is joyous, at each bed that she passes heads swivel to eye her. Polly is in a crib at Elaine's side. "Oh —" says Kath. She leans over the crib; she is very still, absolutely intent — there is something in her eyes that startles Elaine. "Oh . . . you." She looks at Elaine: "Could I hold her?"

Elaine lifts Polly from the crib; she puts her into Kath's arms. And Polly opens her eyes, her tiny crumpled face comes alive. For a moment she and Kath seem locked in intimacy.

Elaine reaches out. "I'll take her," she says. "She's due for a feed."

Kath and Polly were always as thick as thieves. And, yes, I was sometimes jealous. Kath descending like the fairy godmother. Polly going on about Kath says this, Kath does that. Kath was everything I wasn't, it seemed.

Is that what Nick felt too?

This thought flies in as Elaine is on the home straight, almost at her own door. It contaminates the relief that she always feels at the end of a demanding day, with an inviting, unsullied evening ahead. And this is not what is supposed to happen; Nick is gone, she must not allow such considerations.

But there of course is his car, another thorn. Elaine hurries into the house and sets about the routine inspection of letters, faxes, voicemail, the kitchen

176

blackboard. This nicely disposes of any intrusive thoughts. She is on track once more, busy with client queries, requests, the daily quota requiring her attention. Polly has rung sounding fraught; Nick has not, which is a bonus. Her publisher looks forward to their session together tomorrow, and has some exciting work to show her by a new young photographer. The blackboard points out that the weather forecast for the weekend is excellent and hence that visitor attendance will be high; Jim proposes enlisting a nephew to help with the car parking. Pam too has noted the likelihood of high visitor numbers and has been potting up hellebore seedlings and some cuttings from the greenhouse — hardy fuchsias and penstemons — in expectation of heavy demand on the plant sales area.

Elaine sits in the conservatory with the paperwork on her lap and a glass of wine in hand. Another beautiful evening — *Euphorbia griffithii* glowing ruby-red in the late sunshine, the ornamental grasses shimmering. The sight of these induces reflections on the volatility of taste where gardening is concerned. Nowadays, people do not much care for pampas grass (because people like me tell them that they should not, she thinks . . .); once, it was all the rage. Now, we prefer *Stipa* and *Miscanthus*. The dictation of fashion, of course, but such fickleness invites you to wonder about the whole concept of beauty. A large subject. Elaine plans to include discussion of gardening foibles in the book that is currently at the planning stage; clearly, a glossy publication of this kind is no place for an in-depth review of aesthetics — her concern will have to be strictly limited — but right now she finds her thoughts drifting from plants to people. Knowing as they do so that once again Kath is moving in.

Kath was defined by her looks; she was immediately noticed. Would that have been so a hundred years ago? Two hundred? Elaine thinks of Victorian faces, of eighteenth-century beauties. Are there abiding aspects to a woman's charm — certain proportions, a particular quality of eye, of mouth? With Kath, it was the entire package — not just a face, but her stance, her movements. Even I could see that, thinks Elaine, and I'd been seeing her since she was — well, since she stepped out of childhood and became this surprising new person. She remembers that fifteen-year-old Kath had seemed suddenly like a stranger. "Why are you looking at me like that?" she had said one day, to Elaine. "Is something wrong?" And then — puzzled — "People keep doing it." She hadn't known, back then, genuinely had not known.

And later? Later, she knew. Well, she knew in theory, but it was something she pushed aside, turned away from. Even when Elaine was at her most grudging, she would never have accused Kath of vanity.

She hears Kath. Kath is not speaking to her, but to someone else; this is an overheard conversation. "It's no big deal," Kath says. And now the other half of the conversation comes floating up — what the other person had said. "What's it like to be so incredibly attractive?" The other person is not a man; this is a woman, asking out of genuine interest and curiosity.

And Kath had replied thus; she is not being evasive, or arch — the reply is as genuine as the question.

When was this? Where? Who? Elaine has not heard this exchange before, or, if she has, she has not paid attention to it. Now, she wants to know more. It seems to her that this took place at the old house, at some gathering, one of those many occasions when there was a crowd of people for Sunday lunch, or one of those impromptu book launches that Nick used to organize. Who is this other woman? She does not really matter, but her anonymity is irritating. She seems to be a relative stranger — perhaps someone meeting Kath for the first time, striking up an acquaintance that day. The question could be taken as presumptuous, intrusive; but Kath is apparently not offended. She gives her honest answer.

And what was I doing? wonders Elaine. She imagines the scene — the kitchen full of people, herself moving to and fro with plates, food. Yes, that would be it — she passes Kath and the woman, and picks up this fragment, which hangs on to this day, as such things do. Why that snatch, rather than some other? It had caught her attention, presumably: the directness of the query, the oddity of Kath's reply. No big deal. What does that mean? That her looks meant nothing to her, or did nothing for her?

The paperwork has been set aside. Elaine sits staring out into the garden, seeing Kath. Is that what I always wondered myself? How it was to be Kath? To be in possession of that guarantee of instant attention and interest? But of course I never asked her. We never talked like that. I was her sister, but probably knew her less well than her friends did. I never cared for that kind of heart-to-heart stuff; I'm not cut out for intimacy.

And as she thinks this, Elaine finds other Kaths crowding in. These Kaths are not clear and precise, they do not say anything that she can hear, they are not doing anything in particular; they are somewhere very deep and far, they swarm like souls in purgatory, disturbing in their silent reproach. Child-Kaths are mixed with grown-Kaths, so that the effect is of some composite being who is everything at once, no longer artificially confined to a specific moment in time — no longer ten years old, or twenty, or thirty, but all of those. This is a hydra-headed Kath, who is nevertheless entirely convincing; a multiple Kath who is the continuous, changing person who was there through all of Elaine's life, all that she can remember, and then suddenly was not. This Kath is not happy; these Kaths are not the brimming, busy Kaths of life, but mute witnesses to something unspoken. There is this abiding sense of appeal: "Talk to me . . ." Does she hear this? "Be *nice* to me . . ."

Unsettled, Elaine drives these Kaths away. She sweeps up her papers and goes through into the kitchen to fix herself a meal. She puts a quiche to heat in the oven, sets about making a salad. There is some Stilton, and wholemeal biscuits. She lays a place at the table, and as she takes down one of the old Provençal plates from the dresser, there is a small seismic heave of memory and she knows when it was that Kath replied thus to the question from that woman, because the same woman had commented on the plates: "I've got some like that. You must have been to Aix." And Elaine hears herself say, "No. Heals in Tottenham Court Road, I'm afraid." Furthermore, she knows now that the woman was the wife of the author of a book being celebrated that day, some recent find of Nick's, a man who was the last word on pub signs. Elaine does not give a damn about either the man or his wife, but she is suddenly interested in when this took place, because a further seismic jolt has told her that this was just after the time Kath was ill. She had vanished, in the way that she did, and then one day was on the phone: "I've been ill. I'm fine now. Can I come on Sunday?" And this illness was never defined. "Nothing much," says Kath. "All done with now." And Elaine knows that she never probed, never asked further.

Young Kath, that was. Well, quite young Kath. Twenty-something Kath. When, exactly? This arbitrary memory is now disturbing Elaine; it has brought with it uneasy glimpses of other matters. She wants to push it away, shelve it — but there is also a maddening compulsion to nail it more precisely. Nick would know. Nick remembers all his past publications, he cherishes them to this day. She turns to Nick to say, "That pub sign book . . . When did you do that series?"

But Nick is not there, and for a moment she is startled, confronting the empty kitchen.

The proposal for Elaine's new book lies on her editor's desk, all three pages of it. A skimpy thing, thinks

Elaine, eyeing it as Helen picks it up, puts it down, continues to enthuse. Helen Connor knows little about gardening, but she knows all that there is to be known about the production of a lavish publication that will sell nicely up and down the land, rich with illustration and sealed with the stamp of Elaine's marketable name. Right now, she is handing Elaine a sheaf of photographs — wonders of light and shade, depth, detail, composition. This young man is a genius, he'll do the most amazing job, I'm really keen to use him, what do you think?

Elaine thinks that if she is not careful this book is going to become the vehicle for some adventurous photography. What she has in mind is text, substantial text, supported by constructive and appropriate illustration. She wants to extend her range in this book, to move away from design and plantsmanship into discussion of garden fads and fashions, the social significance of gardening practice, gardens as icons, and indicators. She is bored with telling people how to create a bog garden, or cope with shade, or use challenging colour combinations. She has shot her bolt on such matters. She is more interested now in what she has seen and learned over the years of looking at other people's gardens, and wondering why they do what they do. She has done with the practicalities of gardening and wants to consider theory.

Helen is making all the required noises of enthusiasm, but it is evident also that theory has her running scared. Her solution is to temper things with sumptuous presentation — the quality, style and quantity of the photographs will persuade the reader that this is a standard work. Their gardens will profit if this lies about on their coffee tables.

Elaine knows quite well that she has a bargaining counter. There are other publishing houses out there. Maybe it will have to come to that, but there would be certain inconveniences involved; she will go as far as is possible with negotiation. So she and Helen will be engaged now in a delicate skirmish, neither of them prepared to concede all, both unwilling to part company, each privately considering some gestures of compromise.

Two hours later Elaine emerges from the publishers' offices. She is neither satisfied nor dissatisfied. She will not be looking for a new publisher, but she has had to curtail her proposed text, give up a potentially rewarding chapter. ("It's going to get a bit *wordy*, don't you think?" says Helen.) Helen has been persuaded to pull some proposed full-page spread photographs in favour of a more subdued and relevant approach. Elaine can see that she will have to fight her corner throughout the production process, but the book has yet to be written. For the moment, she can relax on that front; she is reasonably content with the outcome of this meeting. Though she will mark up a few reservations where Helen Connor is concerned.

Elaine has in mind a quick foray to the Royal Horticultural Society's fortnightly show in Vincent Square before heading for home, but first she needs a break. She buys some coffee and heads for a nearby Bloomsbury square. Only when she is sitting there on a bench, amid the patrolling pigeons and the great presiding plane trees, does the place become resonant. She and Kath were here once.

She hears herself: "I'm not your mother." And she hears Kath. "I know," says Kath. "I haven't got one any more."

Kath is eighteen; Elaine is twenty-four, and a working woman. Today she sees and hears the occasion as though at the end of some time tunnel. The leafy presence of the square is stronger than the two of them; she does not know how they looked, what they wore, but she remembers that even as they talked she was nothing the plane trees, with their splayed elephantine feet and their peeling bark. The trees are exactly the same today; thirty-six years is a mere trifle to them. She picks up an echo of that distant self, eyeing the trees and talking to Kath — a distant, muffled voice declaring that, yes, exactly, they are on their own now, they are *grown-up*, for heaven's sake, and Kath must face up to this, must buckle to . . . Words to that effect.

"I suppose it's all right for you," says Kath. "It isn't for me."

Their mother had been dead two years. Elaine sees Kath with her, intimate in a way that she never was. Hugs and kisses, those long cosy consultations, laughter. Elaine could never be like that; she was impatient with their mother. She saw her as dull, she saw home as a place from which you had to move away. And their mother in turn became wary of Elaine, conscious that she was measured and found wanting. She stood back from Elaine, she mollified, she apologized. But with Kath their mother was someone different; she was at ease with herself, confident, comfortable.

There is more to that meeting under the plane trees. Something that came earlier. Kath ·on the phone: "I can't go on living there. Jenny doesn't like me. Can I come and see you?" Elaine has heard this often, over time, but now she is hearing herself as well. Not words, or phrases, but a jumbled effect that comes across clearly enough today, also conjured up by the square, the pigeons, the trees: well if you can't you can't, but I don't see what you're going to do, I mean it's not as though you were at college or something, had a *base*, you're talking about drama school, well, fine, so long as you realize there's no job guarantee attached . . .

I'm not your mother.

Elaine finishes her coffee, disposes of the container in a rubbish bin. She is rattled, bothered, she is experiencing a further and different level of disquiet. She is angry with Kath: what did you think you were doing? *Nick*, for Christ's sake . . . And Kath has nothing to say; she is safe, beyond reproach. But she is also forever there, and forever provoking some new testimony.

Saturday. Garden opening day. And it is all that was promised by the weather forecasters: Wedgwood-blue summer sky with trails of rippling cirrus, warm sunshine, the lightest of breezes. And there is a steady flow of cars from the lane into the paddock car park; Jim's nephew is kept busy. So is Pam, dodging between the plant sales area and the till in the shop. They are short-handed today; the girl who usually helps out with sales phoned in sick, so Pam must deal with that side of things rather than provide a cheery and informative presence in the garden. Elaine herself is doing garden duty. There have been the usual idiot queries, and a woman presuming to offer advice on epimediums, and various unrestrained children, but also the gardening correspondent from one of the broadsheets, which might be promising, and several genuinely well-informed and appreciative punters. So she is in reasonably good humour when she finds herself confronted by a person in straw hat and sunglasses, who places herself foursquare in Elaine's path, saying warmly, "*Hello!*"

In the person's wake is a girl, also hatted and shaded, but with something about her that causes Elaine a faint stir of disquiet. Elaine offers the woman a somewhat frosty smile, and at the same instant she sees that this is Linda. Cousin Linda — whose Mum, Auntie Clare, was Elaine's mother's sister. And still is — festering in some nursing home, one has heard.

"Oh — hello." Elaine's greeting is barely more robust than her smile. She has not set eyes on Linda for many a year and has had no particular desire to do so. She remembers Linda — ten years her junior — as a pasty, importunate child and Auntie Clare as an occasional tedious visitor with whom her mother engaged in mild competition over cookery skills, dressmaking and the charms of their respective children. In adult life, she and Linda have exchanged Christmas cards from time to time and that has been about the size of it.

Linda now lives in the west country, it seems, and is on her way home after a trip to London: "And Sophie was looking at the map and said, Hey! Auntie Elaine's famous garden is on the way — why don't we look in? So here we are!"

Sophie steps forward, demure. Elaine knows now whence the disquiet. There is a whisper there of Kath. She is not Kath, she is not even a pale shade of Kath, but there are flickers and glints of Kath: the curve of a nostril, the tilt of an eyebrow, a way of standing. Genes have skipped sideways and downwards, and surfaced in dumpy Linda's offspring.

"How nice," says Elaine. Few would be fooled, but Linda beams appreciatively. She waves a hand vaguely at the surrounding garden — at the terrace with its clouds of roses and clematis, at the grass walk edged with tree peonies, at the rill and the ginkgos and the lawn sweeping away to the ha-ha. "You've made it really nice here. I must get you to come and sort out our little patch — we've not got green fingers at all, I'm afraid."

Elaine sees that she is going to have difficulty keeping civil. She looks round for help. Why does no one come up to ask what that blue flower is called, or why their roses keep getting mildew? But the garden is ticking over nicely, with little groups of satisfied customers cruising to and fro.

Linda's attention has shifted. "We've been looking out for Nick, too."

"He had to be somewhere else today, unfortunately," says Elaine. No way is she going to explain to this intrusive relative that she has recently required her husband to leave home because he once had an affair with her sister.

Linda is disappointed. "What a shame. Sophie wanted to meet Nick. She's working in publishing, you see." She shoots a proud glance at Sophie, who glimmers prettily. No, she is not like Kath — it is just that there are these eerie reflections.

Linda asks what Polly is doing. Elaine counters with web design. At least this is saving her from any more crass garden observations, though she is uncomfortably reminded of her mother and Auntie Clare trading child achievements.

Sophie pats her mother's arm: "Don't forget . . ."

"Oh —" Linda reaches into her bag. "I've got something for you, Elaine. We were going through old photos and I found one I thought you'd like. I dare say you've got lots of her. But still —" There is a respectful lowering of the voice; she holds out an envelope.

Elaine knows what is coming. She feels like saying: thank you, but I've seen enough old photos of Kath to be going on with.

This one is inoffensive enough. Kath sits in a white plastic garden chair, under a striped sun umbrella. She looks directly at the camera, with an air of compliance. Some obligatory photo call.

"In our garden," says Linda. "A couple of years after she was married, I think. She dropped in, quite out of the blue — off to see friends in Cornwall. But I gathered she'd just had that nasty little upset, poor dear, so she was rather under par." Linda gives Elaine a furtive look — regret, and complicity. "Such a shame —"

Elaine thrusts the photo into her pocket. "Thank you. How kind." She becomes brisk. "Have you been down to the woodland garden yet? At its best in spring, of course, but the *Astrantia* are just coming out. I wish I could take you indoors for a cup of tea, but I should be around in case anyone needs me." She is ignoring what she has just heard, and also stashing it away for future contemplation.

But Linda is not to be disposed of quite so easily. She is talking about Kath. It becomes clear that this was not an isolated meeting. Elaine is surprised; apparently Kath had kept up a spasmodic relationship with Linda, over the years. Why? Linda is not Kath's style at all, she has probably never set foot in an art gallery or a concert hall in her life, she would never attend an arts festival, she does not pot or paint or take arty photographs. She is the opposite of the kind of people Kath sought out as friends. So why did Kath bother with her?

Linda is saying it was always a red-letter day when Kath breezed in, a real tonic she was ... Kath is cocooned in clichés as Linda talks and Elaine is further exasperated. Can't the woman see that this is a travesty of Kath? She is reducing Kath to her own humdrum vision, she is recreating her as some cheery health visitor. She has no right to this tone of knowing intimacy. She has no right to Kath.

And now the winsome Sophie chips in. She simply loved Kath. I mean, Kath was just *so* cool, she always looked so marvellous, and she was such fun, she'd turn up with these lovely silly presents.

"Actually," says Linda, "we think Sophie has something of Kath about her." A fond glance at her daughter, and a shift to the tone of regretful respect. "Sophie was devastated when — When she — So sad. We couldn't believe it."

Enough. Elaine can stand this no longer. These two helping themselves to Kath. It is an invasion, a presumption. "I'm sorry," she says. "I'm going to have to leave you. I need to check out the car park. Do go and see the woodland garden. Nick will be sorry to have missed you."

Later, she cannot think why she said that. Nick did not give a toss about cousin Linda. And Nick is not here, he is no longer a part of the place. Why did this hollow remark insert itself, as though she needed the armour of marital solidarity, of normal service?

Later, she hears Linda again. That nasty little upset. Under par.

But later is on hold until after six, when the garden empties, the customers and the cars depart, Jim and his nephew pile into the red truck, Pam goes off to the pub with an admirer from the village. Alone, Elaine checks the ticket sales and is quietly pleased with visitor levels, locks up the shop, goes into the silent house. Only then does that other aspect of the afternoon come bustling in. Cousin Linda hangs around all evening, saying that again. And again.

★ ★ ★

Something is happening to the empty house, the Nick-free house, the tranquil and compliant house. Initially, it had been just that: there was no longer the hovering irritation factor, the Nick-generated annoyances, the intermittent requirements and provocations. Elaine's grateful relish of solitude is marred by some subliminal disquiet. She is fine, just fine; she is sitting there at the end of a demanding day, a glass of wine in her hand, something simple in the oven, and then a creeping malaise sets in. The place is too still; its small disturbances are all mechanical — the phone rings, the fax clicks and grinds, the microwave beeps. Its blankness makes Elaine restless; she finds herself wandering around, turning on the television — the background chatter that always so exasperated her in Nick's time. She makes phone calls just for the sake of it, needing to be occupied and purposeful.

She keeps the phone on answer, in case Nick rings, but hovers near to listen, picking up at once if it is not him. When she hears Polly's voice she experiences a mixture of pleasure and apprehension, but is clipped and careful in her responses. Polly's voice brims with agitation and concern, which frequently spill over into further exhortations and appeals.

"Please," says Elaine. "Can we not talk about this."

"But, *Mum* —"

He doesn't know what to do with himself, says Polly. (Did he ever? thinks Elaine.) It's pathetic, says Polly, and I mean *really* pathetic. He doesn't shave some days and incidentally he's buggered up my washing-machine

— I had no idea he was so untechnical. And he won't go and look at flats, in case you're wondering, he says he'd rather be here.

I can't believe my *father* is living with me, says Polly.

Actually, Elaine can't quite believe it either. Much of the time she is on course, she is calm and cool and ordered. She deals with each day in a systematic manner, as she ever did. Her attention is on the matter in hand, whether it is a session with Sonia over paperwork or a client visit or a stint at the drawing-board on some design. She is operating at full strength. But then there come those moments when she is suddenly adrift. She is dazed by events, and she is confused. What exactly is it that has happened? Nick is no longer here, apparently because she sent him away. Kath is in her head more than ever before, but her response to Kath swerves wildly. Sometimes she is angry with Kath: "Why Nick?" she demands. At other times she is trying to recover a shadowy, elusive Kath who seems to be saying something that she cannot quite hear, and occasionally she is startled by some uncontrollable reaction of her own. She had been affronted by cousin Linda, jolted into resentment by that tone of casual intimacy; Linda was nothing to Kath, nobody, she had no business talking that way.

After a long day visiting a health retreat under refurbishment, for which she is designing the grounds, Elaine returns home and at once has the sense that something is not quite right, even as she turns in at the gate. There are a few moments of disorientation before she realizes that Nick's car has gone. The Golf is no longer sitting in the drive.

Elaine goes into the house. Sonia has left the usual pile of letters and memos; there is no reference to Nick. A note on the kitchen blackboard tells her Pam has detected some suspected honey fungus on one of the old chestnuts; below this, there is Nick's scrawl: *Sorry you weren't here.*

He has taken a few more of his clothes. The almost bare wardrobe is disconcertingly eloquent, as is the empty space on the driveway where his car is not.

Children talk a lot about love. "I love you," they say. "Do you love me?" they ask. Elaine remembers this of Polly. As language began to flow from Polly, there came this word, flung casually around, in a house that had not much heard it hitherto. It is a word with which Elaine has always had some difficulty; it did not much pass between her and Nick. Polly's carefree usage had reminded her of Kath, when Kath was young. Kath too had bestowed love in all directions, and had asked for it in return. "Do you love me?" she would say, appearing suddenly at Elaine's side, interrupting her homework or her hair washing or her preparations for an outing. And she hears herself: "Don't be silly, Kath."

Don't be silly, you're my sister. That is what she had meant. Sisters don't talk about love. And anyway I don't talk about love. I'm not that sort of person.

Polly and Nick

Listen, I'm not seeing Dan any more. It wasn't going anywhere. As of last week. All perfectly sensible and grown-up — at least I was. So that's that. A free woman. Though actually there's this guy ... No, there *might* be this guy. Early days yet — I could be quite wrong. So enough said.

Yes, my dad's still in the flat. I mean, I'm really sorry for him but it's driving me crazy. Here I am, I'm thirty and I'm apparently living with my *father*. Yes, of course I've tried that, the place is ankle deep in stuff from rental agencies, he won't even go and *look*. He says he needs to sort himself out first, get his head together. What does my dad do? You mean work-wise? Well, basically, my dad doesn't really do anything. He talks about doing things, and messes about with ideas that might eventually lead to doing something. It wasn't always like that. He had his own publishing company, way back. Rather successful, actually. But Dad wasn't so hot on the money side, got overstretched or something, and it folded. And by then my mum was doing so well ... Actually, my dad's lovely, in his way. I mean, he's still about ten and a half — fifty-eight going on ten and a half. It's always rather driven Mum round the bend, I can see that, but that's how he is, like a sort of overgrown boy, enthusing away about this or that, and actually it's eating me up seeing him like this. Mooching around. Not talking much. Looking *old* suddenly.

My mum? Well, frankly, I think my mum has flipped. I mean, I'm just hoping and praying it's temporary, because my mum isn't a person who flips. My mum is someone who has been on course since she was about five. Well, yes, of course it's *about* something, but all this is so over the top because what it's about is over and done with. Long ago. I won't go into it but . . . well, I do feel a meal is being made of it, and everyone just needs to calm down. God, *families* . . .

Ah — step-parents. No, I don't know about step-parents. We're the old-fashioned nuclear family. *How* many? Wow! A serial marrier, evidently, your mum.

Anyway, so there it is — my dad on the sofa and beer cans in my fridge and dirty shirts all over the bathroom and various arrangements on hold and my mum saying can we not talk about this. Plus, I've got some really complex client stuff going on right now. I mean, I just don't *need* this.

Listen, I'll have to go — oddly enough they pay me to work here. That's another thing — I can't really talk to people from the flat any more. It's not that he's listening — it's just that, well, I've lost my personal space.

Actually, no — tomorrow evening's no good. I'm seeing this guy Andy.

Don't jump to conclusions. I've said — it's early days. We'll see.

★ ★ ★

Oh . . . *hi!* No, this is just fine. Yes, I enjoyed it too. Oh . . . No, no, that wasn't it at all . . . Look, this really is crossed wires.

This is so embarrassing. The thing is — I couldn't ask you up to the flat because my *father's* there. He's — well, sort of staying with me at the moment. It's a long story. That's why. That's absolutely why.

Oh, I *see*. You thought . . . God no. Definitely not. I mean, yes, I've been in a relationship but that's over. Actually, this is quite a difficult time for me — nothing to do with that, that's not a problem at all, we just weren't going anywhere — no, this is, oh . . . *family* stuff. Look, I'm not going to load this on to you, when we hardly know each other.

Are you? Well, I think that's nice. I mean, a lot of men don't want to, frankly. They'd rather not know. Listening's just not their thing. Actually, that was a big problem with . . . with this person I'm not with any more. I just felt he wasn't there for me whenever I had something going on. Know what I mean? Oh, God, I'm making myself sound like I'm in perpetual crisis, it's not like that at all, it's just that, well, when you're involved with someone, you expect . . . Look, I'll have to go — I've got a client meeting in half an hour.

Thursday? Yes, as it happens I could do Thursday.

Mum? You all right? Well, good, because everything's not all right here. First of all, I've realized I can't bring people to the flat because of Dad — well, not some people, if you see what I mean. And actually that's really inconvenient just at the moment because . . . well, there's this man I may be interested in.

Oh, Mum, I *told* you I'm not seeing Dan any more.

And then last night I came home and he wasn't here. No, no — not the man — and he's called Andy, by the way. *Dad.* Dad wasn't here. I mean, usually he's just sitting in front of the telly every evening — and incidentally he's drinking too much. I wasn't going to mention that except frankly I think you should know. But he wasn't here, and at eleven o'clock I'm like some mother with a teenager out at a disco, watching the clock and thinking accidents and stuff.

The car? Yes, of course the car was gone. And he doesn't understand about parking in London — he leaves it on yellow lines and gets a ticket just about every day. And by the way he was really pissed off you weren't there when he went to get it — that was the point of going, if you ask me. Seeing you, not getting the car.

Oh, he came back, yes. Nearly one o'clock. By which time I'm climbing the wall, about to start ringing for the police. He's been out of London, he says. Someone he had to see. And it was a long drive and he stopped off on the way back and he got a bit lost. And then he went to bed, and of course I'm so wound up I can't go to sleep, and now I'm wiped out today, just when I've got a panic on with a job that's overdue.

No, he wasn't drunk.

Mum, don't mind me saying so, but if you need to know whether he's remembered that the car is due for its MOT I think you should ask him yourself.

Oliver and Nick

"No!" Oliver abandons his screen, swivels round in his chair. "I'm not here!"

Sandra is unsympathetic — downright uncooperative, in fact. "Mr Hammond rang earlier," she says, the receiver held out at arm's length. Does she realize who Mr Hammond *is*, by any chance?

Oliver attempts to face her down, and fails. He crosses the room, takes the phone. "Ah. Nick. Hello there."

He is in a lather. Not more of this blasted business? First Glyn. Now Nick. Heaven preserve him from Elaine. He can hardly follow what Nick is saying. Nick rattles away. Something about wanting to catch up, out of touch for far too long. Must meet.

"I'm pretty tied up just now," says Oliver. He talks of deadlines, urgent schedules. "Maybe in the autumn." Sandra is listening with interest.

Nick forges on. He talks in broken sentences. He seems to be saying that he is not at home right now, that he has had a few problems recently, that he'd like to have a talk about the old days. He sounds slightly manic.

No! wails Oliver — speechless, defenceless. Nick is saying that he's got nothing much on today, as it happens, so he'll drive over. Be with you about six, OK?

198

Pick you up at your office — I've got the address. Take you out for a meal.

Well, unfortunately . . . protests Oliver. This evening I . . . But Nick is no longer there. And Sandra is gazing at him, speculative: "Remind me just who this Nick Hammond is?"

When Nick walks into the room Oliver is horrified. This is not Nick, surely? This paunchy figure with thinning hair? With melting jaw-line and bags under his eyes. Yes, we've all of us matured, some rather more than others, but Nick? Nick was eternally young, it seemed, stuck forever at about twenty-eight, as the rest of them hit forty and edged towards the big five-oh. Well, evidently even Nick is not exempt.

Nick is talking as soon as he is in the room, without preliminaries — a feverish account of his drive, and some difficulty with a recalcitrant clutch, and being jinxed by the one-way system. He is on edge — that is immediately apparent.

Oliver gathers himself. Sandra is observing intently; she has found that for some reason she needs to work late and thus is still there when Nick arrives. "Well, *hello*," Oliver says, genial but not over-intimate, for Sandra's benefit — the greeting appropriate to an associate. "Good to see you. Sandra Chalcott — my partner." He turns to Sandra: "We'll be off then. See you later."

"Is a curry all right with you?" he says to Nick. "There's a place just near." He steers Nick along the street. Nick talks. At least in that sense he is the old Nick, but his talk skitters off in all directions, it is

199

dog-legged, herring-boned, it leaps from one unconsidered trifle to another. He is in London a lot these days, he says; possibly he may do a book on London squares, fascinating subject — London squares; Polly sends greetings, at least Polly would if she knew he was seeing Oliver but come to think of it she doesn't; Elaine is extraordinarily busy these days — one doesn't seem to set eyes on her from one week to the next; he has been thinking of writing something on Brunel, but is finding it hard to get down to it, things get in the way so . . .

Eventually, over a plateful of chicken tikka masala, he falls silent. He stares at his plate. His hair no longer flops over one eye, Oliver notes; it has somehow peeled back from the front. Without that pelt, Nick seems exposed, laid bare.

Nick looks up. He puts down his fork, picks up his beer, drinks deeply. "The fact is, I'm a bit bothered about something."

He shoots Oliver a wild look. He seems now like a school-boy in disgrace; a chastened sixteen year old peers out from the softened jowls and the pouchy eyes.

"Ah . . ." Oliver assumes an expression of neutral interest: continue if you must.

"Elaine's got herself into a terrible state about a photo. Do you remember a photo of me and Kath?"

Oliver contemplates his lamb korma. "Yes," he says, at last.

Nick pushes his plate to one side. "There's the most awful fuss, actually."

"I know," says Oliver.

"You know?"

Oliver sighs. Bugger it all! "Glyn came to see me."

Now panic flies across Nick's face. "Oh, Christ! What did he want?"

"He wanted to know if Kath went in for . . . for that sort of thing. For having affairs with people."

"What did you say?"

"I said I didn't know. What would you have said?"

Nick hesitates. He seems to be reflecting — not a process Oliver associates with Nick. "I'd have said the same."

Silence. "All very unfortunate," says Oliver, at last. "But I don't see what I —" He starts to eat again, determinedly. No doubt he is going to be picking up the tab, so why let a good meal go to waste?

Nick now lets fly. He bursts out with a spasmodic, incoherent litany of concerns. Well, of course Kath must have had affairs, he says, I mean — there were always men around, weren't there? After all, she was *so* pretty. But not for the sake of it. Not in a *frivolous* way, right? Any more than I did. Frankly, Olly, I don't know what got into me. Or her, come to that. Crazy. Stupid. But the point is, it's over and done with, so why, now, all this? I mean, it's so unfair. Elaine's being . . . Well, I won't go on about it, but I wouldn't be surprised if I weren't heading for some sort of breakdown. I'm in a terrible state. Someone's got to do something.

Oliver is barely listening. He is thinking of Kath. She has become like some mythical figure, trawled up at will to fit other people's narratives. Everyone has their way with her, everyone decides what she was, how things were. It seems to him unjust that in the midst of this to-do she is denied a voice.

He interrupts. "Did you love her?"

Nick's spiel is chopped off. He looks shocked. "Well, of course I —" he begins. "Naturally, one . . . I mean, when you're caught up in this sort of thing that's not quite —" He retrieves his plate and picks up his fork.

No, thinks Oliver, sadly. You didn't.

Nick has recovered himself, in so far as this is possible. "The thing is, it might help if you had a word with Elaine."

Oliver stares. "What about?"

Nick sighs — a nervous, juddering, confessional sigh. "She's thrown me out, Olly, that's the long and the short of it."

Startled, Oliver considers this. He is surprised at such emphatic action on Elaine's part. Time was, he had always thought that Elaine rather let Nick get away with things. Admittedly, this must have been quite a bombshell.

"I want to go home," says Nick. He sounds like a querulous eight year old.

Oliver is now seized with desperation. He would like to snap at Nick that he is not in the marriage guidance business, but he is held back by some irritable sense of responsibility that he recognizes from their former partnership. But, for Christ's sake, he is no longer responsible for Nick or anything that Nick does or has done.

"After all," says Nick. "You took that photograph."

Oliver bounces in his chair. "No!" he cries. The people at the next table turn and look at them.

"But you did."

"I mean — no, you can't start blaming me for all this."

"I'm not blaming you," says Nick, in tones of sweet reason. He seems now very much in control of himself. He is shovelling down his food, and pauses to finish a mouthful. "I'm just saying that you are involved, after all."

"I am not," says Oliver sullenly.

"Elaine always liked you."

"I haven't seen her for years."

"She was always going on about how sensible and level-headed you were. As opposed to me. I think she used to feel sometimes she'd be better off married to you than to me." Nick grins. "It's OK — I didn't mind. I could always sort things out with Elaine then."

So sort this out, thinks Oliver sourly.

"But she seems to have gone completely off the rails about this. All it needs is someone to sit down with her and have a friendly talk. You, Olly."

Oliver glowers.

"It's just a question of getting her to see that I don't *deserve* this," says Nick plaintively. "Right? I mean — OK, it was silly and wrong, but that's *all* it was. There's absolutely no point in everyone going berserk. Glyn charging around. Elaine behaving as though I'd robbed a bank."

"*No.*"

"No, what?"

"No, I won't talk to Elaine."

Nick gazes across the table in silence. He becomes reproachfully dignified. "As you wish. Entirely up to you. I would have thought you might feel . . . well, a certain involvement. Never mind. So be it."

The meal is finished to the accompaniment of a few constrained exchanges. When the bill arrives Nick has fallen into a depressed silence; Oliver pays it.

They part outside the restaurant. "Good seeing you, Olly," says Nick. He manages to appear generous, forgiving, and leaves Oliver experiencing a grating mix of guilt and resentment.

Oliver and Sandra

"So what was up with your friend?" enquires Sandra.

"Oh, nothing really," says Oliver.

"Come on — I know a man in a tizz when I see one."

They are in bed. There is no escape route. "He always was a bit like that."

"First that Glyn someone," says Sandra thoughtfully. "Then this Nick Hammond. Your former partner, right? And Glyn was married to Nick's wife's sister? Her that died?"

No possible escape. Oliver agrees that this is so.

"And suddenly they're all needing to see you. Has something come out of the woodwork?"

Fleetingly, Oliver considers telling Sandra about the whole business. Well, you see, the trouble is that Glyn found a photo taken by me which indicated that at one point Nick had an affair with Glyn's wife Kath. He knows immediately that he will not. Bald facts are a travesty, a distortion. That is what happened, but it is also misleading, confusing. Left out is what Nick was like, and what Glyn was like, and above all who Kath was, and how she was. Without the ballast of personalities, of how things were back then, such an account is threadbare, it invites a knee-jerk reaction. He knows just the sort of comment that Sandra would make.

She is waiting. This is evidently to be one of those rare occasions on which Sandra decides to pay close attention to Oliver's past. He knows those indications of terrier-like purpose.

"It's just a question of clarification," he says. "People need to get straight about some dates — that sort of thing."

"A publishing matter?" says Sandra. "To do with the business?" Her tone is deceptively bland.

Oliver is no liar. He is fluttering now. "Well, in a sense, I suppose . . . Not absolutely specifically. Sort of indirectly."

There is a telling silence.

"I see," says Sandra. Then: "That Glyn — striking-looking man. Laid on the charm, too. An academic, you said?"

"That's right." Oliver contrives a suggestive yawn. "I'm wiped out, love. I think I'll —"

"The wife," says Sandra. "The one who died. Kath — is that right? I don't have much impression of her, except that she was very attractive. You knew her well, I suppose?"

Oliver is now in full flight. He lays a calming, propitiatory hand on Sandra's thigh, turns away from her with an exaggerated sigh of weariness, and hopes for the best. After a moment, Sandra too rolls over, and is silent.

It is a long while before Oliver sleeps. They all come crowding in — Nick, Glyn, Elaine. And Kath above all. He sees and hears Kath fresh and clear; "Hi, Oliver!" she says, breezing into his office back in the old days.

"Where is everyone?" She sits on the window-seat in Elaine's kitchen, plaiting Polly's hair. She is beside Nick in the group at the Roman villa that day; he raises his camera. And when eventually he drifts on the interface between consciousness and sleep, she is still there, but now she has become very young — a girl-Kath that he never knew — and she is talking about love. He cannot follow what it is that she is saying.

Glyn and Myra

It is Glyn's birthday. He does not remember this until he notices the date on his newspaper. Birthdays never rated highly with Glyn. But he knows how old he is — sixty-two. This reminder of the relentless process is unwelcome. The passage of time is indeed his stock-in-trade, but when applied personally it is as though there were someone out there gleefully chuckling: you too — oh, dear me, yes, you too.

It is Saturday. He plans a weekend dealing with paperwork and ordering his thoughts on a projected article. This will be therapeutic. Glyn is in a curious state these days. He recognizes this, knows that he is not operating normally, that application requires an effort, that his mind wanders, that it is wilful, that he cannot seem to control its direction. He has always been able to work; work has been the imperative, ever since he can remember. He has been able to switch into work-mode under any circumstances. Now, it is not like that. He stares for long minutes at the screen, he does not turn the pages of the book in his hand, or he reads without comprehension.

Kath. Her fault. Except that something odd has happened also with the attribution of blame. He is finding that his former drive to discover her guilt, her duplicity, her involvement with a raft of suspected lovers has evaporated. His various encounters — with Claverdon and his companion, with the Hapgoods, with Kath's portrait and its courteous guardian — have eroded his sense of purpose. They have left him feeling uneasy, even chastened. He is no longer interested in that obsessive pursuit of what she may have done, in whom she may have known. He is not even much interested in Nick, he finds.

He thinks about Kath. She rises up in front of the screen, she is superimposed above the page. He listens to her.

But this morning he will work. Grimly applied, he heads for his study.

The front doorbell rings. It is Myra. With a birthday smile on her face and a present in her hand, which turns out to be a rather nice piece of early Victorian china. He receives both with the best possible grace, but she is out of order. Very definitely out of order. The unstated terms of their relationship are that it is conducted at her place, and there alone. She has only visited this house on two or three previous occasions. If he runs into her in the university he gives her the polite greeting he might give to anyone else on the staff; no doubt their association is known to some, but it is not to be asserted. On the rare occasions that they go out somewhere together, he ensures that it is well away from common ground.

Glyn takes her into the kitchen and makes coffee. He could hardly do less. And, truth to tell, her arrival has given him a lift. The significance of the date had induced a mawkish feeling of self-pity, a sense of solitude quite alien to his usual stern defence of privacy.

Myra is in her late forties, veteran of a failed marriage that Glyn does not wish to hear about; he has made this plain. She has dark, ripe good looks and a vivacious presence that he finds invigorating at the right moments. And the moments, normally, are chosen by him; during the several years of their association, Myra has acknowledged its boundaries. If she once sought a firmer commitment, she has now abandoned any expectations. And, equally, Glyn accepts that if something more satisfactory to her came along, he would no doubt be required to relinquish Myra. He does not think much about this; and if it happened, well, one would have to look around.

Glyn enjoys sex with Myra; Myra too gives every indication of satisfaction. There is a degree of intimacy between them, tempered by the recognition that this is an arrangement of mutual benefit, and that is all. When he is with Myra, Glyn obliterates any thought of Kath. It is not that Myra is no substitute for Kath, it is rather that she is not on the same plane as Kath, nor ever could be.

"You were working, I suppose," says Myra.

"I was." But some uncharacteristic note of apathy in Glyn's voice gives her the advantage.

"Such a nice day."

He notices that it is indeed. He begins to see where this is leading. And within a minute or two, he has somehow fallen in with Myra's scheme. An outing. A sortie into the landscape. A walk, maybe — lunch at the pub. Or . . . As it happens, she has been doing a spot of research and there's this country house which is open today. But I expect you know it already.

He does not. And actually he wouldn't mind having a look at it. Myra is in luck. He agrees, surprised at himself. But first he must have a spell at the desk to deal with a few urgent letters.

Myra is entirely happy about this. She'll find something to do. And within the next hour she has scoured his saucepans, removed various mouldy items from the fridge, bagged up the rubbish and had a run-around with the vacuum cleaner. This is just the sort of thing he has always anticipated, where Myra is concerned, and one reason why he has kept her away. His gratitude is not effusive.

She picks up on this, and is tactfully apologetic. "I'm afraid I got a bit carried away. You know what I'm like." He does indeed, and she is reminding him that the appeal of her own place, for him, apart from the solace of her bed, is the provision of home comforts. "And you haven't got the time or the inclination, have you? Your cleaning lady seems to have a few blind spots. Of course your wife would have —"

Now she is really transgressing; Kath is a forbidden subject. Glyn cuts her off: "Kath didn't do that kind of thing," he says shortly.

Myra is baffled, as well she might be. Does he mean that Kath neglected her domestic duties? Or that she was above such trivialities? But she sees that she has overstepped the mark and makes a judicious retreat by

211

producing a road-map with the suggestion that they check out a route to this country house.

Glyn realizes that the excursion has been well planned; he cannot but admire her strategic skills. He has been ambushed. That said, he is not as resistant as he would expect to be. Once again, he recognizes his own abnormal state. He has allowed himself to be manipulated by Myra, something which does not happen. But there is this unusual lethargy, where work is concerned, and he would not be averse to an inspection of the house which, he recalls, has fourteenth-century origins and will undoubtedly throw up something worth his while.

Glyn drives. Myra navigates, making much of it; she is exuberant with the success of her plot. Perhaps she sees this small triumph as an erosion of Glyn's position, where the conditions of their alliance are concerned. At any rate, she fails to note that he is quieter than usual and she rattles on uncurbed. Her talk skates the surface of things, as always, glancing from one train of thought to another; this has never too much bothered Glyn, for whom her conversation is not her appeal and who is abundantly well qualified to dominate where talking is concerned, when he so wishes. But today he does not so wish, and Myra has full rein, until arrival at their objective and the dictation of a guided tour eventually force her into silence.

A country house, for Glyn, is a fine assemblage of coded references. The roped-off furnishings and the artworks pillaged as successive generations undertook the Grand Tour are of little interest to him; he is busy sniffing out the implications of this accumulation of wealth and patronage. How has this particular pile affected its environment? What has been obliterated by its parkland and its lake? How far has it determined the local economy?

For Myra, it becomes apparent, a country house is merely the decorative extension of a decent cafeteria and an inviting gift shop. The tour is the necessary preliminary, an agreeable enough hors-d'œuvre which she undertakes in a businesslike way, with housewifely attention to detail. She is gratified to spot a cobweb or a grubby surface. But she does pay attention to the pictures, and joins Glyn as he inspects the art displayed in the building's most lavish public room.

The paintings are all about either sex or fame, except for the few that celebrate a woodland scene, a vase of flowers or some idle arrangement of slaughtered animals. Sex comes in the guise of mythology; but there's no doubt what it's all about, thinks Glyn, wandering from a rosy recumbent nymph being eyed up by Bacchus to an ivory-fleshed Leda tucked beneath a sinuous swan.

"Oops!" says Myra. "What's going on!"

He ignores her, thinking now of fame, which blazes all around. A giant cloaked Napoleon glowers from a rocky crag; Nelson dies on a bloody deck; an armoured Caesar glitters amid a thousand spears. Glyn has never paid too much attention to fame, being more concerned with the effects of the toiling masses, but as he prowls from painting to painting he sees that fame displaces its subjects — they float free of any context and become iconic figures. Everyone knows them, but as images, as symbols. This is how these people are perceived, and thus are they portrayed, for ever.

Myra is getting a mite restless. She wants her lunch. She draws Glyn on through the next room, and the next. He is unusually compliant, intent upon his own thoughts, which are no longer directed towards the surrounding display — the tapestries, the weaponry, the inlaid cabinets — but in feverish pursuit of quite other matters.

Myra sorts things out in the cafeteria. She installs him at a table and goes off to forage, returning with a tray of food and a couple of glasses of wine. Glyn pulls out his wallet, reminded of decent procedure.

"Birthday treat," says Myra expansively. She raises her glass: "Here's to it!"

Now she looks closely at him. "You seem off colour. You're not coming down with something, are you?"

Glyn gives himself a shake. He replies briskly that he is fine, fine. Myra has occupied quite enough new ground today. He is not going to cede any more. Confidences are out of the question, and ever have been. All Myra knows from him about Kath is that she died. No doubt she knows a fair amount more from others.

He forces himself back on course. He remembers where they are. He gives Myra a simplified account of the changing fortunes of the landed gentry since the middle ages, to which she listens with apparent interest, though she asks no questions. His intention is to clarify her perception of this place, but by the time he has got to the Victorians his own commitment is waning. Myra takes advantage of a pause to suggest coffee, and goes off to fetch it. She returns talking determinedly of her son, who is reading engineering and about whom she needs Glyn's advice. Glyn has always resisted being thrust into any sort of pseudo-fatherly role and avoids visiting Myra when the boy is in residence. His only defence now is to speed up the coffee stage and suggest that they get out and see the gardens.

Myra goes off to the Ladies. Glyn wanders out on to the wide terrace overlooking a green vista of southern England, and as he does so he is joined by Kath. She comes with a rush, not just in his head, but all around him, it seems, so that he is with her as he once was at some similar place, to which he hustled her during that ferocious accelerated period of courtship. They stand at a stone parapet, overlooking tree-studded parkland, and she puts a hand on his arm: "There's something you never say." And then, "Never mind —" This rings now in his head: "There's something you never say —"

Myra appears, and they start their tour of the gardens, a couple enjoying an outing amid all the other couples and the families and the straggling coach party. The weather remains idyllic, the roses are out. Myra is high with satisfaction. "Well!" she says. "This *was* a good idea."

For Glyn, it is no longer Myra who is at his side, but Kath: Myra talks, but anything she says becomes irrelevant background interference; he reaches beyond it for Kath.

"You're not *listening*," says Kath. But he is. He is listening with all his might. Listening and seeing. And along with the familiar signals that endlessly repeat themselves, the reliable structure of the years with Kath, the received interpretation, there come odd vagrant challenging flashes — like the hitherto undetected stars that periodically excite astronomers. But Glyn is not excited; he is disturbed, perturbed, awry.

He hears Kath on the phone — a low voice that falters, crumbles. Is she *crying*? He comes into the room, and she is putting the phone down: "I'll have to go, Mary." Her face is odd, distorted. He is in a hurry, he is leaving for a conference in the States, and he has mislaid a crucial paper. He cannot dwell on Kath's face, that shrivelled look, but he must have stashed it away because now, here, today, it comes swimming up to him.

Elaine and Polly

Long ago, Elaine considered not having Polly. That is to say, she considered not having children at all. Being childless. There is a choice. She could see that life is a good deal less cluttered without that. One would be able to get on with work a lot more easily. She looked around at her contemporaries and took note. There were those who toiled from day to day, burdened with sleepless nights and howling days, and those who cruised free, accountable only to themselves.

It could have gone either way. For a couple of years, she thought of the matter from time to time, but would push it to one side. And then she noticed that if she forgot to take the pill, she was not particularly bothered about the lapse. She forgot quite often.

When she knew she was pregnant, Nick said, "Oh, good. What fun." She had never discussed with him her own doubts about becoming a parent. Of course there were two of them in this, but it had seemed to her that in the last resort the issue was a personal one. She knew who would be taking the brunt.

Nick was not a bad father. When he was around, and had nothing better to do, he fathered with a boisterous enthusiasm. From the age of about two, Polly saw him as some kind of engaging but wayward family pet — good for a romp, but not to be taken entirely seriously.

As she grew older, this attitude firmed up into one in which affection and amusement rode upon an undercurrent of mild exasperation: "*Typical!*" "Trust Dad —" Polly seemed to shoot past him, becoming the responsible and efficient adult while he remained in a time-warp of feckless adolescence.

Polly's phone calls are now more circumspect. She has given up on direct appeals, defeated by Elaine's polite deflection: "Can we not talk about this." Instead she skirmishes around the edge of the subject. She mentions the trouble involved in fixing the washing-machine ill-treated by Nick. Elaine offers at once to pay. "It's not the money," says Polly. "It's the *bother*." She describes how she has hauled Nick into the offices of a rental agency: "On Saturday morning, when actually I had a million things to do . . . And we went to see this really nice flat and he said, yes, OK, fine. And then as soon as we're back at my place again he does a U-turn and it's, no, he's not sure, maybe, he'll sleep on it. And there's my Saturday morning down the drain." She makes dark references to drinking sessions. She says Nick has lost weight: "Not that he couldn't do with that, but all the same —"

All this has an effect on Elaine. She is distracted. Her resolve is faltering. Instead of concentrating smoothly upon work, upon the demands of each day, upon future plans, her thoughts come homing back to what Polly last said. She pictures Nick wandering aimlessly around London. She wonders about this weight loss, and the drinking.

Polly visits. She visits at short notice, as usual, dashing down on a Sunday. "Dad knows where I've gone," she says pointedly. "He . . . well, he sent his love."

She and Elaine sit and eat lunch in the conservatory. "I can't believe Dad's not here," says Polly. "I keep expecting him to walk in. All right, all right, I'm not going to start up again. Just . . . well, it's so *unreal*."

Elaine agrees, but she is not going to say so. Polly talks about a man. This Andy. "Not that I'm rushing into anything," she says. "But it's *interesting*, put it that way." She looks speculatively at Elaine. "Did you and Dad fall in love with a great wham, or what?"

Elaine is thrown. She is not open to this kind of exchange, nor is Polly in the habit of such questioning. Have normal family conventions been abandoned?

"Oh —" she says. "It's such a long time ago."

Polly is having none of that. "Oh, come on, Mum. Everyone remembers falling in love."

Elaine is busy over the salad. "All home produce," she announces. "This is a kind of rocket I've never tried before. Grows like a weed." She piles herbage on Polly's plate. "And the first baby beetroot. Here —"

Polly eyes her. "Mum, don't mind me saying so, but you'd feel better if you let go a bit more. You're *so* buttoned up. I mean, I know it's the way you are, but it can't be good for you."

Elaine is used to being scolded by Polly. Polly has been scolding her ever since she was about three. Usually it has been over questions of diet, or dress, or

219

household management. Now, it would seem that she is going for basics.

"I seem to remember a process of gradual drift," she says.

"Drift?" yelps Polly. "*Drift!* For heaven's sake, Mum!"

Actually, Elaine is trying to be honest. That is what she remembers. She searches for passion, and something does come smoking up: an incandescent day when she and Nick walked on the Sussex downs, not long before they got married, and she had brimmed with well-being, with anticipation — yes, with love.

"Well, there was more than that."

"So I should hope," snaps Polly. She becomes reflective. "I mean, I've been in love, but I'm accepting that I haven't been definitively in love. Not the full five-star menu, the earth moving, the real thing. Just a few appetizers. I'm waiting."

"Plenty of time," says Elaine. "How's work going?"

But Polly is not interested in talking about work. "Was Kath in love with Glyn?"

Why is Polly so exercised about love? Is it love in the past, or love in the future that concerns her? Elaine's love, or her lack of it? Or a potential love of Polly's own? Whichever, Elaine is uncomfortable.

"I suppose —" she begins. "Well — she seemed very happy."

Kath comes down the Register Office steps, again and again, smiling and smiling. She smiles into the camera, at Elaine on the other side of the road. Her skirt is crooked.

"When didn't Kath seem happy?" cries Polly.

Elaine wants to stop this conversation, if conversation it is, but can see that Polly is in a relentless mood. Nor can she say, "Can we not talk about this," because Polly is not doing so; she is keeping the matter of Nick at arm's length.

But now Polly plunges in another direction. "The thing is, I don't *understand*. I don't understand how people can be so . . . *mysterious*. I don't understand *people*. You think you've got them pretty well sewn up, and then they go all flaky on you. They fly apart. They even fly apart in your *head*, for goodness' sake! I don't understand Kath. I mean, I knew Kath. I don't understand Dad. I look at him — and he's a real mess these days, Mum, I can tell you, grubby shirts, needs a haircut, doesn't bother to shave — I look at him and I don't know *what's* in his head. And I don't understand you, Mum. Absolutely I do not."

There is a butterfly tapping against the conservatory window, beating furiously up and down; a tortoiseshell. Beyond, in the garden, the sunlight sifting through the crab-apple trees has turned the lawn to a brocade of green and gold. Pam wheels a barrow across the end of the grass walk; some stuff falls off and she stoops to pick it up. Elaine is aware of all this, the stable and consoling backcloth to her daughter's discordant presence. Polly no longer sounds thirty; this wail is coming from a person of eight, or ten, or twelve.

"I don't understand how everything can suddenly go completely off the rails. I mean, the point about life surely is that it moves on. It goes forward. On and on, regardless. It doesn't . . . loop backwards. Which, as far as I can see, is what yours is doing. Yours and Dad's. There's Dad, and he's a zombie. He's completely out of it. I'm beginning to think therapy. There's a woman I've heard of —"

Elaine is jolted into reaction. "No. Definitely none of that." She stares at Polly, who has pushed her half-eaten lunch to one side and is managing to look both martyred and mutinous.

Elaine realizes that what she is now experiencing is guilt, and that she has perhaps been experiencing this for some while. She is feeling guilty about Nick. How can this be? She is the one who is sinned against, but there has been a reversal of roles. It is Nick who is apparently some sort of victim, who is at risk, who invites concern. Whereas she is unreasonable, implacable, unkind.

She says, "You do remember what this is all about?"

"Oh, *Mum* . . . of course I do. But, look at you . . . Frankly, Mum, you're all over the place. I mean, I can tell — you're twitchy, you've got baggy eyes, you're not you."

Is this so? Elaine thinks of the way in which Sonia glances at her, from time to time. She remembers Pam's solicitous offers to take on extra tasks. Is this how she appears? Is this, indeed, how she is?

There is a silence. "There —" says Polly. "That's all. I'll shut up." She reaches for her plate and starts to eat again. "The salad's good. Can I take some of this rocket stuff back for Dad and me?"

222

Kath

Oliver finds himself thinking about Kath's men. Those who came with her when she turned up at Elaine's house. They are a shadowy crew — for the most part he can no longer put a name to a face, and frequently the faces too are lost. There were not that many of them — four, five, six maybe, over the years. A couple who came only once; others more tenacious, who have left a stronger impression. An assorted lot — taller, shorter, younger, older — but the common denominator that Oliver remembers is a certain triumphal quality. They were men in possession of a trophy, successful competitors in some contest with which Oliver was not involved. Oliver knew that he was not the sort of man who aspired to a woman like Kath. These men were better-looking, rich with confidence, purposeful. Kath was their purpose of the moment, apparently. They accompanied her with complacent ease; she was their due, they were owed someone like this.

He remembers an actor whose name he vaguely recognized, a roguish charmer; he remembers an urbane fellow with a BMW convertible. Both of these turned up on more than one occasion. And, homing in on recollections of these men and on the way in which they melted away, over time, he finds himself in Elaine's garden, with Kath, companionably gathering windfall

223

apples. She has come alone this time: no man. Polly darts round them, busy with apples. She rushes up, laden: "Look how many I've got!" "Clever girl!" says Kath. "Put them in the basket."

"Where's Mike?" demands Polly. "He promised he'd give me a ride in his car without a top."

And Kath replies, "Mike's not coming any more." Offhand, inspecting an apple. Polly pulls a face and goes back to the apple hunt.

Kath turns to Oliver. Was he betraying interest? Or surprise, or sympathy? She smiles: "It's all right, Olly — my heart is not broken. Did you like him?"

And Oliver, flustered, prevaricates — unable to say that so far as he is concerned they are jammy beggars who don't know their luck, the lot of them.

Kath sighs. She polishes an apple on her sleeve, takes a bite; he sees her white teeth against the shiny red. "The thing is, to move away before it's too late." Is she talking to herself, or to him? He does not know that look: something anxious about it, lost.

"Too late?" he says firmly, to bring her back.

And she smiles — familiar cheery Kath. "Before they change their minds. Have you got a girlfriend, Olly?"

How did Oliver reply? Oh, he can guess. He would have floundered about, and Kath would have laughed, and teased him, and they would have gathered up the apples, and Polly, and gone back to the house for lunch, or tea, or supper.

Indeed, the whole scene is now a fluid mix of imagery and supposition. He sees Kath, and small Polly flitting about in the long grass, and experiences the satisfaction of lighting on a perfect apple — no bruising, no scabs or holes. He sees that alien look on Kath's face. Snatches of what is said ring out: "My heart is not broken . . . The thing is to move away . . . Before they change their minds." The rest is unreliable — perhaps that is how it was, perhaps later wisdoms have imposed themselves, perhaps the need for narrative and sequence has stepped in. Suffice it that he was there, then, with Kath, and it was thus, or very like.

Polly does not remember the day of the apples. It is subsumed into the crowded simultaneous present of her childhood, when she is just a pair of eyes and ears — seeing, hearing, storing. She has stored Kath many times — she can conjure up different incarnations of Kath. Kath gets smaller as Polly gets larger, until eventually they are shoulder to shoulder. Kath is now like some kind of big sister.

Once, Polly wanted her to be something else. She wished that Kath was her mother. This is no reflection on Elaine, it did not mean a repudiation of Elaine, it meant simply that Polly wanted to have Kath with her all of the time, in an attentive, available, mother role. She remembers this longing and she remembers also an accompanying guilt; she knew she must not voice this need, least of all to Elaine.

Nowadays, Polly can see this with adult wisdom. She had doted on Kath, and so, naturally enough, wanted more of her. But she had been sufficiently mature — at six? seven? — to realize that there was a whiff of infidelity in this: you can only have one mother, you should love your mother most of all.

And I did, she thinks, as one does. In the last resort. I suppose.

Not that there was anything particularly maternal about Kath. You could not imagine Kath pushing a buggy, dishing up a family meal, waiting outside the school gates. All of which Elaine did as a matter of course, alongside her other concerns. Polly recognizes this, and gives Elaine her due.

Once, Polly and Kath sit drinking coffee in Polly's college room, during her student days. Kath has come to visit. Polly has shown her off, displayed her around the campus, and now they are having the leisurely heart-to-heart that Polly so relishes. She lays out various friends for Kath's inspection. She is heady with the whole student experience. But she is working, she tells Kath sternly, she is working like crazy. Already, there are objectives, there are goals. She will maybe aim for business, for finance, for the City. Or possibly journalism. Web design has not yet raised its head, though Polly is a whizz with technology.

Kath listens. She sits cross-legged on the bed, with a mug in her hand, as to the manner born. She could be twenty, not forty-something. She listens, apparently rapt. "Lucky you," she says, and there is an unfamiliar note in her voice. Polly is brought up short: lucky? her? But it is Kath who is lucky — just for being Kath. To look like that, to be like that — breezing through the days, through life.

They talk about love. Polly thinks she may be slightly in love; not madly, desperately, mind — but there is a definite disturbance. She is interested in her symptoms, and questions Kath. There is no sleep loss, but she does find that she thinks about him a lot and in . . . um . . . a sexual way. She cannot help making a point of engineering that their paths cross. Is this a low-grade response, unlikely to escalate? Do you know at once when it is serious? She is assuming that Kath is an expert.

Kath laughs. "Oh, all *that* —" She says that she first fell in love when she was five, with the postman. And then with the Rentokil man and with the vicar and eventually with the boy at the paper shop when she was fifteen and that lasted all of two months. But Polly is not interested in this juvenile stuff, and she senses flippancy. She is after informed guidance. But now Kath seems to withdraw; she is not so much evasive as oddly muted. "All I know is that I'm no good at it," she says. "Mistakes, mistakes —" She stares at Polly: "The thing is, do *they* love *you*?"

Nick thinks that he has slept with six women, apart from Elaine. That seems modest enough. There is a possible seventh when he was eighteen, but he is not at all sure that she counts; it was a particularly inexperienced session. But this is not the track record of a libertine, is it? And three were premarital encounters that can be viewed as perfectly normal steps in sexual development. The other three are indeed infidelities and cannot be explained in any other way, though one is a borderline case, he feels, being a shortlived lapse triggered by getting drunk at a party and fetching up in this woman's flat. The liaison with a publishing associate long ago is more reprehensible, looked at with detachment; but Elaine never knew, no one got hurt, the thing is dead and buried.

His eye has wandered, during married life — he is quite prepared to admit that. He has looked, and occasionally lusted. He has entered into understandings that have somehow stopped short of sex, and he would admit also that these might well have progressed, if the opportunity had arisen.

It is not a particularly admirable record, but neither is it despicable, surely? There are worse husbands, for God's sake.

If it had not been for Kath, Elaine would have reacted otherwise, in all probability. If that photograph had shown some other woman — some neutral, impersonal figure — Elaine would have been angry, he would have grovelled, but he would not be here in London, exiled.

Why? he asks himself. Why did it happen? But he knows. He looked at Kath one day and saw her afresh. And now he cannot see her thus any more. That fatal compulsion is quite gone; the Kath he experiences today is neutral, and the Nick to whom she responds is not himself.

Kath sits on the window-seat in the kitchen at the old house, with Polly on her knee — an infant Polly. This is in the time of innocence, long before he looked differently at Kath. Nick has come into the room and he thought at first that this was Elaine. He says as much. "I thought you were Elaine," he says, or must have said. And Kath looks at him over Polly's head: "No. It's me." She says it thereafter, again and again, and he is arrested still by her tone, by how she is. She is not vibrant Kath, but is suddenly bleak.

Glyn took Kath to the Lake District for their honeymoon. There was a strategy to this choice; he was interested in early hill farming at the time and needed to do some fieldwork on boundary systems. That week is now a blur, one image melting into another: Kath lying on her stomach to drink from a tarn, the attentive gaze of people in a pub, as she comes in through the door, her rain-wet hair glinting in the light. She follows him up a valley; he looks round and sees that she has stopped, her back to him, hands on hips, wearing a scarlet jacket, a small vivid figure, like some romantic affirmation of human existence against the spread of sky, lake and hills.

They climb; the steep grassy slope, the winding trail. "Does this thing have a name?" she asks. "They all have names. This is Cat Bells." There is soft caressing wind, and sunlight that flees across the hillside. She comes close and wraps her arms around him. They kiss. Pressed up against him, she runs her hand down and finds his erection: "I think we'd better get off this mountain," she says. They skid back down the track. Somewhere below there is a low stone wall, sheep-cropped grass and bushes beyond. They are over the wall; she is laughing, she says, "I can't take *all* my clothes off — it's freezing!" He spreads his coat on the grass, puts her down on it. She kicks off her trousers. It is the most urgent sex he can ever remember, a glorious immediacy, pinned forever in that place — the wind, the smell of crushed grass, some small piping bird, sheep moving about. Afterwards, he is suddenly euphoric, richly alive; he hugs her to him, pushes his hands under her sweater, feels her warm skin. She is laughing again: "Oh yes," she says. "*Yes*."

And now, today, he is filled with outrage that all this survives only in the head. He wants to retrieve the moment. He wants to retrieve Kath, as never before.

"I'm going to have five children," says Kath. "Mostly girls. A couple of boys — twins maybe. Not just yet. In a few years."

Elaine listens with cynicism. She is pregnant: heavy, hampered, irritable. Kath has blown in; soon she will blow away again, off back to her unfettered life, to whatever it is she is up to these days.

Elaine observes that Kath may find that she requires a husband.

"Oh yes, definitely. I'm looking for one." Kath is twenty-four. And spoiled for choice, Elaine assumes. On occasion, she is accompanied by some attentive man. Not today.

This is a time when Elaine's feelings for her sister rampage from one extreme to another. If Kath disappears for weeks on end Elaine is on edge about her. Why does she not phone? Where has she got to? When she shows up, need is replaced by a gust of annoyance: there she is — carefree, the fiddling grasshopper amid the striving ants, her beauty a repeated surprise. One had forgotten its effect.

"Well, look carefully," says Elaine. She has little faith in Kath's judgement. She sounds sour, and knows it.

Kath laughs. "Oh, I do. You've no idea how careful I am." The laughter stops, abruptly. She is suddenly concentrated, serious. Her glance sweeps the room — the cluttered domestic place. It homes in on Elaine's fecund belly. "Is it wonderful?" she says. "All this?"

Voices

"Look," he says. "It's Nick. I know I'm absolutely the last person in the world you want to have on the end of a phone and I don't blame you if you hang up, but I had to give it a try, OK? I just felt if you and I could talk a bit, and frankly you've every right to tell me to piss off, but I thought — no, I bloody well will, I'll ring him up, there's nothing to lose, things are bad enough anyway, at least they are at this end. And, Christ, I know what *you* must have been feeling. Believe me, Glyn. What I'm trying to say is — and I know you must be thinking this is a bit rich coming from me — I'm trying to say it's . . . well, I'm trying to say it's not absolutely what it looks like. I mean, I know it must look pretty wretched from your point of view, but that's where I feel if I could only have a chance to explain a bit, just kind of talk it through, you might be able to see it differently, see *me* differently. It's a question of perspective, really. The thing is . . . Are you still there, Glyn?"

Glyn growls that he is still there — wondering in fact why the hell he is.

"Oh, God, thanks. Thanks for giving me a chance. Look, what I'm trying to say is . . . it was all so bloody stupid, it wasn't such a big issue, it was a crazy sort of *mistake*. I don't know what came over us — came over me. Oh, that's what people always say, isn't it — except I'm sure you don't, you've got more sense, I always thought you were such a level-headed sort of bloke, knew what you were doing, which is why I thought, let me just try to *talk* to him."

"You seem to be doing just that," says Glyn. "To what end?"

"Ah. Well, it's kind of several things, you see, Glyn. I mean, firstly, me and Kath. What you've got to understand is, it was all over almost as soon as it began. It wasn't some great long drawn-out business. And it made absolutely no difference to — to other things. Me and Elaine. You and Kath. Those were what mattered, believe me. We both knew that, at the time. She . . . well, I tell you honestly, and I absolutely mean this . . . I always knew her heart was never in it. And for myself, well, I got carried away. She was after all incredibly . . . I just sort of lost my head. But only temporarily, that's what I'm trying to say. It was just this brief kind of lunacy. And that's really the point of my getting in touch, Glyn. I mean, it's long since over and done with and Kath's not here to . . . Surely the sensible, reasonable thing is just to bury it, let it be, and all of us get on with life —"

Glyn interrupts to say that, personally, he is doing precisely that.

"And that's where you're so sensible, Glyn. I mean, you're seeing it in proportion, you're being rational about it and frankly I'm so relieved, talking to you, thank God I did phone, and, believe me, I've had to screw myself up to this, but I feel so much better now.

But the real trouble is . . . Elaine's taken it rather differently, and that's what I wanted to talk about, too. She's really gone over the top about it all, completely over-reacted. Actually, Glyn, she's thrown me out."

Glyn has swung from extreme irritation through contempt to boredom. Now, he is interested. Well, well. That's a turn-up for the books.

"I'm staying with Polly. I don't mind telling you, Glyn, I'm in a pretty bad way. It's so . . . well, I just feel it's so extreme. I mean, yes, of course, I can see how she feels, but does it have to be like this? She won't talk to me — nothing Poll says has any effect. What's occurred to me, Glyn, is . . . Elaine always had a lot of time for you, she respects you, I know that — maybe what's needed is someone a bit more detached, like yourself, to sort of have a word, put it to her that she's going too far. I just have this feeling that she'd pay attention to you, Glyn."

"Do you, now?" says Glyn.

"And of course it was through you that she knew about it."

"Oh, I see. It's really all *my* fault," says Glyn.

"Christ, no — that's not what I mean. I can entirely understand why you felt you had to —"

"Good," says Glyn. "Just as well."

". . . of *course* I understand that. And you and Elaine have known each other a long time — though I wish you'd come to me first, if you and I could only have had a talk at that point —"

That does it. "Quite," snaps Glyn. "Elaine and I go way back."

234

"Sorry?"

"We . . . considered one another for a while. But you may be aware of that."

"Actually, no — I wasn't."

"Again, no big issue, put in perspective. You take my point?"

Afterwards, Glyn has no idea why he said this. Exasperation? Mischief? Somehow, the words just fell out.

"Oh," says Nick. "You and Elaine —" And is silent.

"So, I could, I dare say, have a word, as you propose — but on the whole I think it inappropriate. You have to deal with this for yourself, if I may say so."

"Mum? Look — I'm worried about Dad. Nothing new about that, but I'm differently worried. He's gone all quiet. Not that I see him that much — I'm flat out this week, working all hours, someone's off sick and . . . oh, never mind — but when I do it's as though I'm not there. He just looks at me — as though he's miles away. I'm thinking therapists again, frankly."

"It's me. I've got to talk."

When Elaine puts the phone down she can hardly believe that this conversation with Nick has taken place. In which she has had to agree that, yes, she and Glyn were once . . . interested in one another . . . that, yes, she met Glyn on a few occasions. But that, no, they were never lovers. She is experiencing a brew of emotions: fury at Glyn, embarrassment, defensive cool with Nick, who has bypassed the answerphone because she forgot to put it on. But now that their exchange is over, and she is angry and undermined, she realizes that Nick's tone was not what she might have expected. There was neither challenge nor reproach; rather, he seemed bemused, incredulous. He was not out to make capital from this, it would appear. The phone call was to seek confirmation: "I thought he might be making it up."

And whatever had Nick been doing talking to Glyn? She can hardly believe this, either: "I wanted to ask him to speak to you about . . . everything. Put in a word for me."

Only Nick could have come up with such a ruse, or only Nick in some manic state. Provoking Glyn to this backhander. It is as though we are all possessed, she thinks.

Glyn goes back to basics. Research. A hunt is on once more. He trawls directories, he harries the Crafts Council, he picks up false leads and goes down dead ends, but eventually he is able to make a phone call, and arrange a visit.

Elaine finds that she needs urgently to call in on a well-known garden in Gloucestershire which she has not seen for some while; it would be professionally remiss not to check up on their new water garden, and see what the tree peonies are like this year. This trip will take her very close to Winchcombe, where there is someone she would rather like to talk to, right now. She picks up the phone: "Hello. This is a voice from the past. Elaine — Kath's sister. I was wondering if by any chance —"

Oliver goes through old address books. He does this furtively, of an evening, while Sandra is in the kitchen or the bathroom, slamming them quickly back in the drawer when she returns. This is one of the aspects of coupledom that is always a trifle irksome — the fact that any harmless little activity that one does not wish to have to explain must be circumspect. Where basics are concerned, you cannot fart or pick your nose. At another level, anything that may give rise to casual queries that one would prefer to avoid becomes surreptitious. Whyever should he be feeling guilty about a search for the phone number and address of an old acquaintance?

Eventually, he is successful. Here it is, not in any address book but scrawled in the back of a notebook, amid jottings about printers and suppliers and pages of figures and costings. All this dates from the Hammond & Watson days. And next to her address he has written "photos", and circled the word. He must have scribbled this down at the very end of the picnic at the Roman villa; he must have promised to send her photos. And presumably did so, though that he cannot remember, but in making the selection he would have come across the fatal frame. Which he presumably did not include in the batch that he sent to Mary Packard.

Nick cannot get rid of Glyn's voice. It reverberates in his head, a voice not heard for a number of years, but at once entirely familiar — a dark voice with a lilt to it, conjuring up the man himself. "Elaine and I —" The sound of it flings Nick back into that other time, when Glyn was a frequent visitor, with Kath, always talking, holding forth, quenching Nick himself, whose role that had been. Even then, Nick was prepared to admit himself out-talked.

Elaine's voice rings loud, too. What she said. How she said it: frosty, but with an undertow of confusion. Nick himself is in a turmoil now, but it is in some ways an oddly reassuring turmoil, actually, he is feeling better rather than worse, though he cannot quite work out why, and maybe it doesn't matter anyway. Glyn has refused to be drawn in as an intermediary, and Nick wonders now how he can ever have imagined that he would, but instead Glyn has thrown this bombshell. Or is it just a small firework? Nick is trying to get himself sorted out about this. What does he feel about it? Well, he is surprised. Elaine and *Glyn*? Though it would seem that there wasn't all that much to get excited about. But even so . . . Does he feel angry, jealous? Well, not exactly. Though perhaps a little . . . upstaged. And it puts a rather different complexion on things, does it not?

Most of all, Nick finds himself plunged suddenly into endless replays of Glyn's voice. Not only now, but back then. That day. When Kath. He hears him then, sounding the same, but different. The phone rings again, and it is Glyn: "I need to speak to Elaine."

That Day

A Thursday. Glyn left early for the university on account of a nine o'clock seminar. He had woken late, reached for the clock, said, "Bloody hell, look at the time!", and saw Kath lying wide-eyed beside him.

"Why didn't you wake me? I've got to get in early."

Everything about that day stood out in bold relief, later. What was said; what was seen.

He showered, he shaved. He saw his own face in the mirror, foam-flecked, and a reflection of Kath passing behind him — a bare shoulder, her profile. When he went back to the bedroom, she had gone; he dressed. Downstairs, she was in the kitchen, wearing that blue towelling bathrobe, making toast; bare legs below the bathrobe, her hair brushed behind her ears. There was coffee on the table. She said, "Boiled egg?"

"No, I haven't got time." He went into his study, gathered up papers he needed, returned to the kitchen, poured coffee, glanced through a student essay.

"A boiled egg takes four minutes."

"No, no —"

Afterwards, he would home in on this repeated offer; usually, it was take it or leave it — or he fixed something for himself.

In the garden, the sound of an autumn robin. He looked up from the essay: the grass freckled with fallen leaves, the skinny branches of the trees.

She said, "How about we go out for supper tonight? The Italian place?"

"I shan't get back till nine or so — there's something I have to go to. Bit late —"

"OK. I may go to the pictures with Julia." She had friends in the city; people he hardly knew, people she saw on her own.

She was sitting opposite him, reading the front page of the newspaper; the shape of her face, its perfect planes — intensely familiar, but always catching the eye.

She looked up, held out the paper. "Did you want it?"

"No, thanks. I'm off in a minute." He went back to the essay.

She said, "It's nothing but death and disaster." He saw a headline about famine in Africa, the wizened features of a ragged child.

"It was ever thus. This student is telling me — somewhat inadequately — about the demographic effects of the Black Death."

Kath said, "I wish I was one of your students."

He did not know what she meant, nor would he do so subsequently — examining the words. "Why?"

"Oh . . . just, they know someone I don't. Do you get fond of them?"

"Some leave an impression. It's a relentless tide, you know. One lot goes, another comes." He swept the pile of essays into his briefcase, took a final swig of coffee. "Right —"

"Glyn —" She put her hand out as he stood up, as he moved past her towards the door — she touched his arm. He paused: "Yes?" Hurried, distracted.

"Nothing." And there was nothing in her face, nothing that he could see then, or would see later. A smile. "You get going. See you —"

Thus, that morning. The beginning of an autumn day, a working day, unexceptional. Her voice, her presence, as on a thousand other mornings. He went out of the front door, heard the robin again, got into the car. He may have glanced back at the house, in which Kath was sitting in the kitchen, drinking a cup of coffee, reading the paper. Perhaps picking up the phone to say, "Hi! What about a film this evening . . .?"

At the university he gave a seminar on eighteenth-century agrarian reform to third-year students. In his office he went through the mail, wrote some letters and a student reference, took a completed paper to the departmental secretary for typing. He stopped to chat with her for a minute: Joy, a chirpy young woman who served as the hub of local activity, pestered by staff and students alike. At twelve, he lectured.

What did you do that day? While she was home, alone.

At one o'clock he went over to the cafeteria for something to eat, joined a couple of colleagues, got into an argument about student expansion, discussed a proposed new course, had a beer. At one-fifty he returned to the department in haste, to collect a file on his way to the library. Joy beckoned as he passed her open door: "Your wife rang. She tried your direct line, but you weren't there. She asked if you could call her back."

He picked up his file, and was at once waylaid by an importunate student; the student occupied his attention for ten minutes, driving other thoughts from his mind. At two-twenty he was on the steps of the library, and briefly remembered Joy's message. The phone call to Kath would have to wait — he had only an hour and a half in which to finish off some crucial checking of references.

In the event, he got back to the department five minutes late for his four o'clock appointment with a research student, already waiting patiently outside his door. That session overran, which meant that by the time the man left, Glyn's five o'clock seminar group was also camped in the corridor.

At a quarter past six he was through with them. There could be a further quick foray to the library before the inaugural lecture and ensuing reception which he planned to attend. He was going to this not out of intellectual curiosity and support of a colleague, but in order to confirm his view that this appointment, which he had opposed, was a disaster. He was halfway down the stairs when he remembered that he should phone Kath.

He went back to his office, made the call. No reply. He listened to the ringing tone for a minute or so then hung up. Gone out, presumably.

A useful hour in the library. Then the lecture, which was satisfactorily poor. Finally, the reception, at which he stayed for rather longer than he had intended, carried away by a couple of glasses of wine.

At ten past nine he arrived home. The hall light was on — but he knew at once that there was no one here: the inert feeling of an empty house. He went into his study, dumped his briefcase. Then to the kitchen for a glass of water; the breakfast things were still on the draining-board. He looked in the fridge; some cold meats, and the wherewithal for a salad. Kath would no doubt eat out.

He went up to the bedroom to shed his jacket and find a sweater. He switched on the light, and saw that the bed was occupied.

She lay on her side, turned away from him so that he could not see her face. He knew, as he stood there. He knew before he went over and touched her, looked at her. There was no one here; the room was empty of life, just as the house had felt barren as he entered.

When at last he walked over to her — looked, touched — it was as though she were a husk. This was Kath, but also it was not Kath at all; the face hers, but also a mask, a void. She had vomited; her mouth was open, there was a mess on the pillow. He wanted to cover her up; no, there were things that had to happen now. He saw the glass on the bedside table, the little capless brown bottle, some empty packets. He seemed to be acting like an automaton; he could move about, respond, but at some other level there was rampaging disbelief. This was not possible. Impossible that he was

243

here, in these moments, with this around him; the proper place to be was hours ago, back this morning, dressing in this room while downstairs Kath made toast and coffee, picked the newspaper up off the mat. That was real, this was not.

The ambulance came, and went. Later the police arrived, two of them, a man and a woman. They went up to the bedroom, incongruous invaders, and came back down with the things from the bedside table. They sat with Glyn in the kitchen and asked a few questions — dispassionate, perhaps apologetic.

What did you do that day? While she . . .

The woman asked if there was anyone he would like them to call. He shook his head.

When they had gone, he sat there; the automaton struggled with the rampaging disbeliever. He made a cup of tea, but never drank it.

Then he reached for the address book and looked for Elaine's number.

That morning, Elaine was planting the two *Sorbus cashmiriana* which had arrived the day before. Perfect circumstances; crisp dry late autumn weather, the ground still nicely workable. She and Jim moved the young trees from position to position until they had it right, dug the holes between them, carted compost. It was an hour or so before the job was done, the stakes in, the two stems of future promise standing bravely alongside the grass walk to the orchard. Returning to the house, she turned to look back at them, visualizing how they would be ten years on — tall, sturdy, with those jewelled snowy clouds of autumn berries. To garden is to harness time.

Eleven o'clock by now, and the day snapping at her heels. Sonia needed guidance, Nick wanted to talk about buying a computer, which would give him a head start with this exciting new scheme he had to tell her about, there was a tricky phone call to be made to a new and exacting client. Elaine set Sonia straight, deflected Nick, was relieved to find the client unavailable, and turned at last to her largest current project — landscaping the grounds of a refurbished country house hotel. She spent a couple of hours on design and costings.

A sandwich lunch in the kitchen with Sonia and Nick ("The thing about the technology, sweetie, is that in a couple of years it's paid for itself, in terms of cost efficiency"). By now Elaine was watching the clock; she planned to catch a train to London. In the early evening there was the reception and press launch of the new wing of an art gallery, for which she had designed a courtyard garden, and before that she intended to visit the Royal Horticultural Society's Lindley Library, in pursuit of information about an extinguished Edwardian garden of which she had once seen photos, which might prove inspirational for her current project.

Nick drove her to the station. He had given up on the matter of the computer; both he and Elaine knew that he would return to the subject and that Elaine would probably have to concede, and provide the money, given that he was indisputably in tune with contemporary thinking on this matter. Well, the thing could be set against tax. At the station, he dithered for a moment with the thought of coming with her, tempted by the notion of the champagne extravaganza at the art gallery, and then decided he couldn't be bothered. He would pick her up when she got back.

At the library, Elaine was instantly immersed in her search, absorbed with catalogues and a growing pile of books. An hour later, breaking off to take stock, she realized that she had forgotten to ask Sonia to get together and despatch some papers needed urgently by the accountants. Not too late to get her before she left at the end of the afternoon.

Elaine found a public phone, got through to Sonia, sorted things out. Sonia reported on a call from a client: "Oh, your sister rang, too."

Back with the books, Elaine filed this away; she could ring Kath when she got home. Or tomorrow. The afternoon was nearly gone; the gallery festschrift loomed.

The press photographers were gratifyingly attentive to the courtyard garden. And indeed it did her credit, a vibrant floodlit oasis at the heart of the austere quadrangle of the gallery. She received compliments from an assortment of strangers. There were several indications of possible future commissions. She took a close look at the garden, which she had checked out only a few days before anyway, decided that a *Corydalis* was wrongly sited and made a note to get it moved. After forty minutes she left to catch the train.

Nick was not at the station. She waited, irritated, until the car came sweeping in ten minutes later: "Sorry, sorry, I forgot the time —"

During the course of this day Elaine thought about Kath three times — but thought is not the right word for that involuntary process whereby a person surfaces in the mind of another. Rather, she experienced Kath. As she planted the trees, the worm tumbling from a spadeful of earth brought a sudden glimmer of Kath as a small child, crouched intent over a flowerbed, crying, "Look, look! A *thing* —" Not thought so much as consciousness. Later, in London, a woman glimpsed through the window of a bus had Kath's stance, her shape, and briefly Kath flowed in again — a concept, not deliberate thought — and was chased away almost at once by consideration of how to find an account of this half-remembered garden in the library.

After the phone call to Sonia she did indeed home in upon Kath. Kath occupied her full attention for . . . a minute, perhaps longer. It was several weeks since Kath had last rung. There had been talk of a visit, which did not happen: "Maybe I'll come over next Sunday. Depends what Glyn's up to. I'll let you know." But there had been no subsequent call, and Elaine had been mildly irritated: typical Kath. She intended to phone, but the days had piled up, and the call was never made. But she would make it now — this evening, once she got home.

It was a quarter to nine when they reached the house. Elaine put the oven on to heat the remains of a casserole. Then she went to the telephone.

There was no reply from Kath's number. No answerphone, either, but Kath seldom remembered to put it on. Glyn also out, presumably.

The casserole was eaten. Elaine read the paper, joined Nick to watch the news. She had a bath. She was drying herself when she heard the ringing phone: it stopped — Nick must have picked it up downstairs. She came into the bedroom and heard him call: "It's Glyn — for you." She went over to the bedside phone.

Glyn said, without announcing himself, without preliminary: "I've got to tell you something terrible." And at once she knew. Not how, or why — but what. Kath.

For much of that day Nick was thinking about computers. If he had one of those things — a really good one with masses of giga-whatsits and the latest whatever it was, software — then undoubtedly he would be able to do just so much more. Indeed, the equipment would be inspirational in itself — it would be a stimulus, it would give him ideas. You couldn't work without this technology, nowadays. Especially not in his field. With it, he would be able to . . . well, he'd soon see what could be done once he was up and running.

Elaine was going to take a bit of persuading, that was clear. But Nick felt reasonably confident. If he went about it the right way — calm, businesslike, knowledgeable — she would eventually capitulate. Yes, these things were quite pricey, but it wasn't going to break the bank — not the way Elaine was pulling it in these days, and all credit to her.

Fired by these considerations, he drove into town after he had dropped Elaine at the station, to do some reconnaissance on the different makes. He spent an hour in a big office supplies place, where the twitching screens were a bit intimidating, and he could not understand a word of the sales talk. Never mind, he'd get his head round it all soon enough.

Back at the house, he made himself a cup of tea and took one to Sonia. It was nearly four now, so there was no point in getting down to anything today. He settled himself in the conservatory with the tea and a book. At one point he went back to the kitchen to forage for a snack, feeling peckish. Sonia was on the phone as he passed her door; she held the receiver aside to say, "Kath, for Elaine. Do you want to —?"

He shook his head. Not that there was any *problem* with Kath since ... since that time. Absolutely not. Everything was always quite normal and natural. Just they both sort of avoided any one-to-one situation.

He got hooked on a TV programme, and was a tad late meeting Elaine's train.

Judiciously, he made no further mention of the computer. Elaine was in a good mood, quietly chuffed from the praise apparently lavished on her art gallery garden. They ate a companionable meal, watched the box for a bit; she went up to have a bath.

Glyn's voice on the phone was terse: "I need to speak to Elaine." Nick called up to her from the bottom of the stairs. He returned to the sitting room, decided he'd had enough of this programme, switched off the television. He wandered around for a few minutes putting out lights, and then went up. When he came into the bedroom Elaine was standing with the receiver still in her hand, and an expression on her face that he had never seen before, a look that gave him a jolt of wild unease.

By the time Polly heard about Kath, that day was yesterday. She was visited by a sense of guilt, of culpability — all these hours in which she had gone about her business unknowing, carefree, while elsewhere Kath . . . Polly could not bear to think of that.

Polly was a working woman. She was twenty-two years old, she had a degree, an overdraft, three credit cards and a studio flat in Stoke Newington. Her feet were planted firmly on the bottom rung of the Prudential Insurance Company, which might not turn out to be the best place to have put them, but it would do for now, while she sniffed the air, took stock.

And so, that day, she had breezed through her work, which was not exacting — not exacting enough, indeed; she had socialized usefully with colleagues, she had conducted an interesting flirtation over the photocopier with a guy from the sales department. In her lunch hour she had bought a pair of expensive shoes without which she could not live for a moment longer. After work she had met up with an old friend from college and had luxuriated in an extended gossip over a pizza.

She had been occupied, intermittently interested, she had been stimulated, entertained, uplifted by the flirtation and the shoes; at one point she had walked amid the city lights, the bustle, the energy, and had experienced a surge of well-being. If asked, she would probably have said that she had been happy that day. She had once or twice been irritated, she had remembered the overdraft with compunction when buying the shoes, she had had a flicker of envy for the friend, who was in the throes of an ecstatic love affair. None of these add up to unhappiness.

When Polly looked into that day — Kath's day — she knew that she was staring at something far beyond her experience, beyond even her conception of experience. Kath, that day, had visited some terrible place that Polly found unimaginable. Kath — so intimately known, so familiar, so . . . well, in a way so ordinary, except of course that ordinary she was not.

Polly realized that she had never known someone die. Someone close, someone in your life. And she was incredulous — not so much grief-stricken as in a state of incredulity. No, no . . . this could not be. Impossible. Not Kath. There must be some absurd mistake.

When eventually she knew that there was not, all she could think was — but where has she gone? Where *is* she? Where, where? She imagined some great dark void, and Kath out there in it, helplessly drifting, unreachable.

When Oliver read Elaine's letter his first reaction was one of shocked recognition: yes, it never occurred to me, but, yes, this was always on the cards. He found himself searching for times with Kath, and each sequence that arrived was subtly changed by what had happened; that day last week had kicked away old assumptions — what had seemed unexceptional was now quite other. "Are you happy, Oliver?" asks Kath.

He mourned Kath. He read the letter, which told him little, the bare facts — when, where, how. But not, of course, why. He read, and then he put the letter down and was filled with sadness. He had not seen or spoken to Kath for years, but he realized that there had always been a sort of quiet satisfaction in knowing that she was out there, somewhere. And now she was not.

He did not wonder why; he did not want to know why. He saw — dimly, inexplicably — that in some disturbing way what had happened was heralded, that there had always been something troubled about Kath, something that set her apart. Behind and beyond her looks, her manner, there had been some dark malaise. But nobody ever saw it, back then, he thought. All you saw was her face.

Mary Packard

Mary Packard watches each of her visitors as they arrive: the car pulling up in the lane outside her gate, the driver getting out, looking around, checking that this seems to be the right place. Coming up the front garden path between the lavender bushes towards the cottage door, while Mary observes from the window of her studio to one side. She will emerge when the visitor puts a hand on the knocker: "Hi," she will say. "I'm in here."

To Glyn Peters, to Elaine, to Oliver — whose other name she always used to forget, and still does. Not all at once, of course; separately, spread out over the course of several weeks, this curious little epidemic of arrivals, each preceded by a phone call — brief and purposeful (Glyn), diffident but determined (Elaine), equivocal (Oliver). After the first, she had no longer been surprised by the others.

Mary's studio is a converted dairy, detached from the cottage; cool in summer, cold in winter, whitewashed walls, tiled floor, large strategic window that floods the room with light. There is a sink, and a great cluttered table, and the clay and the wheel and shelves of finished pots. Mary's work is displayed in galleries and craft centres; it is expensive. It seems astonishing that those poised shapes can have arisen from the dumpy glistening mound of clay. Kath used to say: "Can I just sit and watch?" She would be over there, on the old cane chair — a silent, companionable presence.

Mary is short, compact, sturdy. She seems to have more in common with the clay than with the elegant reincarnations that she conjures from it. Today, years on from the time when Kath was often here, her cropped dark wiry hair is badger grey. She is alone; various men have come and gone, which is fine by her. The man of the day at the Roman villa is so effectively gone that she has to hunt around for an image of him, when Elaine makes some reference: "Oh, he's someone I'm not in touch with any more," she says.

This is a woman who is self-sufficient. Which does not imply egotism, or complacency, or indifference to others; just, she is one of those rare and perhaps blessed souls who are able to make their way through life without the need to be shored up by companionship, or dependants, or love.

Mary has both received and given love; but when love is not around she is able to do without. She is childless, and takes pleasure in children; she acknowledges that perhaps she has missed out on something significant there, but sees no point in dwelling on the matter. She is astute, she is generous, she is warm; she is also gifted with the power of detachment.

People have always eddied around Mary, recognizing some strength that they cannot identify. Or that most cannot identify. Some have had a shot: "You've got ice in your heart," said one man. He was wrong; not ice within, but armoury without. Mary has a sound shell into which to retreat; those less well-equipped are inclined to hover near her, like scuttling crustacean claws in search of a safe haven. Mary accumulates lame ducks, hangers-on, some of whom have been men who had to be gently dislodged when the level of dependency became ominous. Sometimes there have been studio apprentices, girls whose need was not so much to learn how to throw a pot as how to live. Which is something that cannot be taught, as Mary has come to realize. Nowadays there is no one enjoying official waif or stray status, just various people who turn up on a regular basis — friends for whom Mary has been the reassuring backstop, and an assortment of needy neighbours and local connections.

Mary dispenses brisk sympathy, wry advice which is not always heard as such, coffee, cheap wine and her spare bed. She listens well — the kind of uncommitted listening that induces a sense of catharsis. Those who have leaned on Mary for a while are left feeling cleansed, relieved; their problems look a bit more manageable, as though set in perspective. In fact, Mary has indicated little and said less. Sometimes, her own thoughts would surprise and dismay those who bend her ear. She cannot help feeling a certain impatience with the way in which people allow themselves to be dragged through the fires of hell by others. At the same time, she recognizes that her own immunity is unusual. Since this state is not one that she can transmit to anyone else, all she can do is hear their tales of woe, and reserve judgement. This restraint is quite hard for her at times, when she hears another saga of betrayal from some apprentice who brought the whole thing upon herself, in Mary's view — couldn't she see that the guy was stringing her along? Or when a neighbour's tale of financial woe reveals a sub-text of feckless outlay. Mary herself lives frugally, and always has. Those who conspicuously consume must accept that they may be consumed, she thinks — but says nothing. People who pour out their woes to others require commiseration, not admonition.

Mary met Kath at a craft fair long ago. Kath was manning a friend's stall; Mary looked across and saw this exquisite woman behind a display of fired enamel dishes and a rank of mesmerized customers. The run on enamel was phenomenal. Mary came over to chat; they took a lunch break together. Mary said, "Would you care to sell pots next time?" They beamed at each other, each recognizing an unexpected confederate. "I am your exact opposite," Mary would remark, idly, at some other time, much later. "Yes," says Kath. "That's the whole point. But really I want to be you. Swap?" Spoken as a joke, but in fact not a joke at all.

They were a conspiracy, a tacit alliance. Weeks and months might go by without contact, and then they would resume the association as though they had parted yesterday. Phone calls were elliptical, each knowing how the other would react. "Why aren't you a man?" said Kath. "Or why can't we be gay? Then that would be me all sorted out." If any of her men met Mary they shied away, sensing some sort of competition that they could not match. Kath never asked what Mary thought of this man, or of that; she would just say, eventually, "He was no go, of course." And they would talk of something else. She was blithely agreeable to Mary's occasional lovers; when they were gone she would say, "Poor him. But he wouldn't do. And you don't even need him, do you?"

Over the years, they were close, yet also far apart — separate lives linked only by the crucial semaphore of friendship. Kath observed the lame ducks, the hangers-on, alert to their status; but when such people were around Mary she was at her warmest, her most friendly. Once, when they were alone after a succession of such importunates, she said, "Am I like that? Come on, you can be honest." And Mary had said, "You never could be. Whatever happens to you, that's impossible."

She knew what happened, from time to time. Not always. On occasion, she knew from Kath's shuttered look; she saw that beneath the surface gaiety something darkly thrashed. She knew also not to ask. She saw Kath as in perpetual flight from enquiry, from scrutiny; whatever it was that went on there could only be glimpsed. But once in a while she would learn in full: "Sorry about this," Kath would say. "But I need to dump on someone, and it seems to be you. Actually, there is only you."

Glyn Peters and Mary Packard circled one another like suspicious dogs. On the first occasion that they met, Mary felt her own rictus of welcome to be more like bared fangs. Why him? she was thinking. Why this one? Why now? She had noted Kath's state of tension. She saw Glyn as some kind of opportunist marauder, a sexual freebooter. When Kath told her — when she announced, "Actually, I'm going to marry him" — Mary had said, "You're not pregnant, are you?"

Kath went suddenly still. She looked away. "Oh, no," she said. "Oh, *dear* me no." There was a silence. Then Kath spoke again — a small quiet voice. "I think he loves me." Mary could find nothing to say.

And so, on this day so much later, when Mary watches Glyn get out of his car, look around, open the gate and walk up her garden path, she sees a man who carries baggage — the baggage of all those years. He is freighted with her own initial mistrust — mistrust which gave way eventually to tolerance. She sees a man she once disliked, and then got used to, because there was no alternative and he was by then an unavoidable feature of her friend's life. She sees a man she sparred with, on occasion, a man she thought too ready with an opinion, a man inclined to talk everyone else into the ground. She is startled to see that this man is now an older man, and then remembers her own grizzled head. All the same, he is palpably the same man, and all around him there float other times, and other people. He brings Kath; he brings Kath's voice saying, Glyn this, Glyn that, Glyn's away for a few days so I'm going to play hookey and come to see you, right? He brings that house of theirs in Melchester which Mary seldom visited and always found in some way a house without a heart, a house in which two people came and went but in which they somehow did not live. He brings Elaine and Nick and their place — gatherings in that crowded kitchen, Kath with Polly dancing

attendance, Elaine dishing up food to a dozen people,
Nick on a roll about some project, Oliver whatsit
hanging about at the edge. He brings . . .

Glyn arrives at the cottage door. He lifts a hand and
knocks. Mary opens the studio window. "I'm in here,"
she says.

When Glyn opens the garden gate, he is pitched into
uncertainty. He no longer knows quite why he has
come to see Mary Packard. What on earth got into him?
Why did he make that impulsive phone call, so essential
at the time?

He rallies. He takes in his surroundings; he sees a
limestone cottage with mullioned windows, seventeenth-
century with brick chimney and slate roof of a later
date. He heads up the garden path and knocks at the
door. And a voice comes at him sideways. He looks
round, and sees her. Oh, it is her all right, though he is
surprised to see that she too has . . . well, moved on.

"Ah," he says. "Mary."

Afterwards he will try to piece together what was said
and will find that what he has is an accumulation of
language and of feeling; her words, his mute responses.
His own words are not much in evidence; he is
conscious of having spoken at the outset and then
fallen silent. At one point she too stops speaking and
the silence hangs in the room — Mary's deeply
inhabited room which is kitchen, sitting room, office, in
which an old railway station clock softly ticks and the
dresser is crammed with sea shells, lumps of rock,

grasses and a sheep's skull. "I seem to have rather shut you up," she says. "Sorry about that." And he remembers spreading his hands in a gesture of . . . what? Defeat? Concession? Repudiation?

That would have been way on into the afternoon. After the initial niceties, the move into the cottage, the making of coffee. After his opening moves, Mary sitting there, saying nothing, that look in her eye. After he had made his pitch; after he had been careful, candid, persuasive.

Some while after that. After Mary had begun to talk, had been talking for what seemed a long time. Talking about Kath. You want to know about Kath? she had said. Right, then, I'll tell you about Kath.

Actually, I'm not fooled, Glyn, she said. Stuff this memoir. There isn't any memoir, is there? I don't know what it is that's bugging you — but, whatever it is, you've become obsessed with Kath, haven't you? Obsessed in a way that you never were when she was alive, I suspect — at least not after you'd married her.

This is when the words begin to pile up, when he simply listens, despite himself, when he is conscious of kaleidoscopic emotions. A tide of resentment ebbs, and is replaced by something else that will surface fully much later on — tomorrow and tomorrow. Mary talks about a Kath whom Glyn seems not to have known. This is when she talks about the miscarriage. You never knew about that, did you? she says. Kath told me you didn't. She wouldn't have you know. You were away somewhere when it happened — in the States, I think she said. She was going to tell you about the pregnancy when you got back. It was a while ago — two or three years after you were married. She was working for some Arts Festival at the time.

You hadn't realized she wanted a child. How much she did. Neither did I, until then. Afterwards, she said — maybe just as well, Glyn wouldn't have taken all that kindly to the idea. But it wasn't just as well, it was just about as bad as anything could have been.

It was the second. The second miscarriage. The second non-baby. The first one wasn't yours. Way back, that was. When she was in her twenties. She told me about it once in an offhand way — that way that always set alarm bells ringing. I asked her if she'd have stayed with the father, if things had turned out otherwise, if she hadn't lost the baby — and she said, oh yes, for that I would have. You bet. Anything, for that.

You want to know about Kath's friends? Mary says. Well, that's me, mainly. But you always knew about me. You want to know about Kath's men friends, don't you? Is that what's bugging you? If so, you're on a hiding to nothing, Glyn. There was no string of lovers. There's nothing under the carpet.

So he tells her what is bugging him. At least he has a card to play.

Yes, I knew, she says. Afterwards, I knew. When she was busy hating herself. Hating herself even more than usual.

She told me. She said, I've been doing something so stupid. So bloody pointless. Nick. She said. *Nick*, of all people. I remember her sitting there, looking utterly bleak.

And no, I don't know why. The sort of thing that brings the analysts out of the woodwork, isn't it? What I can tell you is that it didn't go on for long, and when it was over it was over. Nick, of course, is . . . well, you know Nick as well as I do. Better, indeed. Nick blows with the wind, doesn't he? A seize the day man, Nick. And there was a streak of that in Kath — more than a streak. But with her it was because it was the only way she could keep the demons at bay — whatever they were, whatever it was that boiled away there, every so often. She had to keep on the move — get out, go somewhere, do something.

So that's what's bugging you. I remember the picnic at the Roman villa. She was staying here for a day or two and either Elaine or Nick rang up and suggested we all meet up. You were off somewhere, presumably. The photo call I do not remember.

Mary's voice conjures up the photograph, which Glyn does not want to see, ever again. He side-steps, he backtracks.

Hating herself . . .?

You didn't know about that? Well, she was good at smoke-screens. Maybe there was a touch of acting talent after all — perhaps she shouldn't have quit drama school so precipitously. Most people would never have known. But you . . .

You were married to her; you lived with her for ten years. This is unspoken, but rings out between them.

Again, don't ask me why, says Mary. I don't go in for amateur shrink stuff. But that was how she was. Not always. Sometimes she could coast along fine. Then . . .

wham! Oddly, she was often at her most beautiful when she was like that. Kind of glowing. Oh, you'd never have known. I only did because she told me. Once, just once. And after that I watched her.

I'll tell you why she married you, Glyn. Out of all the men who went after her. She thought you loved her. Mary looks intently now at Glyn, and he finds that he cannot meet her eye.

And at some point then Glyn has had enough. He can't manage any more of this, he wants out, he wants to get in the car and head away from Mary Packard, from what she has said. Except that nothing can now be unsaid, her voice will be there always. He must walk down her garden path with her words in his head, and take them home with him.

Elaine knows what she wants of Mary Packard, but she does not know how she will go about getting it. What she wants is precise in her mind, but is also impossible to specify. She wants to hear someone talk about Kath — someone who is not Polly, or Glyn, or Oliver Watson, or Nick — least of all Nick. Who is not maddening cousin Linda. Someone who, like herself, speaks with authority. But something has happened to her confidence in that authority, over the last weeks; there have been subversive voices, there have been suggestions of lacunae, glimpses of things she does not understand.

She wants that confidence restored. She wants to hear that the voices are misleading, that she has not heard what she thinks she may have heard, that everything is as it always was.

She just wants to talk for a while about Kath to someone who knew her well. That is all she wants. Isn't it?

And so she steps briskly from the car, opens the gate, walks up the path between the two little hedges of *Lavandula augustifolia* "Munstead" and raises her hand to knock on the door of Mary Packard's cottage, which is thickly clad with *Clematis tangutica* and *Rosa* "New Dawn".

"I'm afraid I'm a bit of a bolt from the blue," says Elaine. "It's been quite a while —"

"Not at all," says Mary Packard. "I thought you'd come."

Which is not what she should be saying, and Elaine is disconcerted.

That was at the beginning.

At the end, when Elaine walks away between the lavender hedges, she has this odd feeling that much time has passed, instead of an hour or two, during which she has become someone else. In one sense she is herself, but in another she has been entirely altered. The past has been reconstructed, and, with that, her own old certainties. She sees differently; she feels differently.

The non-babies are now loud and clear, who did not exist a couple of hours ago. Kath's non-children. Because of them — because of these beings who never were — there is a new flavour to much that was said, much that was done. When Kath speaks now, Elaine hears a new note in her voice. Kath says the same things, but she says them in a new way.

Why didn't you *tell* me? says Elaine.

She sees Kath with Polly, dancing with her — small Polly, grown-up Kath — she sees her plaiting Polly's hair, she sees her coming into the kitchen with Polly and a brimming basket of windfall apples.

I always thought you didn't particularly *want* children, says Elaine. She speaks to the wheel of her car, to the driving mirror, to the tail-gate of the lorry ahead of her, to Kath.

The non-children eclipse much else. She hears the non-children louder than anything that has been said. It is the non-children above all who have skewed things. They keep coming back — faceless, formless, significant.

Mary Packard knew, and Elaine did not. Friend; sister. Mary is perhaps embarrassed by this: I hadn't entirely realized . . . she says. I knew that Glyn . . . but I thought that probably you . . . I see. Well, Kath would have had her reasons, I suppose, says Mary.

Quite, thinks Elaine. And the principal reason was probably me. How I am. How I was with her.

There is more, though. There is a subversive flow that occupies her as she drives mindlessly in the direction of home. The thing is, says Mary Packard, Kath always wanted to be someone else. She wanted to be you. She wanted to be me. She was stuck with the dictation of what she looked like, which pretty well determined her life, one realizes. If she hadn't looked like that, quite different things might have happened. Different men. Different directions. She might have set to and learned a trade, like you and me. She once said — sitting out there, in my studio — she once said, there isn't a single thing that I can do well, I've fiddled away at this and that ever since I can remember.

She wanted to be loved. Most people do, I suppose. But her more than most.

Your mother dying when she did. That accounts for much, says Mary. Didn't you know? There is an edge to her voice; Elaine is uncomfortable.

The business with Nick . . . says Mary.

And Elaine, who would not have spoken of that, goes rigid. Oh, so Glyn has been here. I see, no wonder I was expected.

That sodding photograph, says Mary. Yes, I remember that day. Who? Oh, him. Someone I'm not in touch with any more.

Forget it, says Mary. That business. Nick. A crazy aberration. God knows why. Do we need to ask?

Halfway home, stationary at a crossroads behind a line of traffic, Elaine discovers that she does not need to ask. This news comes as a relief, a release from something oppressive, and adds to her sense of a change in perception. When the line of cars advances, and she gathers speed once more, it is as though she were moving into some new age, a time when things would be apparently the same but also rather different.

266

★ ★ ★

What the hell am I doing?

Oliver sits in his car, outside Mary Packard's gate, and for two pins he would start the engine up again and be off. What is he doing here? This is daft. Embarrassing. Entirely unnecessary. Except that for a few hours, several days ago, it seemed an imperative.

He gets out, locks up, opens the garden gate.

He had forgotten quite what Mary Packard looked like, but she is immediately familiar. Of course — that shock of hair, that cool, calm manner. And as soon as he is sitting in her kitchen, with a mug of tea in his hand, it seems quite reasonable and straightforward to be there.

The thing is, he says, I can't get all this out of my head. Ever since . . . Well you see, there's this bloody photograph that turned up.

I know about the photograph, says Mary Packard. And she tells him why she knows, but Oliver has an eerie feeling that this woman might know everything anyway, by some osmotic process, like the wise woman of folk tales.

It's all my fault, says Oliver. I mean, it isn't, of course — but actually it is because I took the photo and then like an idiot I gave it to Nick instead of just throwing it away and saying nothing. If it weren't for me there wouldn't be all this fuss. I've had Glyn on my back, then Nick. Elaine threw a complete wobbly, it seems, and gave Nick the push.

Yes, says Mary. People do seem to have been on the move.

Is it my fault? says Oliver.

Of course not, she tells him. And you know perfectly well it isn't. You didn't come here to ask me that, did you?

Oliver agrees that he did not. They have become oddly companionable, he and Mary Packard, as though they were old friends, though Oliver cannot recall that back then they ever exchanged more than stock civilities. There is now some shared unstated vision.

It was a crying shame, says Oliver. He is no longer talking about the photograph, or Glyn, or Nick. Her, of all people, he says. The blessed of the gods, you'd have thought. But she wasn't, was she? One of the damned, more like.

I keep thinking about her. I mean, one always did, but not quite so — compulsively. Was there anything to be done?

Probably not, says Mary.

The afternoon has turned to evening. The mugs of tea have been replaced by glasses of red wine. Oliver and Mary Packard talk about other times. About Kath, especially. They remember this and that; they bring Kath back to life, passing her to and fro between them — looking at her, listening to her. They are clear-eyed; they do not remember with sentimentality. Oliver hears of things he did not know, and the Kath of whom he talks is subtly changed even as he does so; what he saw and heard is infused with a different understanding. But he is somehow soothed. It is as though in this consideration of Kath they are also performing a kind of ritual, they are paying tribute. He has no idea if this is what he came here for, but he is glad that he did. The visit has served a purpose, if not perhaps the one that he sought — if indeed he knew what that was.

She had an effect, he says.

She still is having an effect, says Mary.

Conclusions

"Can you remember what date Mum and I got married?"

"Actually, I wasn't there," says Polly.

"It was July, I'm pretty sure. And it's July now. But what *date*?"

"You don't *know*?" cries Polly. "All this time, and you don't know?"

Nick replies that he does know. Well, he sort of knows. He knows sort of whenabouts it is — just, the exact day he sometimes forgets.

"Well, then, let me tell you. It's the nineteenth. This Friday. And, frankly, Dad, I'm astonished you don't know. I think you should ask yourself how on earth it can be that you don't know. And listen, Dad, I'm going to be away this weekend. I'm going to the country with . . . with a friend. *Please* remember to take your keys with you when you go out."

Nick goes shopping. He stares bemused into windows, glowing caverns in which watches have been tossed carelessly amid folds of satin, in which headless velvet necks display swags of gilt or shining stones, and miniature crystal trees are festooned with gold chains. Since he cannot imagine going into one of these places and entering into some negotiation, he passes on, and

270

eventually ends up in a department store, where he cruises helplessly up and down escalators. He hasn't been to such an emporium since his mother used to take him on forays to acquire school uniform. He could do with his mother right now; she would have known how to deal with this.

Nick wanders from Electrical Appliances to China and Glass, through Haberdashery and Lingerie, into Furnishing Fabrics, up to Sports and Garden Furniture, down by way of Babywear and Gifts. He is a boat against the current, bumping up against hordes of purposeful people; everybody here knows what they are doing except for him. He is immeasurably dispirited; it seems possible that he will go mad here, pitched finally into the purgatory that has loomed since Elaine told him to go. The store has become a mocking metaphor for a world in which others head confidently for their chosen slots. They know that their destiny is with Lighting or with Hosiery, while he can only drift feckless among them, unable to identify either need or direction. It is all uncomfortably near the knuckle, a parody of some true experience, except that in its way this is indeed real — he is here, by choice, and does not know where to go or what to do.

There are signals from ordinary life. In Kitchenware he passes a kettle like the one at home. He finds himself staring at a chair identical to one in Polly's flat. He brushes past a girl wearing big hoop earrings like Kath used to wear, but immediately slams Kath out of his mind — there is not time nor space for her, she must be put aside, for now and perhaps for ever.

Occasionally he comes up against himself, a mirrored glimpse of this distracted man — too bald, too old — and is further disoriented. This cannot be him, but apparently it is.

He comes to a halt at last by a desk. A woman sits at the desk; a calm, benign woman who smiles at him — the first human contact he has experienced in this place. The woman has a sign above her head: she is Customer Services.

There is a chair in front of the desk. Nick sits down. The woman continues to smile invitingly. Later, it seems to him that he bared his soul to her.

"It's the nineteenth," says Sonia. "And we still don't have an estimate for the hard landscaping on the Surrey place. Two weeks overdue."

Elaine registers this — the date rather than the errant estimate. So? she tells herself. So it's the wedding anniversary? Well, it would be, wouldn't it? They come round, like bulb planting or pruning time. So?

Later, when she has snatched an hour to work in the garden, the date lurks, prompting various reflections: that Nick seldom remembered it, and, if he did, invariably got the day wrong and proposed a celebratory dinner a week too early; that this always riled her; that the wedding occasion itself is now something of a blur. How can such a seminal event have dissolved into a few hazy impressions? Aunt Clare's hat, the rock-hard cake icing that resisted the knife, Kath in a floaty green dress.

Elaine plants out some pulmonarias and tries to concentrate on current projects. She has plenty of work in hand, but since her visit to Mary Packard she has felt disoriented, unable to fix her attention where it is required. It is not so much that she has been dwelling on what she learned from Mary Packard; rather, it is a question of coming to terms with a revised vision, with a new set of responses.

The day proceeds. Elaine spends time on a garden design, and even more time on the phone. Sonia comes in and out with queries, as do Pam and Jim. Elaine achieves a further spell in the garden and, eventually, after five, everyone has gone and she is alone.

Nick's arrival is nicely judged. Elaine has had a bath and is through in the conservatory when she hears a car in the drive. She goes to the front door, and there he is, with a package in his hand.

Elaine is so taken aback by the sight of him that she just stands there. Possibly she says, "Oh —" Polly is right — he is thinner. Otherwise he is simply Nick, and moreover, Nick wearing the furtive expression that normally heralds a long process of exculpation.

He proffers the package.

"It's a scarf," he explains. "It's got flowers on it. Actually, a nice woman in the shop helped me, I must admit. You know I'm not good at shops. I told her all about you, and she thought this one with the flowers. It's Italian, apparently. Silk."

Elaine continues to stand there, now holding the package. An entirely fresh image from that day thirty-three years ago has swum into her head: she sees

273

Nick's hand above hers as he puts on the ring. She remembers her startled recognition that she was now part of a unit of two, whatever that was going to mean.

Nick is on the doorstep, expectant.

"Well," she says. "You'd better come in." She knows as she speaks that he will not be leaving again, and that this will be all right, or as all right as it ever was.

"You know how everything was completely fouled up for me?" says Polly. "Well, now it isn't. Honestly, *life* . . . First of all, I think it may be serious — with Andy. We went away for the weekend and — let's just say it was pretty good. What? Yes, of course there was amazing sex, but that's not the whole picture, is it? The thing is, he's just such an understanding person. You can relate to him. He's not — well, he's not like the men I usually end up with. Oh God, just talking about him's making me feel all peculiar. Do you know — this may be it.

"And there's more. My dad's gone back to my mum. Or rather my mum's let my dad come home. I got in late on Friday night and there's this message saying, actually he's at home now and he'll come and pick his things up next week. Just like that. Sorted, apparently."

In youth, Oliver was good at Latin. Occasionally, a shred of Virgil or of Caesar can still float into his head. These days, he is haunted by *lacrimae rerum* — those plangent words. He remembers that the Latin master considered the phrase untranslatable. He would chalk it up on the board, with some suggested renderings: the pity of things, the tears of the world. "Not right, are

274

they?" he would say. "A beautiful expression, the ultimate in poetry — and it has to be left as it is."

Lacrimae rerum. Oh yes, indeed, thinks Oliver. Admittedly, run-of-the-mill distress such as he has in mind is hardly on a par with the fall of Troy, but nevertheless the language seems apt, and a curious kind of solace. He allows the words to float, and one afternoon he lets them fill his monitor also, in many different colours and fonts — red, purple, yellow, green, bold, italic, Symbol, Tahoma, Times New Roman, you name it. He shuffles them up and moves them around.

Sandra, crossing the room at one point and glancing over his shoulder, says, "What on earth are you up to?"

"Doodling," says Oliver. He clears the screen. "Right. Now am I doing the Rotary Club job or are you?"

Glyn works. Of course — that is what Glyn does, what he has always done. Term is over, so there is no longer the dictation of students and colleagues; he spends long hours in the library and in his study, preparation for a far-reaching new project on transport systems. He thinks prehistoric trackways and salt and cattle and coal; he thinks road, water and rail; his mind's eye is concentrated upon the map of Britain, a network of communication, layer upon layer, piled up, intersecting, making nonsense of chronology. He does not think about himself, he does not think about Kath; or he believes that he does not.

That photograph is back in the landing cupboard. Glyn does not wish or intend to look at it again. He might as well destroy it, but the destruction of archival material offends his deepest instinct. Let it lie there.

Glyn works, amid this tide of paper — books, periodicals, offprints, maps. He reads and writes, he marshals information, he interprets and reinterprets. Even when he takes a break he is pondering the route of a canal, the advance of a railway; as he makes a cup of coffee, river systems are imposed upon the kitchen counter; as he walks to the shop to buy a newspaper he is considering connections and survivals.

But every now and then this detachment fails him. He is flung inexorably into contemplation of other things. That day, above all. The day he returned in the evening to this empty house. He moves through the day again and again, and at the end he sees what he saw then. The sight is the same as ever it was, except that it is informed by new wisdoms, and he looks differently.

Glyn knows now that he has to find a new way of living with Kath, or rather a way of living with a new Kath. And of living without her, in a fresh sharp deprivation.

Martin Sixsmith was born in Cheshire and educated at Oxford, Harvard and the Sorbonne. From 1980 to 1997 he worked for the BBC as a foreign correspondent, and from 1997 to 2002 for the government as director of communications and press secretary to various MPs. He is now a writer, presenter and journalist.

SPIN

It's the year 2011. The New Project Party is in power and on a moral revival campaign. Selwyn Knox is at its helm. Sonya Mair, his political adviser, is helping him call the shots — along with some more personal matters . . . They've selected the team with dossiers on each member . . . Sir Robert Nottridge, Permanent Secretary: married, no children — or so his wife thinks. Christopher Brody, director of policy: a gambler with debts up to his eyeballs. Nigel Tonbridge, director of strategy and communications: ex- journo and keeper of some dark family secrets and disturbing political ones that might taint Saint Selwyn . . . But for now, they must do as they're told, and get down to administering morality.

MARTIN SIXSMITH

SPIN

Complete and Unabridged

CHARNWOOD
Leicester

First published in Great Britain in 2004 by
Macmillan
London

First Charnwood Edition
published 2006
by arrangement with
Macmillan Publishers Limited
London

British Library CIP Data

Sixsmith, Martin
   Spin.—Large print ed.—
   Charnwood library series
   1. Labour Party (Great Britain)—Fiction
   2. Journalists—Great Britain—Fiction
   3. Great Britain—Politics and government—*1997 –*
   —Fiction 4. Satire 5. Large type books
   I. Title
   823.9'2 [F]

   ISBN 1–84617–238–1

Published by
F. A. Thorpe (Publishing)
Anstey, Leicestershire

Set by Words & Graphics Ltd.
Anstey, Leicestershire
Printed and bound in Great Britain by
T. J. International Ltd., Padstow, Cornwall

This book is printed on acid-free paper

This novel is an amused and affectionate look at the worlds of politics, journalism and big business.

The incidents and characters in the book are not real . . . yet.

Acknowledgements

Thanks are due to my family,
Who suffered with me stoically;
To Ed, and DavidMariaKatieLiz
at Macmillan,
Who all performed heroically.

PART ONE

1

SEPTEMBER 2006

'Jon Adams?'

'Here.'

Oh, when the fog comes down . . .

'Julie Braeburn?'

'Here, sir.'

. . . the thick, the clinging fog, the fog that swirls and blackens thought . . .

'Peter Dalglish?'

'Yeah.'

. . . does it come to smother our faults, to hide our deeds from human eyes?

'Rory Fenton?'

'Present.'

Dan Curragh, sixty-four, decades a hill walker, never so seized with the cold mountains' dread.

'Jenny Haddow?'

'Here.'

Dan the teacher, Dan the leader.

'Evie Kilburnie?'

'Present, sir.'

Dan, whose voice was shaking.

'Sally Lawless?'

Sniggers.

'Yeah. Here.'

And now the fog and now the night beginning.

'Leanne Lockerbie?'

'Yeah.'

How can this be? How can this be?

'Philip McNab?'

'Here.'

To start with twelve and return with eleven?

'Paul Nisbett?'

No reply.

'Paul Nisbett?'

So is it him?

'Paul Nisbett?'

Paul the tough guy, Paul the swaggerer?

'Paul, are you here?'

Dan felt a shock of relief.

If it's him, he'll make it.

Of all of them, he's the one to beat the mountain.

'Paul Nisbett? Is it him who's missing?'

A quick infusion of hope after panic.

'Nah, sir. He's over there having a fag.'

Hope dashed.

Back to the nightmare.

'Cathy James?'

'I'm here sir, but it's Clare — Clare's not here.'

'What do you mean, Cathy?'

Don't panic, Dan.

'She's not here, sir. She's not here any more.'

Don't panic, Dan.

'Are you sure? Has anyone seen Clare?'

Silence.

'Cathy, you're her best friend — '

4

'Yes, sir. I don't know where she is.'

OK. OK, Dan Curragh. Think.

The fog's thick; she could be here.

'Clare! Clare O'Leary! Are you here?'

Clare the quiet. Clare the timid. Don't let it be her.

'Cathy! You two are always together. When did you last see her?'

'I don't know, sir. It's the fog. And Clare's gone. I'm scared, sir!'

Sit down, Dan.

Take stock.

One child down.

No way we can go back with one child down.

'Ian, we need to call Mountain Rescue. We need to get them out here right away. That's the first thing. Right? Then we need to decide who goes looking and who stays here. OK? . . . And where's Selwyn? What's he doing? . . . No, wait. Wait. We mustn't move from here till we talk to Mountain Rescue. They'll tell us what to do. Have you got the mobile? Come on, Ian! Ring them now!'

Ian Murray. Ten years younger than Dan. New Project, like Dan.

'Right, Dan. OK. What number do I ring?'

Why does my back hurt?

What am I doing here? What's down there?

I want to go home.

5

Home.

'What do you think, Frank? It's getting dark. Do you think they'll still be up in the mountains? I hope they're all right.'

'Of course they're all right, Eileen. It's organized by the council. It's the youth club. They know what they're doing. Stop worrying.'

'Hello, nine nine nine? What? . . . No, I don't want any of those. No . . . Yes, it is an emergency. I want Mountain Rescue . . . Yes, we're up in the mountains . . . What? It's Ian Murray. I'm a councillor. I'm one of the leaders of the trip.'

I'm scared.
It's too dark. It shouldn't be this dark.
I want to be at home.
Top of the Pops *is starting.*
Why can't I feel my legs?

'We'd better record *Top of the Pops* for Clare, Frank. They're not going to be back in time now, are they? Can you do it, please? Get up off your backside and do something, Frank!'

'You're asking me what my phone number is? I don't know. I'm ringing on a mobile, of course . . . Yes, it is my mobile . . . No, I don't know the number.'

I've got to look down. I can't.

It's the only way out. I can't climb back up there.

I must have fallen.

Why is it dark? The last I remember it was light.

'No, I don't know exactly where we are. It's completely fog-bound up here and we've been going round in circles. But we've got a child missing. Can you please hurry up and come and help us? . . . I think we're near the top of Ben Donnan.'

'It's The Darkness on *Top of the Pops*, Frank. Have you put a tape in for Clare? What, have you just been sitting there? I can't believe it. Put the bloody tape in, Frank!'

'Yes, I told you: I'm Ian Murray . . . I'm a Project party councillor from Exxington District Council. It's our youth scheme . . . we've got eleven children here . . . we started with twelve.

'And we've got an adult missing too. We haven't seen either of them for about two hours now.

'The child's called Clare O'Leary. She's twelve. I'm worried about her . . . she's not very tough. Very timid . . . quite frail, you know.

'The adult's Selwyn Knox . . . he's a New

7

Project councillor, too. He's the one who runs the youth scheme . . . It was his idea to bring this expedition up here . . .

'I wish we hadn't come on the bloody trip. It's too late now, but I wish we'd called it off when the weather warning came out. It's just, you know . . . Yes, OK . . . Sorry . . .

'Well, yes, *we're* all OK. No injuries, no . . . Yes, we're all warm and safe here. We've got food, but I want to find Clare and get this lot down as quick as possible.'

I can't look down.

I want my Mum.

Mummy, it's Clare! Can you see me, Mum?

'Frank, I'm really worried about Clare. Perhaps we should call the school.'

'It's got nothing to do with the school, Eileen. It's the council youth scheme or something. And, anyway, we haven't got their number. So just calm down, they'll be back in a bit.'

'Oh, Selwyn, there you are! Where the hell have you been? We've been going spare here.'

'Hi, Ian! Don't worry, Dan — I'm fine. I've been looking for Clare, but I don't think we'll find her in this fog.'

'What do you mean, you don't think we'll find her? We've got to find her. We can't go

8

back without her! Ian's been on the phone to Mountain Rescue. They're going to send a helicopter. Then they're going to get the rest of the children down out of here.'

'Oh, right. So when's the helicopter coming, Dan?'

'I don't know, Selwyn, for Christ's sake! Ian's on the phone to them. They'll be coming as soon as they can.'

That's funny. I'm starting to feel warm again.
Why am I feeling warm?
It should be freezing here.
And I'm feeling warm.

'You know Clare O'Leary, don't you, Selwyn? You're in charge of the youth scheme. Do you think she'll be all right out on the mountain on her own?'

'I don't know, Ian. She's quite little and she's very nervy. I'm worried about her.'

'But she'll be all right won't she, Sel? She's not going to die out there or anything, is she? She's not, is she? Sel? Why did we come on this bloody trip, anyway?'

I'm getting warmer.
I feel OK now.

'This is BBC Radio Strathclyde. Some pretty atrocious weather conditions out there tonight. There's a weather watch in force for the whole of western Scotland, so if you're driving please do take extra care.

'Now, we're getting reports of a party of local school children stranded on a mountaineering expedition. The Mountain Rescue service has been alerted and a helicopter is reported to be on its way to pick up one child who's said to be injured. We have no further details on that breaking story, but we'll keep you informed as soon as we hear more.'

'That's the phone, Frank! Can you get it, please? I've got the dinner cooking here!'

Please, let me go home . . .
  If you let me go home, I'll never argue with Lily again.
  I'll never be cheeky to Mum and Dad.
  I want to go home.

'Mountain Rescue here. Is that Ian Murray's phone? . . .
  'Oh, OK. So who's that then? . . . Selwyn Knox did you say? All right. Hello, Mr Knox. The helicopter's on its way to you now.
  'We'll be looking out for your party, so can you please make yourselves visible. That means spreading out as much brightly coloured material as possible on the ground where you are. Use tents or groundsheets — anything bright. And please light a fire so we can spot you as

10

quickly as we can. I don't suppose you've got any flares with you, have you? . . . OK, not to worry. We'll be there soon.'

'Eileen, it's your sister. She says she's been listening to Radio Strathclyde and there's been something about a school party in trouble in the mountains. I told her not to worry because Clare's not on a school party, it's the council youth scheme.'

I'm getting warmer again.
   And now I know how it's going to end.
   I read it in my book; I'm just not sure what sort of bird it is.
   It looks like an eagle, but I know it's not an eagle.

'I can hear the helicopter, Ian. Can you hear it, Selwyn? I'm sure I can hear something. Listen carefully. This damn fog muffles the noise.'

'Oh, Frank, I'm worried. It doesn't matter what they call it. School, youth club, council — it's school children up in the mountains. And I'm sure it's Clare. I just know there's something wrong.'

'Ten o'clock. BBC Radio Strathclyde news. This is Nigel Tonbridge at the news desk.

'Our headlines tonight.

'A party of Strathclyde school children is reported missing on a hiking expedition in the Ben Donnan area. The party, organized by the Exxington District Council youth scheme, set out this morning before weather conditions started to worsen. It's thought the party of twelve children, reported to be aged between thirteen and sixteen and led by three council members, were caught in the dense fog that descended over the region in mid to late afternoon. Mountain Rescue helicopters are now scouring the area, but there are unconfirmed reports that one child may be missing.'

It's an auk!
That's what it's called! An auk.
I remember it now from my book.

'Yes, it is the helicopter, Ian. I can see its lights now. Can you see it, Selwyn?

'I think it's going to try and land.

'Children! Everybody stand up and start waving.

'Here's the helicopter. It's coming to rescue us, so everyone stand together in a group and start waving so the pilot can see us.

'Move over to those rocks, children. The pilot wants us to move over there, so he can land on this flat bit of ground. Quickly, children! Go now!'

12

An auk.

A great auk! That's it.

He's coming to take me home.

When little children get lost, he always comes to carry them back to his nest, where it's warm and soft and safe.

'Hello, is that Mrs O'Leary?

'Hello, Mrs O'Leary. It's the duty officer at Exxington District Council here. I just wanted to let you know that there's been a bit of a problem with the youth scheme expedition. Now you don't need to worry. We're doing everything we can and we've got the Mountain Rescue people out, so everything's going to be all right.

'Mrs O'Leary . . . ?'

'Hello, I'm Captain Peters. Who's in charge here? Which of you is Mr Murray?'

'Hello, Captain. I'm Selwyn Knox and I'm in charge. Let's get the children on board, shall we? And let's get everyone home as quickly as possible.'

'Yes, I'm here . . . I'm here. I'm sorry . . . it's just I can't take it in. Clare's only twelve, you know. She's so little. And she shouldn't really be going out hiking like that, only it's organized by the youth scheme, you know, and Mr Knox said it would be safe. But now we've got the newspapers ringing us and saying Clare's been

13

injured or something. I just don't know what's going on and I'm so worried . . . but you did say she's all right, didn't you?'

'Yes, Captain, I know we've got a little girl missing, but we have to be logical about this. We need to get these children back to safety or we'll have more of them dying from cold or frostbite. We can't help Clare O'Leary at the moment, but we can help the others. So let's get them all back home while the other helicopter and the search parties carry on looking for Clare, all right?'

'Hello, Mrs O'Leary. It's the council duty officer again. Just to say that the Mountain Rescue people have been on. They've located the main party now and they expect to have them back here in an hour or so. Unfortunately, they haven't found Clare yet, but they say you shouldn't worry because they've got search teams and two helicopters out looking for her and they say they hope to find her as quickly as possible. So don't worry, Mrs O'Leary; the best thing you can do now is stay by the phone and wait until I ring you again, or the Mountain Rescue people or the police get in touch. Is that all right? . . . Mrs O'Leary — ?'

'Is that Selwyn?
'Selwyn, it's Bob Travers here. Thank God you're back. And thank God we've got most of the kids back. But what the hell's

14

happening about Clare O'Leary?

'We're all very worried about this. It's not looking good for the council, you know . . .

'We were the ones who set this thing up; and we're the ones who're going to get blamed if anything's happened to the girl . . .

'I've already had the media ringing me, Selwyn, and it's pretty unpleasant, I can tell you. As council leader, I'm getting it right in the neck. They want to know why we let the trip go ahead in such bad weather and what safety measures we took.

'You know, they're saying we breached government safety guidelines. But I've checked: there are no bloody guidelines! So I don't know what they're on about, really.

'But that hasn't stopped London getting on the phone to give us a bollocking. The leadership are absolutely furious. They say we're a major New Project council and this could hurt the government's image. I've told them that's nonsense, but you know what control freaks this New Project lot can be.

'Anyway, they're sending somebody up here for a meeting first thing in the morning. What? . . . No . . . no, I don't know who it is yet. We'll find out in the morning. Anyway, they want the whole of the Project group here without fail. So make sure all three of you who were up on the mountain get in here by eight o'clock, OK? Tell Ian and Dan. All right?

'Yes, I know you've got to make a

15

statement to the police. Go and do that now, then get some sleep. But you need to be here in the morning to tell this guy from London exactly what happened. They've really got it in for the council — and that means me and you. We're in trouble if we can't give a good account of ourselves.

'And another thing, Selwyn: the media are camped outside the O'Learys' house. They know it's Clare who's missing. So keep away from there, OK?'

'This is BBC Radio Strathclyde with the seven o'clock news.

'Just one headline this morning and it is, of course, the continuing story of the little schoolgirl who's missing in bad weather following a hiking expedition that went disastrously wrong.

'Clare O'Leary, who's twelve and comes from the Exxington area, is still missing this morning, despite intensive rescue efforts, which have continued throughout the night.

'Search teams are combing the area near the last sighting of Clare, but the Mountain Rescue helicopters, which would normally lead an operation like this, have not been able to operate since fog and driving sleet forced them to return to base. Earlier one helicopter managed to bring back eleven other children and the three Project party members of Exxington District Council, who had taken the expedition into difficult mountainous territory despite weather warnings from the Met Office. No council spokesman was available for comment this morning, but on the line now is Captain John Peters from the Mountain Rescue service: Captain Peters, can you tell us what went wrong?'

★   ★   ★

'Gentlemen, can I call this meeting to order, please? I'd like to start by introducing Geoff Maddle, Geoff's here from party headquarters in London. The national Project party — or the government — which is it, Geoff? . . . OK, the national Project party it is — they're the same thing, of course, but Geoff's officially from the party, even though he's an adviser to the New Project government, is that right? . . . OK, Geoff. Thanks.

'So London have sent Geoff here to help us deal with the way we, er . . . deal with this very unpleasant incident.

'As council leader, I'd just like to say that it was most unfortunate that this expedition ended in the, er . . . unfortunate way it did.

'But I'd like to add that we mustn't give up hope. The missing girl is still missing. So she isn't dead and we can only hope that things turn out all right after all. I think we have to hope that — '

'Get real, Bob. The girl's dead. Even the Mountain Rescue people say she couldn't have survived a night out in weather like this. Didn't you hear them on the radio this morning?'

'Just wait a minute, Tommy. Wait! You weren't up there on the mountain. It's no good jumping the gun here. I think we have to have a policy to follow in case she's alive and a policy in case she's dead.'

'What do you mean a policy? This is a little girl we're talking about here, Bob. How can we have a policy? We've cocked things up and we have to say so. We can't play politics with a little girl's life.'

'No, of course we can't. We've all got children . . . or we've all got mothers and fathers at least.

'So we're people first and foremost, of course, but we're also the public face of the New Project party and Geoff is here to make that point to us all.

'So before we all get carried away . . . no, wait. We can't all talk at once!

'We'll all get the chance to have our say.

'Order! Gentlemen! Wait! Please —

'What we have to do first is introduce ourselves so Geoff knows who we are. And then I think we'll hear what Geoff has to say.

'And, don't forget, Geoff is speaking for the Prime Minister. Whatever Geoff says to you all this morning, it's the same as if Andy Sheen was saying it himself. Is that clear, everyone? That's right, isn't it, Geoff?

'Right, let's tell Geoff who we are. First of all, I need the three of you who were leading the expedition to make themselves known to Geoff.

'First, Dan Curragh. This is Dan Curragh, Geoff.

'Dan's been a mountaineer for very many

18

years. There isn't anyone more experienced at mountain walking than Dan in the whole of the region, is there? And Dan was in the SAS, weren't you, Dan, so he knows all about survival and rescue and things . . . What? The TA — OK. The TA Dan was in.

'And second, here's Ian Murray, Geoff. He's a master butcher and he's been a member of Exxington District Council for fifteen years — fifteen is it, Ian? So he's very experienced as well.

'And last of all is Selwyn Knox. He's the leader of the council's youth scheme, so he knows a lot about young people and to some extent it was his idea to take this expedition out there, wasn't it, Selwyn?

'Selwyn? . . . where's Selwyn?

'He was here earlier, wasn't he?

'I know I talked to him on the phone. I'm sure I did because I told everyone on the New Project group they had to be here. Does anyone know where Selwyn is?'

★ ★ ★

Selwyn Knox had not slept during the whole of that terrible night.

After two fraught hours at the Mountain Rescue HQ, talking to the search leaders on the radio link and trying to guide them to where Clare might be, then giving endless statements to one police officer after another, all the while churning over the events in his head, he could not sleep even when he got back to his flat at three a.m.

19

As mug of coffee followed mug of coffee and the night ticked away, Selwyn brooded on the images of sleet, fog and rock that were burned on his brain and gave him no peace: the thought of Clare; the blackness of the fog descending on the mountain; sight extinguished; sound deadened; no voices, no cries; then returning to the group; Dan's voice; the dread cold of fear in his heart; the mental rally as he attempted to take control; the celestial apparition of the helicopter; the surge of adrenalin; the return of lucidity in conversation with the pilot —

Now, Selwyn, now!

Stay focused — stay calm!

You're facing your biggest test yet so keep the ice in your heart — stay in control.

They're out to get you — they've always been against you — you've only yourself to rely on.

You're down now, they'll try to keep you down. But every setback is an opportunity. Don't just survive this: use it, use it to grow stronger, use it to advance. You're not one of them — you're different, stronger, better. You're marked for the future — don't forget the future — your future will change things — and today is make or break for you.

★ ★ ★

'OK, so it looks like Selwyn isn't here. Maybe he overslept or something. Can someone try his phone, please? Meanwhile, I'm going to hand over to Geoff from party headquarters. And I want you to listen carefully to what Geoff has to say because the way we handle this crisis could determine all our political futures. We've got local elections coming up soon, I don't need to tell you that. And Geoff's got his own concerns about the party's image at the national level too, haven't you, Geoff? I think we all need to remember what Andy Sheen has always said: 'What we do is important, but it won't count for anything if we don't present it right.' So Geoff's going to tell us now how we need to go about presenting this crisis. Geoff — '

'Thanks. Morning, everyone. Sorry I've had to come at such a difficult time. I'm here 'cos the Prime Minister and Charlie McDonald are concerned about what's happened in Exxington. They're both very sad about the little girl and her family, of course, but most of all they're concerned because this was an expedition organized by the New Project party. I'm not saying anyone did anything wrong, I'm sure you all had the best intentions. But when things happen that have the New Project party's name attached to them, we can be sure our enemies will be delighted that things have gone wrong for us. The opposition will be meeting at this moment to figure out how to use this against us. And don't forget we've got Prime Minister's Questions coming up, so Andy Sheen is going to face a grilling in parliament. And that's really why I'm here now: what I need from you is a clear explanation of everything that happened up in those mountains. Then we need to agree a very clear story that we all stick to. We mustn't end up contradicting each other because it'll make us look guilty and that's exactly what our enemies want — we don't need it. We need to stick together. We need to agree a line to take and we need to get your other guy — what's his name, Selwyn Knox? — involved in this. We don't want any loose cannons on this story. OK? So why don't you go first, Ian Murray, and tell us exactly what you remember about yesterday, starting from when the expedition set off, and then talk us through exactly who did what and who went where? All right?'

★　★　★

'You don't have any children, do you, Mr Knox? It's not easy bringing them up. You spend your whole life building them up, creating them, then they start to leave you. Or that's how it feels. The whole time you feel them growing away from you. But if you're lucky you can know they're still yours. They're still with you. When you wake your daughter in the morning she looks like a grown up twelve-year-old, but in that minute when she's coming round from sleep, waking from a dream, you know . . . she's suddenly back to the little one she used to be. It's hard to explain. She's all soft with sleep and when she opens her eyes she looks at you just the way she used to do when she was small. And then you can see that inside she's still the same; still the lovely child she was when she was little; you can see that she's full of goodness and simplicity and love. Oh, Mr Knox, how can this have happened?'

As he walked out to seize his destiny, Selwyn Knox glanced in the hall mirror of the O'Learys' terraced house. He looked stern. He looked determined. He smoothed his beard with the palm of his right hand.

There are moments in a person's life when the future is decided. You need to recognize them, you need to seize them. Only the strongest can seize their destiny. Only the strongest can act with mental clarity and decision — and I have been given that gift — I have been given the talents and the power. I am strong — I won't be looking back in twenty years and regretting opportunities I missed —

'Good morning, ladies and gentlemen.

'You've been here most of the night. Thank you for doing your job with such devotion.

'I know you are all concerned about Clare.

'I know you want to talk to Mr and Mrs O'Leary.

'And I know you want to hear from the council, who organized this expedition.

'Well, I'm here. My name is Councillor Selwyn Knox. Mrs O'Leary is here too, and we'll do our best to answer all your questions.

'But first let me say how terribly stricken I feel this morning. Stricken by the weight of last night's events; stricken by the anxiety and fear of a mother waiting for news of her child; stricken by the force of a mother's love.

'We all know the burden Mr and Mrs O'Leary are carrying as we wait to hear about Clare, as we hope for her safe return from the mountain but fear for her safety.

'So let our first thoughts be with Clare and with Clare's parents. As human beings, we owe that to ourselves.

'But let me say, also, that I am here to answer any questions you may have about the council's role in these events. As a two-term New Project party councillor myself, I can say that I at least have absolutely nothing to hide. This has been a tragic accident. If anyone has acted incorrectly, then I'm as determined as you are to find out the truth and take any action that is necessary. I can say quite categorically — '

'Mr Knox! We want to talk to Mrs O'Leary — '

'Mrs O'Leary, how do you feel about what has happened to Clare?'

'Mrs O'Leary, are you angry at the way the council has handled this?'

'Mrs O'Leary — '

'Wait! All of you! One at a time. Don't shout! Don't you know Mrs O'Leary has been through a terrible ordeal? Now Mrs O'Leary has a short statement to make and then I'll take any further questions. Eileen, are you all right? Are you going to be able to talk? OK, be quiet everyone and listen to what Mrs O'Leary has to say because this is all she'll be saying today.'

'Thank you, Selwyn — Mr Knox, I mean. I just want to say that I love Clare very much. She is my youngest daughter and she is a lovely girl. I know she is in danger, but we are praying to Our Lady to keep her safe. We're praying . . . I'm

24

sorry . . . I'm sorry . . . that's . . . I'm sorry . . . '

'It's all right, Eileen. Don't worry. Just the last bit, remember? The bit about the youth scheme. OK?'

'Yes . . . yes . . . I just want to say that Clare has been a member of the council youth scheme for the last two years and she has always been safe on it. And she has always enjoyed the activities Mr Knox has organized. And we have never had any problems at all. Is that all right?'

'Thank you, Eileen. Now I want to say — '

'Mrs O'Leary, have you been told exactly how Clare went missing?'

'Mrs O'Leary, how did the supervisors all manage to lose sight of Clare?'

'Mrs O'Leary — '

'Now stop that! Stop shouting! Can't you see Mrs O'Leary is upset? She's been very brave coming out to talk to you. You can't expect her to answer all those questions — '

'It's all right, Selwyn . . . it's all right . . . Can I just say to all of you that Mr Knox has been a good friend to Clare ever since she was ten and she joined the council youth scheme. In fact, he's been a friend to our whole family. So I want Mr Knox to answer your questions. He can speak on behalf of me . . . if you'll excuse me, I just can't say anything else just now . . . I'm sorry . . . I'm really very sorry — '

'Right, everyone! Leave Mrs O'Leary alone. You've had your statement. Leave her in peace. Thank you. Now, I just have a couple more things to say on behalf of Exxington District Council.

'The whole of the New Project group are devastated by what has happened to Clare. The decision to take the expedition into the mountains yesterday was made by the council as a whole. It was a collective decision. The trip was led by very professional, very experienced guides. And the decision to set off yesterday morning was made before the bad weather started. There was never any suggestion that the weather was going to turn, and anyone who says the bad weather was predicted by the Met Office is just kidding themselves.

'It is true that I was one of the leaders of the expedition. I can't go into details of what happened up in the mountains because the relevant authorities are still investigating what happened and I cannot be seen to pre-empt their conclusions. But I can tell you that I was not the man who organized this outing. I have no axe to grind and I certainly have nothing to hide. What I can tell you is that I didn't support the idea of the trip. In fact, I had severe reservations about it and I think bad decisions were taken by some of those in charge of the expedition, although I don't want to point the finger of blame and they will have to speak for themselves . . . when the time comes, that is.

'I will just say that when things went wrong up on the mountain there was a lot of panic among those who should have known better. When the weather turned bad — and conditions were atrocious, I can tell you — it was me who took charge, while the others were dithering around at base camp. I went looking for Clare, I did all I could, so my conscience at least is clear.

'As Mrs O'Leary told you, I have known Clare and her family for a long time. It is no exaggeration to say that in some respects Clare knew and respected me as a father to her. So what happened yesterday was absolutely heart-breaking for me . . . excuse me a moment . . . I'm sorry, I just need a moment . . . I can tell you, in all honesty, I loved Clare like a father . . . I'm sorry . . . what was I saying? Yes . . . so, as a result of what I suffered yesterday, I have decided I could not live with myself if I didn't now do everything possible to ensure a tragedy like this never happens again. It's scandalous that despite many promises there are no legal guidelines to ensure that such trips are carried out with the maximum safety for the children involved. So I hereby pledge to all of you that I will not rest until this question has been tackled properly. From today onwards I shall be devoting myself to leading a campaign for new government guidelines to increase safety regulations for trips like this one, whether they be school trips, youth club outings or any other expedition.

'And I can tell you that this campaign will be waged at national level, not just here in Exxington but at Westminster! Because there can be no higher cause than the safety of our children, our children who are the future of our whole society. And I can tell you that I, Selwyn Knox, will be at the heart of that great campaign.

'Thank you very much, everybody. I would like to end by asking us all just to take a couple of moments of silence to turn our thoughts to

Clare O'Leary, who is missing in the mountains, for believers among us to pray for her salvation, and for all of us to express the hope that Clare will be found safe and well and that she'll be back here soon with her loving parents.'

★ ★ ★

But what Selwyn Knox could not hear at that moment was the voice of Clare herself, poor Clare, lying in the mountains —

'I know he's coming. I know the great auk is coming,' said Clare, her eyes now burning from the pain and fever, but burning too with hope and looking to the happiness that lay ahead.

'The great auk is coming.'

And Clare was right, because what happened next was exactly as she had foreseen it.

With the utmost gentleness, the great auk swooped down to the ledge where Clare was lying.

Even though a tear was running through the feathers round his noble eyes, he smiled his great auk smile at her and Clare felt comforted.

And then, just as she had known he would, the great auk cradled her in his powerful claws — taking infinite care not to crush or hurt her.

With a mighty beating of his powerful wings, he rose from the sluggish pull of the earth and hovered briefly over the mountain ledge.

Clare felt the relief and thrill of weightlessness.

Then the great auk soared into the sky, carrying his precious cargo to the safety and warmth of his noble nest.

★ ★ ★

In Exxington, outside a terraced house on a council estate, a mobile phone rang moments later and a member of the media listened to a message from his newsroom.

'Mr Knox . . . Mrs O'Leary. I'm sorry to interrupt. We've just heard. Clare's been found.'

2

Geoff Maddle was watching the television in the council leader's office with a growing sense of anger.

The story had been too late to make the papers, so that was OK.

On the radio the *Today* programme had given in to its current anal fixation with the faltering economic situation, running item after item slagging off the government for things that any reasonable person knew were beyond its control, like the state of the stock market, the crisis of British manufacturing or the collapse of Marconi and all the other crap news.

Geoff had felt his usual fury with the insidious John Humphrys and his weaselly undermining of all the government's achievements, his fixation with attacking it over GM, and his refusal to give any government minister a fair hearing in interviews more like public lynchings than exchanges of views.

It was further confirmation — if confirmation were needed — that the PM was right to spurn the *Today* programme in favour of *Richard and Judy* and *Tonight with Trevor McDonald*. They were the shows real people followed and took notice of. Not like *Today*, with its audience of sad bastards in the Westminster village, the saddo journalists and political observers who were more concerned with observing the fluff in their

30

own navels than doing anything relevant to the real concerns of real Britain.

Anyway, the consequence of all that — all those sad *Today* programme obsessions — thought Geoff with some relief, was that the dead-girl story had actually come well down the programme's running order and that it had been played low-key, with no opposition spokesman and no real attempt to exploit the political implications of the New Project council connection.

So not bad, a score draw there, Geoff thought.

But then he had switched on the end of *Breakfast* news to keep an eye on how the story was playing on the telly and — to his amazement — had come in on the middle of Selwyn Knox's impromptu press conference at the girl's family home.

Geoff found it hard to believe his ears.

In all his years as a professional media director, in all the hundreds of stories he had managed for New Project, he had never heard anything so badly controlled and so ill-disciplined as this. What had happened to the 'culture of no surprises' the party had inculcated in all its workers and officials?

This was exactly what he had warned those bloody councillors *not* to do!

Not to go off spinning a line that hadn't been cleared by Downing Street; *not* to start shooting from the hip with freelance versions of the story, however convincing and however clever.

Geoff Maddle's fury with Selwyn Knox grew as he heard Knox expand his maverick line of

31

special pleading and self-justification. Yeah, right! That all sounds pretty good for Selwyn Knox esquire, Geoff fumed, but what's it going to do for the rest of us? What's it going to do for the party? It won't take the media long to spot that Knox is dumping on his colleagues; it won't take them long to come round here asking who's to blame, who it was that made all those mistakes superhero Selwyn had to try to put right — what a fucking shambles!

'Bob! Bob Travers! Get down here now! Have you seen what's running on the telly? It's your man, that bloody Selwyn Knox. He's on *Breakfast* news and he's off spinning his own line on this story. It's bad news for you guys, I can tell you. You're the council leader and he's dropping you and the New Project group in the shit. This is exactly what I was sent up here to stop happening. You get him on the phone right now, mate, and tell him I want him here in this office in less than half an hour. Tell him I'm going to have to ring Downing Street about this and it's not good news for you or for me or for anyone — '

★ ★ ★

'Good morning, Downing Street.'
'Put me through to Charlie McDonald.'
'Who's calling, please?'
'It's Geoff, Geoff Maddle.'
'Good morning, Mr Maddle. Putting you through now.'

32

'Charlie, is that you? . . .Yeah, OK, mate. How you doing?'

Geoff Maddle had known Charlie McDonald for twenty years.

They had worked together as junior reporters at the Brixton Newspaper Group, where Charlie's colour — a deep West African brown — and his size — six feet seven inches in his undarned socks — had helped protect Geoff's pasty white, scrawny English ass on numerous occasions in a variety of professional and personal scrapes. In the bars of Brixton, they had shared more pints than they cared to remember, more stories than most hacks get through in a lifetime and more women than either recalled or would admit to. Both of them were New Project through and through and fired with a grim determination to get their party into power 'by hook or by crook — whatever it took!'

Geoff had gone on to work for the National Union of Journalists, fronting its PR effort and doing his best to defend its anaemic leadership from the overwhelming opinion among hacks that, when it came to standing up for its members, the NUJ packed all the punch of a blancmange.

And Charlie had taken the job as chief political correspondent for the *Daily Mail*, a move that had prompted much amazement and ribald hilarity among his friends and colleagues. Charlie's reply, when challenged over how a pillar of the black community and the Project party left could write for the right-wing *Mail*, was to laugh and ask whether his questioner had never heard of the fifth column or the then much-vaunted tactic of entryism.

It was the run-up to the 2005 general election that had brought the two of them back together.

As a political journalist, Charlie had long moved in elevated political circles, getting to know and admire national figures like Alastair Campbell and Hugh Gavno. He had a high intellectual regard for Campbell's political writings and a more physical appreciation of his outpourings in certain male-orientated organs — the sort of writer whom one reads, in Alfred de Musset's memorable phrase, with one hand.

Charlie's ethnic and social background — the archetypal ghetto boy made good — and his undeniable physical presence had earned him a high profile among the chattering classes.

His job gave him access to high places and he spent the late nineties and early noughties cultivating his links with the coming men of the New Project party. His friendship with Andy Sheen, the young lion who was rescuing Project from the unelectable doldrums of Militate, proto-communist trade unions and self-destruct-button squabbling, was reflected in a noticeable softening of the *Mail*'s tirades against New Project.

Charlie was even credited with suggesting the party's Procter & Gamble-esque brand name, New Improved Project (or NIP, as it was joshingly called by Old Project diehards), and the PR campaign that went with it. Privately, he used to say that New Project was located somewhere between the party he had grown up in and the newspaper he was now working for, and he didn't mean it entirely as a joke.

When the election was announced, Andy Sheen had asked Charlie how he would feel about coming to work full-time for the party. Sheen's explanation of the role seemed nebulous, but Charlie immediately spotted the potential it offered. Few people in those days realized how powerful the New Project spin doctors were to become, how much influence the imperatives of presentation would soon have over the substance of party policy-making. But from Andy's sketchy job description Charlie knew that he could be at the pinnacle of that power and influence. He was delighted.

After a little diplomatic hesitation, Charlie McDonald went back to Andy Sheen with a few additional demands about his title (director of strategy and communications), office (next to the PM in Downing Street with a window overlooking the garden) and formal powers. Sheen promised him the incoming Project party government — no one had any doubt they'd be elected — would give him all the power he needed.

When New Improved Project were duly voted in, Andy Sheen became the voice of the country's conscience, a righteous, ethical, trustworthy Prime Minister, and he took his protégé with him.

As a non-elected official, Charlie McDonald's job was supposed to make him a back-room boy, but his colour, his attitude and his size meant he didn't stay in the shadows for long. His natural street-wise, no-nonsense authority had worked on the streets of Brixton and it worked equally well in Whitehall. It wasn't long before even the toughest MPs and ministers understood that when Charlie spoke they needed to sit up and listen.

Having thus secured his own future, Charlie McDonald set about recruiting the people he wanted to work for him.

Few were surprised when his first port of call was Geoff Maddle. Charlie wanted people he could rely on in a tight corner, people who would punch their weight in a scrap and who wouldn't be too squeamish about some of the things they might be asked to do in the name of the party. Geoff had all of these qualities: in Charlie's eyes he also had the invaluable attributes of complete trustworthiness, complete discretion and complete devotion to the cause. His experience in PR at the NUJ was a bonus, as was the fact that he was so pissed off there that he leapt at the chance to work with his old mate.

In the months since New Project had come to power, sweeping Labour out of Downing Street, the two of them had built a ferocious team and an equally ferocious reputation. Now Downing Street had become the most efficient, most revered and most feared PR outfit in the whole of Europe.

Foreign governments sent their Charlie McDonald wannabes to study at the court of the master: to learn how carrots, sticks, black eyes, blackmail, saccharine and smears, seduction and schmooze can all be deployed to keep the government at the top of the news agenda; how the media could be flattered or cowed into submission; how difficult journalists could be neutralized; and how inconvenient stories could be killed by kindness, by cunning or by cutting some bastard's balls off.

It was Geoff who had become the most accomplished exponent of the last technique. He was Number Ten's fireman, despatched to quell the flames of any hot news that looked in danger of singeing Andy Sheen's immaculate coat tails. His work was behind the scenes and all the more effective for it.

Success for Geoff Maddle was when a story did not appear; when a dog did not bark. For him no news was most definitely good news. Let Charlie and the others do the clever stuff, plant the positive stories, manipulate the facts to make them fit the government's preferred agenda, mould journalists and editors until it became second nature to them to know what Andy Sheen wanted and simply to write it. Let Charlie get on with all that; Geoff was happy going out and twisting a few arms, stuffing a few mouths, keeping his nose and Andy Sheen's arse as clean as possible.

And that was why he was here now in the back of beyond, in Exxington, where a New Project party council's stupidity had got a young girl killed.

'Listen, Charlie, have you seen what's going down this morning?'

'I saw the GM story on the front of the *Guardian* — ugh; the usual crap from Humphrys

37

on the radio; and we've got a few helpful previews for Andy's speech at the Guildhall tomorrow. Your dead-girl story turned out OK, I thought. Is there something else I should know about?'

'No, Charlie. It's the dead girl I'm ringing you about. We kept it low-key overnight. It didn't make the papers, at least not in a big way. But we've had some stupid fucker from the council mouthing off.'

'What do you mean from the council? Is he a councillor?'

'Yeah. It's a bloke called Selwyn Knox and he's just done a presser outside the girl's house here. You must have missed it — they carried it live on *Breakfast* news.'

'Right; I've just come back from the eight-thirty meeting, so I haven't had the telly on. I've heard of this guy Knox, though: he was at the party conference last year making a big fuss about himself. Not a bad operator. What's he been saying?'

'Well, he's been defending himself, of course; saying that it wasn't his fault and he'd tried to stop the expedition before it set off — which is a bit rich, considering he was the one who ran the youth scheme and considering we know it was his idea to take them up into the mountains.

'Anyway, I suppose that's fair enough; but the thing that pisses me off is that he's trying to blame his mates and the council as a whole for the cock-up. He's talking as if we're doing some kind of cover-up here, as if we've got something to hide.

'And the worst thing is that he's trying to cover himself in roses by attacking the government for not having proper safety rules for school trips. He's setting himself up to lead some sort of campaign for legislation to regulate youth expeditions and that sort of thing. So he's coming out of this looking like the good guy in the white hat.'

'OK, Geoff. We don't want that. Not today of all days. Andy's speech tomorrow is the top story on our News Grid for more than a week. We can't afford to have that overshadowed by some loner promoting his own political career.'

'Yeah, that's definitely what's behind all this. It's the Selwyn Knox show and 'Notice me please . . . I want to be an MP.' That's what Knox is up to, Charlie.'

'Right. Let me just think about this for a minute. The first thing we need to do is put out a news sponge to soak up some of the hacks' attention. I'll think of something — maybe we could do the Alice Sheen starts nursery school story, or perhaps I'll use the stuff about that Tory MP and the backhander allegations —

'Anyway, don't worry about that; that's not your problem. What *you* need to do is neutralize Knox. You need to stop this school-trip legislation campaign before it starts, Geoff. I don't know if you've followed it, but we've been having a real ding-dong with the education select committee over school trips ever since those lads were killed canoeing in France.'

'Yeah, I saw that. Some problem with the unions, isn't it?'

'Basically, if we introduce regulations, we'll have the teaching unions down on us like a ton of bricks; they're shit scared we'll use any legislation to prosecute their members every time little Johnny gets his knee scraped on a school nature ramble. It'd mean teachers and youth-club leaders would down tools and refuse to take children out anywhere. And we can't have that happening.

'Anyway, the PM doesn't want to hear another word on the subject: we've managed to slip the select committee a few sweeteners to keep them quiet, but if this guy Knox starts up the fuss again, we'll never hear the end of it. So we need to shut him up. Will you see what you can do with him? Have we got any useful information on Knox from the records?'

'No, we haven't. That's the problem, Charlie. While I was travelling up here last night, I got the boys at headquarters to run a check in Lancelot, to see what we could dig up on all the Exxington rednecks. I ran the check on all the council members 'cos I didn't know which ones would turn out to be the troublemakers. Anyway, we've got something on nearly all of them. The one with the biggest list against his name is a bloke called Ian Murray, by the way: he's a dab hand at fiddling his expenses and we know he's used his influence on the Exxington housing committee to get council houses for at least three of his relatives. So he would have been easy; we could have screwed him over, no trouble. The problem is that Knox came out completely clean. You know, I think that's the first time I've ever seen Lancelot not come up with something on a subject: Christ knows, we spend enough time and effort collecting and sifting all the dirt we keep in there!'

'OK, Geoff. Don't worry. If you can't threaten him, you'll just have to reason with him! And if that doesn't work, try a bit of sweet talking. Tell him Andy Sheen knows who he is and rates him as a future MP or something — all he has to do is agree to drop this barmy campaign idea he's talking about. Think that'll do the trick?'

'I'm not sure. You said yourself Knox is good at making a fuss — I take it we're not really going to offer him a seat, are we?'

'Mmm — ' Charlie McDonald hesitated. 'I don't know, Geoff. Maybe, maybe not. I told you he did well at the party conference. And I know it's a pain in the arse what he's been up to today, but you have to admit it shows he's got guts. You've got to hand it to him: he's turned a pretty bleak story into something potentially very positive for himself. That's a talent we could use. It's not everyone who has the nous to do that sort of thing. And it's not everyone who comes up clean after we've dug through their records in Lancelot! Ha! I dread to think what you and I would have against us if they ran a check on us, mate! Anyway, just size up the situation. See what you can do to keep him quiet without promising him anything. But actually, you know, if you can't manage that, Andy *has* got a couple of safe seats going spare for the next election. Come back to me if you think we'll need to use one of them on Knox. OK?'

41

'OK, Charlie. I'll see what I can do — '

As he put the phone down, Geoff Maddle felt a surge of anger. He didn't know Selwyn Knox, he'd never even met him. But instinctively he disliked the man.

Geoff was still smarting from Knox's TV appearance, which he saw as a deliberate challenge to his own authority: he'd told the councillors to keep their mouths shut and Knox had gone shooting his mouth off; he'd told them they had to agree a party line and Knox had gone to the press with his own version of events.

So, no team player — that was for sure!

But at the same time, and it pained him to admit it, Geoff was impressed with Knox's performance. It had been clear to him from the outset that Knox was the man in the hot seat and that if anyone was going to get blamed for Clare's death it was Knox. Knox was the man who ran the bloody youth scheme and — according to everyone except Knox himself — the man who had organized the trip to the mountains. And yet here he was on the TV, as bold as brass, painting himself as the hero of the hour: not only had he counselled against the trip, he had — in his version of events — kept his head when all around him had lost their marbles.

And how clever of him, thought Geoff, to do all that emoting on camera: in the eyes of the media, Knox was pretty bullet-proof now, a friend of the family, a father to Clare and almost as upset by her death as the mother herself. How could anyone be callous enough to suggest that maybe Selwyn Knox should take some — if not all — of the blame for what went wrong?

And Geoff couldn't help admiring the final master stroke of Knox's performance: leaving the media with something to throw the story forward, something to distract them away from Selwyn Knox and someone else to chew on. By dropping in the safety campaign right at the end, Knox had shifted the spotlight away from himself and straight onto the government. Now the government was the villain for not having regulations to stop accidents on mountains! What a devious bastard!

★　★　★

Nine fourteen a.m. 'Ride of the Valkyries' ringing on the mobile.

Always a welcome event for Selwyn Knox.

Always a sign that someone wanted him, needed him, was taking an interest in him.

'Knox here.'

'Selwyn, it's Bob Travers and it's bad news. You'd better get down here pronto. The guy from London is hitting the roof. He's on the phone now to Charlie McDonald in Downing Street and he says he wants to see you right away. Can I tell him you're on your way? You are on your way aren't you, Selwyn?'

'Yeah. Tell him I'll be there. It's about my statement to the press, is it?'

'Damn right it is. You've put your foot in it there, good and proper. You're not going to be London's blue-eyed boy any more after this, I can tell you. You can wave goodbye to a seat in parliament.'

'All right, Bob, keep your hair on. We'll see. Tell Maddle I'll be there in a couple of hours; there's a few things I need to do first.'

'A couple of hours? He's not going to like that. He says — '

Knox cut the connection.

★ ★ ★

The Valkyries were riding again.

And this time the ring was tinged with something else.

Not fear. Not panic.

But apprehension — an unaccustomed doubt whether the summons from the outside world would be the harbinger of new glories, accolades, promotions.

'Hello, Knox here.'

'Oh . . . hi, Selwyn.'

The voice was familiar, but somehow hesitant. 'Who's that?'

'It's Nigel — Nigel Tonbridge from BBC Radio Strathclyde.'

'Oh, Nigel. Of course. How are you?'

Selwyn was back in his stride now. A local journalist. Something he knew how to deal with. 'Do you want a quote on the tragedy? What happened was awful and we need to learn the lessons for the future. Safety on school trips and youth club outings needs to be codified and policed by the government. Is that OK?'

'Yeah, that's fine, Selwyn. I got all your stuff

from the news conference as well, so we're OK on that. I'm just ringing about something different.'

'Oh yeah. What's that? Fire away.'

'It's a bit tricky, Sel. I'm not sure how to put this.'

For the first time in the conversation, Knox hesitated.

'Well, I can't guess what it is, Nigel. You'll have to tell me.'

'OK. I've been speaking to Ian Murray.'

'Yeah . . . and? What's he saying?'

Murray the councillor, old school Project party . . . Knox knew from council meetings that Murray was a plodder. Thorough, but lacking imagination. No future in the New Project party. Not like Selwyn Knox.

'Well, he had a couple of things to say about you, Sel. He said you broke ranks with the council; he says you didn't turn up for the councillors' meeting on the Clare O'Leary tragedy — '

'Yeah, so what? Somebody had to get out there and talk to the press. Those old farts don't realize you can't spend hours wittering away to yourselves when the media needs to be given some proper information. They'd still be in there now if I hadn't gone and done it — that's not for quoting, by the way.'

'Yeah, Sel, I know that. But what Murray's saying is that you went out on a limb. You didn't stick to what the council wanted to say about the tragedy.'

'Oh yeah. Like what?'

45

'Well, you know Murray. He won't go into details. He's a bit old schoolish. But he didn't sound happy with you at all. In fact, he sounded pretty angry.'

'Yeah? So what?'

'Look, Sel. Reading between the lines, I think they're all a bit pissed off with you. Partly because you've come out of this looking like the hero of the hour, partly because they've all been made to look stupid. And partly because they're shit scared the council's going to get blamed for the whole thing. If you're the only one who actually went out looking for the kid after she went missing and all the others just ran round like headless chickens, it doesn't look good for them, does it?'

'I can't help that, Nigel. I've made my position clear — that I was against this trip in the first place. That I wasn't convinced it met even the most basic safety standards. And that I did everything in my power to find poor little Clare when she went missing — despite the panic in the group leaders' ranks. And now I'll be lobbying hard for national legislation to make school trips and youth club outings safe in the future. It's going to be my crusade, Nigel, and I'll take it to the national press, to parliament and to the government. We need proper guidelines for the supervision of children when they're taken out on trips like this. I'm going to make sure something is done about this scandal.'

'Yeah, I know, Sel. It's a good issue to take up. It'll do you no harm either. But what Murray is saying is more to do with what actually

46

happened up there on the mountain.'

Selwyn Knox hesitated again, and this time Nigel Tonbridge noticed it . . .

'What exactly is Murray saying, Nigel? I need to know what he's been saying to you.'

'Well, what he says, Selwyn, is that he saw no evidence of your heroics up on the mountain.'

'Of course, he didn't. He was pissing around at base camp while I was out looking for the bloody girl.'

'Yeah. Murray doesn't dispute that. He's not trying to make himself a hero. But he is saying that you hadn't been with the party for quite a long time before they noticed Clare was missing. And that you only came back much later.'

'Nigel! You weren't there. I was. Conditions up there were atrocious. You couldn't see a yard in front of your nose. No one knew where anyone was. We all got lost and started going round in circles. It's no good one member of the team trying to stir up trouble for the others.'

'I don't think Murray is trying to do that. OK, he's pretty annoyed about you missing the councillors' meeting to speak to the press. But he's not trying to do a whitewash on this. I think he's unhappy at the way you've been portrayed as the good guy in the white hat and made all the rest of them look like idiots.'

'OK, so he's not proud of messing up. What's that got to do with me?'

'Listen, Sel . . . the thing is — Murray's saying that you and Clare both went missing *before* the fog came down. And that you came back much, much later, on your own. So for one thing they had no idea what you were doing all the time they were regrouping. And for another Murray claims that when you came back you said straight away you'd been out looking for Clare. He says no one had told you anyone had gone missing, so there was no way you could've known about Clare — *unless you were with her when she got lost!* Were you with her, Selwyn? How did you know Clare was missing? Were you with Clare O'Leary when she disappeared? . . . '

There was a pause on the line. Then Knox, his voice strained, rattled.

'Look, Nigel! I'm not going to stand here and listen to you calling me a liar! I know what I did! I tried to save Clare!'

Selwyn Knox was flustered. He knew he was flustered and he knew it was showing. He was angry with himself for letting it show. He prided himself on not letting things show.

'The others can say what they like, Nigel. They messed up. It's their fault. And I did my best to put things right. I'm still doing my best to put things right. To stop this sort of thing happening again in the future. So how dare they try to blame me? How dare they try to excuse themselves and blame me? They've got absolutely no evidence of anything . . . of any of what they're saying . . . they're trying to drop me in it to save themselves, Nigel. That's what they're doing!'

'Look, it's not me who's saying this. It's Ian Murray. He's Project party. He's your colleague. All I'm doing is telling you what Murray has said to me.'

48

'And all I'm saying is that if you broadcast any of this you won't have a leg to stand on. There's nothing behind all this. Nothing at all. Murray and the others have got no proof of anything. I'll string the bastards up if they repeat it again — and I'll string you up too!'

'Look, Sel — '

'They've got no evidence of anything. What can they say? They were all pissing around doing nothing at base camp and I was out there trying to save the girl. What can they say against that?'

'Look, Sel, don't have a go at me — '

The phone call was abruptly terminated. Nigel Tonbridge was left with a dialling tone and the first vague suspicions that he might actually have a story.

3

Selwyn Knox didn't arrive at Exxington District Council until eleven o'clock. Two hours, five strong coffees, a lot of thinking and numerous phone calls after Geoff Maddle had first summoned him.

Geoff Maddle was not happy.

Geoff Maddle was not used to being dissed by redneck councillors from the back of beyond. Even if they might become Charlie McDonald's or Andy Sheen's little favourite.

'Where the hell have you been? I told you to get down here straight away!'

'Good morning, Mr Maddle. My name is Selwyn Knox.'

'I know what your bloody name is, mate. Don't piss around with me. You know who I am and you damn well know who sent me here. So you'd better start explaining what the hell you think you're up to.'

'I'm not sure what you want me to explain. I've been doing my best for Exxington District Council and for the Project party. I take it you know that I've been comforting Clare's parents in my role as youth scheme leader?'

'Too damn right I do. Me and several hundred thousand other people saw you all over the television this morning. And who gave you permission to do that? No one bloody did! I didn't. Charlie McDonald didn't. Andy Sheen didn't. So what do you think you were up to?'

'All right, Geoff. I know I should have cleared it with you, but it just happened, really. I was at the house trying to help the O'Learys — I thought you'd approve of that, showing the Project group in a compassionate light and so forth. But then all the media and the TV crews turned up and they kept asking Eileen O'Leary to go out and talk to them. Now I knew we needed to control the situation — you guys are always telling us we should control news situations and not let the story get out of hand, right? And I knew that if Eileen went out on her own she could have said some very damaging things, you know, about the council — and about Ian Murray not doing anything to make sure Clare didn't wander off and get lost up there in the mountains — so I had a quick word with Eileen and told her that she should just make a short statement. I told her not to answer any questions because the media always try to distort whatever you say. I said I'd answer any questions on her behalf, and she agreed because she trusts me. I've known Clare and her family for two years now under the Project group's 'Help the Community' initiative — we've been doing some pretty good work on that, Geoff, I'll have to tell you about it sometime. It's certainly got New Project a good name with the poorer voters, New Project voters, Geoff, people who are going to keep Exxington New Project — '

'Look, Knox, cut the crap! You know what I'm talking about. It's all the stuff you've been saying to the media that's got Charlie McDonald pissed

51

off — and Andy Sheen too. They want to know why you made yourself out to be the hero in all this and left the council to carry the can.'

'Geoff, I had to do it! No one else from the council was standing up to be counted so someone had to talk to the press. Otherwise they would have just written whatever they wanted and that wouldn't have been good for the Project party. Your guys in London, all the New Project spin doctors, they're always telling us, 'Never leave a story without a comment. Never let the hacks write unguided because they'll get it wrong.' Now that's just plain good sense. And that's all I was trying to do! I mean, let's get real on this one: there's been a pretty big cock-up; it's some of our councillors who are to blame, and the flak's coming our way. So I reckoned the best thing was to be up-front, to say, 'OK, someone made a mistake, mistakes happen, mistakes are human; Ian Murray is basically a good guy, but he should never have been leading that expedition up in the mountains. He messed up, but — hey — there was nothing evil about what happened up there. He just took his eye off the ball.' And you know, Geoff, I think people will respect us for that sort of honesty. They'll see we're human too. So it's no longer Exxington Council that made the mistake, it's no longer the New Project party that's in the dock: it's just one old codger who bit off more than he could chew. And another thing: can I tell you why I was a bit late coming here to see you, Geoff? It's because I've spent the last two hours giving exactly that message to all the media — '

'You've what? You mad bastard! Who told you to do that? You must be joking! You've been doing all the press calls — ?'

'Yes, Geoff, but don't get angry. Let me tell you what the response has been. It's been really good — '

'Wait a minute! Why does Exxington Council employ a press office? And why have I just spent all morning telling that press office what to say if the press ring for a comment? Why have you been doing a job that someone else is trained to do . . . and . . . and paid to do?'

'Oh, Geoff, if you knew the council press office the way I do, you'd know you can't rely on them for anything. I always do my own press work. That way you can be sure the message gets across without any intermediaries and without any cock-ups. I don't want to tell you of all people how to suck eggs, but I always find the media respect a politician much more if he talks to them direct instead of hiding behind press officers, you know. Anyway, let me tell you how this story is running with the media. I've talked to virtually all the nationals and our local contacts, and they all agree this was an unfortunate tragedy and nothing more. One or two of them are going to have a go at Ian Murray, but not as a councillor, just as a bloke who got out of his depth. And the overriding emphasis in all the papers is going to be on poor Clare and the human tragedy. It's not going to be a political story, I can promise you that. You can relax — '

Geoff Maddle thought for a moment.

'Are you completely sure of that, Selwyn? You're not spinning me a line, are you? Because if you are — '

'Absolutely not, Geoff. Absolutely not. The press are swallowing what I've been telling them. But I'll be completely honest with you — there's just one guy who's got me a bit worried. We've got a reporter at our local BBC station up here — name of Nigel Tonbridge — a bit of a wanker, really, too big for his boots, real bigot, anti-Project, poodle of the Tories. He's been out to get the New Project group for months now and I think from talking to him he may have a go at the council for lax safety practices on this trip — '

'What makes you say that? Has he got something we don't know about? What's his angle?'

'I don't think he's got an angle exactly. He's just talking in general terms, you know, about the council's record on safety and how they shouldn't have let the expedition go up the mountains. That sort of thing. But I know Tonbridge and he's likely to use this as a political football. I'm pretty sure he's going to have a go at the Project party for not introducing proper safety legislation for school trips — '

'Oh, shit! That's exactly what we don't need. That'll really stir things up. And that's something else I need to speak to you about, Selwyn, by the way, about this daft idea you've got for some sort of safety campaign. We're going to have a problem with that one. But look, first things first. First we've got to knock this Tonbridge guy on the head. How did you leave things with him?'

'Well, we've got a bit of time, Geoff. His show's on air this evening at five o'clock and I said I'd get back to him with something this afternoon. But to be honest, I think we need to do something about him before then. I think we need to put Nigel Tonbridge back in his box! Actually, there is one thing I was just wondering about. You've got that computer at headquarters, haven't you? What's it called? Lancelot, isn't it? — the one that keeps all the useful information on politicians and people you think might be anti-Project? Do you think there's any chance you could have a look on it for something on this Nigel Tonbridge guy? We'd have to be pretty quick, though, that's the only problem — '

'Hah! Don't worry about that, mate. Lancelot is quicker than quick! I could put the call in now and we'd have all the gen on Nigel Tonbridge back with us in no time at all.'

'Well, do you think you could do that for me, Geoff? It would be really useful — and then I'll get back to Tonbridge a.s.a.p. and make sure he doesn't dump on the Project party. And then perhaps we could talk about my campaign for school-trip safety legislation — ?'

★ ★ ★

There are few feelings in the life of a journalist to equal the intensity of emotion involved in tracking a scoop. When that scoop combines the pathos of human tragedy, the revulsion of human depravity and the whiff of political scandal, the

55

emotion can be overwhelming.

Nigel Tonbridge was on a high.

His thoughts roamed incessantly between the horror of Clare's lonely death, the enormity of the allegations he alone was privy to and the possibility that a man like Selwyn Knox could actually be a murderer. Selwyn Knox the youth scheme leader, Selwyn Knox the pillar of the community, the sanctimonious holier-than-thou puritan with a gleaming future as a New Project MP? Surely not.

And even as Nigel churned over all the implications of what he knew, or felt he knew, another thought lurked in the back of his mind — consciously repressed, constantly resurfacing — a premonition that this story could be the turning point in his own career, the breakthrough all journalists seek and few achieve. The anticipation of what it could lead to filled his mind with images of fame and success: Nigel Tonbridge, the investigative journalist; Nigel Tonbridge, the righter of wrongs; Nigel Tonbridge, the guest of chat shows and national TV debates. It was a somewhat ignoble thought when a young girl had just died, but he found it hard to shake off.

First, though, he had to convince the guardians of BBC Radio Strathclyde that his story was kosher and that he, Nigel Tonbridge, should get on the air and tell the world.

Nigel's news editor, George Young, was one of those hacks who probably enjoy being referred to as hardbitten, the type of journalist who's been round the houses and come back with a few bumps and scrapes to prove it. For George, scandal was not new. Forty years in the BBC, forty years of competent, unspectacular news processing had left him, if not exactly cynical, then at least hard to impress. And George knew his journalistic law. He was the man who'd been copy-tasting on the BBC's general news desk in Broadcasting House in London the night news of John Profumo's affair with Christine Keeler had broken. George had dropped the story because he wasn't going to risk the Secretary of State for Defence suing the Corporation for defamation. Ever since then he had been known as 'the man who spiked Profumo'. Nigel knew he would have a fight on his hands.

'Listen, son,' George replied, after pausing to digest the story Nigel had breathlessly spilled out, 'I'm going to give you some good advice. That's a pretty good story and it'd be hot as mustard for any journalist who can stand it up. But right now it's a passport to disaster. Just think about it for a minute. You've got a girl dead up a mountain. You've got a local councillor, Calvinist pillar of the community — no previous, no fangs, no dribbling saliva — and you're going to tell the world he's a child murderer? Not on my radio station, you're not! I'd need a lot more proof than you've given me before I'd let you loose on the airwaves with that story.'

'But, George, you think about it, too. This is the biggest story we've ever had up here — well, except for the spy in the shipyard last year. You know it's our chance to put Radio Strathclyde on the map. This Selwyn Knox is a big fish in the

57

Project party. He's going to be an MP pretty soon, you know — some people are saying he's a natural to be a minister in the government. So are we going to let him get away with it? Are we going to let someone like that run the country when we know he abused and killed a little girl? You can't let that happen, George. We've got to run with this story.'

'Keep your hat on, son. I didn't say I want to let him get away with anything, *if* he did it. And that's a pretty big if. Look, what have you got? You've got a councillor who says he thinks Knox took the little girl off and didn't come back until she was dead. But did anyone see him molesting her? Did anyone see him do her in? No. And has your councillor told the police about it? I thought it was *their* job to keep monsters out of government, not mine.'

'George, he's been to the police and they told him to get lost. The problem is Knox is best mates with the Exxington cops — I think he's best mates with everyone who has any clout round here. Anyway, Murray was basically told to keep quiet. The police and all the other journalists I've spoken to have decided this was just a tragic accident and that Selwyn Knox is the best thing since Mother Teresa. It's no good hoping PC Plod will sort this out for us because he won't.'

'OK, I can see that, Nige. But put yourself in my place, lad. If the police are saying it was an accident, then in my book that means to all intents and purposes it was an accident. We're not paid to go out on a limb to contradict the

58

strong arm of the law. That's not our job, is it?'

'Well, maybe it isn't, George. But how will you feel tonight if you go to bed knowing you were the only person who could stop a child abuser and murderer getting away with it and you'd done nothing?'

'Hang on a minute, Nigel. I didn't say we weren't going to do anything. I've got grandchildren, you know. I'm as upset as you are. It's just that I don't want to go off half-cock with a story that's going to collapse and drop us all in the shit. So you just calm down a bit and tell me again exactly what you've got. For a start, will your councillor — what's his name? Ian Murray — will he back us up if we do go public? Will he come on air and repeat what he's said to you? Can you get the girl's parents to finger Knox? Will Knox say anything himself?'

'George, look, I'm chasing all those leads. I've got calls in to everyone. But this is a difficult story and it's not going to be handed to us on a plate. At some stage we're going to have to be brave and start the ball rolling. We may not get it cut and dried before we hit the air with it, but once we go public I'm dead sure we'll get people confirming what we say about Knox. He must have abused other little girls too, I reckon. We just have to be the ones to start the ball rolling on this story.'

'Well, you probably haven't come to the right man if that's what you want to do, son,' said George with a wry smile. 'I'm the man who spiked Profumo, remember? Anyway, I'll tell you what I think. If we're serious, we're going to have

59

to clear the story with the BBC lawyers; there's no way we can avoid that, whatever way you look at it. And at the moment I haven't got a leg to stand on if I go to them with what you've told me. At the very least, you're going to have to go back to Ian Murray and get him to put something on tape. Then you'll need a statement from the family. And you'll have to run it past the police. OK? Do you think Murray will stick to his guns?'

'Yeah, I know he will. He was absolutely certain of what he was telling me. He said he'd discussed it with Dan Curragh, the other councillor who was up there, and they both agreed it was really fishy about Knox and the girl. But let's get this straight: if I get Murray to go firm on this, you'll let me put something out on air?'

George thought for a moment and grunted. 'Yes, I suppose so. It was a terrible thing about that little girl. If there really is something going on, someone's got to stand up and be counted.'

★ ★ ★

He didn't show it — he never did — but Selwyn Knox had an anxious few hours while he waited for Maddle and McDonald to interrogate Lancelot, waited for the dirt on Nigel Tonbridge that would put God back in his heaven and restore Selwyn Knox's universe back to its usual, pristine, calculated order.

Five o'clock was the deadline. The five o'clock show on BBC Radio Strathclyde — 'Drive Time,

60

Tonbridge Time'. It was coming fast.

And he had a few shocks to deal with in the meantime.

The Valkyries now were bringing Selwyn calls he would rather not receive.

'Is that Mr Knox? Hello . . . Selwyn? Yes, it's Eileen here, Eileen O'Leary. I'm sorry to bother you. It's just we're very upset . . . we're very upset about Clare, you know . . . and we need to ask you something. Is that all right? We've had the police on the phone. They took us to identify Clare's body . . . oh God, oh, Holy Mother of God . . . I can't . . . I can't . . . no, it's all right. Wait a minute, Mr Knox . . . what I need to ask you . . . the police have asked us . . . asked me and Frank, you know . . . asked us if we want an autopsy done on Clare — '

'What? When did they ask you that? That's ridiculous. I talked to the police and they said they wouldn't be doing one. Who told you — ?'

'No, Selwyn. They didn't say they have to do one. They just asked us if we want one. They said it was usual to do one in the circumstances.'

'Yes, usual but not strictly required. That's what they told me.'

'That's right. They told us the same. They aren't obliged to do one because there's no foul play involved or anything, and they say they don't want to put us through more than we've already been through — '

'Yes. That's right, Eileen. There's no need for an autopsy. Did you tell them that?'

'Yes, we did. That's what we thought too. But they said we had the choice if we wanted one.

61

And, you know, I just thought: what if there has been something wrong up in the mountains? What if it wasn't just an accident?'

'Eileen, look, I was up in the mountains. I know nothing happened to Clare. It was just a terrible accident. And you know I loved Clare like a father. So I just want what's best for her and for you. Think of her. Her poor little body has been through enough. We don't want anyone cutting her up with a knife, do we?'

'No . . . I suppose . . . no . . . you're right, Mr Knox. We'll tell them . . . OK. That's decided, then . . . I'll tell Frank to drop the idea . . . OK . . . right . . . I'm sure you're right. There's just one other thing . . . can I ask you about it? We've been refusing to talk to the press, like you told us, you know . . . but there's just one of them who's been pestering us . . . and actually we know him, and we'd like to talk to him if you don't mind . . . it's a boy called Nigel Tonbridge, who was in my little brother's class at school and now he's working for the BBC. He says he wants to talk about Clare and what she was like and things — '

The sharpness of Knox's response took Eileen by surprise.

'Listen, Eileen! There's no way you or Frank should talk to Nigel Tonbridge! He's not interested in Clare or her memory. We're the only ones who respect Clare, who loved Clare. You, Frank and me: we're the only ones. Tonbridge is like all journalists. All he wants to do is exploit Clare's memory and your tragedy to make his name as a journalist. He's only thinking about himself, take it from me. There's no way you should talk to him — all right? You trust me, don't you, Eileen?'

'Yes, but — '

'So you're not going to talk to him, are you?'

'No, I suppose not — '

'If he rings again, just tell him you can't talk to him and that I'm handling all questions so he should talk to me, all right? In fact, I'll ring him now, so you don't have to worry — '

'All right, Mr Knox. Thanks . . . thanks very much.'

★ ★ ★

'BBC Radio Strathclyde, Nigel Tonbridge speaking.'

'Yeah, hi. It's Selwyn Knox here.'

'Oh, yes. Thanks for ringing, Selwyn. I need to talk to you — '

'You've been pestering the O'Learys!'

'What? No I haven't. I just rang them for a comment. I was at school with Eileen Bates, Eileen O'Leary, that is — '

'I don't care. Just stop it. Stop ringing them. Enough has happened to them. They don't need people like you pestering them at a time like this. I've got a statement on their behalf. You'd better write it down because this is all you're going to get. Are you ready? 'Mr and Mrs O'Leary have suffered a great loss. Clare was a lovely child and will be greatly missed. The best thing now is for everyone to let Clare's memory rest in peace.' And that's what you'd better run tonight, Nigel.

That and nothing else. I'm referring to our earlier conversation. You know what I mean.'

'Well, look, Selwyn. I can't do that. You know I can't. I've got a pretty heavy story here, you know, the Ian Murray allegations and all that, I can't just drop it. Not unless you can tell me what really happened up there in the mountains. I need the truth, Selwyn. Can you give it to me?'

There was a brief pause. Then Knox, emollient now, suddenly helpful: 'OK. OK. Look, Nigel, don't do anything rash. I'll get back to you this afternoon. You're not on the air till five, are you? Don't do anything before then, OK? If you play this properly, I may have something for you in an hour or so. Something really big. But you have to hold on and not run the rubbish you've got from Murray. OK?'

'Yeah. OK, Selwyn, I'll wait. But you're going to give it to me straight, aren't you?'

'I am, Nigel. That's a promise. Just wait until you hear from me. OK?'

★   ★   ★

'Hello, this is Ian Murray's voicemail at Exxington District Council. I'm not here at the moment, so please leave a message and I'll get back to you as soon as possible. Please talk after the tone — '

'Murray, it's Selwyn Knox here, you bastard. It's one o'clock. You've been speaking to the press. You know what I'm talking about. Well, it's all crap that you've been telling them. It's absolutely untrue. There's not a shred of

64

evidence and you're making some really libellous allegations. Oh, and another thing. Don't think I don't know about your expenses' scam: it's up to about twelve thousand pounds now, isn't it? And how your sister-in-law jumped the queue for a council house. I don't think those little facts would help your career if they got out — in fact, *you* probably wouldn't get out for six months minimum! So think about it — and you may decide you want to get on to Tonbridge and tell him you made a mistake. Which you most certainly did — '

★ ★ ★

'George, can I talk to you?'

Nigel Tonbridge was bringing his editor bad news.

'Yeah, come in, Nige. Had any luck standing up your big story?'

'Well, it's a bit tricky. It's sort of 'good news, bad news'. The first thing is that I've just rung Ian Murray again to ask him if he'll put something on tape.'

'And?'

'Well, I think he's been nobbled. He won't talk to me any more. He says he made a mistake when he rang me this morning and he's retracted everything he said.'

'Oh, well, that's the end of that one!' To Nigel's annoyance, George Young sounded mightily relieved. 'To tell you the truth, I never thought we'd get the story past the lawyers. It all sounded so tenuous. And Selwyn Knox, well

65

. . . he's such a respected man; such a big fish in this town — '

'Yeah, but hang on a minute, George. For me, this doesn't kill the story. I think Murray's been warned off. He was so certain this morning. And now he's saying exactly the opposite, contradicting himself. It doesn't add up unless Knox has scared him off somehow. Anyway, the other thing is . . . I told you there was good news, bad news. Well, the good news is that Knox rang me himself, unprompted. So I reckon he's pretty worried about this story. At first he tried to warn me off; but when he saw I was serious he changed his tone completely and he's promised to ring back this afternoon before the show goes on air. He says he's got something really big to tell me. So if you'll authorize it, what I'd like to do is set up a tape to record his conversation with me — you know, covert taping. It's a bit tricky under BBC guidelines, so we'll have to testify that it's in the public interest. Is that OK? Then I'll get him to talk about what happened on the mountain and if we can get him on tape in his own words, we can definitely run something on the show, can't we, George?'

'Hmm. Maybe — ' George Young looked dubious.

Nigel Tonbridge took it as a yes and went to set up the tape recorder.

★ ★ ★

'Good afternoon, Nigel, Selwyn Knox here. I promised I'd ring you back and I always keep my promises.'

'Oh, great. Thanks, Selwyn. Just wait a minute while I go to another phone. Don't hang up if the line goes dead for a moment. OK? . . . Right. Here we are. Now, Selwyn Knox . . . what do you have to say to me, Mr Knox?'

'Just a couple of things, Mr Tonbridge. The first is that you have been threatening me in a most scandalous way. Your allegations are, of course, completely false and what's more they are highly libellous.

'You have no evidence, no witnesses and no testimony to support your allegations. Since I am completely innocent in this matter, I can only put your behaviour down to a highly unprofessional political bias on your part against the New Project party, a bias that does you and the BBC no credit at all.

'My second point is that if you persist in repeating the sort of thing you have been saying, and in particular if any mention of it is ever made on air in any shape or form, I will see you in court in less time than it takes to say 'record libel damages'.

'And don't think you'll be able to count on any support from your corrupt and prejudiced former informant on the council because you won't.

'Finally, just in case you are recording this conversation, Mr Tonbridge, I want to make something very clear to you. I want you to know that I am aware of things about you and your past that show you in an extremely unfavourable light.'

Nigel felt as if a charge of electricity had

surged down the phone line and rattled his headphones.

'What's that? What did you say?'

Knox's voice was calm, exaggeratedly deliberate.

'I said I know about your guilty secret, Nigel. I know what happened with you and your father — '

Nigel felt the electric shock in his ears; felt it burning in his brain.

'I don't know what you mean — '

'Oh, but I think you do, Nigel. I think you most certainly do.'

★　★　★

At four p.m. a white-faced Nigel Tonbridge was in George Young's office for the regular pre-show planning meeting.

'Sit down, Nigel. You look whacked. How's the big story? Did you get anything on the tape?'

For a moment Nigel sat motionless, deep in thought. Finally, he looked up and mumbled, 'No. I guess you were right, George. There's nothing in the story. There's nothing on the tape. In fact, the machine didn't work. And anyway Knox seems pretty innocent. He didn't really have anything to tell me. Nothing we could use. I must have got a bum steer from someone. I think we'd better forget it, if that's all right with you.'

Not surprisingly, it was more than all right with George Young, the man who spiked Profumo. 'OK, that's that, then. Now, let's have a think about a new lead for the show. I think the Clare O'Leary story has pretty much run its course. No one else seems to be covering it any more, so I think we can drop it. Now, if you agree, Nigel, I think we should lead the show on the investigation into the state of the town swimming pool. Apparently, there are loose tiles and dangerous seating. It seems someone had to have tetanus jabs after sitting on a rusty nail. So let's see if we can get the public health inspector to come on the show — OK?'

★   ★   ★

That evening in the Exxington Arms, Geoff Maddle was finally starting to loosen up. The dead-girl story had gone away with no damage to the party and Geoff was toasting his success with what was either his fourth or his fifth whisky.

'Anyway, well done, Selwyn, mate! I don't mind telling you, I listened to the opening headlines on that Nigel Tonbridge show with a bit of trepidation. So when they led on the swimming pool and the fat lady with the rusty nail in her arse I was well pleased! And not a mention of dead girls or New Project party councils. Charlie's just been on the blower from Number Ten and he says the first editions of tomorrow's nationals are looking pretty good, too. So well done. We got a result there. We'll have to get rid of that dope Ian Murray, of course. You know that, don't you?

Don't you lose sleep over Murray, mate! I've told him he has to step down on health grounds. No great loss, if you ask me. The only thing is, Selwyn, you'll have to drop your bloody school-trip safety campaign — it's a pain in the arse, to tell you the truth. It's really embarrassing the government, you know. Andy's in deep shit with the teachers' unions and the select committee, so he's asking you as a favour — and Charlie and me are asking you, too — to drop it, mate. OK?'

Knox was a man to recognize his chance when he saw it. He thought for a moment, smiled and said, 'Hey! If Charlie McDonald and Andy Sheen want me to drop it, what can I say? But listen, Geoff, we're all politicians and we all live in the real world. I've done you one favour today and now you're asking me to do you another one. So what do I get in return?'

'Well, you've got balls, mate, that's for sure! You were pretty ruthless dealing with the media too — pretty ruthless and pretty smart. And, you know what, that's the sort of attitude we like. I reckon you could go far. I know Charlie and Andy think pretty highly of you too. So if you're looking for a pay-off for today, why don't you think about coming to join us, say, on the media-management side of things — down in London, I mean. Get out of this dump, eh?'

But Selwyn Knox had his sights set on bigger things. 'I was thinking about a seat, Geoff. I'm a natural for an MP. Can you give me that?'

Geoff Maddle broke into a grin. 'Hey, hey! Somehow I thought you might say that. Well, that's not something yours truly can deliver, but you know what? I do know a man who might be able to. What do you think? Shall I get him on the mobile and see what he says?'

Geoff Maddle dialled a familiar number, went through a familiar switchboard, heard a familiar voice and passed the mobile to Selwyn Knox.

★   ★   ★

The following day, 11 September 2006, two hijacked planes crashed into Canary Wharf, wiping out Britain's tallest building and two thousand lives.

In Whitehall, a New Project party special adviser sent an email suggesting it was a good day to put out some of the difficult news stories the party would prefer the media to overlook.

In Exxington, Clare O'Leary was buried; so was Selwyn Knox's school-trip safety campaign.

★   ★   ★

In Downing Street three weeks later, Prime Minister Andy Sheen found time to sign — although not to read — the note that Charlie McDonald had written for him to welcome their latest recruit.

Dear Selwyn,
    Terror and war are looming again. We need determined, ruthless people like you. Come

71

and join us as an MP. Help us protect the values of our society.

Yours,

Andy Sheen

PART TWO

4

FEBRUARY 2011

Selwyn Knox gazed at his own image in the brightly lit mirror of the chrome and glass en-suite bathroom attached to his ministerial office.

Knox liked the new Department of Commerce building on Marsham Street: it was clean and bright; it was sparse, bold, modernist; it looked to the future; it was not mired in the past.

He used to say the building mirrored his own character.

It was four years since he'd shaved off his beard and he felt the clean-shaven look was in keeping with the dynamic, pared-down, stripped-for-action image he and the New Project party were striving to convey.

It was four years since Selwyn Knox had become an MP.

The Canary Wharf tragedy had enflamed Prime Minister Andy Sheen's lust for revenge and in February 2007 he'd called a snap election on an 'Endorse the Next War' ticket.

At Sheen's invitation, Knox had contested and won a difficult campaign in a Scottish constituency vacated by an Old Project dinosaur who Charlie McDonald had helped persuade to step down.

And it was now two years to the day since

Knox had landed his first cabinet post, rising by way of junior ministerial jobs in education and environment to become one of the youngest — if not the youngest ever — Secretary of State for Commerce.

As he stared into his face in the mirror, Knox reflected on his rise and rise; but his gaze did not soften with emotion. It remained hard and inscrutable. If his progress were to continue — which he knew it must — those eyes would have to stay cold, stay ruthless, stay merciless.

★ ★ ★

Knox did not blink even when Sonya Mair, his political adviser, tapped gently on the bathroom door.

Another minute went by. He passed his hand over his face, switched off the bathroom light and walked in darkness through the connecting door to his office.

As he slumped into the leather armchair, Sonya shrugged her shoulders and let the slip she was wearing slither to the carpet.

In the evening gloom, her body was silhouetted in the moonlit window and her luminous skin glowed like a siren's, calling men to their doom. The languor of her movements, her sensuous grace — at once serene yet arousing — were the language of her siren tongue. Her flesh voiced pleasures that men with eyes and ears unbound were fated to struggle against and then succumb to — ineluctably to drown.

She sensed Knox's eyes lingering on her flesh. Her body moved faster; her nails brushed hurried patterns on her naked skin.

She slid across the room, moving closer, still not looking him in the face.

She enjoyed this foreplay, this moment of maximum exposure. She enjoyed unveiling her naked flesh to a man's probing stare; she enjoyed hiding her eyes to allow men's gaze unhindered access to her body, to its intimate vulnerability, its welcoming secrets.

Sonya knew that this moment of anticipation, of contact achingly delayed, could not often be prolonged, that physical invasion rapidly followed the invasion of men's eyes.

Now, though, she waited and as the waiting was drawn out she began to sense something other, a deviation from the rite's habitual course.

Now the moment of transition — the moment of turbulent, fleshly onslaught — was slow in coming.

Knox's gaze was on her — she knew it, she felt it, but where was his expected touch? Where were his hands invading her body? Why was her anticipation not eliciting a response?

She risked a furtive glance from under lowered eyelids.

She saw her boss on the green leather armchair, slouched, as when she had last looked at him. His eyes were fixed, intent, rapt almost, but devoid of desire, devoid of expression.

Her flesh shivered under Knox's gaze.

She was puzzled, unused to this absence of complicity, alarmed to discover his lack of

77

participation in the rite she had been performing — and had mistakenly believed he was sharing.

She drew closer to her boss; she leaned over him, tall, slender, naked.

'It's no good, Sonya,' Knox said petulantly. 'It's not right . . . we need to try something else — '

★ ★ ★

'Jack! Your car's ready! The driver says the police barricades are all operating between here and Downing Street, so you'll need to leave soon if you want to get there on time. Shall I tell Tim?'

Jack Willans did not look pleased. The prospect of a stop-start drive through the anti-terrorist searches all the way from Dock-lands to Whitehall was bad enough; the thought of the grilling that lay in store for him from Andy Sheen and Charlie McDonald was infinitely worse.

'Yeah, OK, Linda. Tell Tim to hurry up. And tell him to bring the Operation Colditz papers with him. I'll meet him downstairs in the garage.'

2011 was shaping up to be a crucial year for DRE plc.

The fallout from the early struggles over Iraq in the first half of the noughties, back when Labour was in power, and the subsequent Allied invasions of Iran, Syria and Saudi Arabia had been a disaster for most of the top FTSE 100 companies. The Stock Exchange had fallen dramatically and had still not recovered signifi-cantly.

But for defence stocks the lengthy series of Middle East Wars, now universally known as the MEWs, had been a godsend.

Years in the doldrums following the Cold War had been replaced by full order books and production lines working at a pace not seen since the heady days of the Second World War.

As chief executive of Britain's number-two defence company, Jack Willans had made his own name and a fortune for his shareholders.

DRE's weapons systems had been deployed in virtually every phase of the long-running MEWs, from the initial air war when DRE laser-guided bombs had wiped out the bulk of the region's industrial base, through escalating deployment of ground forces, when DRE's night-sights and battlefield communication systems had been widely used in the fierce hand-to-hand fighting, to the still continuing guerrilla wars, in which DRE's short-range ground-to-ground projectiles were repeatedly unleashed against the mosques and so-called 'civilian hospitals' sheltering enemy troops.

So for a long time DRE had been flavour of the month, the darling of the New Project party and exploited relentlessly by government ministers whenever they needed an example of British enterprise to hold up to the rest of the world. For Jack Willans, success had brought a seat in the House of Senators and the self-interested but nonetheless prestigious attentions of a gushing Andy Sheen.

Flattering profiles in the country's leading journals had been followed by nominations as

Businessman of the Year and a middle-rank place in the *Today* programme's Man of the Campaign awards.

Through it all genial Jack had kept his feet firmly on the ground, shrugging off the adulation of the City with a ruddy-faced smile and his frequently repeated claim that 'I was just in the right place at the right time.'

In fact, Jack Willans had never been much of a publicity seeker.

When the MEWs had really hotted up and business began to boom for DRE, the board had brought in a top PR man, Stephen Hadley from Granwick Communications, to handle the deluge of media attention. With requests for press and broadcast interviews pouring into DRE's Docklands headquarters from leading media figures in virtually every country, Hadley used to say his job was money for old rope.

But even Stephen Hadley couldn't crack the Jack Willans nut: instead of seizing the free publicity as Stephen constantly urged him to, Jack would respond with a wry grin and a slightly pained expression. 'But, you know, I did a pile of media engagements last month. Let's give the public a bit of a rest from my ugly mug, hey?'

When the media became insistent and the PR people told him he really should reconsider, he would reply, 'Why don't you get Tim to do them?'

But using the irascible Tim Stilwell, the finance director who ran DRE's mergers and acquisitions division under a rule of terror, substituting barked orders and tantrums for Jack Willans's charm and charisma, was a suggestion Stephen Hadley and his communications directorate were never keen to take up.

★　★　★

Tim Stilwell's secretary leaned her head round the door and coughed quietly. Stilwell did not look up.

'Er, Tim — '

'What is it, Deirdre?'

'Er, Senator Willans says it's time to go. You've got your Downing Street appointment at nine. And he says will you bring the Colditz strategy paper, please?'

Tim Stilwell uttered an oath and grumbled his way from the fifth floor to the basement garage. As he slumped into the back seat of the BMW, his greeting to Jack Willans was less than effusive.

'So we're off to see the lovely shiny Sheen, are we? I hope he's not going to give us any shit over Colditz!'

'Me too, Tim. But I don't think he's going to be very happy — '

'So what's he going to do? Take your senatorship back?'

'Oh! Don't mention the senatorship, Tim!' Jack Willans smiled wryly. 'I reckon they only gave it to me so I'd be their tame businessman — backing the PM's loony schemes and helping them bash the unions, you know. And I keep getting slagged off for not going to the House of

Senators enough — I think I went twice last year. Did you see that article in the *Guardian* saying I've got the worst attendance record of any of the new appointed senators since the Upper Senate was created? I have been loyal to Andy, though, so he can't fault me on that — it should be useful when we tell him about this Colditz thing.'

'It had bloody well better be, Jack. By the way, let me do the talking in Downing Street. If Sheen and McDonald give us any grief, I'm not going to roll over and surrender just because you're a pal of Andy Sheen's. OK?'

Jack Willans depended heavily on the hyperactive Tim Stilwell. A charismatic chief executive was one thing — and Jack was genuinely popular with the staff — but everyone in DRE recognized that it was Stilwell who pulled the strings in terms of the financial aggression, deal-making and marketing strategy that had brought DRE its very profitable relationship with the UK military and the Ministry of Defence. What was more, Tim Stilwell was well aware of Jack's dependence and treated him accordingly.

'Look, Jack, the first thing we need to say to Sheen and McDonald is that they owe us one for everything we've done for the war effort. They'd be in even deeper shit than they are now if we hadn't fixed those night-sights for the occupation forces. How many British soldiers are dying in Iraq and Iran and Syria? About a hundred a month, isn't it? Well, without our night-sights I reckon we'd be losing a hundred a day and that's no lie. So the first thing to get straight is that they are in our debt, not the other way round. Then we need to remind them that DRE's success is about the one bright spot in their crappy economy at the moment. And who is that success down to? It's down to us, Jack. So when we tell them it's time for a change, they'd better believe we know what we're talking about. The plain fact is that the defence market has changed, and it's not our fault — '

By now the BMW had negotiated the army checkpoints and police chicanes along the Embankment and was drawing up to the armoured gates at the Whitehall end of Downing Street. The Portakabin which had previously housed the Number Ten security screening unit had been replaced after the failed Stinger attacks of 2008 by a permanent installation of brick and armoured glass: a business-like army captain briskly relieved Jack and Tim of their mobiles, belts and writing implements and exchanged their shoes for pairs of standard issue slippers. He apologized for this latter precaution, explained that it had been introduced in response to the growing spate of shoe bombers, but he said they were welcome to keep the slippers as souvenirs when they collected their belongings on departure.

Once inside the front lobby of Number Ten, the two men felt as though they had entered another world. After the impersonal efficiency of the security checks, the homely familiarity of a largely unchanged Downing Street was a pleasant token of continuing normality. The policeman checking their laissez-passer was reassuringly genial. Young policy unit officials wandered back and forth in casual shirts and sweaters, Tracey Emin wood-and-wire sculptures stood on rosewood tables and nine-year-old Alice Sheen sat on a hard-backed chair in the corner waiting for her driver to take her to school.

Within a few minutes, a smiling secretary had appeared to usher Jack and Tim along the corridor to the back stairs and up to the first floor. Depositing them in an empty, pastel-coloured conference room overlooking the garden, she took their orders for tea and coffee and apologized for the PM's late arrival: he was, she said, on his way back from a working breakfast with the Secretary of State for Commerce at the D of C. On hearing this, Tim Stilwell grimaced and put his hands together in an image of mock prayer: both Jack Willans and the departing secretary smiled at the allusion to the notoriously pious Selwyn Knox.

Tim Stilwell used the delay to give his chief executive a final pep talk.

'OK, Jack, so we tell Sheen we're getting out of defence, we tell him why we're doing it, and we tell him why we're selling to EES. You can do that bit. You can tell him the MEWs were good for us at the time of the big invasions. That's clear and we're not arguing with that. But now things have begun to change, and not for the better as far as DRE is concerned. We've seen an end to the big offensives. Now it's just a war of attrition. A guerrilla war. Skirmishes with the terrorists and all that, but nothing major since we destroyed Damascus and Tehran. So no more need for the big laser-guided bombs, no more need for ground-to-air missile systems. And that's not good news for DRE; we expanded pretty dramatically when the war was at its height and we've overstretched ourselves. We've left ourselves badly exposed — although that's for you to know, Jack, not for Andy Sheen and Charlie McDonald. When we see them, we don't give any hint of weakness, OK?'

At that moment the doors of the conference room burst open and Andy Sheen swept in, followed by the towering figure of Charlie McDonald and a retinue of officials and minders. Sheen was a man who radiated youth and vigour. He dominated the room, just as he dominated every room he entered. He was Britain's boldest, most radical Prime Minister in decades and he never let you forget it.

'Good morning, gentlemen. Jack, how are you? Haven't seen you in the House of Senators for a while — only joking! And you must be Tim. Hello, Tim. I know all about your exploits, of course. Now sit down everyone, please. Let me introduce Charlie McDonald — he's my director of strategy and, as you know, much more powerful than I am . . . ha, ha! And Geoff Maddle. Geoff is Charlie's very capable right-hand man. Now I think we want to keep this quite tight, so Cedric, Billy, Julie, Helen and the rest of you — could you all go and make yourselves useful elsewhere, please? Thank you. We've got an hour scheduled for this meeting and I'll kick off. Now, Jack, I hear you're scheming to get out of the defence market. I hear you want to sell your business to English Electronic Systems, so I'm going to tell you straight away: I don't think that is a good idea!'

Jack Willans's face fell through the floor.

Apart from himself, Stilwell and the three other members of the highly restricted Operation Colditz team, no one was supposed to have any idea of DRE's plans to escape from the contracting defence market — to do a Colditz, as they'd jokingly called it. And yet Andy Sheen knew all about it; he even knew who DRE were planning to sell to: English Electronic Systems, their major British rivals — their only British rivals — the only other major defence firm in the UK.

Jack was almost lost for words. 'Er, Andy, I'm not quite sure what you're telling me here. Do you know about the Operation Colditz plan? How did — ?'

'Jack, I'm the Prime Minister. It's my job to know what is going on in this country and to know it in good time. I know all about your plans. I take it that *is* what you wanted to talk to me about this morning?'

Tim Stilwell told Jack later that at that moment he looked like a rabbit caught in the headlights of an onrushing Ferrari. Far from negotiating from a position of strength, Jack Willans spent the next fifteen minutes firmly on the back foot, outlining all the problems the slow-down in the MEWs was causing for DRE, and revealing how desperate the company was to restructure.

It took a firm kick under the table from Tim Stilwell to get Jack to shut up and hand the floor over to his deputy.

'Thank you, Jack. Thank you very much. Now, Prime Minister, I think I heard you say that you don't believe DRE should get out of defence. But I am here to tell you that that is exactly what we are going to do. And I'll tell you why. The defence market is shrinking. There are no more big orders like the ones we had a few years ago. So DRE has several options. We can retrench; we can cut costs, downsize and carry on with the military communications gear. The night-sights business could break even, too. But it won't maintain the momentum we've had over the last eight years; it won't maintain DRE as the shining light of your ropy national economy, Prime Minister. And it would mean closing factories. It'd mean job losses, too, lots of job losses. Now I don't think you want that, do you? You don't want to see the one company that has done well for New Project and for Britain go down the drain, do you? So I think you should listen very carefully to what I'm offering you this morning. A business like DRE needs to stay dynamic, it needs to move forward to stay alive. So we are going to move forward. We're going to be positive. We're going to get out of defence and into bio-engineering! We're going into gene therapy, life extension and — best of all — into human cloning. There's no doubt whatsoever that it's where the future lies. Bio-engineering and human-cloning technology are what defence was eight years ago: a market about to boom; a

87

market with everything going for it — '

Charlie McDonald looked at Tim Stilwell and couldn't disguise a shudder of distaste. Who was this little runt to come here and threaten the Prime Minister of Great Britain? Who did he think he was talking to?

Andy Sheen, though, was maintaining his usual calm. He knew Willans and Stilwell held some strong cards, the talk of bio-engineering was intriguing and, most importantly, he knew the trap that he and Charlie McDonald had planned for DRE's unruly bosses was still poised to spring shut around Tim Stilwell's bony ankles. He nodded and asked Stilwell to continue.

'Well, just think about it, Prime Minister. The world's been a pretty dodgy place since the Middle East went up in flames. The terrorist attacks here have made people think about life: they've seen Canary Wharf, they've seen the gas victims on the Piccadilly line, they've seen the people killed by poison in the water supplies, and what do they think? They think: it could be me next! I might not still be here by the time Jeb Bush and your good self finally manage to sort the Arabs out! So what's their next thought? They think: maybe I should have a look at this bio-engineering lark; maybe I'll be a goner myself, but at least DRE could help me live on in some shape or form by cloning my DNA. Human cloning — it's a natural human desire and DRE could help satisfy it in a big way. And think about gene scanning: they've got technology that'll read your genes like an open book. It'll tell you what diseases you're going to get, how long you're going to live — it'll almost tell you who's going to win the Grand National. It's the biggest thing around. People want to know their futures; insurance companies want to know their customers' futures. And now's the time to do it! There are three US bio-tech firms and half a dozen start-ups that we've identified as potential takeover targets. It would make DRE Britain's world leader in a market that's going to be the next big thing. Think about it, Prime Minister. It's the way forward. It's good for DRE, it's good for Britain and it's good for Andy Sheen. All you have to do is give us your blessing and not make problems for us over selling off the defence business.'

Andy Sheen looked at Charlie McDonald, then turned back to Willans and Stilwell and smiled. He felt like a man who was about to spring his master stroke.

'Well, gentlemen, I hear what you are saying. I understand why you so desperately need my approval for your plans. Now let me tell you why I shall oppose your defence sale as you are currently proposing it. As Prime Minister, I must protect the interests of the people of this country. And I would not be doing that if I let you sell off your defence business to EES. Why not? Because DRE, as you well know, is one of only two British defence firms capable of filling the vast majority of contracts from the Ministry of Defence. If DRE sells out to English Electronic Systems, it would leave one firm — EES — in such a dominant market position that they would have a monopoly. Every time a big purchasing contract came up, they would be able to hold the MoD to ransom. The taxpayer would suffer, the British military would suffer, the whole country would suffer. Do you seriously think I could honestly countenance such a situation arising at a time of conflict in the Middle East?'

Tim Stilwell's face was darkening ominously.

'So let's be clear, then, Prime Minister. Let's be quite clear. Are you saying you're going to use the Competition Commission to block our plans?'

'Oh, Tim, I'm a reasonable man. I can see how much this means to you and what a tricky position you are in. I want to help, I truly want to help — '

Tim Stilwell heard the note of conciliation, but he also detected a trap. 'So what do you propose? What do we have to do to get approval for this sale?'

Andy Sheen let the trap spring shut. 'Quite simple. If you want me to approve the sale, you sell to the French.'

For a moment there was silence. Then Willans and Stilwell both began to speak at once. Willans put his hand on Stilwell's shoulder. Stilwell knocked his boss's arm aside and elbowed him sharply in the ribs. With a face the colour of an overripe aubergine, Tim Stilwell clasped his hands in a rictus of rage.

'I can't believe you are saying this, Prime Minister! If you know so much about this deal — as you certainly seem to — then you know the French are offering us a pittance! You know

English Electronic's bid is the only one we can accept, the only one that'll give us the equity we need to get into the bio-engineering market — '

'Well, I'm sorry about that, Tim. You know my very strong preference is for a common European defence policy and a common European defence industry. This country needs to do much more to prove its European credentials. In fact, I am on record as having told President Le Pen that any rationalization of the UK defence industry will certainly involve France and Germany too. So if you want to sell — and I sense that you have a pressing need to do so — then the answer is simple: forget EES and sell to the Europeans.'

Tim Stilwell's face had been turning a deeper and deeper shade of purple. Without a word, he rose to his feet, picked up his papers and walked out of the room. Jack Willans was on the point of saying something to Andy Sheen, when Stilwell reappeared at the door and yelled, 'You ungrateful bastard, Sheen! You bastard! Come on, Jack. We're leaving — '

★   ★   ★

The following morning Tim Stilwell and Jack Willans were trying to pick up the pieces of their shattered business strategy. One fraught hour in the pastel-coloured meeting room in Downing Street, one moment of rage from Stilwell, had left Operation Colditz in tatters and DRE's future looking bleak.

'It's a bugger, Jack, and we need to do

something about it pretty damn quick. That bastard McDonald will be spinning their version to the Sunday papers even as we sit here. I just hope Stephen Hadley has enough guts and enough clout to get our story about the frigates into the press. We've got to show Sheen that we can play hardball with them and that we're not just going to roll over and die. At the moment, the only hope I can see of saving Colditz is to kick the government in the balls and keep kicking them until they beg for mercy — '

★ ★ ★

On the floor below DRE's director of communications Stephen Hadley was drinking tea with the company's chief engineer.

'Milk and one sugar, please, Peter. Thanks for seeing me. It's a bit urgent, actually. Jack and Tim have just had me in and they want me to put out a story to the Sunday papers. It's a bit hush-hush, so keep it under your hat, all right?

'Now Tim wants us to get this story in the *Sunday Times* and their deadline for copy in the business section is tomorrow afternoon, Friday. I don't know why it's so early — to do with sharing the presses in Wapping, or something. Anyway, that's the way it is. So what I have to do is get all the facts together a.s.a.p. and give them to Matthew Koblenz — he's the business editor and I know him from way back — so that he can get the story on the front page if possible. That's where you come in. It's the MoD frigates story I want, and you were chief engineering manager

92

on that project, weren't you? Not a happy time, by all accounts. What I'm after is the stuff about the cost overruns and the MoD's cock-ups that kept changing all the specifications . . . you know, all the stuff we kept quiet about at the time to save the government's face. Well, now we're out to rub the government's nose in it, so don't hold anything back.'

★　★　★

The following Monday it was a grim-looking Charlie McDonald who strode into the eight-thirty meeting in the Downing Street press office, clutching his Arsenal mug and a copy of the *Sunday Times*. As he threw the paper on the table in front of him, McDonald made a show of holding his nose between the finger and thumb of one hand and pulling an imaginary lavatory chain with the other.

'So who's responsible for this, then?' he growled, glaring at a front-page headline: 'Government Wastes Taxpayers' Millions on Frigates that Can't Sail Straight'.

'This is dirty work from someone and I want to know who!' McDonald looked menacingly round the table. 'No one knew about the steering-gear cock-up. Or at least no one did until yesterday morning. So was it some wanker at the MoD who leaked it, Toby?'

McDonald stared accusingly at Toby Singlet, the overawed-looking press chief from the Ministry of Defence.

'Er, no, it wasn't anyone at our end, Charlie.

93

In fact, we're all so ashamed of the frigates story that I can't imagine it would even cross anyone's mind to speak to the press. I did a quick mole hunt yesterday, just to make sure I was right. Our guys are clean. Actually, the *Sunday Times* have got so much detail that they must have seen a copy of the enquiry we carried out with DRE once the faults were discovered. And I know for certain that all our copies of the report are accounted for, and the only other people with copies are DRE themselves — '

★　★　★

A few hours later, up in Marsham Street, Selwyn Knox was preparing for his working lunch with representatives of the driverless vehicle industry, when Sonya Mair poked her head round the door. 'Phone for you, Sel. It's Charlie at Number Ten.'

Knox picked up the receiver and nodded to Sonya to listen in on the spare extension on the coffee table.

'Hello, Charlie. Selwyn here.'

'Hi, Selwyn. Just check your people aren't monitoring this call, will you?'

Knox replied quickly and deferentially — the tone that everyone adopted with Charlie McDonald. 'It's OK. I've sent Jeremy out to lunch and I can see there's no one in the outer office. It's just me and Sonya here. So fire away.'

'It's about this DRE proposal to sell off their defence business, you know, and go into bio-engineering and cloning technology or whatever.'

'Yeah, yeah. I've seen the advance reports. I would have thought that's going to run into trouble on monopoly grounds. It'd leave English Electronic Systems as the only defence manufacturer and that'd put the poor old MoD over a barrel every time they ordered a new tank. I can't see that being approved.'

'I'm sure you're right, Sel. And that's good news for me and for Andy. But what I'm saying to you is that when the deal comes to your people for approval, you need to make sure the Competition Commission turn it down. Don't leave it to chance — tell them there's only one decision they can make. OK?'

'Yeah, Charlie, sure; but you know . . . technically, things have changed since the old days of the Monopolies and Mergers Commission. The Competition Commissioners are independent now, they aren't directly answerable to me as Secretary of State any more. So I can't actually tell them what to decide, like we used to do with the old MMC. If the CC decide to block a deal on monopoly grounds, that's their decision; and if they decide to let it go through, it's their call and theirs alone. We made a big thing out of saying we wouldn't interfere — a bit like the Bank of England and interest rates, really. I suppose I could tell them what to do, but it would be breaking all the rules — '

'I don't think you heard me very well just then, Selwyn. I said when the deal is referred to you, you need to make sure the CC vetoes it.

And that means one hundred per cent sure
— OK?'

'OK, I get it. I hear you loud and clear,
Charlie. I was just explaining the legal position,
that's all. You know I'll make sure everything
turns out the way you and Andy want it. In fact,
I don't think there's even going to be a problem
in this case. We don't have to worry: I've already
had a look at what DRE are proposing and I can
tell you there's not a cat in hell's chance of the
Competition Commission letting it through. The
monopoly supplier argument is so strong the
commissioners will block it for sure. So take it
easy, the sell-off's going to be blocked. Tell Andy
it's a done deal.'

'That's the stuff, Sel! Great. And thanks very
much. I'll let Andy know we're OK for knocking
back Willans and Stilwell. And it couldn't
happen to two nicer blokes, right? See ya, mate!'

5

Jack Willans and Tim Stilwell were men in despair. Operation Colditz was looking increasingly hopeless with every day and with every phone call to Downing Street and the Department of Commerce.

All the good will from Jack's past service to the New Project cause seemed to have gone out of the window following their disastrous meeting at Number Ten. Tim Stilwell calling the Prime Minister an ungrateful bastard to his face had certainly done little to foster warm emotions and a helping hand for the defence sell-off.

Downing Street was now using its tame poodles in the media to attack DRE with more venom than Jack — or any FTSE 100 chief executive for that matter — had ever experienced at the hands of New Project's mighty spin machine.

Charlie McDonald had responded to DRE's leaked story about the faulty frigates with a long and savage series of articles planted in the business and political press. All, without exception, were aimed at undermining DRE's previously high reputation: exposing the faults in DRE's gear which had 'put our boys at risk in the heat of battle'; and — most damaging of all — pointing out the unacceptable harm that would be inflicted on the UK's war effort at a time of international crisis if Senator Willans and

Tim Stilwell were allowed to sell their defence business to EES.

As the man on the receiving end, Jack was taken aback by the firepower Charlie McDonald and his spin doctors were able to muster.

Even more was he taken aback by the complicity of the British media in reporting what Downing Street and McDonald dictated.

It seemed that the journalists who had queued to fête him and sing DRE's praises for the past eight years had suddenly forgotten all that had gone before; now they were falling over themselves to do him and his company down. The only explanation, thought Jack, was that the hacks were either hopelessly beholden to McDonald and his crew for past misdeeds, or they felt an overwhelming need to curry favour with the man who distributed coveted news from Number Ten exclusively to his favourites.

Most willing to do his master's bidding — and this was no surprise to those who knew him — was Dave Sopwith, political correspondent at the *Chronicle* and so intimate with Downing Street that ribald journalist colleagues used to swear they could spot Dave's nose and blinking eyes protruding from the crack of Charlie McDonald's arse.

It was Dave Sopwith who delivered the coup de grâce to DRE's hopes of completing the sale to EES. In a malevolent splash, he 'revealed' that DRE had 'deliberately ripped off the taxpayer on a series of defence contracts to the tune of £750 million'. The article was stuffed with damning details of inventory pricing, purporting to show that DRE had overcharged the Ministry of Defence for tanks, missiles, rifles, machine guns and virtually every item of kit the British army had ever ordered from them. At the same time, Sopwith claimed, the company had failed to deliver much-needed consignments of body armour, whose absence had left the troops badly exposed. As unanswerable proof of DRE's demonic cupidity, Sopwith printed a 'secret' government memo showing that the company had charged the MoD 'fifty pounds per roll' for every pack of desert-proofed toilet paper our boys had taken into battle in the Middle East.

The government, Sopwith informed his readers, was seeking an immediate freeze on DRE's financial operations — including the buying or selling of any business assets — until the overcharging scandal had been explained to Downing Street's complete satisfaction.

Jack Willans knew Dave Sopwith; he knew Sopwith had exaggerated and distorted the facts; he knew the source of Sopwith's information was the man sitting at Andy Sheen's right hand; but he also knew that for DRE the game was up — Operation Colditz was dead. DRE and with it Jack Willans were on the downward slide to disaster.

★ ★ ★

Sonya Mair fixed her lipstick and strolled into Selwyn Knox's office, closing the door behind her and settling her shapely rear on the arm of the easy chair in which her boss was stretched out reading Dave Sopwith's front-page exposé of Senator Willans's evil deeds.

'Hi, Sel. Everything OK?' she whispered, making a pretence of not disturbing his concentration.

'Yes it is, thank you. I've just about sorted out the Rover sale. Looks pretty certain that the Cambodians are buying it. We should do a photo opportunity with their Trade Minister and the Cambodian board members in front of the Churchill statue on Parliament Square. Apparently they're going to drop the Rover name and rechristen it CamCars. Quite clever, really — gets the Cambodian reference in without reminding people they're actually buying something that's going to be made in the paddy fields and jungles, eh? Anyway, Rover's been a millstone round our neck ever since George Simpson sold it to the Germans in the nineties — and ever since Stephen Byers got his knickers in a twist when BMW decided they wanted rid of it too. But enough of that. What good news is the lovely Sonya bringing me?'

'Well, a few things. I've got Rachel Thomson to agree to profile you in the *Telegraph*. She says she's particularly interested in where you buy your clothes and have your hair done. I told her she can come and have a look at the labels and inspect your parting! I said we don't want it to be totally girlie, though, and that we'll withdraw the interview if she doesn't write about your political ambitions. Rachel's fine, actually, but she won't write a heavyweight piece. In the end, I did a deal with her: I told her if she'd include the line, 'Selwyn Knox, increasingly seen as a credible successor to Andy Sheen as Project party leader,' we'd let the photographer do a shot of you changing your shirt. And she bought it. That's OK isn't it, Sel?'

'Yeah, I suppose so. Did she ask about Ruth?'

Sonya Mair gave a fleeting but undisguised grimace at the mention of Selwyn Knox's long-time live-in girlfriend, or partner as he called her.

'Yes she did, actually. She asked if she could do the interview at your flat or at the house in the constituency, with Ruth there in the background. But I said no. It's not that I've got anything against Ruth, Sel. It's just that there's such a lack of chemistry between you two that things are painfully obvious. Rachel might start speculating — or write something dodgy, you know what I mean. And then Ruth's looking so, well — so old these days. It just isn't quite right for your image. You know there was all that gossip last year about her being just a 'token girlfriend'? The last thing we want is to start all that running again. So, anyway, I told Rachel we'd do the interview here in your office or not at all. So that's fixed.

'Now, the other thing is the civil servants. I've been having the same trouble again . . . some of them are getting really bolshie. Most of them'll do what I tell them all right, but there are one or two who've started quoting the civil service code at me, or whatever their prissy little bible's called, saying they're not obliged to take orders from party political advisers like me and that they have to be neutral and non-political and ethical and all that crap. Well, it just won't wash, Sel! I know that's the formal position, but they should know Andy and Charlie have made it pretty clear they don't give a toss for their code of ethics. It's New Project that calls the shots now and the bloody civil service had better do what we say. Anyway, if I tell you who the troublemakers are, will you haul them in here and tell them they have to do what I tell them? Actually, there's one in particular I think you'll need to get rid of: can you give him his marching orders, please? Then I thought we might make an evening of it tonight. What do you think?'

★ ★ ★

The civil servant whom Sonya Mair had fingered to the Secretary of State as a hopeless troublemaker was sitting in the sanctuary of his poky office in an outlying annexe of the Department of Commerce.

While the department's Marsham Street HQ was clean, bold and forward-looking, this backwater would have been recognized with no difficulty at all by civil servants of the Northcote — Trevelyan era. It was dark and dusty, cramped and slightly malodorous, but it was here that the big issues were examined: issues like which strategic business deals, disposals, takeovers and mergers would be allowed to go ahead and which would be blocked; issues which affected the UK's biggest conglomerates and the future of the UK economy itself.

For some time now Barry Clynes had been looking hard at an application from DRE to sell its defence arm to English Electronic Systems.

From the moment the application had dropped on Barry's desk he had known there was no chance it would ever get past the Competition Commission. The country couldn't allow itself to end up with a single defence manufacturer cornering the market — the new heavyweight EES, bulked up from swallowing DRE's plants, patents and production lines, would have eaten the poor old MoD for breakfast.

Perversely, though, Barry had left the DRE application to gather dust for some weeks now. Not because he had any doubt about its outcome — it had to be blocked — but because for some reason he had found himself the target of an annoying campaign, led by Selwyn Knox and Sonya Mair, to bully his team into making the decision they were going to make anyway.

Barry was a bluff Mancunian and he didn't take kindly to being leant on. He believed that if the British civil service was meant to be independent and not subject to the whims of party political apparatchiks, and if the government had agreed that the Competition Commission should be objective and impartial in its decisions, then that was how things should be.

Barry despised the blatant crassness of Charlie McDonald's spin campaign to demonize DRE through the media; he resented Sonya Mair's attempts to tell him what to do; he hated New Project's arrogance in assuming that the civil service could be used for its own party advantage instead of serving the interests of the nation as a whole with political impartiality and integrity.

After repeated sessions of nudging, cajoling and threats from Knox's hyperactive political adviser, he had coined the nickname by which she was now universally known: 'Miss Night-Mair'. When they saw him looking careworn, sympathetic colleagues would ask, 'Been Night-Maired again, Barry?'

But even Barry Clynes's stubbornness had a limit, even Barry Clynes's prickly principles were not immune to the brute force he was now subjected to.

The day after Sonya Mair and Selwyn Knox had their conversation about difficult civil servants, Clynes was summoned to the Secretary of State's office and told to veto DRE's application. If he didn't, Knox told him, he should prepare himself for a transfer to a new post adjudicating disability allowances at the Benefits Agency in Leeds.

The following day Knox and Mair had their way. The document Knox wanted was on his desk and all was well with the world — the application by DRE plc to sell its defence business to English Electronic Systems plc was to be 'disallowed by the Competition Commission on monopoly grounds' and the decision could 'be announced by the Secretary of State for Commerce at a time convenient to him and his department'.

Selwyn Knox smiled a smile of satisfaction and picked up the phone to Charlie McDonald.

'Good stuff, Selwyn.' McDonald sounded delighted. 'Well done. Don't make the announcement just yet, though. I need to look for a prominent date for it in the News Grid. We don't want this being overshadowed by any other big news from another department, do we? Talk to ya later — '

★ ★ ★

Sonya Mair was a New Project true believer.

She had believed in and worked for the Project ever since her earliest experiences of student activism at Redbridge University. A close personal and political friend of Andy Sheen and Charlie McDonald, she had performed the remarkable feat of maintaining good relations with the man in Number Eleven at the same time. Harold Delph, the Chancellor of the Exchequer, was a very different kettle of fish from Andy.

Where Andy was visionary and inspired, Harold was down to earth and pragmatic; where Andy believed in moral imperatives and his mission to improve society, Harold believed in a strong pound and watching the pennies; Andy wanted to be remembered as a crusading Prime Minister, Harold wanted to be remembered for balancing the books — he certainly wouldn't let Andy Sheen drag the country into the Euro if it was going to throw his accounts out of balance.

Even on the war issue the two men took different routes to the same conclusion: Andy believed in expanding the war in the Middle East because that was ethically the right thing to do; Harold had at first opposed the war on grounds of cost, only coming round to the idea once Washington had promised him that any expenditure he incurred would be more than reimbursed by spoils and oils from the conquered countries.

In the tensions that existed between Numbers Ten and Eleven, between Andy and Harold, Sonya Mair was an invaluable, irreplaceable go-between. For Knox, having Sonya as his helpmate was like a platinum-plated entry card to both camps and to all sources of influence in the government — few ministers could say they enjoyed the same access.

But Sonya was also something more. Her feminine instinct was as powerful as her political instinct. Her charm could be switched on and targeted like a laser-guided missile. Few could resist her and she knew it.

Strangely, the objects of her charm offensives were usually acutely aware of the deliberate and calculated nature of the way she was treating them — Sonya Mair rarely, if ever, did anything without thinking it all through in advance — but, astoundingly, they didn't seem to mind. The phenomenon was worthy of study by the anthropologists — seasoned politicians and hard-nosed journalists would melt in the sunshine of Sonya's smile, even while a small internal voice was saying, 'Watch her, mate, she's not doing this because she likes you; she's doing it because she's after something.' The problem was that a louder voice at the front of their mind was saying, 'Never mind about that; look into her eyes and let yourself drown!'

If she wasn't hammering you to death, Sonya was achieving the same result with a smile and a flutter.

She brought Knox something that no one else had ever done or ever could do. She brought him the secrets of other men's minds.

★ ★ ★

At DRE, things were going from bad to worse.

When the nerve-racking weeks waiting for the Competition Commission's decision grew unbearable, Jack Willans decided he must confront Tim Stilwell to discover the reason for his obsessive insistence that Colditz was their only possible salvation.

Jack and Tim had spent the morning in the City trying to reassure their big investors — pension funds, unit trusts and insurers — that DRE remained a good bet in the long term. Jack had spoken warmly about future prospects if the move out of defence was completed — it was, he said, a potential gold mine for investors who could buy low now and watch the share price rocket when cloning technology and gene scanning came online. But when he started to argue that the prospects remained good even if DRE were forced to stay in the defence market, he suddenly noticed Tim Stilwell's face had lost its usual composure and his lips were mouthing something that Senator Willans could only guess at.

In the company BMW on the way back to

headquarters, six years of accumulated annoyance and resentment with Tim Stilwell boiled over into sudden anger.

'Look, Tim, what the hell is going on? I need to know what you're up to. Why are you so worried about our defence business? What's wrong with it?'

Tim Stilwell had obviously decided he too had had enough of the pressure. 'Well, Jack, you asked for it. You want to know what's up? I'll tell you: we're broke! We've got nothing left. Everything's gone down the pan and if we can't flog the business to EES you and I are finished. If Selwyn Knox and the bloody Competition Commission announce they're blocking it, you and all the other suckers can wave goodbye to any future at all.'

The rest of the journey passed in silence. After thirty years at the peak of British industry, Jack Willans was staring disaster — unmitigated and terrifyingly final disaster — in its leering face.

★ ★ ★

As the BMW pulled into DRE's underground garage, and at the very moment Jack stepped out of the car to walk to the lift, Albert Topping died.

Albert was fifty-nine, a smoker, a drinker and a former miner.

The doctor told his widow it was perhaps no surprise the heart attack had been so violent. Even if medical help had arrived the moment Albert collapsed in his constituency office, it was unlikely anything could have been done to save him. As it was, it had been a quiet afternoon and it was probably one or two hours before Albert's constituency agent had arrived and discovered the body.

Andy Sheen was informed thirty minutes later. 'Oh no, Charlie. Did you hear that? Albert Topping's died. He was only fifty-nine, I hadn't realized. I guess he just looked so much older. Means a by-election I suppose. Safe seat, though, isn't it?'

'Albert Topping? He's Tyneland East isn't he? Yes, he is. Oh, fuck! That's where the bloody shipyard is, Andy. What's it called . . . Schoerner's. And you know what that all means. We're really up shit creek now!'

★ ★ ★

Selwyn Knox was feeling pretty pleased with himself.

The Rover deal had been completed and he had had a very good press. The Churchill statue pictures were flattering and had been widely used. Rachel Thomson had included the key phrase in her *Telegraph* piece as Sonya had promised, and he'd had several calls from political hacks asking him if he saw himself as a future leader of the Project party.

To all of them Knox had used the time-honoured phrases: that he was not seeking any other job than the one he was currently doing to the best of his ability; that the party had an outstanding leader in Andy Sheen; but that if in the future, for whatever reason, his party were to call on him, he would be ready to answer that call.

The one sour note had been a telephone call from a dyspeptic Harold Delph, who reminded him that leadership questions were not something any minister should be commenting on and that it was in the party's best interests to discourage press speculation on the subject. Knox had, of course, concurred, but when he put the phone down Sonya Mair, who'd been listening on the other extension, burst out laughing. 'What he's really saying, Sel, is that it's OK for Harold Delph to talk about the next party leader, but it's not OK for anyone else! Unless they're tipping Harold Delph for the job, of course!'

The two of them glanced around. They both knew there were civil servants in the outer office for whom loyalty to Knox was not number one priority, so it wouldn't do for them to know too much about his ambitions, or those of his right-hand woman.

'I'm off to Number Ten now, Sel,' Sonya said. 'Charlie McDonald's having a drinks party for the press. He wants me to reward the helpful hacks with a glimpse of cleavage and cane the bad boys until they beg for mercy. OK? I'll see you this evening: don't forget.'

★　★　★

It was a subdued Andy Sheen who put in an appearance at Charlie McDonald's media drinks party. Sonya thought Charlie himself was in his

110

gloomy, overhanging eyebrows mood.

Dave Sopwith was there, doing his best to cheer up his mentor and protector, but McDonald wasn't having any of it. Hacks who asked what the matter was were told the news about Albert Topping had dampened the mood, but Sonya knew that neither Andy nor Charlie gave a monkey's about Topping, an Old Project fart who had never got with the new party. Sonya knew there must be something else, so she deliberately stayed behind after the party to find out what was on Charlie's mind.

'It's bad news, Sonya. Old Topping's gone and died at the worst possible moment. The daft bugger, he could never do anything without fucking up! The problem is Schoerner's, the Germans — you know, the ones who're closing the naval shipyard up there? Well, fuck me if it isn't in Tyneland East, Albert's constituency! The Krauts wanted to close it nine months ago, but we got them to postpone it while we tried to look for a buyer. Well, you know all that — we couldn't find anyone daft enough to buy the place, 'cos the MoD aren't placing the big naval contracts any more. You can't sail battleships across the Iranian desert! So, anyway, Schoerner's called us two weeks ago to say that they've waited nine months while we faffed around and they're closing the place down now whether we've got a buyer or not. They're making the announcement next week in Hamburg and we've not been able to make them change their minds.'

'So it's the by-election that's the problem

then, is it, Charlie? How many redundancies are we expecting?'

'Twelve fucking thousand when you take all the support industries into account. It's meltdown time up in Geordieland, Sonya girl, and it couldn't have happened at a worse time. There's going to be a lot of angry voters up there.'

'Yeah, but come on, Charlie: we're not going to lose the seat, are we? It's safe New Project, isn't it?'

'Yeah, in theory. But ever since the formation of this NewLib party, we aren't as invincible as we used to be. Bloody Ken Clarke leaving the Tories and taking all the pro-Europeans with him caught us on the hop. If he'd just set up some Tory-wet-pro-Euro party, we couldn't have cared less. But he was pretty smart. Linking up with the LibDems and the Labour rump was a fucking master stroke. Together they're a real opposition now and we haven't been used to that, have we?

'Crap name, by the way, 'NewLibs' — sounds like something I'd have dreamed up fifteen years ago. Anyway, they're on a roll and they know it. They're really popular up in Tyneland even without this Schoerner close-down and if we don't do something, we reckon the NewLibs are in with a real chance. If we can't get someone to buy the yard now, and if half the constituency get thrown on the dole, the anti-Project protest vote'll hand it to the NewCraps on a plate. And if we lose Tyneland, think of all the other seats we could lose. We could see the heartlands going down

112

like dominoes. It could set the whole New Project edifice crumbling — '

★ ★ ★

'How did the drinks go, Sonya?'

Selwyn Knox looked up from his papers as Sonya Mair walked into the office. It was ten o'clock and Knox was doing his usual late-night swotting.

'Not good for Charlie and Andy: they're down in the dumps. But I've got an idea that might do you and me some good, Sel. Can I go off and do a bit of freelancing this week?'

★ ★ ★

Jack Willans had been trying without success to talk to Sonya Mair for the past two months. He knew the influence she could wield over the Competition Commission's decision. But every approach, every phone call and letter, had been met with a wall of silence or a curt instruction to make his request 'through the proper channels'.

Now here was the woman herself, sitting on the black velvet sofa in Jack's office and looking even more gorgeous than her pictures in the papers.

When Jack emerged briefly to collect the two white coffees his secretary had prepared for them, even Linda couldn't help commenting — and only half in jest. 'She's a bit of a looker, Jack. You'd better stop panting and keep your wits about you if you don't want to end up doing something you might regret.'

113

Jack smiled sheepishly and went back in with the coffees. His pleasantries about how hard she was to get hold of were met with an arch smile. 'You can get hold of most things if you try hard enough, Senator Willans.'

Amid the banter and the flirting — Jack was aware he was being targeted by the Sonya Mair charm, but like most men he was more than happy to step eagerly into the role of willing victim — her opening gambit was delivered in a deceptively offhand aside. 'I see DRE's in a bit of a mess, isn't it, Senator Willans?'

Jack almost fell through the floor. 'Er, no, not that I know of, young lady. What makes you say that?'

'Well, it seems I must know something you don't know, then. Didn't you know your accounts are up the spout and you'll be lucky to survive another six months?'

'Er, that's not my understanding. May I ask what gave you that idea?'

'Information is my business, Senator Willans, but it's your problem, not mine. I'm not here to threaten you, I'm here to help.'

Sonya Mair slowly crossed and uncrossed her legs. She looked fixedly at Jack Willans's ruddy, battered face to see if his eyes would wander down towards her carefully exposed thighs. They did. Sonya smiled.

She continued: 'Just imagine something for me for a moment, Senator Willans — Jack. Just imagine that I am Father Christmas and that I'm bringing you what you most want in the world at this very minute. Think of the one thing that

114

would make you happier than anything else. And imagine I'm here to tell you that I can get it for you. What would you think about that?'

Jack Willans's jaw dropped open and his white coffee spluttered onto the black velvet of the sofa.

★   ★   ★

After that things happened very quickly indeed, as they often do in the pragmatic worlds of politics and big business.

As soon as questions of personal fortune — financial or political — come into play, it is instructive to note how quickly and easily deals that once seemed unthinkable can be struck; how gratifyingly everyone's vital interests can be protected.

★   ★   ★

Jack Willans called a full board meeting of DRE plc in the company conference suite and explained to a flabbergasted array of non-execs, managers and accountants that he had decided to buy the Schoerner shipyard in Tyneland East.

The board's objections, expressed in a flurry of horrified speeches from around the table, ran broadly along the following lines.

— We need a shipyard like a hole in the head.

— That particular shipyard is an even bigger white elephant than most because it's geared for exactly the deep-draft naval vessels that the MoD has said it's got no intention of purchasing for at least the next decade.

— Schoerner's is losing money hand over fist.

— The yard's pension commitments are enough to bankrupt us on their own.

— The workforce are wreckers and skivers.

— And, anyway, our plan is to get out of defence and into bio-engineering and human cloning, so why the hell would we buy another military shipyard?

Jack listened to them all patiently and told them the deal would be signed the day after tomorrow.

*   *   *

At about the same time, Charlie McDonald rang an astonished Dave Sopwith to tell him he had to write a new splash on the DRE question. This time, the *Chronicle* needed to explain that DRE was actually an outstanding exemplar for British industry, that its management team were among the most gifted in the world, and that the company's proposed move into bio-engineering and human-cloning technology would put the UK at the forefront of a vital sector in the future development of the world economy.

*   *   *

Selwyn Knox called Barry Clynes into his office for another meeting.

He showed the gob-smacked Mancunian a 'redraft' he had made of Barry's earlier announcement on the DRE — EES deal. There

116

weren't many differences between the two texts, Knox told him, but one that Barry spotted straight away was that the word 'disallowed' had been replaced with the word 'approved'.

On seeing what Knox had done, Barry Clynes muttered, 'Bugger this for a bowl of cherries — I resign,' and walked out of the Secretary of State's office never to return.

★ ★ ★

On the night New Project won the Tyneland East by-election, Selwyn Knox took Sonya Mair back to his pied-à-terre in Dolphin Square, Westminster. She was still there the next morning. In north London Sonya's husband noticed her absence again and gave a resigned sigh.

★ ★ ★

That evening Andy Sheen called a smirking Selwyn Knox to Downing Street to congratulate him on a job well done. Over a glass of pink champagne, the blue-eyed boy asked if the PM had shared Harold Delph's annoyance at seeing Knox spoken of in the press as a future leader of the Project party. Andy Sheen looked at Charlie McDonald. Both of them looked at Knox, shook their heads and smiled most encouragingly.

6

The movie mogul Sam Goldwyn used to say a verbal contract was not worth the paper it was written on.

For weeks after Selwyn Knox's celebratory meeting with Andy Sheen and Charlie McDonald, the jibe haunted him with increasing bitterness. It was unlike him to be carried away with the excitement of the moment. He had, he felt, broken his own golden rule at Downing Street that night: he hadn't pinned Sheen and McDonald down to an undertaking they could not renege on. It was all very well for them to give him a nod and a smile; it was all very well for them to hint at his prospects for advancement — but where was his guarantee? Where was the proof? Where was the route map to the destiny he knew should be his?

It was another month of anxiety and self-reproach before Knox finally discovered his worrying had been unnecessary. Andy Sheen and Charlie McDonald were as good as their — unwritten — word. On a sunny Tuesday morning in Downing Street, the Prime Minister unveiled the first instalment of Knox's advancement with grace and no little panache.

'So look, Selwyn. You and I go back a long way, don't we? I can remember back in 2006 when we had that little trouble up in Scotland — Exxington, wasn't it? I don't recall all the details, but I do know you acquitted yourself remarkably well that day. I remember getting notes from Charlie here, and from Geoff Maddle, saying you were MP material. And they were right.

'You've had a pretty rapid rise, Selwyn. Merited, of course. And what I will say is that every time we've come up against a problem of some sort you've not let us down. You and Sonya Mair. So we're indebted to you. We really are.

'Now Charlie showed me something quite interesting yesterday. I've got it here. Here it is. It's the little note I sent you back in September 2006, remember? It was just after Canary Wharf and we were all pretty jumpy at that time. Anyway, this is what I wrote to you: 'Dear Selwyn, Terror and war are looming again. We need determined, ruthless people like you. Come and join us as an MP. Help us protect the values of our society. Yours, Andy Sheen.' Yes. That's it. Now that was a very special time, of course. The civilized world was under attack. We didn't know what to expect next. Emotions were running high.

'I'm not quite sure, by the way, whether I really meant to use the word 'ruthless' there, did I, Charlie? Didn't I mean to say 'dedicated' or something more like that? Oh well, it doesn't matter. If Charlie says ruthless, then ruthless it is. But ruthless in a positive way, ruthless in the sense that we are all ready to do everything necessary to save this country from disaster; we're ready to be ruthless with ourselves, to bear any sacrifice — and ruthless with others, of

119

course, if they stand in the way of our programme.

'Civilized values are under threat in the modern world, Selwyn, and that threat comes from many sources. It comes from the terrorists who seek to destroy our world and our civilization. And we have been ruthless with them. We have borne all the sacrifices that have been demanded of us, including the loss of young British and American lives. I have not flinched. I have remained determined in the face of adversity. I have remained, yes — ruthless, because I know my actions are serving the greater good.

'Now I am telling you all this because I am about to ask you to follow my example. I am about to ask you to take on the same heavy burden of responsibility; the burden of ruthlessness and self-sacrifice in the name of a cause we all believe in.

'I said earlier that the threat to our values comes from many sources. Sadly, international terrorism is not the only threat our society is facing. There is another less obvious, but perhaps more insidious, more dangerous threat. And that is the threat from within our own society. You know, sometimes I look at what we have done in Iraq and Iran and in Syria and Saudi Arabia, and I think: yes, we have protected ourselves, we have protected our values from the outsiders who would destroy what we stand for.

'But what an irony — what a bitter irony — if we were to allow the very values our brave troops have fought and died for in the Middle East Wars to be undermined and corrupted from within. What a terrible indictment, what an insult to their memory, if our lack of vigilance here at home were to negate what they have achieved on the battlefields so far away.'

Andy Sheen paused and looked Selwyn Knox straight in the eye. He had long felt that Knox shared his own moral beliefs, his own dedication and commitment, his own selfless desire to bring succour to the people of Britain. This was a man he trusted as pure, honest, modest and free from personal ambition. Now was the moment to put that trust to the test.

'Selwyn, I want you to do here at home what I have done in the Middle East. I want you to take on the domestic threat in the way that I have taken on the foreign threat. And I want you to triumph in the way that I have triumphed.

'Charlie here will explain all the details. He will tell you how the new Department for Society is going to work. How it is going to wipe out the inner rottenness that is spreading through today's society: the antisocial values that are threatening our way of life; the ungrateful individuals who are spreading poison in the form of dishonesty, disrespect, greed, immorality, laziness and all the negative phenomena such attitudes engender — drug addiction, crime, teenage pregnancies, irresponsible parents, desertion, single-parent households, benefit fraud, bogus asylum seekers — all the things that threaten us — all the manifestations of the enemy who lives among us — the enemy in our midst —

'It is a very big brief, Selwyn. I do not disguise

121

that. Creating a Department for Society is a brave move. People will criticize us. Perhaps they'll say we are over-ambitious. Perhaps they'll say society cannot be saved from itself. Perhaps they'll even say there is no such thing as society. But we know better. The Department for Society. It is a radical concept and we need a big man to be our Minister for Society. Are you that man, Selwyn? Can you step into those shoes?'

Selwyn Knox returned the Prime Minister's unblinking gaze, thought for a moment and nodded his head gravely.

'Yes, Prime Minister. I am — and I can.'

★ ★ ★

Knox's meeting with Charlie McDonald was fixed for ten o'clock the following day. He told Sonya the meeting would be decisive for his future and for hers. If this Department for Society was going to work, he told her, it would have to be thought out properly and in minute detail. He also told Sonya that Andy Sheen's concept had struck him as woolly and a little naive. He was hoping Charlie McDonald would be able to tell him more clearly what it would involve, exactly how its responsibilities were to be defined and where the boundaries would lie between it and the Home Office.

For her part, Sonya was considerably more sanguine. Where Knox saw problems, she saw opportunities: 'Look, Sel, for a start, Andy is going to be on your side in any turf war. He's never been a fan of the Home Office. So you've got the whip hand there, for sure.

'And your other advantage is that our department will be able to take a real overview of the problem. Everyone knows drugs and crime, unemployment and parental abuse, teenage mums, shirkers and benefit fraud are all interconnected, but up to now they've been dealt with by different government departments, and you know the Keystone Kops effect that always creates. All that talk about 'joined-up government' at the end of the nineties and the start of the noughties was just guff.

'What you've got now is the chance to rise above all that. You've got the Olympian overview — you're basically an uberminister, Sel. That's what you are, an uberminister! ... Seriously, though, I think Andy was right about how many social problems can be traced back to this underlying malaise thing. It's down to people who just don't know how to behave as a part of society — all the yobs and antisocial elements — and if we can start to tackle them, I think we can really impress him. And you know what that means for your future, don't you? Andy won't be around for ever: you've got to start thinking about that. I know bloody Harold Delph's thinking about it — he doesn't think about anything else!

'So when you see Charlie tomorrow remember you're in a position of strength. Downing Street has been really rattled by the rise of these NewLibs — we've got a proper opposition now and Charlie told me Andy's pretty scared of them. I reckon he sees you and this new department as the answer to his prayers. So when you see McD, you need to be sure they give you authority over all the departments the Home Office currently works with — police, immigration, employment, social security, health and all the rest. Don't let him get away with saying you'll have a partnership relationship with them — OK?

'Now, I think we'll need to run the department on a unit model. We'll need a parenting unit, a family unit, a new teenager unit and maybe some others too. They're going to put us in the old Cabinet Office buildings, so that's good — it was about time Andy got rid of the bloody Cabinet Office. What a waste of resources they were! It means we'll be on Downing Street's doorstep — and you can't beat that in terms of access.

'But remember, Sel, the key to success in all this is the staff. If you don't get the right people, you've had it. You'll need me for a start obviously! Right? But we'll also need a free hand in choosing the junior ministers, and all the civil servants at grade five and above. That's absolutely vital: there's no way we want to end up with a bunch of no-hopers like we had at the D of C.

'And one other thing — this is absolutely vital, Sel — McDonald needs to agree that we have access to all Home Office and police data as of right now. We can't afford to wait: that's our top demand and it's not negotiable — '

★　★　★

The next day Selwyn Knox got lucky.

His meeting with Charlie McDonald was a complete success.

Knox got everything he asked for from a preoccupied-looking director of Downing Street communications, who did little more than outline the aims, powers and structure of the new department before handing it over into Knox's safe keeping. Even the demand for immediate access to the Home Office and police files went through on the nod. McDonald dictated a brief memo conferring full authority and full security clearance on the new Minister for Society and told him to use it wisely.

The announcement about the Department for Society was to be made on the following Monday and Knox would be put up for the ten-past-eight slot on the *Today* programme, followed by intensive media briefings.

According to Charlie McDonald, the date of the launch had been personally selected by Andy Sheen because it would be the sixth anniversary of New Project's accession to power. The symbolism underlined the fact that the new department was the start of a prestigious and high-profile policy shift that would be crucial to the future of Andy Sheen's government.

'Andy sees this as a way to wrest back the momentum from the NewLibs,' Charlie McDonald said. 'The Tories are history, we all know that. For too long we got used to a world where there was no opposition to worry about. But ever since Ken Clarke took the pro-Europeans out of the Tory party and linked up with the Libs and those Labour oddballs, there's been a groundswell of revival going on. Andy has been looking at the polling data and he knows the NewLibs are strong enough to beat us now. If there were an election tomorrow, we reckon the NewLibs would get in.

'And that's why so much depends on you and the Department for Society. The wars and the foreign agenda have kept us on top of the pile up to now, but that's starting to falter. So it's up to you to get the same effect with the domestic agenda — you'll need to come up with something pretty radical. Andy wants you to go and think the unthinkable, Selwyn, something bold, something big, something to get us moving again!'

As he ushered Selwyn Knox out of the door, Charlie McDonald uttered his own blend of imprecation and blessing. 'Don't forget, Selwyn, we're depending on you. What you're doing is starting a moral crusade. Yeah, that's it — a moral crusade for the salvation of Britain. You should use that. It sounds big! And presentation is everything. What you'll be doing is going to be controversial — the more controversial the better. So I say get the presentation right and the rest will follow. It's up to you now.'

★ ★ ★

Selwyn Knox didn't know it, but the reason he got such an easy ride from Charlie McDonald was that McDonald's thoughts were occupied with another matter, quite as important as the new department but with a much more pressing deadline.

He went straight to another meeting, deep in the bowels of Downing Street, where a group of political advisers and information officials had gathered and were chatting in little groups awaiting the arrival of their boss.

'Mornin' everyone — sorry to have dragged you out of the pub. Sit down, you lot. We've got a bit of business to sort out. Come on, Damon: leave Andrea alone, you're getting greasy pawmarks on her! Where's Graham? Is he coming or not? . . . OK, quick as you can. I want to get started . . . right. I've got a few questions to ask you and I want you all to think really hard about this. It's serious, OK?'

Geoff Maddle was sitting next to Charlie McDonald on the raised podium at the front of the room, spring sunshine streaming over their shoulders from a dusty pavement-level window behind them.

Geoff had known Charlie long enough to know when his mate was worried: worried enough not to have taken him completely into his confidence, which was unusual; worried enough to have called an extraordinary meeting of spin doctors and civil servants from all the Whitehall departments.

'OK, the first thing I want to establish is whether you've all had any unusual traffic from the media in the past week. Any unexpected calls, anything out of the ordinary?'

'I had the *News of the World* asking if any

member of the cabinet had taken drugs or if the PM had taken drugs.'

'So did I. I think they're trying to do a spoiling story on this new Department for Society stuff. You know, 'Ministers who smoked dope are now telling us how bad it is for us.''

'We've had the *Mirror* asking where our man's going on holiday this year — '

'Yeah, we had them too, Charlie. It's a round robin, I think. They're doing a 'conspicuous wealth and New Project's new snobs' story.'

'They've been chasing us about the leadership question. Same old crap about when is Delph gonna be the PM and all that. I told them it was all froth and they should do something more important.'

Charlie McDonald listened to the hubbub of voices with the concentrated air of a man waiting for bad news; waiting to hear his worst suspicions confirmed. 'Right. Let's just talk about the *Mirror* stuff, can we? How many of you have had calls from the *Mirror*?'

Hands were raised by half of those present.

'OK, so quite a few of you. And was it always the same caller? Jim McGee was it?'

Everyone agreed that it was McGee.

'Now. Did all the calls start off about ministers' holiday plans?'

The consensus was that they did.

'Right. What I want you to try and remember now are the supplementaries. What did McGee ask you after he'd done the holiday questions?'

Among the civil servants, Damon Fowler, head of news at the Environment Department, was waving his hand in his usual eager-schoolboy way. Charlie McDonald thought Fowler was a self-serving asshole — he'd told Geoff as much on several occasions — but now he needed any help he could get. 'Yes, Damon. What was McGee really after?'

'Well, Charlie, I know we're not supposed to discuss ministers' movements; you've made that very clear to us and I always respect your guidelines, so I said I couldn't tell him about holidays. So then he started on about our Secretary of State's finances: he said David is quite rich, and I said, 'Yes, he is; so what?' And then McGee started asking about the other cabinet members and I said I didn't really know about them. That all went off OK. But then he got on to Andy, er — the PM, that is. And he said he was interested to discover that the PM owned two homes in the UK and also a flat in New York. Well, I sort of knew this was the truth — but I didn't know whether we were supposed to confirm it or not. But McGee seemed to know it anyway, so I told him, 'Yes, that's right.' And then it was his next question that puzzled me a bit. McGee said, 'Well, we're always being told that Andy Sheen came from a modest family, son of a vicar and all that, and yet here we are discovering that he owns all these properties.' Now I know New Project don't think wealth is anything to be ashamed of, Charlie, so I said, 'So what? The PM is the PM and he's entitled to own properties, isn't he?' But McGee wouldn't let up and he said, 'Do you want to know something interesting, Damon? Andy Sheen bought all those properties a long time ago. In fact, he bought the New York flat in 1981 when he was still a student — so what do you think about that?''

Damon paused to gauge Charlie McDonald's reactions, to see whether he was going to be applauded or rebuked for the way he'd dealt with the enemy on the *Mirror*, but McDonald remained inscrutable.

'OK, Damon. What else did you tell him?'

'Oh well, that was it really, Charlie.' Damon Fowler suddenly had the impression that his chirping was not going down well with the boss and decided it might be time to shut up. Mercifully, Charlie McDonald didn't pursue him but turned instead to the others.

'Well, Damon's had quite a chat with Mr McGee, then. Anyone else had a similar conversation about Andy's finances?'

With a show of some reluctance, two other civil servants and three political advisers, including Sonya Mair, raised their hands and recounted the grillings they'd had from Jim McGee. All agreed that the initial enquiry about ministers' holidays had been just a smokescreen and that McGee's real interest had been in the Prime Minister.

Charlie McDonald frowned and started to bring the meeting to a close.

'OK, thanks very much everyone. Now I've got a favour to ask you. Can you all have a good think about any dealings you've had with Jim McGee in the past? Anyone who has anything useful they can give me about McGee — you all

130

know the sort of thing I mean, *useful*, OK? — will you please come and see me afterwards? Anything you guys have got on the *Mirror* in general or on the editor Cliff Evans will also be gratefully received. And I need this stuff pretty sharpish. One final thing: Geoff and I are going to be dealing with this matter from now on, so any further calls you take about Andy and about his finances, just say nothing. Make a note of the questions and come and tell us. OK? Got that? Thanks very much.'

★　★　★

The following Monday was the anniversary of New Project's accession to power. It was Selwyn Knox's big day too.

The announcement of the new Department for Society had been leaked to the previous day's *Observer* at Sonya Mair's suggestion. She had argued that the bleeding-heart liberals at the *Guardian* and the *Obs* would be the biggest critics of the department once they'd figured out what its real agenda was. So Sonya's plan was to wrongfoot them by feeding them an exclusive story about all the social ills Britain was now suffering from, which a new department was going to be created to deal with. 'The *Observer* lot will jump for joy when we give them this stuff,' said Sonya. 'They'll do a front page saying the department's the answer to all their liberal prayers and Selwyn Knox is the new messiah. So when we actually get the department going and they discover what it's *really* about, they'll maybe

131

have to think twice before slagging off an idea they started by praising to the heavens — '

In the event Sonya's gambit worked reasonably well. The *Observer* was cautiously encouraging and its story set the tone for Monday morning's radio, TV and press coverage. Selwyn Knox's *Today* programme interview was followed by a traipse round ITN, Sky, Channel 4, IRN and the multiple BBC outlets — all fortunately housed together in the parliamentary broadcasting centre over the road from the House of Commons — with Sonya Mair leading her boss in and out of studio after studio.

Sonya told Knox he'd done well. The interviews were largely conducted by presenters who knew very little about the new Department for Society and had had to base their questions on what little briefing she herself had given them beforehand.

The result was a media consensus that the concept behind the department was intriguing and that Selwyn Knox should be given a fair wind to make things happen.

Charlie McDonald had told Sonya there was a possibility of a joint photo op for Knox with Andy Sheen that Monday afternoon. He'd told her this would depend on whether Sheen could clear his diary; but Sonya knew what he really meant was that Downing Street would be watching the tone of the morning's media coverage before a decision was made: if Knox and the department got the thumbs up on morning radio and TV, Andy Sheen would be straining at the leash to join Selwyn in taking credit for the idea; a media thumbs down would almost certainly have meant the PM finding himself just too busy to join his new minister in dealing with the press's criticism. So Sonya was gratified when Charlie rang to say Andy would join her boss at two-thirty on College Green. The photo op went well, the two men smiled a lot, and the Department for Society got off to as good a start as anyone could reasonably have expected.

★　★　★

That afternoon Selwyn Knox and Sonya Mair were settling into their new departmental offices off Whitehall, watching the cleaners clear out the last reminders of the dinosaurs from the late unlamented Cabinet Office, and discussing the key members of the team who were about to join them.

Sonya didn't beat around the bush. 'What we must make sure is that we don't end up in the same situation as at the D of C: we're agreed on that, Sel, aren't we? We need our civil servants to be absolutely loyal to us. That's the only way we'll ever get anywhere with some of the stuff Andy wants us to push through. Some of it's going to be pretty controversial and we can't afford to have officials who are doubters and troublemakers. Am I right? OK. So you know, and I know, that the only way to do that is to make sure we have something over them. Something we can use against them if their tender consciences start troubling them and they start being a nuisance for us. Well, the access to Home Office and police files you got us off Charlie McD was well worth the effort, Sel: have a look at what I've got here. I think you'll like it — '

Sonya Mair opened her briefcase and spilled a pile of red folders onto Knox's desk.

'Pick a card! Have a look at some of the stuff I've managed to find out. It's pretty high grade, I can tell you.'

Knox gave Sonya's hand a squeeze, picked up one of the dossiers from the top of the pile and began to read aloud.

' 'Robert Jenkins: age forty-three; currently Home Office director of drugs policy. Coming to us on 20 May. Married, three children — ' blah, blah, blah. 'First from Oxford,' OK, good. 'Previous departments include Customs and Excise, Transport and — ' ah-hah, this is it, isn't it, Sonya? This next bit is your freelance stuff.'

Sonya Mair smiled and pointed to a paragraph at the bottom of the page. Selwyn Knox read on.

'August 2006; in Soho — in a gay bar! Whoa! That's a good one, Sonya! Picked up by the cops — I wonder what he told his wife and three kids.'

'That's the point, he didn't tell them anything. They don't know. But we do because I took the trouble to find out. And *he* doesn't know we know! He only needs to know that if he ever gives us any trouble. Pretty handy, eh?'

'Certainly is. Can I see the others? Who's this one here? Christopher Brody from the Inland Revenue — coming to us next week. Married, two children. OK, what's the gen on him, then?'

'Look at the bottom of the page, Sel. That's where all the juicy stuff is. It's gambling with this guy. You might think they're all boring grey accountants at the Revenue, but you'd be wrong: this Brody guy has gambled himself into a bigger hole than the ones they had at Passchendaele! He's got debts to loan sharks in the East End; he's taken a second mortgage that his wife knows nothing about; and he's got two County Court judgements against him that he's kept pretty quiet. Any of that stuff could blow him sky-high if we ever needed to use it against him. And let me just show you one last one. This is the big fish, Sel. It's Robert Nottridge — Sir Robert Nottridge, actually, your new Permanent Secretary who's moving in to the office through that wall. Just have a read — '

'OK. Thanks, Sonya. 'Sir Robert Nottridge: born 1953; Eton; Cambridge — nothing obvious there. Married, no children — '

'Right. Stop right there, Sel. Now look down the page. Nottridge's wife thinks he's got no children. But guess what? The old bugger's been knocking off one of his former secretaries, a girl called Miriam McLeish, who lives in a flat in Clerkenwell and — surprise, surprise! — she's got a four-year-old and a two-year-old. Claiming benefits, had to give a father's name — that's how we put two and two together. Nottridge doesn't know she put him down as the father, but it's all in the files. So we've got a double whammy on him: we can screw his relationship with little Miriam by letting on that she's named him to the Benefits Agency, and we can screw his marriage by presenting Lady Nottridge with her two little stepchildren! What do you think of that, then?'

'What do I think? I think you're quite something, Sonya! The stuff you've got in your head is priceless. It's enough to make you bullet-proof — and me too, thank God. There's no way anyone can touch us, you know that. Because we've got the ammunition to fight our way out of any corner. I honestly don't think I could survive without you, Sonya, and I'm not joking when I say that — '

Sonya grinned. 'Too right, Selly baby. Too right. So just make sure you don't cross me, then! You won't be bullet-proof from me, you know. I'm the one with the silver bullet, so you listen to what I say — OK? Right. Now there's one post we haven't talked about yet and it's an important one: with all the media work we're going to have to do for this department, we'll need someone pretty on-message as our director of communications. It's a civil service post, of course, but it's too important to leave to the usual paper-pushers. I think we need to get a journalist in, Sel. We'll have to get him through the civil service selection procedure, but I think we can manage to fix that, can't we? Is there anyone smart and malleable at the same time? I thought of Dave Sopwith — he's certainly malleable; it's just that he's such an arsehole — '

'Don't worry, Sonya. We're sorted on the communications job. That's one post I *have* thought about myself, and I've got the perfect candidate. We're going to go for the BBC politics reporter, Nigel Tonbridge — he's working on *Newsnight* at the moment, but I've known him for quite a while — '

'What? *That* Nigel Tonbridge? He's a good journalist right enough, but isn't he the guy you had a run in with, back up in Scotland?'

'Exactly right,' said Selwyn Knox. 'And that's why he's so perfect for us: I've got *plenty* on Nigel Tonbridge.'

7

Charlie McDonald and Geoff Maddle usually ended their extended working day with a couple of drinks at the Red Lion.

They were both in Downing Street every morning by half-past seven, in time to read over the papers and the radio and TV transcripts before the eight-thirty news-planning meeting. And they rarely knocked off before eight or nine in the evening. How could they? Even if there was no event for them to attend with the PM, no speech, no reception or dinner to go to, there were the TV bulletins to monitor, the late-deadline calls from journalists needing just one last piece of guidance before putting the front page to bed, and worried ministers needing a quick briefing before going on *Newsnight* or else praying Charlie's indulgence for some slip of the tongue, for some deviation from the official line while speaking to this or that hack.

After all that, the Red Lion might have seemed a strange place to seek refuge.

Just over the road from Downing Street and right opposite the old Treasury building, the Lion was the pub where Whitehall, Westminster and the fourth estate met and mingled on neutral ground. Civil servants in shabby suits were there; so were the sharply attired TV faces, the political correspondents and business hacks hoping for a repeat of the legendary Charlie

Whelan's indiscretions, which had more than once thrown the stock market into turmoil. Into this bear pit Charlie McDonald and Geoff Maddle would stride with a nonchalant, 'Hi, you lot. Who's buying?'

For Charlie and Geoff, the Red Lion served two purposes.

If they wanted to plant tomorrow's story in the minds of the press corps, this was the place to do it.

Like most people's, journalists' minds blossom and become touchingly receptive after a few drinks. It was always easier for the spin doctors to take a chosen one to the back of the taproom and whisper in his or her ear than it was to follow the formal channels of a news conference, a press release or even a telephone call in the cold sober light of next morning's newsroom.

But if Geoff and Charlie didn't have a story to peddle, if they'd had a shitty day and just wanted a bit of peace and quiet to chew things over, the Lion was still the place they headed for. On these occasions, though, they wouldn't hail the assembled crowd; they'd nod to the landlady, the endlessly helpful and unfailingly hospitable Marian, and she'd wave them to the private rooms upstairs.

Here the sultans of spin could stretch out and relax. The front room, overlooking Whitehall, was their favourite. Here they could stare hypnotically at the lazy ceiling fan as it wafted their cigarette smoke round and round the grimy, print-bedecked walls; they could help themselves to the drinks that Marian trustingly left on the narrow bar counter at the back of the room; they could escape from the storm outside and gather their frazzled thoughts.

Tonight, as so often, they smoked and drank their way through an initial nerve-calming twenty-minute oasis of luxurious silence. Glances exchanged, sporadic smiles and nods were the outward and visible signs of the inward process of mental digestion they were both going through, thought patterns seemingly following parallel trajectories as they mulled over the triumphs that lay behind or the potential pitfalls ahead.

It was Geoff who finally broke the silence.

'So what's that *Mirror* story all about, then?'

'Yeah, I was just thinking the same thing. It could be nothing — '

'It could be something, though, couldn't it?'

'Yeah. The thing that's got me a bit worried is that Andy doesn't want to talk to me about it. It's not like him.'

'Nah. What's the deal? It's that flat in New York, isn't it?'

'Possibly. I knew he had it, of course. Marie and the kids have been over there a couple of times during the school holidays. I don't think Andy uses it, though. Doesn't really speak about it much.'

'So is it just the *Mirror* on its politics-of-envy kick? You know, 'Why has Andy Sheen got a luxury pad stateside while our readers live in crappy council houses?' There's not much mileage in that, is there?'

'Wouldn't have thought so — '

140

'Well, has McGee phoned to speak to you personally, Charlie, or is he coming at this from some sort of angle? What was he after from all the guys he's been ringing? Why did he ring Sonya Mair, for example?'

'I don't know, mate. Maybe because she knows Andy as well as anyone. I don't know. It is strange that he hasn't rung me, though.'

'It's nothing to do with the 'not inhaling' story, is it? That's not going to jump up and kick us in the balls?'

'Funny you should say that. I asked Andy about that too; but he's absolutely insistent that he just did a Clinton — nothing more. And it's over thirty years ago, when he was a student at Cambridge. I can't see how that can hurt us.'

'Well, let's think it through, Charlie. So Andy smoked a bit of pot when he was at Cambridge. Right. So did everyone. OK, no big news in itself. Smoking dope didn't harm Bill Clinton; it didn't harm those Tories who put their hands up when Ann Widdecombe started rabbiting on about zero tolerance ten years ago, did it?'

'Yeah. The only thing is this new Department for Society that Andy's just got going — with Selwyn Knox, you know. It'd look bad if the papers run a story about the PM smoking dope when he's just launched his moral salvation crusade to wipe out naughty behaviour. We all need to be whiter than white at the moment — '

'Right. That'd be embarrassing, but it wouldn't be the end of the earth, would it? I don't know, Charlie. I've just got a sneaking suspicion there's something more than that

141

going on in Jim McGee's filthy little mind.'

'Yeah, I think you might be right. Andy says we should just forget it, but I don't think it's going to go away, myself. Sometimes Andy needs us to protect him even if he doesn't know it.'

★ ★ ★

As McDonald and Maddle were ruminating in the Red Lion, Nigel Tonbridge was just beginning to feel the pressure.

The problem with *Newsnight*, he always felt, was that the ten-thirty transmission time gave you a false sense of security.

When he'd been working for News, he'd got into the rhythm of churning out piece after piece from the moment he arrived at the BBC Westminster office in the morning to the minute the Radio 4 midnight bulletin went off the air. It was hectic, but in a way it was easier. You just got your head down and went with the flow.

Newsnight gave you too much time to think. Sometimes Nigel would spend the whole day agonizing over a minor element in a story: how to phrase something; which MP to use as the main interviewee; where to go for pictures to illustrate the story. And before you knew it the time would have ticked away and the studio director would be screaming for the cut spot.

Added to that was the pressure to be different; to give a sexy new perspective on a story your viewers might already have watched four or five times on earlier news bulletins; to be hip and cool in that annoying *Newsnight* way; to appeal

142

to the younger audience that Fred Pond the genial D-G was always banging on about.

Recently Nigel had begun to wonder if it was all really worth it.

And another thing — Nigel laughed as he caught himself muttering the telltale phrase of the archetypal ranting nutter — Nigel's 'other thing', the thing that was really starting to get to him about the new-style BBC, was the dumbing down. The seemingly endless quest to seduce a new, less sophisticated, less informed, less interested audience was becoming the bane of Nigel Tonbridge's professional life.

It wasn't just the need to sex up every story with 3-D smart-graphix and a dose of chart music, it wasn't just the pressure to expound every policy initiative in terms of 'what it means for today's urban teenager', or to explain every time you mentioned Andy Sheen that he was the Prime Minister — it was the whole new BBC mentality. In moments of soul-searching, Nigel was honest enough to admit that an additional factor in his dissatisfaction — perhaps even the most important factor — was that his face was starting not to fit.

It was over four years since he had moved from Radio Strathclyde down to Television Centre in London. On his debut as a TV News reporter, he had been acclaimed as a serious heavyweight; four years later and four years older, he was starting to feel like an old lag. He'd done his stint of car crashes, floods and crime reporting, he'd spent three months in the social affairs unit, he'd been to Brussels and he'd done two tours of duty in the various Middle East war zones.

Then he had moved to the BBC's Westminster operation, where he had been taken under the wing of the man he respected more than anyone in broadcasting.

Marc Lemaire was a brooding genius of French-Jewish descent. More than most others he had resisted the Corporation's headlong slide into infantile trivia, reality docu-soaps and news as entertainment. He had fought hard — and failed — to stop the axing of *Panorama*, *Worldview* and *Nation Matters*. He'd put up a valiant rearguard campaign against the dropping of foreign news from the television bulletins. In his own self-defining terminology, Marc Lemaire was a grown-up; but he had been fighting a losing battle with the less than grown-ups who were now running the show.

Over the months, Nigel could see his mentor becoming more and more frustrated, more and more frayed at the edges, as he watched the ineluctable decline of the Reithian ideals that once fuelled public-service broadcasting.

Marc Lemaire had taken early retirement from the BBC on his fifty-fifth birthday in 2010. The TV Centre accountants had announced they needed a thousand redundancies, and had offered beneficial terms and enhanced pensions to the staff the new bosses had fingered as dinosaurs, troublemakers — 'old soldiers rattling their muskets' in the D-G's telling phrase. Marc's name had been at the top of the list — how could it not be? — and the names of

144

virtually everyone else Nigel rated and respected in the Corporation had come just below it.

Since then, Nigel had found BBC Westminster increasingly inimical.

The new reporters and presenters flooding in were for the most part young and pretty — and pretty ignorant of politics, history and world affairs. But theirs were the faces that fitted at the new BBC, not Nigel's. Nigel Tonbridge's generation were starting to hear the tumbrils roll.

Tonight, for example, Nigel was supposedly cutting a four-minute spot on the problems facing British conscripts returning from the Middle East Wars.

He'd wanted to examine the financial and social issues of injuries sustained in the line of duty; of chemical poisoning from Syrian weapons plants, where previously unknown stocks of nerve gas and germ warfare agents had miraculously been discovered; of psychological traumas among the returnees.

But Newsnight's highly regarded young editor, Shayna Kelvin, had told him these were issues with 'no resonance for our audience'. What she wanted — and what Nigel was now reluctantly producing — was a survey of returning squaddies to see how they rated the new music in the charts compared with what had been there when they'd left for the war, how they coped with unfaithful girlfriends and — Shayna was hoping for a little actualité TV here — how they dealt with the blokes who'd stolen their bitches.

At that moment Nigel's phone rang.

145

Looking back later, he realized the only reason he didn't tell Selwyn Knox to go screw himself was that his despair over the BBC and his fears for the future were at an all-time high, while his self-confidence and his resistance were at an all-time low.

★ ★ ★

Geoff Maddle's mobile had gone off in the Gents. He'd told Charlie that the toilets of the Duke of Clarence weren't the best place for a confidential chat and had gone outside to the anonymity of a busy Trafalgar Square.

'Right, mate; we're OK now. What is it?'

'I don't know what to make of it, Geoff. After we'd been talking in the Lion last night, I went back to Andy and told him to stop pissing around. I told him if there was anything else in the drugs story — or anything else he's got tucked away in his past — we needed to know about it now. I told him if there were any skeletons — any shape or any size — they could harm us pretty badly if we don't know about them and things come out in an uncontrolled way. I mentioned all the sensitivity over St Selwyn's new department, like we said, and I told him we might just be able to get away with whatever it is, if he owned up to me right away, but he just kept denying there was anything.'

'OK. Well, that's it then. Shiny Sheen is shiny clean and we can stop shitting ourselves. Right?'

'Yeah, maybe, but I've just got a funny feeling, Geoff. You know, we've always assumed Andy

146

really is Mr Clean. So I was just a bit surprised when he wouldn't look me in the eye while I was giving him the third degree. I'm a pretty good judge of when someone's bullshitting me and I got the distinct impression Andy was covering something up. Maybe we should run a Lancelot check on him — what do you think? It's just it's a bit sensitive running Lancelot on the Prime Minister — '

'Yeah, but I think we should do it. We can't afford any surprises with Andy. We've always promoted him as such a goodie-goodie. Anything that dents that image is bad news for everyone, not just for him, but for the whole party, the whole image we've built, the whole Project.'

'Yeah, I reckon you're right. I just wanted to check that with you, mate. I'll get it done and let you know what spews out.'

'OK, but don't just go after the cannabis thing, Charlie. I want to know why McGee keeps banging on about Andy's finances and the New York apartment. Maybe you should get Damon Fowler back in for a chat. He's a wanker and he can't keep his mouth shut, but he might be a useful way to quiz McGee, assuming you don't want to talk to him directly.'

'Yeah, good idea. If I ring McGee, he'll know he's got us worried. I'll use simple Damon instead.'

* * *

It was after midnight when Nigel got home from his shift at *Newsnight*.

147

Joanie and the kids were all in bed, but Nigel knew he wouldn't be able to sleep. The sound of Selwyn Knox's voice — not on the radio, not on TV, but in person on the end of the phone — had shaken him more than he cared to admit.

For four years, Nigel had tried to forget the Exxington tragedy, had tried to forget little Clare O'Leary, to forget the growing terror he'd felt on hearing Knox's carefully calculated, smirking telephone speech which had killed Nigel's scoop and crushed his self-esteem.

For four years he had carried in his pocket the journalist's notebook he had been using in September 2006, the notebook with the transcript of Ian Murray's allegations, Eileen O'Leary's lament and Knox's gloating mono-logue.

Without him quite realizing it, the image of Selwyn Knox had become an obsession.

The memory of his own attempts to bring the guy to justice, his shame and self-loathing when he had crumbled before Knox's bullying and his subsequent rationalizations, which had half persuaded him to believe Knox was most probably innocent — all this had become ineradicably ingrained in a corner of Nigel's psyche, a corner he had spent four years trying never to visit.

Nigel spotted the blinking light of the answering machine and flicked the Play button. Like a dogged nightmare, the grating voice he had heard in September 2006 and then heard again tonight for the first time in over four years echoed round the room.

148

'Hi Nigel. It's Selwyn. It was good to talk to you tonight. I'm ringing to ask if we can let bygones be bygones. I'm sorry our last conversation back in Exxington was a bit fraught. I've always rated you as a journalist, it's just you got the wrong end of the stick all those years ago. Anyway, I appreciate your integrity over the whole affair. You were big enough to realize there was never anything in those stupid allegations Ian Murray was peddling and I respect you for that. I'm sure you know Murray left the council straight after the accident on the mountain: it was pretty obvious he was accepting the blame for what went wrong — the *Express* and the *Sun* made it clear it was all his fault and I guess he was big enough to put his hand up. I feel a bit sorry for him, actually. That was the end of his career and he ended up a bit of a sad case — drink and things. Died last year, from what I heard. But you've done well, Nigel. What was it after Radio Strathclyde? A stint on the local radio desk down in London and then that posting in Brussels doing EU stories for the BBC regions. Pretty good stuff. And now here you are on national television, working just round the corner from me. Anyway, I won't beat around the bush. I want you to come and work with me on the big project I'm launching. I'm sure you've heard about it. I know you're not happy at the BBC. This is your chance to do something worthwhile, to give something back to society. Come and do it, Nigel. You won't regret it.'

★　★　★

Damon Fowler had been in a flurry of excitement ever since he came back from Downing Street. He had been recounting and embellishing his conversation with 'Charlie' to his colleagues in the Environment Department press office with a glow of pride: 'So Charlie asked me what I thought of Jim McGee and what I would do to deal with the *Mirror*. So I said, 'We're going to have to deal with this guy sooner or later, Charlie; we're going to have to deal with him hard, and I think we should deal with him now before he can do us any harm.' Charlie and I think McGee is a bastard.' Damon looked slightly shocked at his own temerity in pronouncing such a word, but he clearly felt it was the sort of language he should use to impress people and show he was one of the boys.

Damon Fowler's burgeoning self-image was about to get another boost. His phone rang and there was the voice of Charlie himself. Damon made sure his colleagues on the desks around him could hear his end of the conversation and that they were in no doubt who he was talking to.

'Yes, Charlie, I think you're dead right. That's exactly what we need to do. Of course I'll come over to Downing Street, Charlie. I can ring McGee for you, no trouble. I'll see you in about half an hour. Bye, Charlie.'

★ ★ ★

The Department for Society was starting to take shape.

150

Selwyn Knox and Sonya Mair had watched the new officials moving into their offices and played a private little game of matching faces to files, exchanging discreet nods and grins as they spotted the more amusing cases.

The department's top civil servant, the Permanent Secretary Sir Robert Nottridge, was due to arrive the following day: his departure from the Department for Work and Pensions had been delayed by another crisis in the long-running saga over the collapse of the UK's pension system, which had left hundreds of thousands of OAPs without income, food or housing. Knox had fixed a private meeting with Sir Robert, Sonya and himself for the next morning.

For her part, Sonya was not best pleased.

Their new department had inherited the dregs of the former Cabinet Office's press officers, the more competent among them having found themselves jobs in other departments.

Sonya had discovered an operation in disarray.

All the faults of the old regime were present in spades. The press operation was a shambles, with no strategy unit, no media-planning unit, no instant rebuttal unit and an out-of-hours cover system that left much to be desired. Jack Davenham, who had been running the information directorate on a temporary basis pending the appointment of the new director, had been in the business for twenty years and evidently felt no need to improve on what he had grown used to.

Journalists' telephone calls were regularly met

151

with a casual 'I'll have to check and get back to you,' followed by radio silence until after the reporter's deadline had been missed. So newspapers were left to print whatever they liked about the government, with no statement to put the department's point of view or correct misleading facts.

But even worse than the lack of defensive media response was the total absence of proactive planning. Sonya was shocked to find that the department had no strategic planning unit to work up future media opportunities, to identify the best dates for future stories and to coordinate with other departments and Downing Street. This meant there were often clashes when the department tried to put out big news releases on the same day that other departments were presenting theirs.

And even worse than the organizational chaos was the attitude of the civil servants working in the directorate. The place was full of old lags working out their time until retirement who were totally uninterested in improving the way the press office operated.

As far as Sonya was concerned, the place was a shambles. It needed shaking up from top to bottom.

And to do that, Selwyn Knox told her, they needed a director of communications who would do Sonya Mair's bidding, someone who could be made to do what he was told, someone like Nigel Tonbridge.

★ ★ ★

Nigel talked to his wife about the phone calls from Selwyn Knox.

Joanie did not hesitate: she told him it was a great opportunity. He had been so fed up with the way the BBC was going lately that he should jump at Knox's offer. And the six-figure salary was much better, too.

Joanie was surprised when Nigel sounded diffident. And when he could not explain the reasons for his hesitation —

She asked if he had anything against Knox as a person.

Nigel was aching to tell her, to ask her advice about what had happened in Exxington.

But he couldn't: embarking on that story inevitably would have meant explaining the threat Knox had used and could still use to gain Nigel's silent connivance. Several days' thinking took Nigel little further.

Too many questions remained unanswered and — from where he was sitting — unanswerable; questions that could only ever be answered by re-entering the ambiguous world of Selwyn Knox. What was behind Knox's offer? Was it a genuine attempt at reconciliation? Was Knox trying to use Nigel in some way? Would he be stepping into a trap, into some sort of danger, if he were to accept?

He was surprised Knox had come to him after their run-in all those years ago, but he understood why Knox might regard him as useful: he had good contacts in political and media circles, they were both from the same part of the world, and Knox knew his qualities as a journalist.

On the other hand, Nigel still felt anger and shame over those events in Exxington.

The old notebook with the shorthand notes, always in his pocket, Nigel kept as a constant reminder of his own cowardice and inadequacy, a nagging self-reproach, which over the past four years had become a Hamlet-like obsession.

The more Nigel agonized, the more he rationalized, the more he convinced himself that Knox must surely be innocent, that Knox would surely not have approached him now if he really were guilty of Clare's murder, that Nigel must indeed have tried to convict an innocent man in Exxington.

What Nigel did not enunciate to himself was that actually he liked this conclusion because it brought him a sense of relief . . . a happy release from the burden of culpability he had carried with him for four years. If Knox were innocent, then Nigel too could be freed from his own sin of omission, his own guilt by inaction.

Nigel actively wanted Knox to be innocent in order to redeem himself.

And because he wanted his own redemption so badly, he slowly convinced himself that if he accepted Knox's offer he would somehow validate Knox's innocence, he would somehow make real the construct he had built in his own mind: 'If Knox employs me, he cannot be guilty.'

In the end, Nigel's agonized reasoning brought him to the strange conviction that only by accepting Knox's offer could he set the seal on

Knox's innocence — and on his own salvation from the sins of hesitation, weakness and, consequently, complicity in responsibility for Clare's death.

Nigel rang Knox's office to say he would be delighted to apply for the post of director of communications at the Department for Society.

★   ★   ★

As Damon Fowler walked into his office, Charlie McDonald was seized by a powerful wave of contempt. Little tough guy Damon, the pocket braggart who talked the talk but couldn't walk the walk, Damon the big mouth, Damon the tiny dick.

McDonald sighed and waved to Damon to sit down.

'OK, mate. Like I told you on the phone, you're going to ring McGee, tell him that you've been thinking about his call and you'd like to help him. You'll have to say you've got some grudge or other against Andy and you'd like to help the *Mirror* stitch him up or something. The main thing is to find where McGee's coming from. Try and see what his information is; see what tip-off he's had to get him started on the Andy thing, OK? I'll be listening on the other extension. And don't forget: whatever you hear in this office stays in this office. If I hear you've been blabbing about any of this, your future ends yesterday. Understood?'

★   ★   ★

Sir Robert Nottridge had been a civil servant for thirty-five years.

During that time, he had seen administrations of every political hue come and go.

He had worked with good ministers and bad ministers, good governments and bad governments.

So vast was his experience that friends told him he should write a book about it.

The reason Robert Nottridge did not do so was because he took seriously the civil servant's obligation of confidentiality, the oath of omertà that bound him and his colleagues to silence.

In long careers spent in intimate contact with government ministers, he and others like him would hear plenty of evil, see plenty of evil, but undertook to tell none of it to the outside world.

Robert Nottridge believed this was the only way the machinery of government could function. In his eyes, it was the only way ministers could allow themselves the total frankness they needed in their close, daily dealings with their Permanent Secretaries, the best of whom became a cross between father confessor, mentor and butler, the trusted receptacle of the most sensitive knowledge and opinions.

In his years at the top of the civil service, there had been two or three occasions when Robert Nottridge had felt that the malpractice of his minister or his minister's political adviser bordered on the reprehensible and the criminal. On none of those occasions did he speak out about what he had witnessed and he felt no sympathy for civil servants who did. But this dog-like loyalty did not preclude Sir Robert from having his own opinions about the governments he served.

He had despaired of the sleaze and stagnation of previous governments and had privately rejoiced when the New Project government was elected in 2005. He welcomed the new cabinet's energy, resolve and genuine idealism. It had been a good time to be in Whitehall, as the New Project broom began to sweep out the dead wood.

In their first, successful years, the new boys had enacted a swathe of sensible, reinvigorating legislation that had brought new life to the political arena. Even their increasing obsession with PR and spin and their steadily growing reputation for distorting statistics and embellishing news of their own achievements did little to dampen Sir Robert's enthusiasm. He felt this was a good reforming government that believed in what it was doing. He had supported the Middle East Wars, even when the casualties began to mount and the Allies were drawn into invading one more country after another.

His only doubts concerned the way New Project had begun to treat the civil service he believed in and loved.

Since the Northcote — Trevelyan reforms of the mid-nineteenth century had abolished the old ways of cronyism and corruption to establish a non-political, independent service appointed on merit and grounded in the highest ideals of impartiality and integrity, the civil service had loyally served governments of all stripes. In return it had been respected by them and protected from improper political pressure.

Until now no government had asked the civil service to do its political dirty work, no government had forced it to serve party interests at the expense of the wider interests of the nation.

The one flaw with New Project, Sir Robert felt, was that they were so eager to see through the work they had begun, so eager to stay in power, that they had begun to treat the civil service as their own plaything, at New Project's beck and call to help New Project get re-elected.

The antics of some of the party's infamous political advisers, the shock troops of the New Project revolution who were sent into every department to bully civil servants into toeing the New Project line, revolted Sir Robert.

The advisers, who thought they could give orders to his officials, undermining the service's prized impartiality, were anathema to him, and those who ordered civil servants to tell lies and conduct smear campaigns on behalf of the Project party were the worst of the bunch.

Now though, in 2011, Sir Robert Nottridge was prepared to give Andy Sheen and Selwyn Knox the benefit of his good will.

The idea for the new department he had been chosen to preside over struck him as evidence that the party was returning to the idealism and radical thinking it recently seemed to have lost.

His get-to-know-you chat with Selwyn Knox had gone well. He had found the minister enthusiastic and impatient to start the good work. Knox had told him to expect controversial measures from the Department for Society and Nottridge had replied that no omelette was ever made without breaking eggs. His political adviser, Sonya Mair, on the other hand, had struck Nottridge as deliberately unfriendly and cold. He had been told she had no time for civil servants, and she had taken few pains to hide it.

On the whole, though, Sir Robert Nottridge had left the meeting with a good impression of Knox. On returning to his own rooms down the old Cabinet Office corridor, he briefed his Private Secretary on what to expect.

'Knox comes across as a man of integrity, Philip. He seems motivated by idealism and not by personal ambition. I believe he may be the man to make a success of the great initiatives we are now embarking on, to bring back that honesty and generosity of spirit that has recently been dimmed in our political life. I admire him and have great hopes for him.'

For their part, when Nottridge left the room and closed the door behind him, Knox and Mair had looked at each other and burst out laughing. 'Fancy that lump of pompous bullshit having two little bastards hidden away in Clerkenwell! He doesn't look as if he had it in him!'

★　★　★

Nigel Tonbridge received his invitation to an interview at the civil service selection board the following week.

159

He was invited to submit in advance a paper on 'The Problem of Teenage Immorality and the Presentational Issues Surrounding Government Action to Tackle It'. At the selection board, he was told, there would be role play based on a 'typical situation that a director of communications may be expected to have to deal with in a major government department', and an extended interview before a panel of senior civil servants and assessors.

Nigel found the whole project somewhat daunting.

Two days before the selection board he received an unexpected phone call from Sonya Mair. 'Don't worry, Nigel. The board is going to go your way. Selwyn and I want you as our communications director and we're going to make sure we get you. Nothing has been left to chance. You're home and dry.'

★ ★ ★

That evening, Selwyn and Sonya drove to his pied-à-terre. It was here, in Dolphin Square, that the original nightingale reputedly had sung, only for the songwriter to decide eventually that Berkeley Square sounded more romantic. Nowadays the sprawling complex of apartments looked like an upmarket council block. Its less than fashionable position, on the Thames embankment next to Vauxhall Bridge, made prices affordable, while its closeness to Westminster made it a favourite place for out-of-town MPs to stay during parliamentary sessions.

160

Many of them, like Selwyn Knox, enjoyed the fact that wives or live-in girlfriends seldom made the effort to come and stay with them.

Sonya Mair had already uncorked a bottle of red Bordeaux and poured two large glasses. Dinner was on the table by the time she broached the subject that had been on her mind for days.

'You know, Sel, I made all the arrangements to fix that selection board for Nigel Tonbridge. Those civil servants are so prissy about their ethical independence, but you only have to know which buttons to press and they roll over as easy as anything! I went to see the HR guy who's chairing Tonbridge's board and a couple of the board members: they all figured in those dossiers I showed you, remember? So I gave them a little glimpse of what we know about their little peccadilloes and they all jumped straight into our pocket. What a surprise! So Tonbridge owes us one before he even starts the job. But look, I've been thinking. The thing I really want to be clear about is this: are you *really* sure you want Nigel Tonbridge to come and work with us? I think he's too dangerous. He could be a viper in our midst.'

Knox smiled as he replied. 'You've got it wrong, Sonya. If the guy's dangerous, where better to have him than right here where we can keep an eye on him? If we leave him at the BBC, it's going to be too tempting for him to start taking potshots at me once the department launches its crusade.'

But Sonya wasn't convinced. 'Oh, come on,

Selwyn. That's bullshit. He's had plenty of time to take a potshot at you and he hasn't. Why on earth do you want him on board now?'

Knox hesitated for a moment. 'I don't know — you need to trust me on this one, Sonya. I just have a feeling he could be important for me. That's why I'm involving him in what we're about to do. I'm making him our accomplice. I'm binding him so close to me he won't be able to bite.'

Soon, almost unnoticeably, the bottle of wine — and then another — were emptied.

As Knox stretched out by the fire, Sonya leaned across and stroked his neck. He did not respond. Sonya's hand began to slip inside his collar. He remained motionless. Now her hand was unbuttoning his shirt, reaching down to his belt, opening the buckle, slipping inside, slipping down to grasp . . .

Suddenly, Knox leapt to his feet, boiling with anger, all pretence at restraint irretrievably lost in a hail of rage and flailing fists.

'What the hell are you doing? Not that way, for Christ's sake! That's wrong, you bitch — that's not what we do. I need it how I've told you. What are you trying to do — humiliate me?'

Sonya Mair leapt back to protect herself from the blows raining down on her. 'No, Sel, no. It's not that — ! I just wanted to try something normal for once . . . I'm sorry . . . no, don't hit me! Not my face . . . don't hit my face! No. No. I'll do it . . . wait . . . I'll do it, Sel . . . '

And Sonya Mair ran from Selwyn Knox's onslaught into the adjoining bedroom. When she

162

returned, she was no longer the sophisticated, elegantly dressed, carefully made-up thirty-five-year-old who had left the room minutes earlier.

8

Nigel's letter of appointment arrived from the civil service commissioners, informing him of the grade, salary and pension rights attached to his new job.

His title was to be director of strategy and communications at the Department for Society, a grade three post entitling him to membership of the senior civil service and the First Division Association. His three-year contract was renewable by mutual consent. Under separate cover he received a genial letter from Sir Robert Nottridge, welcoming him to the department and inviting him to make an appointment for an introductory chat on his first day in post.

When Nigel phoned Sir Robert's office, an Assistant Private Secretary with a pronounced Brummie accent told him he was expected to start work a week on Monday and the Permanent Secretary could see him after morning prayers that day at ten-twenty.

After so many years at the BBC, Nigel found himself disorientated by the speed with which such defining changes in his life were being made. To BBC colleagues who quizzed him about his new job, and expressed doubts over the characters of Selwyn Knox and Sonya Mair, Nigel replied with a noncommittal shrug. He told them he'd had enough of being a political reporter, constantly on the outside looking in; he cited the example of other journalists who had gone to work for the government and who all spoke now of how closely they were involved with policy-making; and he reminded them of the respect this government accorded its communications officials as privileged participants in the inner workings of the New Project party.

Privately, he told Joanie that his greatest regret was that he would now have to abandon Sir Hubert. As a serving civil servant, he would be barred from making any publications with a political content and he felt Sir Hubert would inevitably be regarded as falling into that category.

For the past six years, Nigel had spent his spare time trying to resurrect his unfinished university thesis, which had recently blossomed into a full-length biography. During that period, Nigel had grown as fond of Sir Hubert Wakely as if he had been a living friend, rather than a long-dead nineteenth-century politician, remembered now — if he was remembered at all — solely for his role in one of Westminster's lesser political scandals.

His affinity for Sir Hubert was due partly to their shared Scottish connections and partly, Nigel sometimes felt, to his own empathy with Wakely's tendency towards melancholia and self-reproach. This darker side of Sir Hubert emerged with great clarity in the private journals he had kept during his reclusive existence at the family home of Clanwinning in Midlothian following his disgrace in 1845.

In his student days Nigel had visited Clanwinning and befriended the then owner of the house, a youngish stockbroker named McIndoe with little interest in history and no use for Wakely's journals, which had lain unopened for over a century. Mr McIndoe had been more than happy for Nigel to beaver away in the former library, which Mrs McIndoe had had converted into a solarium and mini-gym, and to copy down in longhand vast swathes of Sir Hubert's musings.

This prolonged communion with the dead politician had given Nigel a strange insight into the Sheffield & Ironbridge scandal and the devastating effect it had had on its principal political victim. Wakely's journals began a few weeks after his resignation speech to the House of Commons in May 1845, which, he wrote, 'has left me with ringing cries of 'Shame!' from my erstwhile familiars forever burned in my ears, very like we are told the visage and form of the assassin can sometimes be burned on the retina of his victim's eye, there to be retrieved after death and used by the detective seeking to resurrect the identity of the killer.'

It seemed to Nigel that Wakely regarded his life after the railway scandal as a form of living death. Nowhere did he attempt to justify his own part in the events leading up to the twenty-seven fatalities on the Crewe to Warrington line. He accepted the findings of the official inquiry that the derailment had been due to 'the buckling of the rail under the downwards pressure exerted by the passing engine on a section weakened by

166

insufficient admixture in the iron used for its constitution'. And he refused to complain about the treatment he received when he was expelled from parliament.

At no point did Wakely ever deny that he had lied about the Northern Railways share scandal. He had failed to warn investors that the steel used for the new tracks on the Crewe to Warrington line had been ordered from the Sheffield & Ironbridge Foundry Company, despite warnings of impropriety about the firm's directors.

The investigation into the ensuing crash had established that the track failure was due to the adulteration of the iron ore used in its construction, and that Sheffield & Ironbridge had done this deliberately to save money. Wakely had tried to hide this fact in his statement to parliament. Later he had been forced to backtrack on several important aspects of his statement and had then been held up to public ridicule and forced to resign.

What puzzled Nigel was that Wakely never sought to defend his conduct or to exculpate himself. While bribes had been paid by Sheffield & Ironbridge, Wakely himself had never made any monetary gain from the affair.

The government minister who did profit — he was, it later transpired, the first cousin of Sheffield & Ironbridge's chairman — was never charged with misconduct and went on to enjoy a long and successful ministerial career. The only references to this in Wakely's journals are oblique. In the section of his diaries which he had apparently been preparing for publication as a memoir under the title, 'Animadversion on the Nature of Success and Failure', Wakely hinted at his disillusion with former colleagues. 'All I see around does seem to point at me the bitter accusing finger of failure and dishonour. Not least the bounty I see my colleagues enjoy in their careers which, though I estimate such worldly success at nought, I cannot but feel levels reproach at one such as me. I bear my shame with bitter fortitude.'

A close reading of the Wakely journals had led Nigel to conclude that Sir Hubert had other transgressions on his conscience in addition to Northern Railways. The diaries made reference to further episodes involving false statements to parliament both by the author himself and by fellow ministers.

Nigel felt perhaps the greatest merit of his own work on the Wakely case was the light it threw on the culture of lies and deceit which routinely surrounded the political life of the period. But the most shocking result of his research, and the one that affected Nigel most deeply on a personal level, was his conviction that Wakely had not died of the influenza that is customarily given as the cause of his death. From references in the later journals, Nigel had become convinced that the shame Wakely felt after 1845 had led him to plan suicide and that his death in 1852 was the result of self-poisoning with arsenic. Wakely's descendants, apparently fearful of the further disgrace this would bring on the family name, had disguised Sir Hubert's suicide

168

in the commentaries written after his death and had kept the secret for the next century and a half.

★ ★ ★

Charlie McDonald had done his research and had gathered as much intelligence as he felt he could expect to unearth from the comfort of his Downing Street office. Now he sensed the time had come to take the initiative.

Now was the time to brief Geoff Maddle and give him full authority to get out and do something.

'So this is what I've managed to find out, Geoff. First of all, I did the Damon Fowler thing we talked about and I've got a much clearer idea of where Jim McGee and the *Mirror* are coming from. I got Damon to ring McGee and offer to help him dig the dirt on the PM. McGee was delighted: as soon as he thought Damon was going to help him rattle Andy's skeletons, he was falling over himself to explain what he's discovered so far.

'Basically, McGee has been contacted by someone who says that he's a pal of Andy's from way back and that he's got something of interest to tell the *Mirror*. McGee wouldn't tell Damon who it is, where he lives or what he's got on Andy, but I think it's someone who knew Andy at Cambridge. What I do know is that McGee's come across the Sheen-smoked-pot story, and what I think he's trying to do is turn it into something much bigger. McGee told Damon he's chasing something that could blow a few people out of the water — '

'He could be bullshitting, Charlie, he could be trying to put the wind up us. I'm not convinced McGee's got anything. He's on the City pages, remember — that's how he got the info about Andy's flat in New York. But I reckon he's trying to put his name to a big story that'll make his reputation and get him into political reporting.'

'Yeah, that's all these bloody hacks are concerned with — making their own name. All they're interested in is gossip and tittle-tattle and they couldn't give a toss about the truth. But we can't afford to take our eye off this one, Geoff. I wondered why no one had ever run a Lancelot check on Andy, so I ran the program on him like we said. It came up with nothing. Nothing, except the usual pile of opposition smears they've tried to run against him over the years, nothing to stick. What I did do, though, was go to the Police National Computer — I just did it on a hunch. And that's where I got something. Apparently, we have privileged access to the third-back-up, fail-safe hard drive, or whatever you call it, on the PNC — y'know, the one that's never wiped out however many times you pass the official eraser over it, the sort of thing that got that pop star on the child pornography charges all those years ago. Well, take a look at what it came up with: 'Andrew Michael Sheen, Cambridge Magistrates' Court, 11 May 1981' — it's a conditional discharge on a drugs rap!'

'Let's see that — Andy bloody Sheen! I can't believe it. So he did inhale after all!'

170

'Looks that way, doesn't it? He was certainly up in court on a possession charge.'

'So do you think that's the story McGee's got? Is that what he's making all the song and dance about?'

'Could be, Geoff, but I'm still a bit suspicious. For a start, from the way he was talking to simple Damon about it, it sounded as if it was quite a bit bigger than just some hippie on a conditional discharge. And the other thing is: if that's all there is to it, why didn't Andy just put his hand up when I tackled him about it the other day? He must know we can deal with a conditional discharge — it's not going to bring the government down, for Christ's sake.'

'So have you been back and shown this to Andy?'

'No, I haven't, actually. To tell you the truth, I'm getting a bit worried about old Andrew Michael Sheen and I want to find out as much as I can before I confront him again — '

'Well, the only good thing is that McGee won't have seen this PNC stuff, Charlie. The court appearance would have been wiped off Andy's record ages ago: I don't think these things stay active for more than a few years. And if this is the only computer file that exists, then I reckon the *Mirror* haven't got anything on us. If all they've got is some guy spinning McGee a yarn to earn a few bob, they don't have a leg to stand on — '

'Yeah: *if* this is the only record of what went on in Cambridge; *if* this is the only thing that fingers Andy. I'm just worried there could be more of this stuff lying around.'

'Well, there's only one way to find out. Shall I go and have a sniff around?'

'Yeah. Thanks, Geoff. You know you're the only one I can trust to do this. Get down to Cambridge, look at the official records — police, courts, university, newspapers — and do what you can to wipe them before the media get hold of them. A bit of rewriting of history is called for here, mate. I'll give you an Official Secrets Act affidavit in case you need to keep anyone quiet over this — y'know, the old 'I can tell you this, but then I have to kill you' routine — '

'That'll work with PC Plod, Charlie; but what about the guy who's been blabbing to the *Daily Mirror*?'

'Absolutely: we need to find him before he does us any more damage. So find out the truth, mate — and then destroy it! Meanwhile, I'll deal with McGee and the *Mirror*. I'm already collecting some material on Mr McGee — useful material to keep him quiet.'

★ ★ ★

Nigel had been intrigued by the idea of government departments holding morning prayers. When he arrived, early, for his first day at the Department for Society and was met in the spacious lobby of the old Cabinet Office building, his first question to the amused Assistant Private Secretary to the Permanent Secretary, who had been deputed to meet him, was met with a laugh and the explanation that

172

this was actually civil service slang for the daily morning planning meeting, which he, Nigel, would soon be expected to chair.

Nigel's second question — a request for an explanation of the young man's own convoluted title — brought a more considered response.

'Well, the Permanent Secretary, Sir Robert, is the top civil servant in the department. He's 'Permanent' because the here-today-gone-tomorrow Secretary of State (that's Knox at the moment) theoretically can't appoint him or remove him — that's what makes the civil service independent and able to offer impartial, objective advice without fear of reprimand or hope of favours from the politicians. I say theoretically, mind you, because this New Project lot are having a pretty concerted go at cowing the civil service into becoming the Whitehall arm of the Project party.

'Anyway, if you think of Yes, Minister, the PermSec is basically Sir Humphrey and the Secretary of State is Jim Hacker. Now, both of them have junior civil servants to run their private offices — make sure they're always well briefed for meetings, that they see all the documents they need to see, that they wash behind their ears and so on — and these are called Private Secretaries. In Yes, Minister, Sir Humphrey's young helper was the one whose name I can never remember — he was played by Derek Fowlds, I think — so he would be the Private Secretary to the Permanent Secretary. And then, of course, you have the Assistant Private Secretary to the Permanent Secretary, which is me, *et voilà!*'

By this time they had reached the Permanent Secretary's outer office, where a bevy of Private Secretaries — or Assistant Private Secretaries — were hunched over documents and telephones looking ostentatiously busy in anticipation of Sir Robert's return from prayers.

Nottridge himself soon strode briskly into the room, spotted Nigel and stretched out his hand. 'My dear fellow, welcome to the Department for Society. I feel as though I already know you well from your splendid career at the BBC. Do come through and have some tea. Judy, would you fetch two teas, please?'

The senior civil service operates a closely codified status system, involving the size of offices, type of desk chair and soft furnishings allocated to its members. Unremarked by Nigel's untrained eye, but a source of pride to their owner, Sir Robert's pink settee and two armchairs were arranged around a teak coffee table. Nigel sat in blissful ignorance on one chair as Sir Robert launched into his welcome speech.

'I must say you join us at an exciting time, Nigel — we're all on first-name terms here, by the way — except, of course, that one addresses the Secretary of State as 'Secretary of State'. As civil servants, we address the office, not the person, a fine distinction, but an important one. Where was I? Yes, an exciting time . . . I have myself been a civil servant for thirty-five years — a Permanent Secretary for twelve of them — and I have served administrations of all colours. I was saying only the other day to the

174

Secretary of State that this New Project government has done exceptionally well overall, but I do feel its place in history will depend on the outcome of the MEWs and — of more relevance to us here — on its social legislation.

'If we in this department can assist them to revive the idealism and enthusiasm they arrived with in 2005, if we can return them to their early commitments to social justice and fairness, then I believe history will remember them kindly.

'Overall I admire the majority of the ministers in this government: you get a few bad apples in any barrel but, in general, they have been a pretty good crop. So, *courage, mon brave!* The spotlight will be on us; I know the PM regards our work as vital to the fortunes of his administration. Now, Philip will show you to your office. If you have any questions, do not hesitate to come and ask me. In the meantime, I would recommend you go and talk to the head of our policy division, a fellow called Christopher Brody, whom you will find at the far end of this very corridor. You and Christopher will be working closely together and he will be depending very heavily — as we all shall — on your presentational advice and your media expertise in our policy work — '

Nigel's head was beginning to spin from the morning's information overload as he knocked on the door of Brody's smaller but nonetheless well-appointed office. Brody was a gangly, bearded man of about fifty, fretful in his manner and with a breathless staccato speaking style. He waved Nigel to a seat on one of several hard-backed chairs drawn up to a beech veneer table squeezed into the space between his desk and the window.

'Well, welcome to the Ministry of Social Engineering. Glad to hear that you'll be keeping us all on the straight and narrow, keeping us in McDonald's good books — that's the ultimate test of success in this government as far as I can see. Get the *Daily Mail* headlines right and you get a pat on the back, that sort of thing.

'Been to see old Nottridge, have you? Not a bad sort — bit gullible, but there are worse. I'll be frank with you: my problem with this New Project lot is the spin. If it weren't for the McDonalds and the Maddles, they could have made a fist of things.

'People believed them back in 2005; but then they decided they had to have the spin doctors in charge of everything, telling lies when they didn't need to. It's just become a bit of an obsession: why tell the truth when you can tell a lie?'

Nigel smiled wryly.

Brody was in full flow now. 'Worked OK at first, but then people began to see through it. Now, even if government press notices were approved by St Peter himself, people would say, 'Where's the catch?''

Nigel grimaced.

Brody looked him straight in the eye. 'It makes your job as communications director very tricky. You're a civil servant so *grosso modo* you're likely to be telling the truth; but I can tell you it won't be long before you'll get leant on by the

176

political advisers to join them in a few Project party porkies.

'You'll need to be on your toes in this department because our political adviser, woman called Sonya Mair, is a particularly bad example of all that. She's already been round here breathing down my neck.

'She'll have you doing New Project's political dirty work for them and if you object she'll have a few threats to throw at you: I certainly hope you've got no skeletons in your cupboard because, if you have, she'll know all about them and she'll have no qualms in using them against you.'

Nigel felt his stomach clench in an icy knot. He looked to see if Brody had spotted his wave of panic, but Brody was still talking. 'You need to remember that she enjoys Knox's total support — you'd better watch your step with both of them.

'They're zealots, of course, right out of Andy Sheen's academy of messianic missions: the New Project lot have always had a streak of odious piety about them, but now it's become an overweening and very unattractive obsession. They believe that only God and they know what's best for society and since God won't introduce the legislation, they had better do it themselves!

'They've got a dangerous passion for social engineering and saving society — and this department has been given the green light to give it full rein. I think we'll need to keep a very close eye on that Knox fellow, or he'll be deporting the unemployed to Tasmania.'

As Brody spoke, Nigel fingered the old notebook in his pocket and felt a frisson of trepidation that the man whose words were contained within it was now leading the crusade to save society — and that he, Nigel, was working alongside him.

★ ★ ★

Geoff Maddle had half an hour to wait at King's Cross — the Cambridge train had been delayed because of rolling-stock failure — so he settled down with a coffee to scan the morning papers. Several of them were running with Knox's remarks on the responsibility he felt as he embarked on his mission to revive the moral underpinnings of society and combat the enemy within. Geoff balked at the rhetoric — it was too high flown for his taste — but he recognized that it would go down well with the PM. He tipped his hat to Nigel Tonbridge, who was now shaping Knox's media strategy and had obviously picked up pretty quickly on the sort of tone Andy Sheen was looking for.

Geoff's personal opinion of Sheen was distinctly mixed. Geoff had joined the New Project spin machine because his best mate had asked him to. But, unlike Charlie, Geoff had not been sharing Andy Sheen's political bed for the past decade and his residual loyalty to the Old Project party remained much stronger than Charlie's. He knew, though, that he had signed up to the new party for better or for worse, and he knew too that in Cambridge he would do whatever it took to protect the reputation of its leader.

Anyway, Geoff reasoned, we've got to think about Andy Sheen the image as well as Andy Sheen the man. It's the image that we've created and it's the image that means something pretty important to millions of people throughout this country: who cares if the man slips a bit from the ideal, as long as the image remains intact? And, whatever I think of the man, it's my job to keep his image shiny clean: I'm not doing this for Andy Sheen, it's for the good of the party and for the good of the whole country.

★ ★ ★

Nigel Tonbridge had been in post for three weeks now. Things had gone surprisingly smoothly for the launch of such a major government department. Selwyn Knox had wisely avoided any detailed policy announcements at this early stage and had concentrated on talking up the ideological rationale behind the Department for Society.

Nigel had warned him that the press were circling the department, unsure what to make of it and reserving judgement until Knox showed his hand. The liberal media had been brought onside by the first *Observer* profile; the right-wing press were hoping the department would provide the backbone in social policy they felt this country needed.

Neither right nor left wanted to take a

definitive position on Knox and his crusade until they had a better idea of his political direction and its practical application. So Nigel's media handling advice was that the Secretary of State should prolong this initial honeymoon period by keeping the hacks guessing. He arranged a series of interviews and profiles at which he advised Selwyn Knox to commit himself to as little as possible. The tone of moral mission had come from Knox himself, but otherwise Nigel felt they had had a good few weeks in media terms.

★ ★ ★

For Selwyn Knox, this was a period of phoney war, a period of consolidation before the great campaigns ahead.

He told Sonya Mair that he felt he was on the threshold of momentous events in his life; that the all-consuming force he felt within himself was at last on the point of finding an outlet, an application that would channel it to positive ends. Sonya congratulated him on a successful start to the new department's activities; in the scheme of things, she said, it could have been a lot worse.

She acknowledged the role of Nigel Tonbridge in setting the tone for the media coverage; but she could not avoid raising the same questions she had asked her boss before: was he sure Tonbridge was safe? Was he sure he had done the right thing in bringing him to work at the department? And, as on previous occasions,

Knox replied that no one other than Nigel could carry out the tasks that would eventually be required of him; only Nigel could play the role that he, Selwyn Knox, would one day need him to play.

Seeing Sonya's fleeting expression of hurt, he added that she and Nigel were the two beings without whom the future he had planned for his department and for himself would not be possible.

With a little shrug, Sonya changed the subject. 'What are you doing this weekend, Sel? It would have been nice if we could have invented some conference or other and had a weekend together. The problem is that Thomas has got clients coming to dinner on Saturday and I'm going to have to stay at home and play the good wife and hostess — '

'I know. I would have preferred a weekend in a hotel with you, but I haven't been to the constituency for a while and the agent is agitating for more grass-roots activity. Constituency parties are strange: they're proud to have an MP who's near the top of the ministerial ladder, but they get jealous too. They seem to look on me as an unfaithful husband who's been lured away by the flesh pots of Westminster. And a weekend at home will help keep Ruth happy as well. She's very long-suffering, but even she gets a bit resentful when she hasn't seen me for so long.'

★ ★ ★

Geoff Maddle was having a problem with Sharon.

Sharon had been in her job for eleven years. She was clear about the rules, and she was used to applying them with a rigour that any High Court judge would have been proud of. 'I'm sorry sir. These things need to be arranged in the proper way. He's the court registrar and he can't just come and see anyone who walks in here.'

'This is very important. Is he in the office today?'

'Well, yes he is. But, as I say, I can't disturb him just like that.'

The man in the parka thought for a moment. Sharon could see the suit and tie under his rough outer jacket. The language of dress codes was speaking to her, but she was unclear how exactly to place what it was saying.

'OK. Please tell him that I'm here on official business and it's very important that I speak to him now.'

Sharon hesitated. 'Well, why don't you tell me who you are and what you need to talk to us about. Then perhaps I could — '

'No. You go and get the registrar. I'll explain to him. This is a very important matter and it's in his interest to talk to me now. I can't tell you any more than that.'

The tone was peremptory, not used to coming off second best. Sharon frowned, made a gesture of annoyance and rose reluctantly from her chair.

'Well, if you wait here I'll see what he says. I can't promise anything. All right?'

Maddle nodded and took a seat. The otherwise anonymous walls of the reception area were decorated with prints of Cambridge colleges. It reminded him of that detective series that used to be on TV: *Inspector Something*.

Maddle wasn't an Oxbridge man. It wasn't that he resented the Oxbridge types in the Government Information and Communication Service. He knew he had seen a lot more of the real world than any of them. How many of them had spent time sitting in magistrates' courts? How many of them had reported burglaries and car thefts and dangerous dog cases for a local rag?

How many of them could have come here today and done the sort of things he was about to do? Not many. Maddle was the man for this job. He was the one to tidy up the mess.

There was the scrape of a door and Sharon reappeared. 'You can go in now, sir. Mr Hodges will see you.'

Maddle walked into a comfortable, orderly office.

★ ★ ★

What surprised Nigel Tonbridge most about his new job was the level of access he had to the Secretary of State and his official engagements. Old hands in the department's press office, which Nigel was now running, told him this was a development since New Project had come to power.

183

In the old days, the director of communications had been just an afterthought in the policy-making process. The politicians would beaver away among themselves, taking advice from civil servants on legal and factual policy issues, but ignoring presentational questions until the policy was ready to go to parliament. Then and only then would they call in the communications director and present him with the initiative or the legislation that he was expected to go out and present to the media and public opinion.

Since 2005, according to Nigel's press officers, the process had been virtually reversed. Now PR considerations carried a much higher priority. Now no government policy was worked on without first considering advice from the director of communications on how it would play with the media. Cynics said the tail was wagging the dog.

From Nigel's point of view, the fact that civil servants working in the Government Information and Communication Service were now regarded as central to the policy-making process meant that his job involved a disconcerting intimacy with Selwyn Knox. Never a day went by without the Secretary of State calling him into his office to listen to lobby groups or attend strategy planning meetings. He was called in for private chats about policy-presentation issues or to listen in on Knox's telephone conversations with the PM and other government ministers.

Nigel's work on the Wakely case had roused his interest in what makes politicians tick; his

184

run-in with Selwyn Knox, and his obsession with his own failure to call Knox's bluff over the death of the girl on the mountain, had left him with an unsatisfied need to explore the forces that drove this particular politician. A sense that there was unfinished business and his own dissatisfaction with himself were pushing him on.

Nigel knew Selwyn Knox must be aware of this — Knox was a shrewd, perceptive man.

The peculiar knowledge each had of the other's past history, thoughts and obsessions threw a heavy shadow of intimated significance over even the most trivial conversation. It seemed as if each man was constantly peering into the other's soul, seeking out deeper meanings in whatever was said, looking for the hidden thoughts behind every comment. It was like a continuing game of psychological chess, whose significance was known only to the two participants: each making mental thrusts and parries; each defending his inner secrets or baring his inner thoughts.

On reflection, Nigel was sure Knox must have known this would be their relationship if he invited Nigel into his professional life and he was disturbed by the thought that Knox had deliberately chosen to create the situation they were now in. Why had Knox recruited him? Why had he clasped to his bosom the one man who could read his most intimate thoughts and reveal the secrets of a past he would surely wish to conceal from the world?

Nigel could find no rational explanation for

185

Knox's action, no explanation of why Knox had deliberately placed himself in a position of great danger — danger of exposure, danger of humiliation and danger of ultimate shame.

★ ★ ★

Geoff Maddle was on the phone to Charlie and his news was not encouraging.

'So I saw the registrar of the court, OK? And he had no idea what the hell I was talking about. He's only been there ten years. I didn't give him any details of the case, but the judge who would have dealt with Andy back in May 1981 has apparently been dead for ages. Anyway, the guy I spoke to today said there would be no written records anywhere in Cambridge as far as he knows. The only possibility would be the Police National Computer and that was extremely unlikely to have kept any information from that far back. I didn't mention that we'd already been there, done that!

'So the next thing I did was to go down to the *Cambridge Evening News* and check the archives for May that year. There was nothing in the paper, Charlie — I didn't expect there to be. That was the hippie era, wasn't it, or at least the tail end of it? There must have been conditional discharges coming out of their ears.

'What I did do, though, was make a note of who the *Evening News*'s crime correspondent was at the time, a chap called Reg Green. Then I spoke to the current hack who does the courts for them nowadays and I asked him about

186

Green. He said Green retired in 1996. He didn't know where he was now except that he thought he had a house in Royston: that's a place a few miles out of town. Anyway, Mr R. Green of Huntingdon Road was conveniently in the phone book, so I thought I'd pay him a surprise visit.

'He's eighty and he's pretty doddery, but he did remember the Andy Sheen case — he said he'd picked up on the name when Andy was first elected PM. He seemed to think the whole thing was a bit of a laugh — obviously didn't realize it might be a bit embarrassing for a Prime Minister to have a drugs record!

'What he did say, though — and I think this might be what we're after, Charlie — is that he thought there were two defendants in that case, Andy and another student. I just wonder if that could be the guy who's been playing the *Mirror*'s Deep Throat — but even if he is, I don't have the faintest idea how we're going to find him.'

9

Even Selwyn Knox admitted he had been doubtful at first about the task he had been handed by the Prime Minister. What Andy Sheen was asking him to bring about was nothing less than a revolution in the hearts and minds of the British people, a fundamental change in the way individuals think about their relationship with and their place in society.

The more Knox reflected on the challenges that lay ahead, the more he became convinced that this momentous undertaking was to be the pinnacle of his life's work. He began to regard the Department for Society as a personal crusade to rescue Britain from all its faults and sins, in short, to rescue it from itself. He began increasingly to speak of the department as a mission of moral salvation.

Knox admitted he was unsettled by the size of the task.

He was comfortable with the aims — he had fixed his department's targets — but he remained unsure of the best way to set about realizing them.

His favourite metaphor was of himself and his fellow reformers as loving parents who find they need to correct and discipline a wayward child. He spoke of a father's love that had to be sincere but had also to be rigorous and sometimes even cruel.

He was unsettled, too, by the torrents of conflicting advice he had begun to receive from political interests, social lobby groups, the media and the many people from around the country who wrote to him in sackloads offering tales of personal experiences and recommendations for tackling the problems they had identified.

In the face of such divergent pressures, Knox had initially felt unsure about the direction his department should take.

With liberal voices urging him to enact more social welfare policies and provide more help for the disadvantaged, more understanding for offenders and sinners, while conservative forces demanded a momentous crackdown on deviant behaviour and antisocial tendencies, for a while Knox seemed to be caught in the grip of debilitating indecision over the very bases on which his crusade was to be constructed.

He knew he would soon have to start producing more than just statements of aims and intent, more than the generalist moral rhetoric he had so far employed. He felt under growing pressure to move from talk to action, to take the first concrete measures to turn plans into practice.

Finally, after several weeks of agonized hesitation, Knox was about to open his first departmental strategy meeting.

On the day he had arrived at the Department for Society, Knox had asked his top officials to prepare for this meeting. He had commissioned strategy papers from all the civil servants engaged on policy formulation. He had explained the parameters within which Andy Sheen had asked them to work and the goals he had asked them to achieve. He had stressed that he wanted his officials to 'think outside the box', to be radical in their proposals and to throw off the shackles of previous policy constraints. He told them they were operating on a green-field site — the world of social policy had begun anew on the day their department was created — and he reminded them that the PM had demanded they have the courage to think the unthinkable.

But Knox was not fooling himself. He knew all about the baggage the civil service had inherited from decades of conservative thinking — stifling caution and an ingrained unwillingness to do anything that might rock the boat.

As he scanned the faces of the officials who had taken their seats around his ministerial conference table, Selwyn Knox felt few grounds for optimism.

He instinctively mistrusted the civil service and felt he could assign virtually all those present to one of two stereotypes: those like Sir Robert Nottridge, old, staid and stifled by the dust of decades of stale civil service thinking; and those like Christopher Brody, cynical, mocking and unwilling to sign up to anything that went beyond the pragmatic and the workaday.

As he looked around the table, Knox concluded that only three of those present were capable of grasping the real issues, only he, Sonya Mair and Nigel Tonbridge, he thought, would have the breadth of understanding, the vision and the imagination to recognize the true import of what they were being called upon to do.

'Good morning, everyone. Thank you for coming. This is an important and potentially historic meeting. I hope you will not object if I open it with a brief prayer — '

★   ★   ★

As those around the table were responding with varying degrees of enthusiasm to their minister's words of holy commendation, Geoff Maddle was uttering a few choice words of his own.

The basement of the police station was dark and dirty. The low ceiling and absence of natural light reminded Geoff of the times his father had punished him as a child by locking him in the linen cupboard 'until he knew how to behave properly', a memory that had stayed with Geoff and — he thought — accounted for the claustrophobia he experienced when flying or travelling on the tube.

At the moment, though, claustrophobia was the least of his worries.

It had taken him the best part of the morning to persuade the Cambridge police that he was who he said he was and that they should allow him access to their files. The senior officer had been polite, but not over-helpful. Telephone calls to Downing Street had confirmed Geoff's identity, but the superintendent had insisted on written permission from the Home Office, and had only reluctantly settled for a faxed letter of authorization bearing the signature of the Home Secretary with the promise of a hard copy to follow by courier.

The station's record keeper — a harassed elderly sergeant who clearly had better things to do than rummage through files from thirty years ago — had categorically assured Geoff that no written records from 1981 would have been kept, unless the case had been a 'big one' or 'something special'. He said files from that time would almost certainly have been thrown out and it was 'well before we were computerized'.

Hampered by the fact that he could not reveal details of the case he was interested in, Geoff was unable to call on Sergeant Plod's assistance in sorting through the files. He had thus found himself sitting in front of a row of crumbling brown foolscap folders that filled a good thirty feet of shelf space. Decades of rummaging policemen had left big gaps in the dates of the surviving files with little attempt at chronology. By early evening, when the new shift was coming on duty at the front desk on the floor above him, Geoff decided enough was enough and told the departing sergeant that he too was calling it a day and might or might not be back in the morning.

★   ★   ★

After a morning of preliminaries, the inaugural strategy meeting of the Department for Society was going much as Selwyn Knox had foreseen.

192

The opening contributions, including one from Sir Robert Nottridge, had been so predictably dull that Knox had found himself torn between anger and amusement. Nottridge's paper was so elegantly, so impeccably balanced, such a litany of 'on the one hand' and 'on the other hand', that Knox had interrupted on more than one occasion to ask Sir Robert whether he had reached any conclusions or whether he even held any views of his own on the matter.

After half an hour of exposition, the Permanent Secretary had clearly noticed the note of exasperation in Knox's voice and hastily decided to yield the floor to the department's head of policy, Christopher Brody.

Brody's paper — presented in a dry, take-it-or-leave-it tone — consisted of an overview of the precedents for social reform measures in the past decade.

He cited a growing tendency towards the application of laws regulating aspects of life that would previously have been considered private and outside the ambit of government policy, a tendency which Brody said he would, for convenience, refer to as 'legislating for human nature'.

One Secretary of State at a department then known as Social Security (a concept, Brody noted, which had subsequently disappeared not only in the name of the department, but to a large extent in practical implementation as well) had instituted cuts in state benefits to unemployed single parents, meaning, in the vast majority of cases, single mothers. The intention was to provide a political stimulus — a financial penalty in this case — to persuade members of a certain class in society to alter their behaviour. The aim of this behaviour-correcting policy was, it went without saying, to get them to stop sponging and start working.

But the fate of those policies, Brody noted, was instructive. Following protests from liberal and left-wing pressure groups, the benefit cuts were initially withdrawn and the minister was dropped from the cabinet. She had, however, blazed a trail and had implanted in the minds of the public the concept that a government — as long as it had a large majority and pure intentions — should have the right to pass legislation aimed at reforming human behaviour. 'Legislating for human nature' was becoming respectable.

And the sacrifice was not in vain.

Within the space of a year or so, the cuts were reinstated in a slightly disguised form, and similar policies were applied without major protest to several other 'difficult' classes of society.

Subsequent ministers came up with various initiatives to deal with malingerers. The young unemployed were targeted initially, then the middle-aged, then the partners of the unemployed, and finally — most daringly — the disabled. In a policy dreamt up by the then Employment Department, disabled people who were out of work were specifically targeted to demonstrate the government's seriousness of intent. Brody spoke of the 'courage' shown by a government willing to penalize people so disadvantaged by nature that they traditionally fall outside the scope of punitive policies. He said he raised his hat to an administration which believed so fervently in its mission to alter and improve human behaviour that it would even target people in wheelchairs or suffering from cerebral palsy. This, he said, was the intellectual rigour of a Robespierre applied to the modern world.

Sensing the rapidly dwindling patience of the Secretary of State, Brody listed briefly the further social engineering measures which had followed under New Project. He mentioned the withdrawal of civic rights from benefit cheats, the forced repatriation of asylum seekers who were placing an unfair burden on the welfare system, the name-and-shame campaigns to stop teenage pregnancies, the provisions to outlaw offensive or undignified sexual practices including sex outdoors, the boot camps for the hardcore unemployed, the prison schools for habitual truants, and the addict colonies for drug abusers — all measures which had been successfully introduced in recent years.

The concept of legislating for human nature — Brody concluded — had now been established as one of the natural rights of a reforming and ideologically trustworthy government.

Had he stopped at this point, Christopher Brody might just have got away with it. Selwyn Knox was perceptive enough to notice the irony in Brody's presentation, but shrewd enough probably not to make an issue of the head of policy's dumb insolence.

Brody, though, was nothing if not daring; he decided he would deliver the last paragraphs of his presentation, whether the Secretary of State liked them or not: 'In conclusion, however, at the risk of appearing a fuddy-duddy, old-thinking civil servant, I feel it would be remiss of me to end this presentation without pointing out that the smooth implementation up to now of such socially charged legislation by this government cannot — as the financial advertisements put it — be taken as any guarantee for continued plain sailing in the future.'

Brody looked up over his spectacles and smiled sweetly.

'I say this simply to point out that legislating for human nature is not as easy as one might think. Attempting to change people's behaviour is a potentially risky business. The human soul, I fear, is not a rational instrument; there is no telling how it might react to the stimuli we may wish to apply. Our social scientists could tell us that our action will necessarily meet with such and such a reaction — a reaction that will logically move society forward and increase the sum of human happiness for all concerned. We may reassure ourselves that our intentions are pure, the putative results of our actions self-evidently beneficial for the objects of our experiment, that is to say, the citizens to whom the measures are applied. And yet, because the human soul is such an imperfect, irrational and slippery target, the fear must remain that its reaction will be far from the one we predict.'

Brody looked up from his speaking notes, as if deciding whether or not to press on with his argument. His slightly raised eyebrows and faint squeeze of the lips suggested to Nigel a man who was briefly weighing up the difference between a lamb and a sheep before plunging onwards.

'So please indulge me for just a few moments if I end with Shakespeare. You will recall that in *Measure for Measure*, the Duke, a highly principled, well-intentioned ruler, has — like us — identified sin and immorality in his country. I will, if I may, just read to you how Shakespeare describes it. He says it so much better than I ever could:

> We have strict statutes, and most biting
>   laws,
> The needful bits and curbs to headstrong
>   weeds
> Which for this fourteen years we have let
>   slip . . .
> Now, as fond fathers,
> Having bound up the threat'ning twigs of
>   birch,
> Only to stick it in their children's sight
> For terror, not to use; in time the rod
> Becomes more mocked than feared; so our
>   decrees,
> Dead to infliction, to themselves are dead.'

Again Brody paused and glanced round the table as if expecting to be interrupted, hesitated slightly and continued: 'So, you see, the Duke is pained by the moral decay of society and he

197

commands his minister Prince Angelo to wipe it out with strict legislation. I should say, by the way, that Angelo's sanctions for unchaste acts are slightly more draconian than we might be contemplating — sex outside marriage, for instance, incurs the death penalty. But, as we discover, it is Angelo's absolutism, his refusal to allow for human nature, that ultimately undoes him. Shakespeare concludes that no amount of laws can change 'the blood', no amount of laws can wipe out the irrational human drives deep within us. And Angelo is undone by the very human nature — this time his own — that he had tried to legislate out of existence: 'Blood thou art blood,' he says, as his own uncontrollable lust makes him commit an immoral act, one of many for which he himself has prescribed the death penalty. And I suppose Angelo's fate might be a lesson to all of us here in this room today: if we cannot stamp out sin in ourselves, we can never hope to stamp out sin in others: 'Judge not, that ye be not judged. For with what judgement ye judge, ye shall be judged: and with what measure ye mete, it shall be measured to you again — ''

But Knox had heard enough. He was not going to stand for such insolence from a civil servant. His voice was harsh and loud.

'That's enough! Quite enough! I am not in the habit of allowing my meetings to turn into lectures on Shakespeare, or on anything else for that matter. We are here to discuss social policy not fairy tales. I am afraid your presentation is simply not acceptable, Mr Brody. And I am not prepared to continue this discussion until we have agreed some rules of behaviour we can all abide by and respect. I am ending this meeting right now. You can all go away and think again about the way you approach these very serious issues. I am afraid I have not seen any evidence at all of the type of serious, committed thinking this department is going to need. And I can tell you, if you are not capable of producing what I need, I will not hesitate to bring in other people who are better equipped and better determined to do what I ask of them. So go now. Go and think about what I have said. You'll hear from me or from Sonya when I am ready to resume this discussion.'

★   ★   ★

Charlie McDonald was getting worried.

He had not heard from Geoff Maddle for forty-eight hours and he could not shake off the thought that the *Daily Mirror*, in the unprepossessing form of Jim McGee, was probably using the time to dig and delve, to accrete more dirt on Andy Sheen, to tighten its stranglehold on the windpipe of the government.

So when the phone rang and a familiar voice came on the line sounding considerably happier than in previous calls, McDonald heaved an audible sigh of relief. 'I never though I'd be so pleased to hear from you, you old bugger. What have you been up to all this time?'

'What do you mean 'all this time'? I haven't stopped to draw breath, mate. And it's been worth it, I can tell you. At last, I think we're getting somewhere with this bloody story — I think I've got a lead on our second man. And we've got it because I've been hacking away in the basement of a bloody police station for the past two days. Anyway, we were right — there was another defendant up with Andy in 1981 and his name is Harvey Parks. The file on the case should have been destroyed years ago, but it wasn't. It was in a filing cabinet in the basement of the Cambridge cop shop — and I found it! And not only do we have his name; we even know where he is. Once I'd read the file, I burnt it, OK? Like we agreed. So that's all dealt with. But then I asked my friendly sergeant about Mr Harvey Parks. Turns out he's pretty well known in police circles. He lives in the last squat in Cambridge, unemployed, bit of a sad case, says my policeman. Used to be a student here, had a good career in front of him, made a lot of money developing and marketing some medical remedy or something, then he got hooked on drugs and lost it all. They've had him in the station here a few times — pleasant bloke, apparently, very intelligent, or could have been. He wouldn't be any trouble to anyone if it wasn't for the old substances: he's a junkie.'

★　★　★

The Secretary of State's strategy planning meeting and the disorderly circumstances under which it had been so abruptly suspended had

200

become the talk of the department and much of Whitehall.

Civil servants who had been there lost no time in revealing what had gone on to colleagues in the various policy divisions, and they in turn were quick to email the spicy news to friends in other government departments.

It was little surprise to any of those involved that a garbled account of the flare up quickly appeared in the *Independent*. Seasoned kremlinologists noted the tone of the piece —traying Knox as a ranting zealot — and speculated about who the source of the leak might have been. Several civil servants spent an uncomfortable day or so in fear of a summons to the Secretary of State's office, where — if challenged — they would have had some difficulty explaining their conversations and telephone records in the aftermath of the fateful meeting.

But the calls never came.

There was no leak inquiry. And when, a week later, Selwyn Knox finally reconvened the interrupted meeting he gave no indication of the rage that had overcome him when they were all previously gathered round his table.

This time, though, the Secretary of State was at pains to avoid a conflict of views with his civil servants. He achieved this largely by making sure the only views heard and minuted were his own.

His opening remarks turned into a monologue that lasted over an hour.

He began by recapping the list of social policy measures taken by the New Project government. He praised them, but concluded, 'If we look at these measures objectively, they were — I'm afraid — little more than tinkering at the edges of the problem.' He then briefly discussed the memos he had received from his officials setting out their suggestions about how to tackle the problems which had been identified as priorities. These were, he said, 'all very measured and reasonable, or, put another way, the ineffectual pap and typical half-measures of anaemic civil servants'.

What was needed now, said the Secretary of State, was not palliatives, but radical surgery, measures to tackle the underlying causes of the disease that must be applied without delay and with all available force.

'And when we have done that,' he continued, 'the symptoms will start to disappear on their own. Our first task is to identify the source of the moral rot afflicting our society. Now, when I first looked into this question, I asked myself if something fundamental had changed in the psyche of mankind. What was the cause of the uncivilized behaviour that has gripped modern society?

'Had man suddenly become evil? And had this new evil suddenly spread through our ranks, bringing with it all the adverse effects we have witnessed in the behaviour of our people?

'Had war, for instance, degraded the ethical basis of men? Had conflict in the Middle East somehow thrown our moral compass off balance?

'My answer to this was: no.

'Our experience in the past has been that war

actually improved the moral qualities of those who remained at home: the Second World War saw a new coming together of civilian society in this country, a willingness to act in the best interests of society as a whole, the celebrated 'pulling together' of the East End.

'My other conclusion was that the moral decline of contemporary society did not begin seven or eight years ago when war first became a dominant factor in our everyday life.

'The moral decline began long ago, but its most pernicious effects, its most dangerous threats to our society, have emerged only in recent years.

'So I ruled out transient factors. I looked deeper. And that is where I found the answer I was looking for.'

Knox surveyed his audience. His eyes radiated the triumph of a man convinced of his own wisdom.

'The answer, gentlemen, is in our parents: in the way they raise their children; in the values they inculcate into them; in the discipline they instil in them. If our parents do not raise our children in the ways of respect and responsibility, how can society ever prosper? Allow parents to raise children with antisocial attitudes and society will ipso facto suffer. It follows as night follows day. The root cause of the dropouts, scroungers, addicts and criminals who plague our society is the failure of our parents. The nest from which emanates the poison at the heart of our social decline is the parental home, where lax discipline, wrong thinking and absent fathers have thrown our society into turmoil.

'This is not rocket science, gentlemen.

'It is not an earth-shattering revelation.

'It is common sense. And common sense says this root cause must be tackled if our society is to have any hope of surviving and prospering. The rocket science — if rocket science it be — lies in making the bold, decisive step of moving from analysis to action.

'Sociologists, academics and even government ministers have identified the problem of parental failure in the past, but they have never had the courage — or, indeed, the authority — to move from merely identifying the problem to taking the action necessary to deal with it.

'Well, I can tell you that today you see before you a minister who has that courage and — thanks to the outstanding leadership of our Prime Minister, Andy Sheen — also has the power to move from words to deeds. Now, over the next days and weeks, I shall be working on practical measures to turn this vision into reality.

'And I am today commissioning you all to go away, to tear up the short-sighted, feeble policy papers you submitted to me for this meeting and to think again.

'What I need from you by the time of our next meeting is a set of radical new proposals that go to the heart of the problem I have just outlined: I need measures to ensure that our nation's homes cease to be a breeding ground for criminal and disruptive elements. I need practical policy initiatives that will ensure parents change fundamentally the way they raise society's coming generations, policy initiatives that will produce a new generation properly schooled in the needs of society, inculcated with the values we hold dear and cleansed of the undesirable attitudes that result from parental inadequacy — cleansed of the sins of the fathers.

'It is a tall order, I hear you say, and I agree with you. But think of the rewards if we succeed in this great enterprise. Think of the new society we will be helping to create. Think how we will be remembered in history. Bear all these thoughts with you as you go about your work. And come back to me with a programme we can all be proud of. I am depending on you; but most of all the society of this country is depending on you. So I leave you with a challenge. You must ask yourselves: do you have within you the motivation and energy to tackle these great issues? Do you have the force within you to make changes that will be remembered and respected for generations?

'And, so that you are in no doubt, I can tell you quite categorically that I do myself have that inner force, that power and energy, which is welling up inside me and demanding to be turned to practical effect. I have it. I hope you all do too. Thank you and get to work.'

★ ★ ★

When Harvey Parks opened the door of the rundown terraced house in the drab street on the edge of central Cambridge, Geoff Maddle had little or no idea what to expect. Nor had he decided how he would deal with Parks if he did turn out to be the informant who was tantalizing the *Mirror* with promises of dirt on Andy Sheen.

Geoff had no intention of telling Parks that he was from Downing Street — that was a no-brainer: there was no point in inflating Parks's own valuation of any story he might or might not have on Andy. Geoff had toyed with several approaches and was still not completely decided when Parks peered out at him, blinking a little in the sunlight.

'Yeah. Can I help you?'

'Harvey Parks?'

'Yeah. Who wants him?'

'You know who I am, don't you, Mr Parks?'

'Erm, no. Am I supposed to?'

'If I told you Jim McGee sent me, would that mean anything to you?'

'Aw, fuck, man. You're from the *Mirror*, aren't you? You bloody journalists — I can tell you a mile away. Look, I'm really glad you've come, man. I thought you lot were never going to get back to me. Come in — come and have a smoke or something.'

★ ★ ★

Christopher Brody had been expecting a visit from Sonya Mair and he was not disappointed. She had put her head round his door, smiled and said, 'Can I have a word?'

Now she was sitting on the edge of his desk, looking desirable in a tight black dress and heels. Despite himself, Brody felt his eyes wandering towards the expanse of white thigh that Sonya had thoughtfully placed in his line of vision. Chris knew what was about to descend on him — the wrath of a Secretary of State was not something that even he took lightly — but he did find himself thinking how much more exciting and, probably, how much more lethal, it was going to be to take his punishment from Sonya Mair than from Selwyn Knox.

'You can guess why I've come, can't you? We've both been in this game for long enough. You're probably used to taking the piss out of cabinet ministers in front of their officials. You probably think it's all a bit of a joke. And, to be fair, you're most likely right in the majority of cases.

'But what you haven't twigged, I'm afraid, Mr Brody, is that this cabinet minister isn't like all the rest of them. When Selwyn Knox embarks on something, when he talks about making things happen and getting things changed, it isn't hot air. Selwyn Knox means what he says and he believes in what he's doing.

'So you can see, can't you, Chris, that it would be very hurtful — very hurtful indeed — to have some smart-arsed civil servant with an inflated opinion of his own cleverness come in and hold the whole thing up to ridicule.

'So I'm here to tell you that you should stop being such a naughty boy. You should stop playing with things you don't understand. Because this time you are completely out of your depth.

'And just in case you don't believe me, there's

one other thing you should be aware of as you go about your duties. I know you civil servants think you're all invulnerable and that you can get away with saying and doing whatever you like because the poor old minister is only here on sufferance and you're all so frightfully permanent and independent and untouchable.

'Well, in your case, Mr Brody, I'm sorry to have to tell that you're dead wrong. And that's because the minister knows all about your secret, Chris. He knows about your sad little addiction. He knows you can't pass a betting shop at two hundred yards. And he knows you've mortgaged your family's future to feed your pathetic gambling habit. And, just in case you're wondering, he knows about your criminal past too. He knows about the court judgements; he knows what you've got hanging over you. So if you want to keep in with your bosses, if you want to keep your job, if you want to keep your family, perhaps, you know exactly what you need to do. It's up to you, of course. You can carry on sabotaging the work of this department; you can carry on dumping on Selwyn — but you just need to know that if you do that, you will be shat on in a much more unpleasant, much more terminal way. Well, it's been nice talking to you. I think we understand each other. And you can take your eyes off my tits now. Byeee — '

When Sonya Mair had closed the door behind her, Chris Brody sat in silence at his desk. He knew Sonya was right: they did understand each other. And he knew he had been comprehensively thrashed by a ruthless and calculating woman. He should have been feeling humiliated. The strange thing was — and he couldn't quite pin down how or why — the experience had left him with a vague feeling of excitement and arousal.

Brody was still sitting frozen when Sonya reappeared at his door. 'And by the way, don't ever quote the Bible at him again — ever! If anyone's going to read him parables, it's me. OK?'

★ ★ ★

Geoff Maddle refused Harvey Parks's offer of a smoke and settled for a cup of PG Tips.

Geoff couldn't quite pin Parks down: his accent was upperclass Home Counties, but his clothes were from Oxfam or worse; his manners were exquisitely polite, but his language was littered with 'fuck' and 'shit'; he quoted Latin but lived in squalor. Geoff had to make a judgement on Parks; he had to figure out whether the man was a drug-sapped nutter or if some sharper intelligence was hiding behind those junkie's eyes. The way Geoff needed to play the situation, his game plan for the next hour, and perhaps the fate of the whole operation, depended on making the right call.

'So, Harvey, you had a pretty useful conversation with Jim then — '

'Yeah, useful, man. Useful. Useful for him, 'cos he knows I've got something, right? Not that

209

useful for me, though — I told him what would be useful for me if he wanted to hear the whole story.'

Geoff was reading the signals and reading them fast. There was a tick in the first box: Parks had swallowed his visitor's claim to be from the *Mirror*, following up Jim McGee's enquiries. And there was almost a tick in the second box: Parks had told McGee he had something on Sheen, but it seemed he hadn't given him the whole story. That was good, but it was also a warning sign: it meant Parks had enough intelligence to play his hand carefully, so he probably had enough intelligence to rumble Geoff if he put a foot wrong.

'Right, Harvey, I see what you mean. It's the money, right?'

'Yeah, the money. That would be useful for me, very useful — '

'OK. I understand that. But you have to understand where Jim and I are coming from, too. We have to know that what you've got is worth it before we decide to sign any agreement with you.'

'Well, I told your pal I had something really big on old Andy Sheen — something that'll send a bit of a shiver through the marbled halls, you know?'

'Yes, that's right, Harvey. You did. But I'm the man who controls the money. I expect Jim probably told you that, didn't he? And if I'm signing a big agreement with you — and I mean big money, Harvey — I need to know exactly what we're going to get from it. You understand

210

that, don't you? I have to be really careful before I sign anything that commits us to paying you so much money. So what I'd like to do, if you don't mind, is just to recap exactly where we're up to. We have to do this bit by bit; we each have to give something in turn and eventually we'll get to signing the big agreement — the agreement that I've got, er . . . here in my briefcase. OK? So first, what I need you to do — just to be quite clear — is to run through for my benefit exactly what you told Jim when he came to see you. Then we'll be one step down the road and I can perhaps offer you a provisional agreement on that basis, so you can then tell me the whole story about Andy Sheen and then I'll be able to sign the full agreement for you to get your money. Does that sound fair to you, Harvey?'

'Well, I guess so, man. The first step sounds pretty good to me, 'cos that's just the stuff I already told your friend when he was here before. So I'm not giving away anything of the other stuff. But then you've got to give me a provisional agreement before I give you the whole shit, OK? And then you'll see that it's pretty dramatic. And then we'll fix a price for it and sign the real agreement, OK?'

'Yes, OK. That sounds a fair way of doing business, Harvey. But you have to be completely upfront about things. So first you're going to tell me exactly what you told Jim McGee, OK?'

'Right. So what I told him is that Andy Sheen and I were the bosomest of bosom pals.

We both came up to Cambridge in 1877 or 1977 or whatever. And we both got on well — like the old house on fire, you know — and what I also told him is that there were a lot of drugs around at that time, man. It was, like, the seventies, OK? So, drugs — yeah. And the thing I told your Mr McGoo was that he could reveal to the nation that clean Mr Sheen, the man who's wiping the scourge of narcotics from the nation's noses, wasn't all that clean way back when. Because in 1981, when we were both in our final year, Mr Sheen got a little summons to the Cambridge magistrates for smoking a bit of the wacky baccy. So what's that worth for starters, Mr Moneyman?'

'Yes, Harvey, that's good. That's a good start. But there's more to it than that, isn't there?'

'My dear fellow, you see into my very soul. Oh yes, my friend, there most certainly is more than that — '

'All right. And let's just be clear, now: did you tell Jim about the other, erm, material?'

'Did I tell him? Well, to be very clear: I told him there *was* more, erm, material, but I did not tell him what the more, erm, material is. And I didn't tell him that because he did not place any money on my coffee table. I trust that is clear?'

'Yes. Absolutely clear, Harvey. Now the difference between Jim McGee and me, Harvey, is that Jim is a journalist and I am a journalist but also a businessman. So I am in the happy position of being able to place the money — or at least a binding agreement about money — wherever you want it placed. And all you have to do in order for me to do that is to tell me now, in your own words, exactly what you know about Andy Sheen.'

10

Selwyn Knox's post-mortem on the strategy meeting was held the following day with the departmental review group in Downing Street.

Sherry Black had been named as the Department for Society's permanent contact in the Number Ten policy unit and she had brought two colleagues with her. None of them looked a day over seventeen, but all spoke with the absolute assurance and authority which was the exclusive preserve of these creatures of the Prime Minister. When Sherry Black pronounced the phrase, 'Andy wants — ' or 'Andy thinks — ', even the most experienced ministers and officials, some of them decades older than her, would unquestioningly concur with her every thought, comply with her every wish. They might complain privately about the arrogance of the policy unit in issuing such orders — many ministers felt the PU advisers were a little too free and easy in invoking the name of Andy Sheen for what were in many cases their own schemes and demands — but they all knew that any show of resistance would be reported back to the PM and reprisals would not be slow to follow.

For Knox, the meeting with Sherry and the Sherrettes — as Sonya had scowlingly christened them — was thus of seminal importance in getting the prime ministerial seal of approval for his reform strategy.

'Well, Selwyn, Andy thinks you are doing well so far. He likes the press coverage you've been getting. But Andy says you need to start producing some concrete initiatives now. He says you need to define a bit more clearly the direction the department is going to take.'

'Right, Sherry. I'm glad you say that. Because that's exactly what we've been discussing and that's what I want to clear with you today. We're set to introduce our first measures now, and some of them are going to be pretty controversial. Andy asked us to get tough and that's what we're going to do. We've looked at all the social-reform policies of the past few years and some of them were pretty stern, but what we're about to do will make that lot look like a Girl Guides' picnic. What we're going to do will tackle the root causes of the cancer in our society. We are going to identify the people who are to blame — the teenage mums, the absent fathers, the unemployed, the spongers, petty criminals, drug addicts, benefit cheats and asylum seekers — and we're going to ensure they do not perpetuate themselves in our society. We cannot afford to allow generation after generation of these people to contaminate our way of life. These people don't vote, of course. They're not too much of a problem in themselves. There'll be liberal voices bleating about civil liberties and protecting the weak, but decent people are sick to death of being ripped off by social security frauds and immigrants. They know teenage girls get pregnant just to get handouts and a house at taxpayers' expense. They're fed up with seeing beggars and addicts on their streets. They're terrified of the muggers looking for easy money to feed their habit. So we're going to clean things up. We're going to be like a whirlwind sweeping through the whole of society, seeking out the corrupt, the criminal, the work-shy, the lazy, the violent and the antisocial. We're going to cut them out of our society like a cancer out of a healthy body.'

Sherry nodded her approval. 'OK, Selwyn. Andy will like that. We've got an election coming up within the next twelve months and it could be sooner rather than later. The votes we need are in the As and Bs. They're the decent people you're appealing to and they *do* vote. So the rhetoric's right and the voter targets are right. How are you going to handle the image issue, though? You're not going to make yourself popular with the liberal media; and that's where Andy will have to distance himself from you. He'll take the credit for the results you achieve, but he can't afford to be too close to the methods you're using. You'll have to stand up and take the flak on that score; you know that, don't you?'

'I do, Sherry, and you can tell Andy I'm more than happy to shield him from the brickbats. The thing is I believe in what we're doing at the department, so I'm proud to be associated with it. The image question isn't a problem for me. This country needs the firm

216

hand of authority and I'm privileged to be the one who provides it.'

★ ★ ★

When Geoff Maddle got back to Downing Street late that evening, struggling with a thickish folder of longhand notes, a DAT recorder and a pounding headache, Charlie McDonald was in emergency conclave with officials from RAM, the Rural Affairs Ministry, discussing contingency quarantine plans to tackle the latest outbreak of GM-crop-borne tuberculosis.

After pacing up and down in the press office for half an hour, the knots in Geoff's stomach got the better of him. He poked his head into the mauve conference room to signal that Charlie had better come out soonish and hear what he had to tell him.

Charlie wrapped up his meeting and came straight out.

'Right, mate. What's the deal? What's your man in Cambridge told you?'

'It's not good news, Charlie. In fact, it's a bit of a Doomsday. I went to see this Harvey Parks guy — I've got his address and phone number and everything. And I went wired. Anyway, it turns out that Parks and Andy went to the same college together in 1977. I can't remember which one — '

'Trinity.'

'Yeah, that's it. Now they were both doing languages there, Spanish to be precise. And it

217

seems that when you do languages at Cambridge, you do two years in your college, then you do a year abroad to practise your speaking and your accent and all that, and then you come back for a final year.'

'Yeah, I know all that, so what's it got to do with Andy and this Parks fellow?'

'I'm just coming to that. As soon as they met, Parks and Andy got to be big mates. So when it came to the year abroad they both asked to go to the same place.'

'Yeah, Spain presumably, since they were doing Spanish — doh!'

'No, mate. It's not just Spain where they speak Spanish. Andy and Parks went to Colombia in South America. They had a year teaching English at a school in Bogotá. But it seems they were doing other things as well — '

'Hang on. I'm sure Andy's CV says he did his year abroad in Spain. Have you checked?'

'Yes, I have checked. What his CV says is that he spent a year abroad studying Spanish: no mention of Spain.'

'Oh, shit. So don't tell me they were sampling the local herbs when they were in Colombia — '

'Much worse, mate. They were quite the young businessmen. According to Parks, it was all Andy's idea. Well, I'm not sure if he's telling the truth about that, but anyway the two of them got pretty pally with some pillars of the local economy — '

'Drug dealers, you mean?'

'Not drug dealers, Charlie, drug *lords*. These are the guys who keep Colombia going. It's their business that finances the national economy. It's their money that greases the palms in the local councils. They're the ones who finance local services, fund the youth clubs and the football teams; they provide the social security, such as it is, and the people love them. They drive around in flash cars with bodyguards and live in fortified compounds. The police can't touch them. It's not Brixton on a Saturday night like we used to know it; it's institutionalized big business. And that's what got Parks and Andy involved. They reckoned it was a business venture they couldn't turn down — '

'Did you say you were wired while Parks was telling you this, Geoff? Have you got it on tape?'

★ ★ ★

The walk from Number Ten along the old Cabinet Office corridor to his own department had become a well-trodden route for Selwyn Knox. Now, energized by Sherry Black's endorsement of his proposals and her agreement to fix a date for him to present them to parliament, he positively skipped along the flagstones.

Back at his desk, he called through to his Private Secretary and asked him to summon Sonya Mair, Nigel Tonbridge and Chris Brody.

'Tell Sonya to come straight in. Keep Tonbridge and Brody in the outer office until I call for them. And make sure no one tells the PermSec about this until the meetings are over,

219

OK? I'll talk to him once we've decided everything.'

In the end, Chris Brody and Nigel waited for over an hour in Knox's outer office while Sonya and the boss were in private conclave.

Brody, who had of course seen it all before, spent the time scoffing at Knox's missionary zeal and lunatic plans, speaking loudly enough to embarrass the junior civil servants in the room and make them glance constantly towards the Secretary of State's door in case the boss could hear what was going on.

'So what do you think of this fellow, Nigel? Now you've been working here a few months, I bet he gives you the creeps, doesn't he? All his crackpot Calvinist ranting about being a father to the naughty children of the nation who've gone astray — to all the poor sods he's legislating for — makes him sound like the tsar of all the bloody Russias. They had the peasants praying to them and calling them 'Our Little Father', didn't they? Well, in my humble opinion, he's going to come a cropper if he goes through with all this. I've seen it happen before. He's going to earn Andy Sheen's undying gratitude and the nation's undying hatred. As for that Sonya Night-Mair, she's a tough old thing, but even she won't be able to save him. I wouldn't be surprised if there's something going on between them, Nigel — something extra-curricular. I've seen it before, you know; ministers and their consorts — always ends in tears.'

★　★　★

After a struggle, Geoff Maddle located the right section in his DAT voice recording and pressed the playback button. Charlie McDonald raised his eyebrows as the muffled but comprehensible voice of Harvey Parks emerged from the machine on the table.

'It was such an accepted part of life down there, man. Everybody was involved in it or connected with it or benefited from it. It was like . . . business, you know. And here we were — young English businessmen from Cambridge — it was a natural! And it was so easy. Remember, this was before the US got paranoid about the heroin trade. There were no CIA ops helping the Colombians; no helicopters, no nothing. It was just a few local pigs and they were all paid off by the cartels. We spent our time hanging out with Ramòn Echeverria — you may not remember him, the Feds shot him a few years later — but he was Mr Big back then, man. And he was pretty cool to be with. He had money and booze and women. Everyone respected him. And everyone respected us too because we were Ramòn's pals. All that time I think he was testing us to see if we were reliable — like, did we use or didn't we? Were we discreet or did we blab? — that sort of stuff. We did bits and pieces for Ramòn while we were there and it was all a big adventure to us. We did runs down to Cali for him — never touched Medellin, that wasn't our territory, too dangerous — but all the time what Ramòn was doing was seeing if we could help him when we went back to England. And I guess we passed the test! Just before we were due to go back to Cambridge Ramòn took us out one night and told us he liked us and he trusted us — I guess he didn't know I was using; Andy wasn't, he never did — but, anyway, he told us we were going to be his representatives in England and, if we made a fist of it, for the whole of Europe. It was like an import — export business, you know: the imports were in the form of white powder and the exports were mainly pounds and guilders and pesetas.'

Geoff Maddle pressed the stop button and looked at Charlie McDonald.

'If this is true — and I think it is, Charlie — we're talking about meltdown time. According to Parks, the two of them came back to Cambridge, did their degrees like everyone else and spent their spare time setting up the whole European distribution network for Colombia's favourite export.'

★　★　★

When the door to the Secretary of State's inner office finally swung open and a flushed-looking Selwyn Knox appeared, Brody turned to Nigel and winked. 'Get ready now, old boy. He's about to do to us what I think he's just been doing to Ms Mair!'

Knox ushered the two of them, plus Jeremy, his Private Secretary, into his inner office, where Sonya Mair was already installed at the head of the long conference table. Before the scraping of chairs and the rustling of papers had subsided, Knox had already begun.

222

'Right. Thanks for coming. I'd like you to listen carefully. We are about to launch the single most important piece of social legislation this country has seen for over a century. I have just spoken to the Prime Minister and we have been given the go-ahead for a speech to parliament in ten days' time. The centrepiece of the legislation I shall be outlining then will be something that should have been introduced long ago, something this nation *needs* to curb the self-renewing generation of antisocial elements who threaten our values and way of life. I can tell you that my priority now, and the priority for all of you present, will be the introduction of radical new legislation to institute a compulsory, nationwide Parenting Licence. It will be a simple but effective test of parenting skills, a qualification that most prospective parents will find easy to acquire, but a qualification without which parents in the future will not be authorized to produce offspring. No Parenting Licence means no right to produce children. It's simple, it's effective and it's vital to the future of our nation — '

Christopher Brody, whose face had been expressing growing degrees of incredulity, could hold back no longer: with one movement he pushed his chair away from the table, threw back his head and erupted into a prolonged guffaw.

★　★　★

If Charlie McDonald was shocked, he was hiding it well. His only visible reaction to Geoff

223

Maddle's bombshell was to frown a little and scratch his head. But his thoughts were in turmoil. The memories of his Brixton childhood, his struggle to make it as a black journalist in a white man's world, his unprecedented rise to the Prime Minister's side — all this was in jeopardy. Andy Sheen's future was hanging in the balance and so was Charlie McDonald's.

'Right, Geoff. We'll need to think. First of all, what exactly has Parks got against Andy, apart from a bunch of wild allegations, that is?'

'That's the problem, Charlie. He's got everything. Parks was the bookkeeper for the operation and basically he's kept the books! He's got a written record of everything they brought in from Colombia and of all the cash — minus their commission, of course — that went back to Echeverria in Bogotá. Half of it's in Andy's handwriting — his DNA must be all over it. And Parks has got the photos — him and Andy and all the Colombian Mr Bigs you care to name. It's a rap, Charlie, and Andy must know it. Let me play you a bit from the end of the tape. Here's what Parks has to say about Andy when they graduated and left Cambridge.'

Another bout of stop — start playback and Geoff finally found the DAT reference he was looking for.

Parks's voice emerged again like an avenging angel's. ' . . . so like I say, man, Andy was getting pretty well off by now. We looked on it as a start in the business world. All the others were getting recruited by McKinsey's, but we had our own

224

little business venture and business was booming. We rarely had anything to do with the actual merchandise, of course. That was brought in by the mules. But the amount of money that passed through our rooms, man, it was mind-blowing! We disguised it all as a medicines and pharmaceuticals trade. Pharmaceuticals! Yeah — anyway, I squandered all my money — I was already a user when we came back from Colombia and it just got worse. Andy Sheen, though, he was smart. He had to launder his part of the bread, so what did he do? He went and bought a luxury bloody flat in New York! There aren't many students who can do that, are there?'

★ ★ ★

Selwyn Knox fixed Chris Brody with a withering glare.

Brody was a hard man, but even he felt a chill run down his spine and his guffaw stuck in his throat. Sonya Mair gave him a sharp look full of threat; for the rest of the meeting Brody sat in silence.

'So, if Mr Brody has finished now, I would like to explain the thinking behind this measure. Perhaps then you will see why it is not only justified and sensible, but also vital and inevitable. You need to know that the Parenting Licence is aimed at a certain class of people. These are the parents who didn't and don't want their children, people who have their children inadvertently because of a lack of education, by mistake as it were. You can see them everywhere you go. The way they treat their children betrays the resentment they feel for the burden of parenthood; they cannot disguise it. And their resentment is all too readily felt by their unwanted offspring. This sort of parenting breeds resentful young people with a chip on their shoulder, the social malcontents who plague this country today.

'Put at its simplest, the new Parenting Licence will be a caring and compassionate way of prompting these people to reflect before they rush into something that they, their children and ultimately society itself will regret. Now I am not naive, despite what Mr Brody and others may think. I know there will be resistance to what we are proposing. I know people will compare our policies to the social engineering of Soviet Russia or Nazi Germany. But nothing could be further from the truth! These are humane, compassionate policies. The requirements for acquiring the Parenting Licence will be laughably simple. All they will involve will be watching a few government-produced DVDs, a couple of half-hour classes with an official government adviser and the completion of a questionnaire. It isn't a big test by any stretch of the imagination and if you are the right sort of person you will get through it easily. But what it will do is make people think twice before rushing into parenthood. It will make them reflect on the responsibilities they will have towards their offspring and towards society. In the cases we are specifically targeting, it will — I believe — help reduce the numbers of unwanted babies and consequently the numbers of potential future criminals, addicts and scroungers.

Knox paused and gave a half-smile of satisfaction: his audience was interested, intrigued — now he could hook them.

'At first sight, what I am proposing today may seem outlandish, but reflect for a moment before condemning these measures. You will remember that several years ago in the Sexual Offences Bill we moved to outlaw many forms of sex, including sex outdoors and in public places. That was a good start. And the people of this country realized that implementing the Bill was the right thing to do. Now I believe we must go further; but we must be clear about our objectives; we must be clear about what we cannot do and would not wish to do. We cannot, for example, outlaw sex outside marriage, much as we might think it right to do so. We cannot forbid people to have sex, nor would we want to — that is clear. However much we believe that certain classes of people should be prevented from reproducing and perpetuating the ills they have visited on society, however carefully we would pledge to choose those who would be subject to the law, I believe such a measure would not be practicably enforceable. Nor are we talking about enforced sterilization, even for the most undesirable classes of society. That is not something that this country is ready for, although I believe the practice exists in some southern states of the USA for destitute black women — among others — who are taken into the care of state-run institutions. Actually, could someone check on that please and let me know? If it is true, it could be very useful ammunition —

'Anyway, what we are doing is simply introducing a Parenting Licence, a humanely enforced educational programme for people's own good.

'Decent people will have no problem with the concept or with the actual act of obtaining their Licence. The tests will be easy for them to pass and will be an opportunity for them to prove their credentials as good citizens. It is the undesirables who will either fail the Parental Licence tests or seek to avoid taking them. These are the people the Licence is aimed at. These are the people we wish to discourage from producing undesirable offspring.

'In sum, we must send a message to decent people that this programme is not aimed at them. It is aimed at those elements in society whom decent folk fear, despise or wish to see removed, people who don't contribute anything positive to society — and, I may add, don't vote.'

★ ★ ★

Geoff Maddle thought Charlie McDonald was taking the news about Andy Sheen's criminal past remarkably calmly. Maddle himself was in the grip of incipient panic and he was strangely perturbed that McDonald did not seem to share his alarm.

'I don't know what you're so calm about, Charlie. This is nuclear. And don't go thinking that Parks is just a harmless druggie because he isn't. One thing he let drop — and I had no idea about this, maybe you did? — is that Andy has been sending Parks money every month since 1997. 1997, Charlie! That's the year Andy started his career in politics. It's too much of a coincidence that the payments started then. Andy hasn't been sending Parks money out of the goodness of his heart. He's been sending it to keep Parks quiet. It's blackmail money. Andy's been paying the guy off — '

'Yeah, it certainly looks that way. So why has Parks gone to the media now? Isn't he happy with what Andy's been paying him?'

'No, it's not enough for him, that's the problem. Parks has found he's needing more and more money to feed his habit and he couldn't get it from Andy. That's why he approached Jim McGee from the *Mirror*. McGee gave him a few quid and the promise of more. But now he's after big bucks for selling his story. If the *Mirror* won't deal, he's talking about going to the *Mail*. He's no idiot, Charlie. I've kept him quiet for now by giving him five hundred pounds in cash and what he thinks is a contract with the *Mirror* that'll earn him eighty thousand quid for his story. But when he realizes I've been stringing him along, he'll be off to your old paper like a shot, and the *Mail* will lap it up for sure — '

'OK, Geoff, we need to stay calm over this one. Let's have a think. For a start, it's pretty strange this hasn't come out before. How has

Andy got away with it up to now?'

'Well, Parks has kept quiet because Andy was paying him, obviously . . . And when they were dealing back then, Parks says they had Mr Ramòn breathing down their necks, so they weren't going to be boasting about what they were doing. And anyway, they were never 'hands on'. They weren't the ones on the street corners selling the stuff, so no one knew what they were up to. I don't think they even felt they were doing anything wrong: for them it was like a venture capital business enterprise, with a product people wanted and they could supply. Their only slip was the court appearance on that minor possession charge and, as we know, they got away with it. It certainly didn't do them any harm: in those days, half the student population of the UK was up on possession charges.'

Charlie McDonald looked at Geoff, passed his hand over his face and sighed briefly.

'OK, Geoff. I guess it's make-your-mind-up time on this one.'

★ ★ ★

The following day Selwyn Knox summoned his director of policy for a private meeting with himself and Sonya Mair. Christopher Brody did not make any trouble, not even when he was tasked with identifying the priority target groups for the parenting unit's new programmes. Knox told him to trawl the police, Home Office, employment and benefit agency databases. He told him to prioritize people with criminal records, single parents, registered and unregistered addicts, asylum seekers and the homeless. In addition, he was told to run a series of focus groups among social As and Bs with the aim of testing public opinion over who they would most like to see targeted for the new Parenting Licence. Brody shrugged and went away to get on with it.

In a parallel meeting. Nigel Tonbridge was told that he must prepare the ground for the parenting unit by stirring up public revulsion over recent examples of parental cruelty, neglect and abuse. He was instructed to compile a dossier of the most horrific cases, starting with the tale of the little girl who had been tortured to death by her parents. Knox told him he should include the more recent examples of children locked in cupboards and left to starve, the young twins who died on a hot summer's day in their child seats with the car windows closed, and the little boy who died of hypothermia after being deliberately locked out of his house overnight in winter. Nigel was told he must ensure the media ran features listing all the most outrageous details of deficient parental behaviour and linking them with unplanned pregnancies and absent fathers. Knox had already spoken to the department's statisticians and he handed Nigel a sheaf of figures proving that the highest rates of unemployment, criminality, alcoholism and antisocial behaviour are found among children from dysfunctional and single-parent families. Nigel looked searchingly at Selwyn Knox, seemed on the point of saying something, but picked up the dossier and left the room without a word.

★ ★ ★

Four days later, the *Cambridge Evening News* carried a brief item recording the death of a drug addict in a house near the city centre. Harvey Parks was described as a former student of the university, who had once had a promising career as a businessman. In recent years, said the paper, neighbours in Dove End Street, where he lived, had found Parks to be quiet and reclusive, but always polite and friendly. The Cambridge coroner had recorded the cause of death as heart failure brought on by a drug overdose; there were no suspicious circumstances.

★ ★ ★

Nigel arrived first and took the more comfortable bench seat against the wall. Tagliano's was one of several central London restaurants he used regularly for these lunchtime meetings with journalists. In the months he'd been at the Department for Society, he had never really enjoyed the artificial intimacy conferred by sharing bread with reporters, who in many cases were his former colleagues and acquaintances. Their meetings were inevitably strained. He knew they regarded him with mixed feelings: a hack who had gone over to the government, poacher turned gamekeeper, as they constantly

232

reminded him. But he knew also that these seasoned correspondents retained a residual and illogical conviction that they could trust Nigel: in their eyes he had been one of them, a journalist, and therefore he was more likely to tell them the truth than the other PR reps vying to sell them a story. He blushed inside as he reflected on the naivety of this, especially when his task was to convince his lunch partner of policies he himself disapproved of. Nigel was about to curtain-raise a Knox initiative that he regarded with the deepest suspicion, that troubled even his long-blunted conscience.

'Hi, Nigel. Sorry I'm a bit late. I was doing the Andy Sheen New Transport for New Britain initiative — giving it a pretty good write-up, you'll be pleased to hear. Have you ordered anything yet? That wine looks nice — '

Dave Sopwith was among the easiest of the Fleet Street polcorrs for Nigel to deal with. His journalism consisted largely of reproducing what the government told him, so he had been the obvious choice to kick off the grooming of public opinion over the Parenting Licence.

Even Sopwith couldn't hide a gasp of surprise when Nigel told him what was being proposed. 'But, Nige, how are you going to get people to accept something like that? And how are you going to administer it? OK, look: I can see it's a good idea to slash the numbers of these problem children who turn into problem adults, but how the hell are you going to force people to sit this parent trap or whatever you're calling it?'

'Dave, you know I'm a civil servant. You know

I can't leak details of government policy initiatives. On the other hand, I can see you're interested in this story and the department wants to help you. If you can just hold your horses for ten minutes, I'm expecting someone to join us and I think she may be able to fill you in on what's being proposed. OK?'

'Yeah, sure, Nige. Whatever you say — '

Ten minutes later, right on cue, Tagliano's was graced by the elegant, head-turning entrance of Sonya Mair. As Sonya glided through the crowded restaurant towards their table, Nigel stood up and took his leave of a fidgety Dave Sopwith. 'All right, Dave, nice to have seen you. I expect you won't mind me leaving you in Sonya's hands, will you? Give me a ring later if anything isn't clear.'

Sonya Mair slid into Nigel's vacated seat and gave Dave Sopwith a melting smile.

★ ★ ★

Charlie McDonald and Geoff Maddle felt that at last things were now beginning to move in the right direction.

Over lunch in the private upstairs room of the Red Lion, McDonald was assessing the danger still remaining, the poison as yet undrawn from the Andy Sheen story, now that the key prosecution witness was gone.

'So Parks is out of the picture. OK. That's lucky for us, Geoff — '

Geoff Maddle gave a half smile. 'Lucky — yeah, I suppose you could say that. Junkies and overdoses — happens every day.'

'Yeah, it does. So, that's the first thing in our favour. McGee's hand is weaker than it was. He got no documentation off Parks and all the written evidence, all the photos from Parks's files, have been Hoovered and trashed, right?'

'Right.'

'So what has McGee got? Parks told him about the conditional discharge, but he's got no corroborating evidence, nothing on paper. Right?'

'Yeah. You took care of the Police National Computer, Charlie, and I burned the paper record from the Cambridge cop shop.'

'OK. So, if you were McGee, what would you do now? You know there's a story out there somewhere, but you can't stand it up. You're pretty sure Parks was telling the truth about the court appearance and you strongly suspect there was much more where that came from. So do you run the line about the conditional discharge and hope it'll flush out the rest of the dirt?'

'I don't know. He's got to be worried about Andy suing him for libel, especially as he can't call on Parks to support the story any more. I reckon McGee's in pretty bad shape.'

'Yeah, I think he is too. But I don't want to take any chances with him, especially as we've come this far already. I don't think we can risk leaving him out there to shoot at us. What do you reckon?'

'I don't know, Charlie. Depends what you've got on McGee, I suppose.'

'Well, funny you should mention that, actually. Because I've taken the sensible precaution of gathering ammunition on Mr McGee: there's easily enough to get our retaliation in first. You know I was trawling for dirt on the guy? Well, it turns out there's plenty about. You remember the story back in 2005 about financial journalists and that insider-dealing scam? They'd buy up shares and then tip them in their column so the price sky-rocketed? Well, some of them got the chop, but it seems Mr McGee managed to get away with it. And, guess what? Since then, he's been doing it again and no one's been able to catch him.'

'Sounds good, Charlie. But what's the evidence for it?'

'The evidence is the lovely Sonya Mair! Among all the others she's charmed over the years, she has been — how shall I put it? — very close to an important insider at the *Mirror* who knows about McGee's little money-spinner. He's even told Sonya about McGee's latest wheeze, a nice bit of insider trading on the DRE deal. Apparently, McGee bought thousands of DRE shares at rock bottom, just before they got clearance to sell off to EES and go into bio-engineering. Do you think I should ring and mention this to Mr McGee?'

'Well, when you put it like that, Charlie, it does seem sensible.'

★ ★ ★

'Listen, Dave, I'm talking to you off the record, OK?' Sonya squeezed Dave Sopwith's arm.

'What I'm telling you now you need to pin on unnamed but reliable sources close to the government.'

'Of course, Sonya. You know you can trust me.'

'Yes I do know that and I appreciate it. But it's especially important with this story. Because what I'm telling you won't be announced to parliament for another week, I'm technically breaching parliamentary privilege by even talking to you. The Speaker won't like it if this can be traced back to the department and you know how het up Mick McPaddywhack can get!'

'Trust me, Sonya. Just tell me what you want me to write and I'll do it for you.'

'Thanks, Dave. Now, I think you've got the rationale behind what we're doing. The main thing is for you to print all the horror stories of parental inadequacy in the dossiers that Nigel gave you. You need to use his statistics to show exactly who these people are and which social categories they come from. And you need to write the article so your readers recognize how important it is to stop them overrunning our society and our values. We need to have the public demanding decisive action — crying out for our Parenting Licence by the time we make the announcement. I think that's a message *Chronicle* readers will welcome, don't you?'

'Oh, absolutely, Sonya. Don't worry about that. We'll give it a good show. But I'm still not clear how you're going to administer this thing.'

'All right, Dave. As far as the mechanics are concerned, I can give you a broad outline but not the fine details. Selwyn needs to keep those

237

for his speech. What you need to write is that the Parenting Licence is an idea whose time has come. It will be welcomed by all right-thinking people and it is so self-evidently in everyone's interest that the vast majority of prospective parents will need no prompting to sit and pass the simple tests it involves. After all, we sit an exam before we can drive a car, don't we? And how much greater is the responsibility involved in being a parent? I think the comparison is clear, don't you? What you can say, though, is that the government recognizes there will be some people who resent the PL or try to evade their responsibilities. On that, you should just write that there will be a carrot-and-stick approach to the hardest cases: the carrot will be free advice from professional government counsellors and help with how to be a good parent. The stick will be in the form of sanctions, but I can't give you anything concrete on those yet: it would be too obvious that the whole thing has come from inside the department. All right?'

'Yes, of course, Sonya. But could you just answer one question for me? What about people who get pregnant by mistake? You know, good, decent people who just make a slip?'

'Well, this might sound harsh, but we have to be realistic: the whole point of the Parenting Licence is to stop slips and mistakes because slips and mistakes are where the future problems for society all come from. People have to learn to behave responsibly. Unplanned pregnancies are what we are trying to wipe out. But we're not unreasonable, Dave. If good, decent people find

238

they are expecting, they can of course come and sit the PL in the months before the child is born. We are even considering post-facto PL tests, but there's been no agreement on those yet. We're reasonable people, Dave, but we have to make sure this initiative is taken seriously.'

★　★　★

Charlie McDonald was a relieved man.

Jim McGee's agreement to drop his investigations into the Andy Sheen drugs story had restored McDonald's usual good humour, which colleagues thought had deserted him in recent days.

Now, sitting in Downing Street with an Arsenal mug full of strong tea, he was sharing a laugh with an equally relieved Geoff Maddle. The first target for their wit had been the PM himself and those cabinet members who had been in the news recently. Then they had been through the documents that had accumulated in Charlie's in tray during the Jim McGee interlude and exchanged scathing witticisms about their authors. Now they were reading a file from the US State Department, which set out the case for Jeb Bush's strongly held belief that the Allies should extend their zone of permanent occupation to Afghanistan and northern Pakistan.

Charlie remarked casually that one way to convince Andy to agree might be to mention the local trade in certain substances and both men collapsed in a fit of giggles.

Their hilarity was still in full flow when

Charlie's secretary called through to say she had the Director-General of the BBC on the phone. By now, Charlie's mood was such that the prospect of a chat with Fred Pond seemed to promise even more amusement, and he gestured to Geoff to listen in on the spare extension.

'Well hello, Fred,' Charlie smirked into the telephone, 'to what do I owe this signal honour?'

'Ahm, bit tricky, Charlie. Bit tricky. Need to tell you something. Not good news I'm afraid.'

'Oh, come on, Fred. It can't be that bad. What's our favourite D-G got to worry about?'

'Ahm, well. Problem is people are talking, Charlie. Having a go at me and the chairman. Sure you've seen it in the press. Saying we're too close to you chaps. Too soft on the New Project government after all that fuss with the chemical weapons inquiry. Not impartial — '

'And there's nothing wrong with that, Fred. You keep it up! You and Mervyn are our best assets.'

Charlie and Geoff were finding it hard to keep a straight face.

'Ahm, quite. Problem is, the press know about the donations from Mervyn and me. Saying we're New Project stooges. That sort of thing — '

'Oh, surely not, Fred!'

'Ahm, 'fraid so, Charlie. Have to do something to prove we're impartial. Having to screen a bit of a political drama. Bit of a drama based on New Project's first decade in power. Two-parter. Called *The Product*. About the way New Project gets marketed and sold by you spin-doctor

240

chaps. All spin, no substance. Bit critical, I'm afraid — '

Charlie looked at Geoff, grinned broadly and gave a theatrical frown into the telephone. 'Now, now, Fred! We can't be having that, can we?'

'Ahm, got to do it, Charlie. Sorry. Got to. Don't worry, though. Bit of a con trick. Publicizing it as an outspoken attack on New Project's ethics — show Mervyn and I are even handed — not soft on the government. Actually, we're making sure *The Product* is a damp squib. Dead boring. People'll think we're criticizing New Project, but it's so tedious no one will sit through it. So nothing to worry about. They'll be bored to death. Hope that's OK with you, Charlie. You will tell Andy, won't you?'

The fun that had seemingly vanished from the spin doctors' lives had at last returned.

Charlie McDonald was back on form and ready to tackle the remaining letters in his overflowing in tray.

'Let's see what we've got in here, Geoff. Who else can give us a laugh? Ah, talk of the devil, here's one from the lovely Cliff Evans at the *Mirror*. I wonder if his boys have had any more ideas for good share tips? Oh, hang on . . . oh, shit! . . . This isn't funny, mate. Have a look at this — '

Geoff Maddle scanned the letter in Charlie McDonald's hand and grimaced.

Cliff Evans was writing to say that it had come to his attention that Prime Minister Andy Sheen had concealed a drugs conviction in his past and that the *Mirror* was intending to run the story

241

the following Monday. Evans's letter admitted that he had no written evidence of the PM's conditional discharge, but said that as editor he was sufficiently convinced of the story's veracity to be prepared to run with it.

Geoff Maddle's immediate response was angry. 'McGee promised he'd drop this, Charlie. But they're still running it. We need to screw McGee now!'

'No, it's gone beyond McGee. The editor's found out and he's the one we need to reckon with now.'

'Bloody hell, Charlie. Why is all this happening to us? It never would have happened when Tony Blair was Prime Minister. He and Alastair Campbell played things straight.'

'Maybe, Geoff, but we're here now and we need to deal with Cliff Evans. What do you think?'

'I think he's bullshitting us. Look, he says himself he can't stand the story up. I bet he'd never risk running it. He's trying to panic us or blackmail us into giving him something.'

'Mmm. I suspect you're right, Geoff. But can we take the risk? That's the question. I suppose we could just let him run the Sheen-smoked-dope story. It'd be embarrassing but it wouldn't be fatal. The danger with any drug story, though, is that it could bring all sorts of things out of the woodwork, it could open a whole can of woodworms. I think we need to play safe, we need to negotiate with Evans. What do you think?'

'Well, maybe. Yeah. You might be right,

242

Charlie. What can we offer him as a sweetener, though?'

'It shouldn't take too much. Evans doesn't know the real story about Andy so he doesn't know his bargaining power. He'll probably settle for a bit of a scoop from us in return for dropping the drugs thing.'

'Yeah. What, though? What can we give him?'

'Well, maybe I can think of something. How old is Marie Sheen now? About thirty-nine?'

'Forty-one last birthday, mate. Why?'

'Hmm. It could work, but it'll need a woman's touch. I think we'll get Sonya to give us a hand with this one.'

★ ★ ★

Nigel Tonbridge had spent his week carefully leaking details of Selwyn Knox's impending policy launch to various newspapers and broadcasters. As is often the case with major announcements, the broad lines of the Parenting Licence had now been reported and picked over in the media well in advance of its official presentation to parliament. The object of this was to lessen the shock of such a radical initiative and to forestall the firestorm that might otherwise engulf the Secretary of State on launch day. In addition, Knox now had a good idea of the reaction he could expect and the questions he would be asked when he rose to his feet the following Monday. Nigel had few qualms about this breach of parliamentary etiquette, but he did have real and growing concerns about the aims

243

of the policies he was helping to promote. The more he reflected on the work he was doing for the department, the more he was puzzled by Knox's motives in bringing him to work there. Nigel was sure Knox was aware of the distaste he felt both for him and for his policies and he had become increasingly convinced that Knox had had another, hidden motive for recruiting him. In his more fanciful moments Nigel had begun to suspect that Knox wanted him close by solely because of their shared experience in Exxington; he was the only one who shared the intimate burden that haunted Knox's every waking moment — the knowledge of past sins. At times, Nigel wondered if Knox had brought him close because somewhere deep down he longed for Nigel to expose him, to unmask the darkness within him. Did Selwyn Knox have a purpose for Nigel? An unexpressed desire for the painful light of exposure? A death wish that only Nigel could grant?

★   ★   ★

At Charlie McDonald's suggestion, Sonya Mair rang Cliff Evans and told him he needed to drop his misguided allegations of a drugs offence in Andy Sheen's past. For a start, they were completely untrue. For another thing, the *Mirror* had no evidence and no witnesses for the story, and if Evans ever did run it, Downing Street would see him in court. But just because she liked him Sonya said she was also offering a trade-off in the form of an exclusive. Evans said

244

he was prepared to deal and Sonya gave him the scoop on Marie Sheen's late and unexpected pregnancy. The next day, the *Mirror* splashed this on the front page. No mention of drugs and the Prime Minister ever saw the light of day.

11

Nigel Tonbridge felt himself sinking into one of his periodic bouts of self-loathing. He had suffered from them long enough to recognize their onset and had learned from experience to resign himself to their chill embrace.

Joanie said his black-dog episodes had got worse since he turned forty; Nigel joked about the male menopause.

Familiarity had taught him the symptoms, perhaps the causes, but never any solutions. His bouts of depression flooded him with self-doubt, convinced him of his own worthlessness, of the waste he had made of his life.

As a young man, Nigel had never had time for self-examination. He had been focused on the next story, searching for the elusive scoop, rising up the ladder of journalistic success. He had had a goal and a defining purpose.

Promotion, praise, fame and money were an easy structure against which to judge his worth. As at school, success and failure were well marked out; things seemed comprehensible, generally fair, always transparent. And while he was progressing towards the next target — the next correspondent's post, the next pay rise, more recognition — he felt he was on course and was satisfied.

But in recent years the stable points in his life had been kicked away. Now the ready-made, prêt-à-porter values against which he had measured himself, the fixed targets, were all gone.

In his bouts of depression, Nigel felt at sea in a world without benchmarks. Now he had to create his own moral checkpoints, define his own acts of courage or cowardice, success or failure, good or bad behaviour. And he did not like it; he had to judge himself and he had no idea how to.

Now he lay awake in the middle of the night, recalling with regret the certainties and energy of the past, looking with trepidation on the challenges of the future, tormenting himself with the memory of what had passed between him and his father — the secret he had concealed from everyone, including even his wife, but which Selwyn Knox had once intimated he had somehow uncovered.

It was in this state of mind that Nigel now tried to confront the dilemma which had begun to obsess him.

The immediate trigger was clear. In recent weeks, he had begun to feel increasingly uncomfortable with the responsibility Knox had given him for promoting the department's policies. In meetings with journalists, Nigel had heard himself describing how Knox's ideas would cleanse and regenerate society, how they would restore moral values and bring people together. And as he spoke, he had realized with growing clarity that he loathed and detested the policies Knox was proposing. He felt gripped by a deep internal contradiction between his own views and the propaganda he heard himself spouting — and he had no idea how to resolve it.

His first reaction was to use the 'obeying orders' strategy: he was a civil servant so he could not object to the official policies of his minister, he had to accept and promote them unquestioningly because his minister told him to do so. The civil servant's code, as understood by Nottridge and most of the others he worked with, was to do blindly and die blindly. Their consciences, if they had them, were eased by the service's vow of unquestioning loyalty.

But Nigel's conscience would not go so quietly.

He began to think of himself as the only man who could halt the progress of Knox's insidious policies, the last remaining Hollywood superhero who could save the world from the evil genius at the helm of the Department for Society! He laughed, but the wrestling with his conscience continued.

'Hello, Nigel? It's Jeremy here. The Secretary of State would like you to come up to his office in half an hour. We've got an NCCL delegation arriving for a chat about the new Parenting Licence, among other things. They'll be here at ten o'clock. Can I tell him that's OK with you?'

The delegation, it turned out, was in fact a coalition of concerned activists, led by the National Council for Civil Liberties but embracing other campaigning bodies such as the League of Churches, the Humanist Council and the Fellowship of Human Responsibility.

Their spokesman, Alastair Barber, was an NCCL lawyer with twenty years' experience of civil rights issues and a string of successes in opposing government policies that he and his colleagues saw as a threat to freedom of speech or action. He had led the campaign to oppose mandatory fingerprinting and DNA sampling of the whole population; he had fought and won when the Home Secretary had proposed the return of the death penalty; he had opposed but failed to halt the return of universal military service.

Now Alastair Barber made no secret of his outrage at the leaked stories in the press foreshadowing the policies which Knox was about to announce.

'Well, thanks for seeing us, Mr Knox. At least you've done us the courtesy of hearing what we have to say. I just hope you'll take note of the alarm and anger that has been generated by the stories about your Parenting Licence proposals.

'First, I would like to put on record that the NCCL and the other groups represented here today have deep concerns about the whole concept of a Parenting Licence.

'We feel it infringes basic personal freedoms. This country has a proud tradition of guaranteeing liberties to citizens to the extent that they do not impinge on the liberty of others. And this is a principle that goes back as far as Mill and Hume and Locke.

'We are, however, realists.

We recognize that public opinion today is such that revulsion against crime and the antisocial phenomena plaguing our society has fostered popular support for your proposals where it probably would not have existed in the past.

'We are even prepared to concede that the damage inflicted on society by the elements you are seeking to curb may theoretically justify certain proposals to curtail civil liberties in order to protect the liberty of others.

'I say this to show that we are approaching this discussion with a reasonable and open mind; and I hope you will respond in kind.

'After extensive debate, and in light of the arguments I have just outlined, we have decided we will not oppose the overall principle of your proposals.

'What we are determined to do, though, is ensure you are held to account in everything you do, that the details of the legislation you introduce are compatible with the protection of the weak and the vulnerable in society. We are determined to police this legislation in all its minutiae, Mr Knox, and to oppose it wherever it oversteps the limits of acceptable civilized law.

'So I'd like to start, if I may, with a series of questions, and my colleague here will minute your responses.

'I should tell you, also, that if we are not satisfied with the undertakings you give us in reply to our concerns, we will have no hesitation in taking this issue to direct action and to popular protests on the streets.

'I hope it will not come to that, however; it is in your hands to give us the assurances we require if we are to avoid such an outcome.

'Now, the first undertaking we need is that the obligation to pass the PL will be applied equally and fairly to all social groups and that there is no intent deliberately to target specific social categories.'

'Yes, Mr Barber, I can give you that absolute assurance.'

Selwyn Knox was firm and frank: he looked Alastair Barber in the eye; he was a man to be trusted.

'Thank you. The second assurance we need is that proper counselling will be made available to all who need it and that there will be no penalization of those who fail. In other words, that this will be a programme enacted with a carrot, not a stick.'

Again, Selwyn Knox was frank. 'Yes, I can give you that assurance.'

Barber looked slightly surprised, relieved even. 'Thank you. We also need an undertaking that there will be no stigmatization of single parents, children born out of wedlock, asylum seekers or other disadvantaged groups.'

'I can give you that undertaking. The programme will be compassionate and benign. All we are seeking is the enhanced well-being of those who are affected by it.'

'Thank you, Mr Knox. We have several other concerns that I will send to you in writing. But I do have one major assurance I shall require from you now if the NCCL is to give its provisional approval for your plans. I must have a categorical undertaking from you that the data you gather from the PL programme will not be misused in any way. You will understand that the people most likely to come under the aegis of your

251

parenting counsellors will be vulnerable groups, many of them from ethnic minorities, whose mother tongue may not be English; people who have difficulties coping with authority, difficulties of a financial, addictive or legal nature. Can you give me your word as a government minister and as a man of honour that your department does not intend to share the information these people vouchsafe in confidence to your advisers with agencies such as the police, immigration or tax authorities, agencies where such data could be used to penalize the participants of your Parental Guidance scheme?'

'Mr Barber, I can give you that undertaking and I am prepared to stand by my word. I shall do my utmost to satisfy your concerns and I hope as a result that you will accept the good intentions behind my PL proposals. I hesitate to mention religious beliefs in such distinguished company, but I am — like Andy Sheen — a committed Christian and I can assure you that my conscience is clear. All the measures I am proposing are of the highest moral standard; all are conceived solely for the good of the people they will apply to.'

'Thank you once again then, Mr Knox.' Alastair Barber looked delighted, overjoyed almost, with the outcome of what had promised to be a difficult meeting. 'I accept your assurances on behalf of all those I represent and I can tell you that the NCCL at least is now prepared to give its provisional approval to your plans. Thank you.'

As the NCCL delegation left the room,

Selwyn Knox signalled to Nigel and Sonya to remain behind.

Nigel's first reaction was to congratulate Knox on the reasonableness of his approach and on the assurances he had given about the Parenting Programme, but Knox and Sonya Mair were already rummaging through files of papers and pulling out documents which they proceeded to lay on the conference table.

'OK, Nigel, you need to move fast.' Knox looked up and put his finger to his lips to silence Nigel's half-uttered remarks. 'Barber's not going to be happy when he finds out what we're really up to with this PL programme, so we've got to make sure he doesn't start turning nasty on us — '

'Wait a minute, Selwyn.' Nigel looked questioningly at his boss: 'What do you mean 'what we're really up to'? You just gave him a pretty clear picture of how the programme — '

'Oh, come on, Nigel. Don't be as wet as you look. All that softly, softly stuff — that's just to buy us a bit of time. You don't think we're really going to keep all those promises, do you? We can't run this programme with bleeding hearts and woolly liberal do-gooders. But we do need to keep Barber in check and fortunately Sonya has come up with the means to do it. The documents I've got here are Mr Alastair Barber's CSA records and they don't make pretty reading. Look, this one shows the Child Support Agency has had to chase missed alimony payments from A. Barber esq. on at least three occasions. The man isn't a responsible parent, Nigel, and he's certainly not the sort of person who should be lecturing the government on how to run its parenting unit. Now I think it would be quite helpful if you were to get the first of these documents to a friendly journalist and then let Alastair Barber know that we are thinking about including him on our Dead-Beat Dads list. Do you think you could do that, please?'

★　★　★

Only much later that morning was Nigel Tonbridge able to bring some sort of order to his thoughts.

He had had time to reflect on the Secretary of State's request and he knew he was now approaching a line which, if he crossed it, would draw him irrevocably into Knox's enchanted inner circle.

He walked into Sonya Mair's office and closed the door behind him.

'Sonya, I have to talk to you. You know I've been loyal over this PL initiative. I've done all the press work, I've toed the departmental line, I've supported him even when I've had serious doubts about what he's proposing. But there are some things he really shouldn't ask me to do. This Alastair Barber thing is too much. It's a smear campaign against the guy and it's not something I should be doing. I'm a civil servant: I'm not here to do Selwyn's political dirty work.'

Sonya Mair looked pityingly at him. 'Don't be a prat. The Barber job has to be done and you should be grateful Selwyn has chosen you to do it. It means he trusts you, he wants you to be part of the team, Nigel. He's showing his faith in you. So don't start having pangs of conscience now, you're in too deep for that — '

'Oh? And what's that supposed to mean exactly?' Nigel's voice was sharp and strained.

'It means you're in too deep, Nigel. You weren't parading your prissy conscience when you got your selection board rigged for you, were you? You didn't come over all coy then, did you? So don't think you can start lecturing us on moral values now. OK?'

Nigel's head began to spin. Sonya was threatening him and making no secret of it. His hands felt chill and his heart was pounding. Sonya was right, of course: if it were ever revealed that the board had been rigged, he would be out of his job in no time. But then, he told himself, it wasn't his idea to rig the board. Maybe not, but he had acquiesced in it. And how could he cope if he were to lose his job? The BBC would never take him back. What could he do?

In his current state of self-doubt, Nigel felt overwhelmed by Sonya Mair's ruthless self-assurance. Instead of standing his ground, he turned to her for some sort of explanation, some sort of answer to the questions that had been obsessing him for weeks.

'Look Sonya, I can't cope with this right now. I've got a lot on my plate. And I need to know some things from you. Some things only you can tell me. For a start, do you understand why Knox decided to recruit me? He knew I was never going to be on board for all this messianic mission stuff — and why does he insist on letting me see all the dirty tricks he gets up to? Why does he always parade the dark side of what he's doing? It's as if he actively wants me to know how devious and twisted he is.'

Sonya Mair looked at Nigel and for a fleeting moment he thought he saw a glimpse of recognition, a glimpse of sympathy. But her reply was cold and harsh.

'Look, Nigel, you're no different from all the other civil servants here. It's your duty to do what the Secretary of State tells you. So don't start thinking you're something special. And stop trying to analyse Selwyn. He's in charge here. He's a force of nature — he can get things done while other people just flounder around. It doesn't matter if he crosses a few lines and tramples on a few outdated notions of propriety. You do what he tells you to do. OK? It's the end result that counts.'

★ ★ ★

Nigel walked slowly northwards towards Trafalgar Square. He was meeting Joanie for lunch at the National Gallery. The removal of traffic and unauthorized pedestrians under the Congestion and Security Measures Act had turned Whitehall into something between a village high street and a ghost town.

The bright sunshine was helping marginally to clear his head. 'Perhaps Sonya was right,' he thought. 'Maybe Knox really is just a bully,

256

maybe the reason he wants me to know about all his dirty tricks is just his way of bragging, to show me he's the boss, that he can do what he likes, that I can't stop him — '

But something still did not make sense.

'It's as if he wants me to see all the evil he's capable of,' Nigel thought. 'But why? Is he proud of his sins? Is he taunting me? Is he showing me that he got away with Exxington because I was too weak to stop him?'

Joanie saw him across the restaurant and waved. As he approached her table, Nigel gave a little grimace and sank into his chair.

'Hi. Bad day, I'm afraid — '

Joanie knew Nigel was suffering since he had taken his new job. She knew the Department for Society was getting him down. But she did not know the reasons and Nigel had shown no signs of sharing them with her.

'What is it, Nigel? It's something serious, isn't it? You've been down for weeks now.'

Nigel looked at Joanie and felt all the love and affection that twenty years of partnership had created between them. After Sonya Mair's predatory, threatening presence, Joanie's goodness shone like a beacon.

'It is, Joanie. It is — '

'It's that Selwyn Knox, isn't it?'

'Yeah. It is.'

'He's creepy. Those dead eyes . . . that mad, ranting way he talks. He's getting you worried, isn't he? Do you want to tell me about it?'

'Yeah, I do. I can't say I understand it myself, though, really.'

'I know you don't agree with some of his policies. Is that it?'

'That's part of it. But there's more to it than that. I suppose all civil servants have times when they don't agree with their minister. But this is more. It's to do with the man himself, Joanie. I can't figure him out. At times, he seems such a good man, so inspired and so enthused with the love of humanity — he genuinely seems to believe in what he's doing. At others, he seems so cynical. So ruthless, so, well, so immoral.'

'Is he asking you to do things you don't agree with, Nigel?'

'Yeah, he is. Things no civil servant should be asked to do. Smear campaigns and blackmail. But it's more than that, even — I can't quite pin it down. It's something to do with the way he treats *me* in particular. He seems to have something about me.'

'Is it to do with that little girl who died up on the mountain? That was the first time you had anything to do with Knox, wasn't it?'

'Yes, it was.' Nigel looked anxiously at Joanie's face to see how much she had figured out about his run-in with Knox back in Exxington. 'You know, Joanie, I think it does have something to do with that. It's strange: he's never mentioned Exxington the whole time I've been working with him, but I'm always aware — and I think he's always aware — that it overshadows everything we do and everything we talk about.'

'Do you think he feels guilty about Clare O'Leary? It wasn't his fault, was it? I thought Ian Murray took the blame.'

'Yes. Yes, he did. There's something I can't explain, Joanie. Something difficult there — '

From her reaction, Nigel saw that Joanie had no inkling of his secret, the secret Knox had used against him to ensure his silence back in Exxington. He felt relief, but also regret, as he heard Joanie move the conversation away from him and back to Knox.

'So what does he say to you, Nigel? What does he want from you?'

'It's not even so much what he says. It's more the way he behaves with me, Joanie. Look, the really strange thing is that he seems to make a point of deliberately letting me know the underhand, dirty tricks he gets up to — all the shadowy manoeuvring, all the lies and the cheating. And I can't understand why. Everyone says he's a calculating politician, but if he is, why doesn't he keep his secrets to himself? Why is he showing me — a stranger, a potential enemy — the worst side of himself? Why is he giving me ammunition I could use against him? There's no logic to it — '

'It's because he knows you disapprove of him and he's worried about what you might think or do. He wants you to know about those things because he wants to draw you in. If he can make you part of them, you can't denounce him. Isn't that what's behind it?'

'Yeah, I did think that. At first, that's exactly what I thought: he's parading all his sins for me to see because he wants to make me his accomplice; to prove he can get away with it and I can do nothing to stop him.

'But now I'm not sure it's like that, it's more complicated. It's as if he wants me to know something that's hidden deep inside him and he can't get out of. You know, he's overbearing and bullying, and he does his best to intimidate everyone he works with. But at the same time he's somehow pathetic and weak — I can't explain it, Joanie.'

'Well, I'm not sure I feel much sympathy for him. I don't know him like you do, but one thing's clear, which is that you shouldn't get involved. Don't get lured into his schemes. As soon as you do one little thing that's wrong, as soon as you give him one little thing he can use to threaten you, you'll be lost. He'll exploit every weakness, every little fault, to draw you deeper and deeper in. If I were you, I'd go and report this smear campaign thing straight away. Isn't there someone in charge of propriety and that sort of thing for the civil service?'

'Yeah, it's Nottridge, the PermSec. I have been thinking of going to see him.'

'Well, do it now. Go as soon as you get back.'

★   ★   ★

Nigel's meeting with Sir Robert Nottridge that afternoon was one of those difficult, stilted conversations at which the civil service excels.

Even before Nigel had taken his place on the Permanent Secretary's pink settee and placed his cup on the teak coffee table, Nottridge had sensed that his director of communications was bringing him trouble and he listened to Nigel's

260

tale with the air of a man who would rather not hear what he was being told.

'I'm sorry to trouble you with this, Robert,' Nigel began tentatively. 'I wouldn't have come to you if I thought there was another way of resolving it. But I have to tell you that I have grave concerns about the behaviour of the Secretary of State and his political adviser — '

'Ah yes, Nigel. We all have these feelings from time to time. You were right to come to me. I find these things can generally be resolved without too much fuss. But do, please, carry on. Tell me what's troubling you, old chap.'

'Right. Thanks, Robert. It's quite a lot of things, actually. But let me give you an example. You know he had a delegation from the NCCL here this morning — '

'Ah, yes. You were invited to attend the meeting, were you? Strangely, I did not learn of it myself until it had already finished. No matter. Please continue.'

'Well, I was impressed by the Secretary of State's attitude during the meeting. He seemed very reasonable indeed. They were asking him to give some quite detailed undertakings about the new Parenting Licence — reassurances that it will be administered sensitively, that sort of thing. And he just kept saying, 'Yes, I agree.' He gave them every assurance they asked him for.'

'Well, that's quite excellent. And I think it speaks well of the Secretary of State: I do believe some of the criticisms of him have been rather exaggerated, you know.'

'Yes, but that's not my point. What I'm

261

worried about is what happened afterwards. He had me and Sonya in, and he basically said he'd been lying to the NCCL and he wasn't going to keep any of the promises he'd made.'

'Ah, I see. Well, you know, Nigel, these things happen and it's rarely quite as black and white as we may think. Politics is the art of the sensible, old chap. I'm sure he didn't mean to say he was telling lies. I suspect he was just refining what exactly he was prepared to do for the NCCL and he'll come up with a compromise that keeps everyone happy. I wouldn't worry about it if I were you, you know.'

'Well, that may be the case with other ministers, but Knox was absolutely blatant about this, Robert. He told me he'd lied to buy time until the PL is passed into law. And the worst thing is he then asked me to take part in a smear campaign to keep the NCCL guy quiet — Alastair Barber.'

'Now, now, Nigel. I'm afraid I must stop you there. One important thing I have learned in my many years in the service is that we have to take care to be moderate in our language. Smear campaigns are not something we should allege lightly, you know — '

'He asked me to leak details of Barber's CSA records to the press to scare him into keeping quiet. If that isn't a smear campaign, I don't know what is.'

'Well, let's just reflect for a moment. The Secretary of State may well have had a perfectly honourable motive. He may have just been — '

'He didn't, Robert. He's had Sonya Mair

trawling through their Lancelot computer to dig the dirt on one of their political opponents and he's asked me, a civil servant, to leak it. It seems pretty clear-cut to me.'

'Oh, Nigel, in my experience, these things are never quite as clear-cut as they first appear. Politics is a grey art, you know, and we have to consider many things before we go flying off the handle. We need to keep constantly in mind, for instance, that we have to work with our minister on a continuing basis: we can't go accusing him of impropriety, or we'd never get on with him again. And where would that leave us? In the past there have been cases of ministers falling out with their Permanent Secretary and not exchanging a word with him for a year or more, and that's no way to work, Nigel. It can bring the whole department to its knees. I'm certainly not going to let that happen at the DfS.'

'I know what the dangers are and I know you have gone out of your way to be conciliatory towards Selwyn, to make every possible allowance for him. And that's laudable, obviously. But it can't mean we have to turn a blind eye to malpractice in the department. That's in no one's interest — '

'Well, I'm afraid sometimes we have to do things we are not entirely proud of because we have to keep the bigger picture in mind. I'm sorry to have to tell you that I do not regard this case as warranting any further action and I must ask you to return to your desk and carry on with your duties.'

Nigel blinked. Nottridge looked disturbingly serene.

'Let me be clear about this, Permanent Secretary. I have told you about a blatant breach of propriety by the Secretary of State and you are telling me to ignore it.'

'Oh, Nigel, I know it sounds difficult but, believe me, these things happen many times over the years and we have to get used to them. During the course of my career I have been outraged by some of the things I have witnessed. There was all the sleaze under the Conservatives, you know, and then all the deceitfulness under the next government. Few people remember it now, but the Stephen Byers and Jo Moore case, for instance, stirred up tremendous passions. But governments always protect their own, Nigel. And in this case they'll protect Knox and spin against you. Don't stand on your principles and think you can speak out. They'll tear you to pieces. Your career will be over — '

'I understand what you are saying, Robert. But don't you think that's an argument for greater courage and integrity from us? If we'd made a fuss over all the little things, we might have been able to stop the lying over the big things: things like persuading the country to invade the Middle East when there was no real evidence war was necessary?'

'Ah, there, Nigel, I am afraid you go beyond my competencies. War is not one of my subjects. I am more concerned with your well-being, old chap, with your career and — I'll admit it — with mine. I am not ashamed to say that the post of cabinet secretary falls vacant this year and I am regarded as one of the leading candidates to fill it. As you will appreciate, I have been given charge of the Department for Society as a crucial test of my abilities and I intend to pass that test, Nigel. I intend to maintain good relations with my Secretary of State and stable working practices in my department. So I fear I cannot countenance any idea of confronting the minister and Sonya Mair over this. And I strongly advise you to put the thought right out of your head.'

★   ★   ★

In Downing Street at that moment, Charlie McDonald and Geoff Maddle were meeting Sonya Mair to plan Selwyn Knox's parliamentary launch of the new Parenting Licence the following Tuesday. After congratulating Sonya on the smooth passage the PL had enjoyed so far, Charlie enquired about Nigel Tonbridge. Sonya said she and Knox had got him under control, but suggested Charlie might want to call him in for a pep talk. For her part, she congratulated McDonald on the disappearance of the Andy Sheen drugs story, but asked how he now intended to get round the problem of Marie's magical disappearing pregnancy.

'Easy,' Charlie said. 'We just ring old Sopwith and give him the exclusive on Marie's tragic miscarriage!'

Sonya and Geoff laughed, but McDonald put his finger to his lips. 'Andy's not very happy

265

about the way we used Marie on this one, but he can stuff it. We did him a bigger favour than he knows, and one day we might have to call it back in from him.'

12

It was one of those days when the crowded Chamber was abuzz with expectation a full hour before the main event.

The Foreign Secretary announcing the breakdown of yet another round of peace talks on the MEWs was like the warm-up bout at a heavyweight title fight: MPs' attention was desultory, their thoughts had turned to the bill topper ahead, and their lips silently mouthed the speeches they had rehearsed to welcome or excoriate Selwyn Knox's notorious Parenting Licence.

When Knox rose the noise was deafening. Speaker McFadyen's bar-room brogue was barely audible above the cries of 'Bravo' and 'Shame' that rained down from both sides of the House.

'Order! Order, I say! The Secretary of State for Society — order! The Right Honourable Gentleman must be heard. Order!'

From his perch high in the Press Gallery, Nigel Tonbridge surveyed the packed government benches below. His now practised eye suggested that Selwyn Knox had a reasonable majority of back-benchers behind him, although the antis were making more noise than their numbers might have warranted.

Since the opposition benches were on his side of the Chamber and below his line of vision,

Nigel found it hard to judge the mood among the NewLibs. He knew the leadership had latched onto the NCCL's endorsement of the PL to give it their support, but the party's MPs were notoriously and endearingly independent minded and it was all but impossible to guess which way they would swing.

The few remaining Tories were solidly behind Knox, whom Nigel reckoned would probably take the vote with a little to spare.

Much, though, would depend on the speech, and Nigel knew Selwyn had spent the weekend and most of the previous day in conclave with McDonald, Maddle and Mair, polishing it until it shone like a platinum wedding ring.

'Mr Speaker, Honourable Members — '. Knox's words were met with another cacophony of cries. He yielded. Speaker McFadyen called for order. Knox rose again. 'I come here today to announce a policy that will change our society — '

Shouts of 'And not for the better!' were drowned out by a chorus of 'Hear, hear!'

Knox stood impassively, waiting for a lull. His eyes scanned the benches opposite; his shrewd politician's brain was calculating the mood of the House, doing the arithmetic that would judge his speech, calibrating the tone he needed to strike.

'The Honourable Gentleman shouts 'Not for the better', but I wonder what society he is living in. I ask him: is society today the society we would wish to live in? Is it the place we want our children to grow up in? Are we content with a society where people live in fear? Fear of the mugger, the drug addict, the burglar?'

Knox had the gift of pitching his speech to the mood of the moment, making it sound like a spontaneous response to the concerns of the Chamber.

'I ask the Honourable Gentleman: is he content to see towns and cities where people live in isolation, not knowing their neighbours, fearing human contact with their fellow citizens? Where a man will not come to the aid of others because he no longer feels part of the society he lives in?'

Knox was in his stride now. 'A world where the glue of social cohesion has melted away, leaving individuals alone, cut off from humankind because of the fear and suspicion that haunt our society? Where children are failed, abandoned, abused and neglected by their parents? Where teenage girls become pregnant but do not want the child? Where young men get their girlfriends pregnant and refuse to take responsibility for what they have done? Where fathers walk out on their families and fail to support the wife and children they have abandoned?'

The Chamber was quiet now. Knox had passed the first test: his audience was listening.

'So, I say to my honourable colleagues, this is not a society I wish to live in. Nor is it the society my constituents wish to live in. Nor — I am convinced of this — is it the sort of society the people of this country wish to live in.'

The rattle of approbation that swept the House told Knox his audience had warmed to his rhetoric. Now it was time to hit them with the detail.

Knox's adumbration of the measures he was promising was fast and polished, delivered in a relaxed, even tone whose confidence suggested that he at least had no doubts of his ability to deliver on the tasks he had set himself: to tackle the underlying causes of criminality and antisocial behaviour; to regenerate society; to save society from itself.

He listed the penalties he planned to introduce to crack down on absent fathers, single mothers, teenage pregnancies, asylum seekers, the unemployed and the other antisocial elements. He saved his master stroke to the end. The Parenting Licence was what MPs had come to hear about and he did not disappoint them. He outlined the training programme prospective parents would have to undergo before conceiving. He listed the skills they would have to prove they had acquired before the PL would be granted. And he announced that a vast network of counsellors and advisers would be set up to visit problem cases and explain the rights and responsibilities of being a parent. Knox drew gasps as he detailed the scale of the project and the number of counselling jobs it would create.

But as well as the carrot, he added with a slight smile on his lips, there would also be a stick. As well as rights, there would also be responsibilities and, in some cases, people would have to be made to live up to them.

There would, for example, be sanctions on anyone who became pregnant without a proper licence. These would involve the withdrawal of certain state benefits, remedial schooling and the obligation to acquire the PL retrospectively. The fabric of society, Knox said, must be based on every generation's respect for parents, and on future parents' realization of the responsibility they took on when planning to bring a child into the world. Without this there could be no self-respect and no social cohesion.

When it finally came, his conclusion was rousing and drew approval from all parts of the Chamber. 'So I say this to the doubters among you, to the jeerers and the mockers: New Project is not afraid to talk of responsibility and morality, despite liberal voices sneering about 'social engineering' and lack of compassion. Because what this society needs is authority. For too long now people have been used to a system that has grown lax, that has fallen into disrepute, that has lost its bite. And, oh! I am not fooling myself. Some people won't like it when authority is restored. They'll resent me for the discipline I introduce. But it has to be done. The figure of the parent, the symbol of the father, must once again become the source of authority and respect in the lives of individuals and in society. I endorse this new order as a man, as a minister and as a champion of paternal government for all our citizens.'

When the vote was taken, the Parenting Licence was passed with a larger than expected majority.

A late amendment providing for enforced abortions 'in extreme cases only' was voted through virtually unremarked.

An hour after the vote Selwyn Knox was still on a high. Adrenalin was coursing through him as he sat slumped in his darkened MP's office high on the narrow upper corridor of the Palace of Westminster. He was waiting for Sonya Mair to finish her rounds of back-benchers, to finish proffering thanks to those who voted for and admonishing those who voted against.

Another hour passed before Sonya came through the door. He was immediately clutching her, pulling her onto the patched and worn sofa in the corner of his office.

'Sonya, we did it. This is the greatest moment of my career so far — '

Knox was buzzing.

'And they bought it, Sonya. We prepared the way and they bought it. The liberals didn't baulk even when we told them how tough we're going to be. They bought it all. And what they don't know is that we've pulled off a double win: if they think all these new counsellors and advisers are going to be agony aunts and uncles, they're even greener than we thought! The adviser network is a godsend for us. Just think, the cases they'll be concentrating on, the 'difficult' cases, the under class — they're the people we need to watch the closest. The advisers will be there to gather the information we need — on the scroungers, the dole cheats, the petty criminals, the drug users. They'll be my eyes and ears, penetrating every home, every nest of crime and discontent. And they'll be my early-warning system: these people may think the counsellors are there to dish out help and fluffy words, but they're much more than that! They're my way to stamp out antisocial behaviour before it happens — '

Sonya smiled and put her arms round Knox's neck. 'Don't you think that's just the tiniest bit sneaky, Selwyn? Don't you think our clients on the Parenting Programme might be just the tiniest bit resentful?'

'No, they won't be, that's the beauty of it. They won't even know they're being watched. These people are my errant children, Sonya, and I need to keep an eye on them. In time, they'll come to know me as a father figure; a father who watches over them, who penetrates their innermost thoughts — '

As Knox spoke, swept onwards by excitement and euphoria, Sonya Mair was slowly sinking to her knees in front of him.

'When I swoop to stop them misbehaving, they won't know how I get the information I use to discipline them. But they will know I have that information. That I know everything about them — their innermost thoughts. I'll know what they are going to do before they do — '

Now she needed no prompting. Now she knew what he wanted. Now she was taking on the role she knew he loved the best.

'And in time they'll respect me for being the authority and discipline they need in their lives, the discipline they never had before I came to them.'

As Knox talked on and on, in front of him Sonya was becoming the childlike figure of the girl he loved the most, the girl he loved to hurt, the girl he loved to smother with love.

'They never had it because their parents didn't discipline them. Because their parents didn't love them . . . and you know, Sonya, I do love them. It's because I love them so much that I have to discipline them. I have to do it. I have no choice. I can't hold back. And they'll love me for it — they'll look on me as a father, Sonya. They'll thank me — '

★ ★ ★

It was nearly daybreak and the first cleaners and messengers were stirring in the great Palace when Selwyn Knox emerged from his fit, a changed man now, his appetites satisfied, his rage calmed. Now he looked with wondering affection on the soft naked form beside him; now he tended her bruised and lacerated flesh with love; now his tears flowed and he opened his innermost thoughts.

'Oh, Sonya,' he whispered tenderly, 'I feel a force swelling inside me, a great power of nature that must see the day.'

The intensity of the physical and emotional high that had enveloped him was pushing Knox to spill the contents of his heart.

'I can't repress it. It's an energy I can't control, an energy for good or for evil — I don't know which. And I'm powerless before it. I welcome it — I fear it — and I know I must be responsible for the impact it makes. The power of my own nature, the strength of this energy within me, sometimes it terrifies me, Sonya. And that's why I need you to stay with me. Alone, I can't control it. That's why I have bound you to me, you and Nigel. You are the only ones who can help me, help me channel the forces within me that are bursting onto the world. You and Nigel understand me; you and he hold the keys to my nature, you and he can shape me, for evil or for good.'

★   ★   ★

Nigel Tonbridge showed his Government Information and Communication Service pass at the gates of Downing Street and followed the police constable's directions to the fast-track security clearance: it was quicker than the procedure for non-government visitors, but Nigel sometimes regretted not being given the souvenir slippers they could take away with them.

Once inside Number Ten, he turned left to the ground-floor press office and knocked on the door to the panelled antechamber where Charlie McDonald's secretary was sitting typing.

'Oh, hello, Nigel. You can go in straight away: he's expecting you.'

As Nigel entered, McDonald looked up from a file on his desk, smiled and said, 'Sit down. I won't be a minute: I'm just perfecting my *EastEnders* strategy.'

Nigel had no idea what Charlie was talking about, but did as he was told.

A beaming Charlie McDonald, white teeth shining in his rich black face, eventually took off his wristwatch and placed it on the table — a signal that he was taking time out from business matters and honouring Nigel with a conversation friend to friend.

'Well, Nigel, we're all well pleased with you. You've done a great job getting old Selwyn such a good press on this Parenting Licence thing. I have to tell you I was pretty worried when Andy and Sel came up with it, but it seems to be going down a treat. And Andy's grateful, too. I've got a note from him here that he wants me to pass on to you and Selwyn and Sonya and all the team. Now, where is it? Ah, yes; here it is: 'I regard the initiatives from the Department for Society as the keystone of our domestic policy. If this government is to be remembered for one thing, I want it to be for the rebirth of a moral society in this country. I believe we will be held to account on this by future generations and by God. My thanks go to all of you who are helping to make this possible.' Pretty heavy stuff, eh, Nigel? What do you think of that, then?'

Nigel nodded his appreciation, but he could not suppress the nervous reaction that often overtook him in moments of emotion or stress. Instinctively, his hand reached into his jacket pocket to thumb the pages of the old notebook he constantly carried with him.

His response to Charlie McDonald's question was similarly unpremeditated. 'I think it's great,

Charlie. But are you really sure Selwyn's the right man to be in charge of all this?'

A look of amused enlightenment passed over McDonald's beaming face.

'Ah, so that's it, is it? You're feeling the Knox effect! Not very pleasant, is it? A bit creepy, eh? Well, don't worry about that, mate. Everyone feels the same, but it doesn't make him a bad minister.'

'Well, I'm not saying that. I'm just — '

'I'll let you in on a little secret, one that's really helped me in this job.' Charlie McDonald was in expansive mood and he wanted Nigel to share it.

'Basically, a politician's personality is irrelevant. What matters is his image, and that's something that has to be created by people like you and me. Once we've done that, it can be manipulated quite easily and quite independently of the man himself. And I'll give you a tip. Go and read a book that helps me at times like this. It's called *The Hitler Myth* and it's by a historian called Ian Kershaw. If you don't believe what I've just been saying, you will do once you've read it.'

Nigel's face was evidently expressing such horror at this suggestion that McDonald stopped himself to laugh.

'I'm not comparing anyone to Hitler, you idiot. All I'm saying is the techniques are still valid: you cover over the reality of the politician, the man, with a veneer, an image — something you can create and control. You'll understand if you read the book: Kershaw says the Hitler image, the brand, got stronger and stronger until it was the only thing left that united the regime and the country. No matter how many Germans had doubts about what the Nazis were doing, there was always ninety per cent or more who approved of Hitler, or — rather — of the Hitler image they'd been presented with. Think about it, Nige! It's a pretty powerful tool. We use it with Andy, although we don't talk too much about it, of course. You know, Kershaw says that eventually the image wrapped around the Führer got so solid and so permanent that the man underneath it just shrivelled up until there was only a black hole. There was no real person left — just a shell, a cocoon, a myth. And that's how I think of your guy Knox sometimes, you know. He's allowed himself to become the image we've created for him so completely that his existence as a man has had all the juice sucked out of it! Sometimes I look into his eyes and I'm looking into empty sockets. They've got that blank look, like Himmler's eyes — have you seen them in photos?'

Nigel nodded, acknowledging the aptness of the comparison.

McDonald laughed again. 'You know, Nigel, people say Knox is inscrutable, but I'm telling you there's really just nothing there. He only lives when he's being the mask we made for him. He's not a man like you and me, Nige; he's a black hole! I think he only exists for his politics, for his ambition, for his ruthlessness: he's become the image we created for him and the man underneath has vanished. Sometimes I think he's worn the mask for so long that it's stuck to his skin, and if ever we pulled the mask off everything else would come away with it. There'd be nothing underneath! As far as Selwyn Knox is concerned, I can tell you: the man has not just become the mask, the man has been replaced by the mask! And that's great because it makes him untouchable — an untouchable weapon, Nigel. You can't get to him as a man because there's no man there to get to.'

★ ★ ★

Nigel Tonbridge trudged down the old Cabinet Office corridor with a heavy heart. He felt as if he'd undergone a Kafka-like transmutation into a modern-day Chicken Lickin from the children's stories he used to read his daughter . . . Chicken Lickin, whom he remembered as the only animal in the farmyard to see that the sun was falling out of the sky and was about to immolate the known world. And everywhere Chicken Lickin turned to raise the alarm she was told to go away and stop being so silly.

As Nigel arrived back at the DfS deep in thought, his secretary lifted her hand and gestured towards his office in a mime of early warning. Inside he was surprised to find Chris Brody and an unknown visitor sitting at his table, evidently awaiting his return. Brody made as if to speak, but was forestalled by the stranger.

'Mr Tonbridge, is it? I'm glad you're back. I've just been having a bit of trouble with your colleague here and I'm rather hoping you can help me.'

Nigel looked at Brody, who shrugged and made a helpless gesture.

The visitor continued. 'As I explained to Mr Brody, I'm from the Home Office, currently attached to the Metropolitan anti-terror unit and homeland security division, and I need a bit of help from you. I have told Mr Brody that I need to see the lists of priority targets for your Good Parenting scheme and your Parenting Licence programmes, but he doesn't seem to want to help me.'

Nigel frowned. 'And why exactly do you need to see our lists?'

'Because *we* have an interest in those sorts of people, too. There must be masses of Arabs and Asians on those lists, masses of asylum seekers who've gone to ground. People who laugh at the idea of carrying an identity card, all those cases that have slipped through our nets and have got caught in yours. And I don't have to tell you why we're interested in those people. The anti-terror programme is the number one priority for all of us now.'

Nigel made an effort to keep an open mind. 'So if we give you these lists, what exactly do you intend to do with them?'

'Basically, we need them for surveillance purposes. We've got to use every lead we can get to track these people down. But don't worry, we won't publicize the fact we're using your data. You'll be safe on that.'

Nigel thought for a moment and looked at

Brody, who was pulling a face. He made up his mind. 'No, I'm sorry. I can't agree to your request. For a start, these are confidential files. It would be wrong under the Data Protection Act for me to hand them over. And it'd be immoral for me to do it. We're trying to help these people, not betray their confidence.' The official tried to interject, but Nigel was in full flow. 'There are a lot of vulnerable people on those lists. They've told us a lot about themselves — very personal details — because they thought we were there to help them, not to hand them over to the Special Branch. OK, you might find one or two dodgy cases, but essentially these are innocent, disadvantaged people who need help, not the police on their backs.'

Nigel could see that his arguments were making little impression, so he tried another tack. 'And, anyway, think about the danger it'd put our inspectors in: if it gets around that being on the Good Parenting list means you're under state surveillance, think how our advisers are going to be met when they visit people. They'll be treated with suspicion, with threats, with violence even. Who knows what might happen? No, I'm sorry, these lists are my responsibility and there's no way I can divulge them. You'll have to go back and say the answer's no.'

The visitor looked distinctly unimpressed. 'OK, mate, if that's your attitude. But don't think this'll be the last you hear of this. You lot need to start living in the real world.'

★ ★ ★

The following morning Nigel was running late. He was due to meet the Secretary of State in the foyer at nine a.m. to leave for the Dead-Beat Dads launch at the old workhouse in Whitechapel, but he had been held up by a morning prayers meeting that refused to die. As he hurriedly gathered up his briefing documents in the press office, he glanced at the morning papers and burst out laughing as he saw the front-page tabloid stories proclaiming that Andy Sheen was intervening on behalf of Wayne Mitchell. Wayne, of course, was Grant's teenage son, who had mysteriously appeared as if from nowhere a few months earlier and whose reputation had now been falsely tarred by association with his father. Wayne had been wrongly imprisoned for a crime he did not commit, and the viewing population was outraged at his fate.

Nigel now realized what Charlie McDonald had been talking about the previous day: in Wayne's arrest, he had spotted an opportunity to demonstrate that the PM was a man of the people, that he shared their concerns, especially about a character in *EastEnders*.

Nigel read the headline on the *Sun*'s story, 'Sheen Says: Don't Visit the Sins of the Fathers on Our Youngsters', and winced at the way it mimicked the rhetoric of his own department.

Even as he admired Charlie McDonald's cheeky wit, Nigel's disquiet increased. What sort of government is this, he thought, that wants to distract us into a fantasy world where Prime Ministers intervene in soap operas? What are they trying to distract us *from*?

He knew his position as a civil servant meant he should not speak out publicly about his minister's malpractice, but no one he talked to about his worries seemed minded to do anything. He felt the familiar beginnings of the depression he was prey to.

He was coming to the conclusion that he must tackle Knox directly, that he should demand an explanation for all the suspicions he was harbouring. He felt McDonald was partly right when he spoke of Knox as a 'black hole', but he feared an even more repulsive reality beneath it. And into this reality Nigel felt he must now peer.

★ ★ ★

Glenn, the chauffeur, spotted Nigel running down the stairs and motioned to him to get a move on. Selwyn Knox was already in the back of the ministerial Jaguar and the heightened security alert — Amber Special — meant they would have to hurry to make it through the roadblocks to reach Whitechapel by nine forty-five.

The journey passed largely in silence.

The precautions over Alastair Barber and the NCCL had had the desired effect, but Knox was evidently aware that Nigel's reluctance had meant it was Sonya Mair who had carried out the leaks and the warnings.

Knox made no direct reference to this, but Nigel sensed he was annoyed.

In the strained atmosphere in the Jaguar, Nigel

283

had the distinct impression that Knox was silently willing him to broach the subjects that were so much on his mind, to throw down the challenge that Nigel had long been contemplating. But neither man made the first step and the understandings or misunderstandings between them remained unspoken.

★　★　★

The Dead-Beat Dads launch went well.

It had been Knox's own idea to set up the Name and Shame website and he had taken a personal interest in giving the initiative a particularly high profile.

To the strains of 'Love Will Keep Us Together', the DfS's unofficial but popular theme music and a strobe flashing the department's official watchword, 'Respect the fathers and society will respect you', Knox bounded up to the high table of what was once the Whitechapel workhouse's communal refectory.

To the delight of the fifty or so journalists present, he proceeded to give a demonstration of how the site would work.

In a 3-D plasma-ball projected above the audience's heads, he called up at random several of the two million case histories the website contained.

The first few were fairly standard exposés of absent fathers who had failed to keep up with child-support payments, showing their face images, current addresses, bank records, a sentimental life story of the children they had abandoned, and concluding with a section where the children themselves were encouraged to express the pain and resentment they felt over their failure-father's behaviour.

The next example was the official exposé of a man who had got his girlfriend pregnant and then left her for another woman. The blurb included the name and address of the seductress and the fact that the man had infected his child's mother with herpes and gonorrhoea.

When Knox was asked why so many of the case histories he had chosen to show were from ethnic minorities, he smiled smugly and said it just showed how much non-whites were statistically likely to figure as DBDs. Later in his presentation he drew the journalists' attention to the notes at the end of each case history, which revealed those subjects who were HIV positive, drug addicts or criminals with a court record.

Knox took questions and was bringing the press conference to a close when the GBC TV crew asked him to project one final case history to use on the evening news. Knox said he was happy to oblige and hit a button that called up the file on a Mr Alastair Barber.

★ ★ ★

In the crush of bodies in the corridor after the event, Nigel could see the high regard Knox was held in by the media. Journalists crowding round him to expound their own tales of inadequate fathers and abandoned children were met with unfeigned sympathy and practical advice on how to contribute to the DfS's new Internet database, which would record and excoriate social failings of many different types and categories.

Nigel was already at the exit door and had signalled to Glenn to start the engine, when a reporter he did not recognize asked a casual question about Knox's relationship with his own father. For a fleeting moment Nigel saw hesitation on his boss's face and a flash of consternation in his eyes before Knox replied flatly that his father was dead. The reporter said he was sorry and Knox jumped into the Jaguar.

As they crawled along Upper Thames Street, sitting side by side in the back of the car, Nigel sensed an opening.

'I need to ask you something, Selwyn. Why did you say your father was dead? He isn't, is he? I saw the letters from him that came to you at the department. You chucked them in the bin, didn't you?'

Knox stared straight ahead. His stillness suggested he was expecting the question, had been preparing himself for it. He did not turn his head, but Nigel noted a tremor in his jaw.

'No, Nigel, he's not dead, at least not in the sense you mean it. He's alive somewhere — alive for someone, I suppose. But for me he's dead.'

Nigel saw a moistness in Knox's eye, and then his conscious effort to draw back from the intimacy that had suddenly opened between them. 'And, ah, if you get any more media enquiries about my family — about anything in my private life — I would be grateful if you

286

could make clear that it is completely off-limits: tell them it's off-limits and then tell me who's been asking. All right?'

Nigel thought for a moment. A catharsis was beginning to shape itself and he could either provoke it or withdraw.

'Yes, of course I'll tell them. But with the work you're doing, the family measures and all that involves, don't you think the media might see your private life as fair game? And if they do, don't you think I should know about anything in it that could cause us a problem? Is there anything you need to tell me, Selwyn, anything you want to tell me?'

The atmosphere was charged. Both men felt the conversation was leading them onward towards subjects they feared, but somehow felt compelled to address.

When Knox turned to Nigel, his eyes were wet with tears. 'Sonya has been talking to me, Nigel. You asked her why I got you to come and work with me, didn't you? Why I sought you out after what happened in Exxington? I'm not quite sure myself. We're from the same part of the world, aren't we, so we understand each other in that sense. But perhaps we understand each other in a different way, too? There are things from the past I share with you that I don't share with any other living being. We have common memories — do we also have a common understanding of what matters in our lives? Sometimes I think we are both bearing burdens — the weight of the past. Perhaps we also feel the weight of the present and the burden of what might come in the future.'

Nigel knew they were getting close to something important. He knew he must push Knox to explain. 'How do you mean, the burden of the future?'

'I feel a great power within me, Nigel. But it's an ambiguous power. And bearing the responsibility for it is a great burden. If I can't control it, it could be a terrifying destructive force. I don't know if I'm capable of controlling it and that's why I have bound you and Sonya to me. I feel that you have the power to release me from the burden I bear; you alone have that power — I don't have it — Sonya may, but she doesn't know it. And in the same way, maybe I have the power to release you from the burden you are bearing.'

Nigel looked at Knox and half-understood the meaning of his words. He had a troubling sense that Knox was trying to confess something, to relieve himself of a weight that oppressed him, or perhaps prompting Nigel to relieve him of it.

He knew he hated much about Knox and what he stood for, but now he was less certain that Knox was responsible for the death of the girl on the mountain, less certain that the burden oppressing him was the burden from Exxington in 2006. Nigel felt a flush of relief that he had not gone public with his suspicions about Knox; a brief pang of solidarity with the man.

Nigel heard himself talking about his own parents. About his father who endured excruciating pain during the two years he had suffered from motor neurone disease. About his agonized discussions with his mother. About their eventual decision to help his father. About the dose of morphine. About the death that followed mercifully and peacefully.

'That's how it happened, Selwyn. I've never told anyone. Not even Joanie. But somehow you knew about it back there in Exxington, and you used it to scare me. We both have power over each other, don't we, Selwyn? But if one of us pulls the trigger, I think we both die.'

13

Nigel's summonses to the Secretary of State usually came in the form of a phone call or an email from one of the civil servants in his private office.

This time Sonya Mair rang.

Normally their meetings were attended by Knox's Private Secretary, who kept a formal record of the discussion.

This time Nigel found himself alone with Knox and Mair.

It did not take him long to understand the reason why.

Knox's manner was brisk and impersonal; he was no longer the hesitant, confiding man who had opened his heart the previous week in the back of the Jaguar.

'Right, Nigel, Sonya and I have been talking. We can both understand why you had your doubts about handing over the Good Parenting lists to the homeland security people. You were right to point out the difficulties. But now I'm telling you the anti-terror measures must be our absolute priority and they have to take precedence.'

Nigel could tell Knox was set on re-establishing his authority, so he sought to step back from confrontation.

'Of course, Selwyn. Of course that's right. But I'm just trying to be practical. If we hand over the lists, we'll compromise the whole PL programme: think how clients are going to react to our advisers if they know they're working for the police — they'll stop cooperating with us, there'll be a backlash and the counsellors will become targets for violence — '

But Knox was in no mood for reason.

'I'm sorry, Nigel, get real. These counsellors aren't Samaritans. They're already collecting information for me. We're using them to fight drug-dealers, shirkers and benefit fraud; and don't tell me you didn't know. All this means is they'll also be helping wipe out the terrorists and infiltrators. I can't see the problem.'

In the face of this intransigence, Nigel's own reasonableness began to waver.

'Well, the problem is when we get one of our counsellors attacked and killed — '

Knox was losing patience.

'Look, the PM wants this and we're going to give it to him. Sometimes people have to suffer. So we may lose a few counsellors, but what's the problem if that helps save the country from terrorists? We don't want a repeat of the ricin poisoning or the tube bombings, do we?'

'Of course not — '

'So think about it. Let's say we don't give them the lists. We stand on our principles: we protect the privacy of the single mums, the scroungers and the addicts and, yes, we save a few of our people. But then what? The terrorists launch another attack, we get another two thousand deaths — and then we find the bastards who did it were staying at the house of an Arab couple on our lists. They were in our sights and we let them go. So another two thousand decent British people are dead and we're to blame. How do you feel about that?'

Nigel was starting to feel in danger of losing it. 'Don't patronize me, Sel. I know what the issues are. But giving them our lists isn't going to stop the terrorists. And you can't trample on people's civil rights just because it might stop something worse happening.'

Knox was entering his grim, calm mode, fixing Nigel with his stare, making it clear he was ready to crush Nigel once he'd finished his little speech.

Nigel ploughed on. 'Look, Selwyn, of course you might stop the terrorists if you turn the whole country into a police state, if you take away every human right, every freedom. But what's the end that justifies those means? We'll have turned ourselves into tyrants. We'll have become the intolerant, bigoted despots we accuse the fundamentalists of being. OK, we might stop a terrorist bombing; we might protect society from physical violence. But what sort of society would we be preserving? A shackled, cowering society of slaves ruled by bullying potentates sitting in fortified offices in Westminster completely removed from reality? Removed from contact with, or sympathy for the people they say they're protecting?'

Now they were glaring at each other, now neither would give way.

They had threatened each other, now they would have to see it through.

Knox's eyes had the emptiness of a gambler's, a poker player staking his future on the outcome of one hand. The blank indifference, the disdain on his face, were calling Nigel, demanding to see his cards.

He was unblinkingly, terrifyingly calm and Nigel could not match him.

Nigel fingered the notebook in his pocket, hesitated and walked out.

★ ★ ★

An hour later, Sonya Mair was in Nigel's office, her back against his door, a silent reminder he was trapped.

'And this time, Nigel, you do it. No running off to Nottridge, no squealing, no wriggling. This time Selwyn's going to push the button.'

'What does that mean?'

'It means if you don't do it you're dead meat. He's got a written record of your machinations to rig the civil service selection board and it'll be on its way to Dave Sopwith at the *Chronicle*. You'll be out on your backside. And what a shame that would be for you and for Mrs Tonbridge and the kids. Who'd be paying the fees at that little public school you've got them into? And the two hundred thousand mortgage on that nice Victorian house in Battersea? I don't think Joanie would be too pleased — '

Nigel hesitated and Mair saw it.

'Come on, Nigel. Don't make a fuss. It's not worth it. You're not going to go public and make a big show of principle over this. Downing Street would crucify you. You wouldn't get any sympathy. And, anyway, think what we're asking you. You know we have to fight the terrorists. We're talking about people's lives now, not just some little smear campaign. Handing over the lists would be an act of public service. OK, you'd put a few counsellors at risk, but you'd be protecting society. You don't have to feel bad about it, you'd be doing the right thing — and you'd be saving yourself and your family a nasty bit of bother.'

'Look, Sonya, I'll have to think about it. And if I do give you the lists, it needs to be in confidence — between you, me and Selwyn.'

Sonya smiled.

'That's the stuff, Nige. I knew you'd make the right decision. Come on board with us: help save society. You know it makes sense.'

'I said I'll think about it.'

'OK. But don't think too long. I need the disks in my office this afternoon.'

★   ★   ★

That afternoon, in Sonya's office, Nigel was looking for something in return, some explanation of the world he felt he was slowly being sucked into.

'I think you know what I need, Sonya. I need to know what Knox expects from me, what he wants me to do. You know everything that goes on in the man's mind, the same way he and I recognize each other's thoughts. So what is it that's bound us into this triangle? And who's

294

pulling the strings? Is it you? Or Knox? Who holds the cards?'

'I don't know what you mean, Nigel — '

'I think you do. I think you and he both know I've got one card — and it's a big one. I don't know if I can ever play it. But the strange thing is I sometimes get the impression he actually wants me to: do you feel that? He hides nothing from me because he wants me to see his secrets. He wants me to see his ruthlessness, his conflicts and his pain. And he wants me to *judge* him. He's showing me the contradictions and darkness inside him because he wants me to be his *judge* — is he trying to goad me into blowing the whistle, Sonya? Does he *want* me to expose him?'

'You understand some things, Nigel. But not everything. Selwyn's a good man. He has ideals and great plans. He's inspired by noble motives. And he's a Christian. He believes society can be brought back from the moral death it's sunk into. He believes people can be redeemed; he believes in salvation.'

'And what about himself? Does he believe *he* can be redeemed?'

'All I can tell you, Nigel, is that when he and I are together, he asks me to read to him from the gospel, and when I read the story of Lazarus, he cries.'

Nigel recognized in Sonya's words the need he knew Knox was feeling, the need to explain and excuse, to reveal the truth about himself and be held in the balance.

'That's it, Sonya. Selwyn wants us to be his

judges. I tried and failed to judge him five years ago in Exxington. Now he wants us to complete that process. But he's asking us to do the impossible. I don't know if the devil can be judged. Can the devil be pardoned? Can he be redeemed?'

Nigel left, not knowing whether Sonya really believed what she had told him.

Could she really think Knox was a force for goodness and purity? Or was she spinning the usual cynical lies? And if she knew Knox was evil, why did she stay with him? Was she addicted to the man? To the power he wielded and she shared? Or was she too scared to leave him? His thoughts about Sonya, about her intentions towards him, remained ambivalent. Nothing was resolved.

★ ★ ★

The *Mail on Sunday* dropped through Nigel's letterbox with a thump. Usually it woke the household, provoking angry barking from the dog and howls of protest from the children, but today the kids slept on.

Over breakfast, Nigel and Joanie flicked through the sections one by one. Nigel was immersed in the arts coverage, trying vainly to take his mind off the stress that had followed him home from the department. Joanie had the news section and was reading out extracts from a follow-up article on Marie Sheen's miscarriage. She had skipped the front-page story on the Internet paedophile investigations: so many similar tales had been doing the rounds in recent months that today Joanie hadn't bothered to read past the first paragraph.

When Nigel eventually got the news section, his eye alighted on a line that grabbed his attention. 'Among the twelve thousand names included on the credit-card lists confiscated from the Meet-a-Babe Agency of Bethnal Green, police sources say they have found several leading businessmen, actors, barristers, MPs and a serving government minister.'

He gestured to Joanie and began to read aloud. 'The sources, who have seen the confiscated lists, have not revealed the identity of those involved and a police investigation is currently under way. They caution that some of the names used by clients of the agency, which allegedly supplied both paedophile pornography and access to under-age child prostitutes, are clearly false. But the vast majority of customers using the services of Meet-a-Babe did not bother to disguise their identity, in the mistaken belief that their credit-card details would remain confidential — '

Joanie looked at Nigel and grimaced. 'I can guess who some of the MPs are, can't you? And I bet the minister is old Trautberg: he's always given me the creeps.'

★   ★   ★

The following morning, Selwyn Knox was in Charlie McDonald's study in Downing Street. The conversation had been strained and Knox was starting to lose patience.

'Charlie, I told you I only used the agency for research purposes. We're doing a lot of work around child abuse for the Good Parenting programme and I needed to see some of the things these paedophiles get up to. It was for official business — '

'Right, so you registered what you were doing with the Data Authority before you started logging on, did you?'

'I told you, Charlie. I didn't do that because I'm a cabinet minister. I shouldn't need to have to do that — '

'And you used official departmental credit lines to pay the site fees?'

'No. I've explained all this. I used my own credit card because it was more convenient.'

'And how many transactions do the lists confiscated from the agency show you've run up?'

'Well, quite a few, obviously. This is a long-term project — '

'Look, I want to help you, Selwyn. But you're not making it easy. You know as well as I do that your record with these Meet-a-Babe people dates back to before you ever went to the Department for Society.'

'Charlie, I want you to think carefully about this. You know how much store Andy sets by what I'm doing at the DfS. You know how much he values me. I know Andy will want to protect my good name and protect the department.'

'Yeah, sure, Selwyn, but — '

'Wait till I've finished, Charlie. You need to

think this through. Andy will expect you to do that. Now, the *Mail on Sunday* haven't seen the actual lists. They were tipped off by some low-grade twerp at the Met, and the police have taken him out and dealt with him. The lists are safe now; there aren't going to be any more leaks. So that's the first thing. The second thing is the Trautberg factor. You know as well as I do that people have thought for years that Trautberg's a pervert. The press would have written the story ages ago if they hadn't been scared of what you guys would say. So when people read the story yesterday, everybody, but everybody, assumed it was him.'

'Yeah; you're right there, Sel. Melanie fingered him straight away — '

'See what I mean? So let's think, Charlie: what's the silver lining in all this? Trautberg's an Old Project dinosaur. The last of them. Andy's been wanting to get him out of the cabinet and out of his hair for years. He hasn't done it because the Old Left have backed Trautberg. But do you think they'd still back him if the media were fingering him for this Meet-a-Babe story? It's a gift, Charlie. Andy needs to take it — for his own good.'

★   ★   ★

Down the hall from McDonald's study Andy Sheen was enjoying a cappuccino with a prawn sandwich as he ran through the sitreps from the government delivery departments.

He'd seemed rather gloomy in recent weeks,

so his secretary was pleased to hear him chuckling.

She didn't know the cause of his good humour, but Andy Sheen had just read the report from the Department of Commerce detailing the filing DRE was about to make to declare itself officially bankrupt. The report writer traced the DRE management's travails from the time they'd used the billions of pounds from the sale of their defence business to buy a string of bio-engineering and human-cloning firms in the USA. Two months later their biggest purchase, HumanBioTech Solutions of Lincoln, Nebraska, had been shown to be the brainchild of tricksters, based on technology that was little more than a fake and accounting practices riddled with scams.

The US regulatory authorities had shut them down, with a disastrous impact on the new DRE. Lord Willans and Tim Stilwell were being sued by thousands of investors and were personally bankrupt.

As a side-bar on the story, the government analyst who'd compiled the D of C report had added a note about Jim McGee of the *Daily Mirror*. 'This financial journalist,' said the report, 'was the newspaper's specialist on DRE. He personally sold thousands of shares before writing the front-page story which ignited the adverse speculation about DRE's fortunes and sparked the disastrous share-price collapse. As in previous instances, insider trading by Mr McGee is suspected but not proven.'

★ ★ ★

Andy Sheen was still chuckling when Charlie McDonald threw open his door and lurched up to his desk in a foul mood.

'Andy, we've got trouble with Selwyn. He's in my office now and he wants me to ask you something.'

★ ★ ★

For Selwyn Knox, left to pace the boards in Charlie McDonald's office, the waiting was agony. His thoughts flitted wildly from the personal friendship Andy Sheen had always shown him — they were both Christians and both believers in the moral imperative to improve mankind — to the catastrophic incongruity of the offences now stacked against his name.

One moment he found himself hoping and believing that Andy's personal goodness and the affection he had for his Minister for Society would persuade him to take the Trautberg route; the next he was in a gut-churning turmoil of despair, foreseeing his own political death and personal disgrace. How could the good name of a reforming minister, he kept asking himself, be squared with public whispers, with insinuations of immorality and worse?

As the minutes stuttered onwards and McDonald's desk clock ticked off half an hour, then three-quarters, then a full hour, Knox began to understand his fate was sealed: if Andy were going to save him, he would have come by now to embrace his errant minister, to absolve him of blame and pardon his trespasses.

But Andy Sheen did not come.

Charlie McDonald came back alone and Selwyn Knox knew his chance of salvation had gone.

'I'm really sorry, Sel' — Knox noted that McDonald's face showed no signs of being sorry — 'but Andy says it's no dice: we're going to have to let you go.'

McDonald talked; Knox heard him without taking it in; his thoughts were in meltdown.

'There's no way we could keep the story quiet in the long run, Selwyn. Trautberg would kick up a fuss; people would find out it was you; it'd do incalculable damage to our moral revival campaign. I'm really sorry, but you just can't expect to stay on as Minister for Society with such a sword hanging over you.'

Knox began to sense that McDonald had stitched him up to the PM.

'It didn't matter when no one knew what you were up to, Sel — when it was all a secret. But it's a different matter now it's in danger of getting out.'

Knox made a last attempt to save himself, to postpone the judgement that was about to strike him down.

'OK, Charlie. Look. Let's forget the Trautberg thing completely. But why can't you just tell the police to wipe my name off the lists, destroy the credit-card records and drop the investigation? I'll chuck the laptop in the Thames. It wouldn't hurt anyone, Charlie, and it'd save the DfS's reputation — it'd allow us to carry on with the work we're doing for Andy and for the party.'

'Selwyn, I hear what you're saying, believe me. It's not going to be easy announcing what's happened to you. It'll hurt the department. But it'll lance the boil. Andy just can't take the risk of being seen to protect a paedophile. Andy loves you, but you've got to appreciate the party has to be absolutely ruthless in defending its own long-term interests. The cause we're pursuing is too important and individuals have to be sacrificed if they get in the way.'

★ ★ ★

Nigel Tonbridge had been due to see the Secretary of State at eleven.

At ten to, the Diary Secretary rang from Private Office to tell him that Knox still wasn't back from Downing Street so he'd have to wait on standby.

Nigel asked her the reason for the hold-up, and she said they were as puzzled as he was: all they knew was that the SoS was in a one-to-one with Charlie McDonald. His earlier meetings had already had to be rescheduled.

Nigel shrugged and went back to the search he had been carrying out on his personal 3DVD.

After years using the same machine, he had been amazed to find that he had accumulated over two thousand Sound'n'Vision files and he'd finally decided it was time to start weeding them out. The only trouble was that each SnV file he examined seemed to hold memories strong enough to make him want to view it before electing to keep or delete. He had viewed SnVs of old press conferences he had attended, interviews he had carried out as a journalist and even the planning meetings he had been to in the early part of his government career.

Mixed in with the official files were sequences from his private life, mainly of the kids at birthday parties, school plays and sports competitions, but also of himself and Joanie when they had wanted to make an e-record of moments that had seemed important at the time, but which now had the inconsequential charm of forgotten voices chattering from the past.

All of them had sparked recollections that kept him occupied throughout the morning and made him neglect his departmental updates and the messages accumulating in his 3-D e-tray.

The SnVs of his late father were particularly poignant.

In the 3-D plasma ball he was projecting over his desk, Nigel watched the frail old man walk towards him as if he were about to walk out of the screen and back into his son's life. He heard his father's voice as he had always remembered it, telling him of episodes from his own youth — swimming in the Thames, returning from Korea, visiting Scotland on holiday, meeting Nigel's mother — all stories Nigel had heard him recount in life.

His phone rang and it was the Diary Secretary again, saying the SoS was back but had gone into a private meeting with Sonya Mair.

He had asked for all his appointments to be cancelled. Nigel could stand down.

★ ★ ★

Sonya had never seen her boss so agitated as when he came back from Downing Street that morning.

She watched his distress.

She listened to him in silence.

She thought of the consequences for Knox, for herself, for the party, for society.

She told him she could save him. She told him what he must do.

★ ★ ★

Nigel opened the SnVs of himself and his mother discussing endlessly the cruel illness that had struck his father and how best they could help him. His mother's distress seemed even more stark than he remembered it in life. He was thankful the files ended a day or so before mother and son had carried out the decision they both knew was right, but both had buried deep in the dark corners of their psyches which they now tried never to visit. Nigel pressed the Delete-All button and watched the SnVs disappear into the void.

★ ★ ★

Knox rang Charlie McDonald to say he needed to see him again.

305

He was running down the corridor gripped by a nervous exultation he had not known since walking out to face the cameras five years earlier — at a house in Exxington.

Knox was hyperventilating; he told McDonald he knew about the drugs.

His chest was tight; he knew about Harvey Parks.

He gulped for air; Sonya had told him everything.

His hands were chill, his vision blurring; he knew Sonya had been made to kill the story.

Little blows of nausea were hitting him in the back of the neck; he really thought McDonald should talk again to Andy Sheen.

Cold, clammy sweat was forming on his palms; he really thought McDonald should do it right away — now!

This time, Charlie McDonald returned within minutes.

Knox spun round to face him.

McDonald looked at the floor. 'You can go and see Andy now, Selwyn. He says it's all right for you to come to him. You're saved.'

★ ★ ★

As Knox left the room, Charlie McDonald's secretary ran in with a live telephone, indicating urgently that he'd better take the call.

It was the Home Secretary, Jimmy Kelso.

McDonald listened; his face darkened; his frown grew deeper.

306

After five minutes of Kelso's whining explanations, McDonald snapped.

The information officers in the adjoining room heard his voice rise menacingly above the hubbub of the press office.

'You keep your pecker in your pocket, you randy goat! You ditch your tart and you stay married — or you can wave goodbye to your cabinet job, mate!'

On the other end of the line, Jimmy Kelso listened in flabbergasted silence.

14

Things were getting difficult in Downing Street.

Andy Sheen was slow to chide. He was quick to bless. But the close shave over Harvey Parks's drugs stories and the pressure of Selwyn Knox's transgressions had seriously displeased him. He had let it be known that vengeance would be his; those close to him were waiting for payback time.

Charlie McDonald had stored away his usual insurance against any fallout that might come in his direction. He felt safe personally, but there was a growing feeling that backs were to the wall in Number Ten. In recent months the joshing and joking had become strained. Now they had the air of febrile whistling in a darkened world, awaiting the impact of an onrushing asteroid.

Charlie and Geoff Maddle were doing their best to keep smiling. With the benefit of retrospect, McDonald's retelling of events had even taken on a patina of humour.

'Poor old Kelso had no idea what had hit him,' he would tell Geoff. 'I was over the top, of course, but don't forget I'd just come back from dealing with the pervy vicar and I can tell you I was raging, mate. I cleared it with Andy, though: he's got no time for ministers screwing their secretaries, never mind wanting to marry them! Ever since Kelso's been meek as a lamb — just caved in, basically. You know, it reminds me of

Goebbels in 1938 — he wanted to leave his wife to go off with a Czech actress, but Hitler vetoed it on the grounds of 'moral responsibility'. Ha! Moral responsibility, there's a laugh. Course, poor Magda Goebbels would've been better off if he *had* buggered off: she ended up swallowing poison with him and their six kids and Adolf in the bunker.'

Now Charlie McDonald's laugh was loud and grim.

★ ★ ★

Nigel Tonbridge, too, had tried to come to terms with the way things were. Unlike Charlie McDonald, though, he was finding it hard to see the funny side.

Nigel had noticed Selwyn Knox's affection for him had become more demonstrative since he had agreed to hand over the Parenting lists. It seemed that the homeland security people had been using information from the DfS's counsellors to good effect and several arrests had apparently been made.

Knox himself seemed on the crest of a wave.

After some administrative problems in the first few months of its existence, his Parenting Licence had been deemed a success and the figures looked good. Official statistics showed a healthy majority of new births were now occurring to parents who had taken and passed the PL short course, designed for couples in the later stages of pregnancy, or had taken the full licence retrospectively. And increasing numbers of prospective parents were now signing up for training in advance of conception.

Talk in the department that Selwyn Knox might have been the minister implicated in the Internet child pornography investigations had quickly died away. On instructions from Downing Street, the police had refused to rule out Frederick Trautberg's name from their enquiries and his guilt was universally assumed.

Knox himself was now invited to attend weekly meetings with Andrew Sheen and Charlie McDonald, an apparent sign of prime ministerial blessing that other ministers regarded with unconcealed envy.

But Nigel's relationship with his boss had grown complex.

For both men it now encompassed hatred, fear and suspicion, with an undertone of complicity and mutual dependence. Nigel continued to sense that Knox expected something from him and was offering him the veiled promise of something in return.

As Christmas approached, Nigel was seized by the nagging conviction that something had to give. He felt increasing pressure to resolve the unarticulated stand-off with Knox and made up his mind to have it out with him.

★ ★ ★

The DfS's 2011 Christmas party was a difficult affair.

Half the department, the true believers, had come in a mood of genuine festive joy, determined to celebrate the successes of the PL and the social experiments they had helped to mastermind. The other half were the weaklings and the cynics: officials like Robert Nottridge, who went along with Knox for reasons of civil service loyalty or personal self-interest, or like Christopher Brody, who feared and despised Knox's policies but kept quiet for their own unspoken reasons.

Both factions were well represented in the department's conference room for after-work drinks — Moldovan beer and the cheap Ukrainian wine that had flooded London since the former Soviet republics joined the EU — and afterwards at the Crown and Unicorn, where the more energetic continued the festivities or the sorrow-drowning.

Knox had not appeared at either venue, but his representative on earth, as Brody liked to call her, was conspicuous by her very attentive, listening presence.

Only towards the end of the evening did Nigel realize he had been drinking steadily and that he was now in a surprisingly jovial mood. Without being exactly drunk, he had reached a state of mind in which the world was beginning to appear manageable and his colleagues in the bar seemed just the sort of people he wanted to share his most intimate moments with.

As closing time approached and the party-goers disappeared out of the door, Nigel found himself sitting alone in a dark corner of the bar.

He was vaguely steeling himself for the cold tube journey home when he sensed a presence

— a whiff of perfume, a rustle of silk, perhaps
— on the bench seat next to him. Nigel had not
noticed Sonya Mair for the latter part of the
evening, but she was here now and she had
evidently been waiting to talk to him alone.

'Are you all right, Nigel? How are things?'

Nigel might be the worse for beer, but the feel
of Sonya's hand caressing his arm was enough to
ring alarm bells.

'Fine thanks, Sonya. Yourself?'

'Mmm. All right, I suppose. Were you talking
to anyone interesting tonight?'

Nigel's suspicions grew: interrogation by
Sonya Mair under these circumstances was not a
prospect he relished. 'No, not really. Just the
usual suspects — '

'Did you talk to Selwyn at all?'

'No, I didn't see him all evening. Was he here?'

'I meant on the telephone. He's away. Gone
off to Ruth. He's spending Christmas with her
up in Scotland.'

Nigel noted the regret in Sonya's voice, but
had enough presence of mind to avoid sympathy.
'Well, everyone seems to have called it a day. I
suppose we'd better be heading off ourselves,
don't you think?'

Sonya looked at him thoughtfully.

In less than a nanosecond, the perceptions
vouchsafed only to the very drunk flashed
through his mind in a series of bewildering
illuminations: 'Sonya Mair is Knox's mistress,'
he thought. 'Of course she is — that's why she's
jealous of Ruth. She's missing him this weekend.
She's coming on to me — '

312

Nigel's consternation at what he had caught himself thinking, coupled with the alarming thought that Sonya could probably read his mind, left him barely able to take in what she was saying.

'Don't go just yet, Nigel. I need to talk to you. Can you stay a bit longer?'

From the front door, Chris Brody, wrapped in scarf and woolly hat, waved a cheery goodbye in their direction and shouted something vaguely scabrous. Realizing Sonya's hand was still on his arm, Nigel waved sheepishly as Brody winked and departed.

'Well, I don't know, Sonya. I should be getting home. Shouldn't you — ?'

Sonya's reply was suddenly earnest; the flirting at least momentarily gone. 'I should, but I don't want to. I can't face it at the moment, Nigel. Would you stay and talk to me? Please?'

Nigel mumbled something about the pub closing and getting thrown out on the street, but he was wavering.

'Look, you don't have to if you don't want to. I know you're probably thinking: what the hell is she up to? Well, I'm not up to anything. I've had a bit to drink; you've had a bit to drink. I just thought we could talk to each other for once, instead of trying to scare each other off — '

Her voice wavered. 'Actually, Nigel, I don't know who I can turn to if you won't — '

Even in his tipsy state, Nigel marvelled at Sonya. Either her appeal to him was genuine, or she was a mistress of the dissembler's art. Either

313

way, he thought, she was a very attractive woman.

'All right, Sonya, it's all right. But where can we go? We can't stay here.'

'Don't worry about that. I've got somewhere we can go. And I've got something I need to show you.'

Unsteadily, they rose to their feet; unsteadily, they walked out onto the pavement. As they climbed into the back of a taxi, Sonya called to the driver, 'Dolphin Square, please. We're going to Dolphin Square.'

★　★　★

Christopher Brody got home after midnight.

The house was quiet and he went straight to the small study on the mezzanine between the first and second floors.

The image of Nigel with Sonya Mair's hand on his arm had stayed with Brody throughout his train journey, on his walk from the station, and was there still as he sat and watched the computer screen flicker into life.

Brody hit the keyboard and began to type. It was something he felt he had to do. He addressed the memo to Nigel Tonbridge.

★　★　★

Selwyn Knox and Ruth Leeming had finished their dinner and were sitting in front of the TV. Ruth had been looking forward to seeing him. He managed to get up to Scotland so rarely

314

these days. Now he was here, though, he seemed distant and uninterested. She caught him looking away distractedly as she spoke. When she asked what was wrong, he snapped at her. The man she had lived with and called her partner was here at her side, but Ruth could see his thoughts were not with her. His eyes were cold as he told her things were getting complicated in London and he might not be able to stay for Christmas after all.

★　★　★

Brody hit the Send button and the memo winged its way through ethernet cables, through routers and switchers, wired and wireless message paths, girdling half the globe before plopping virtually into Nigel's unmanned, unscanned 3-D e-tray.

From: Christopher Brody, Dir. of Policy
To: Nigel Tonbridge, Dir. of Comms
Sent: 17 December 2011
Subject: SoS; Polit.Adv; contradictions

Dear Nigel,
    I reflect on the beliefs which unite and define the monoliths of recent political thought.
    I observe that the great enlightenment currents of the last hundred years have been predicated on the innate perfectibility of man.

315

Communism, Nazism, Maoism have preached that man can be saved.

But that premise has been the greatest instrument of human self-destruction ever invented.

Germany, the USSR, Eastern Europe, Cambodia.

Where politicians believe — or claim to believe — humankind can be perfected, they tend not to falter even at the gates of the concentration camp.

Knox is drawn to this line of reasoning, as is Sheen.

The humanist enlightenment has become an orthodoxy for many, a fanaticism for some.

These latter have seized on the death of God to replace His unshakeable truths with their own.

And their self-belief gives them the right to use every means to impose their utopias.

It gives them the right to despise the people in whose name their utopia is pursued.

They identify with the downtrodden, in whose name they claim to speak, but despise them at the same time.

And here is the flaw.

In their comfortable, self-righteous world, they feel a slight but constant ache.

An ache that nags and cannot be excised; a tremor that shakes the ground beneath them.

If visions of human goodness fuel their fanaticism, knowledge of the worm in the apple serves as an uncomfortable brake on their plans.

Knox claims to believe in human goodness,

but when he looks within himself he sees something different.

He sees in himself the innate fault in man; the original sin that invalidates his politics.

He is committed to his party's brand of utopianism, but he himself bears the mark of Cain.

If he himself is proof of original sin, how can he believe in the perfectibility of man?

He cannot reconcile the two: he is trying to accelerate and brake at the same time.

He cannot resolve the contradiction and it has worn him out.

Knox is a sinner; humankind is sinful. So the question he asks himself is: can Knox be saved? Can the devil be redeemed?

And if the devil is pardoned, what is his place in the new utopia?

Knox understands the conflict between perfectibility and sin, between certainty and doubt.

For an intelligent man in a position of power, this has become a struggle between self-justification and self-hatred.

Vindication through unthinking fanaticism has become his only chance to avenge his own pain.

And it makes him dangerous.

The purpose of this memo is to warn you of this danger.

It is a systemic political danger, but also a personal danger to you, Nigel.

So where I began with the political, I finish with the personal.

By the time you read this memo, you will have formed your own views of Sonya Mair. Tonight I saw you in circumstances that caused me some concern.

What is my conclusion?

The doctrine of unlimited human perfection is the instrument of unlimited self-immolation.

The only antidote, as Kant says, is unlimited respect for the sacred core of the individual. My conclusion is that you should not lose sight of this, Nigel.

I hope you find this helpful.

Christopher Brody

Nigel had little recollection of the taxi ride through Parliament Square, along Millbank, past Tate Britain.

He heard Sonya talk, but he barely responded.

It was her hand on his arm that monopolized his attention; he could not decide whether it was the hand of friendship, the hand of supplication, or the hand of the jailer leading him forcefully to his fate.

The taxi drew into the courtyard and Sonya took control. She paid the fare; she led him into the foyer. She drew him into the lift; she unlocked the door of the third-floor apartment.

In the living room, he saw the photos and mementos; he had already guessed whose flat this was.

Sonya put her arms round his neck and kissed him.

The kiss was tender, almost chaste. Nigel

318

could not discern its meaning.

Sonya moulded herself to him. He felt her body warm against his.

She flowed into his embrace. He could feel the beating of her heart.

Nigel waited. Waited for Sonya to take the lead.

He both desired her and feared her.

Sonya spoke. 'Nigel, I need to tell you something, show you something. Come through here.'

In the bedroom, Sonya opened a wardrobe and Nigel saw Selwyn Knox's sharp, elegant suits. Sonya bent to open the clothes drawer and Nigel saw the crumpled school uniform of an adolescent girl, saw the piles of photographs, the magazines, the downloaded images of children.

His face expressed his horror.

Sonya seized his hand and began to cry. 'I'm lonely, Nigel. He's the one — . There's no warmth in his world. I just needed some warmth.'

Nigel remembered the *Mail on Sunday*'s story; he remembered the government's tacit fingering of Fred Trautberg as the paedophile minister and he was seized with revulsion. Revulsion at the culture of lies that now ruled the government, at Selwyn Knox and at the life that Sonya had let herself be drawn into.

It seemed Sonya had read his thoughts. She began to plead for his indulgence. 'Nigel, don't look at me like that. Please don't blame me, Nigel. He's the one. I'm cut off from human warmth. There's no warmth in his world.'

But months of dealing with a different Sonya Mair, with a hard, scheming, dangerous Sonya, had left Nigel wary. 'Why don't you go back to your husband, Sonya? Go back to Thomas.'

'It's too late for that, Nigel. Selwyn's a hard master. He demands devotion. He's needed me all for himself — and now I've lost everything, cut myself off from everything and everyone.'

'But why did you do it? What reason — ?'

'You know Selwyn. You know how strong he is. He has such massive energy welling inside him, bursting, exploding. And he needs me — it's partly a sexual thing — I think you've guessed that — '

'But what sort of sex, Sonya? What do you call all this — ?'

He gestured at the child's clothing and photographs on the floor.

'It's something I can't explain. It's horrifying, but it's fascinating at the same time. It's to do with sex, but it's about power as well. Don't judge me. You know the power Selwyn offers us — the importance, the significance; He says the power we wield gives a meaning to life.'

'And are you happy with that? Are you content to be part of that?'

'Yes . . . perhaps . . . I don't know. Selwyn says power is lonely and I believe him. He has no other life, no other meaning. If his politics fail, then he fails and there's no right of appeal. They're like a sect of fanatical believers — Selwyn, McDonald, Maddle, Sheen — and I've let myself become part of it. It's exciting, it's arousing, but in the end it's deadly. There's an

320

emptiness at the heart of their power, a lack of values, a lack of substance. Selwyn knows that and he suffers. But he wants to draw others into his loneliness. He's in a deep well of loneliness, Nigel, and he's trying to pull me — and probably you — into it, too. He's pulling us in to alleviate his pain, but he's pulling us in to drown with him.'

Sonya collected herself and sighed. She looked at Nigel. 'But you, I suppose you should go back to your life, back to Joanie. Don't make the same mistake as me — I haven't resisted him, but maybe you can. I see you fight against his pull and I want to see if maybe I can scramble back up out of the well, too.

'But how? We need to save ourselves from his power and we need to save others from it.'

Listening to Sonya, Nigel realized that his decision was made. He knew now that he must go back up to Exxington; back to find the truth about Selwyn Knox. Again, she read his thoughts. Again, she smiled sadly.

'I want to leave him, you know. I've had enough of his power and his exploitation. But I'm worried how he'll take it — '

'Do you mean violence, Sonya? Are you worried about what he'll do to you?'

'No, Nigel, it's him. I'm worried he won't be able to live without me.'

★ ★ ★

Nigel woke with a sore head and cursed the Lord Iveagh.

As he raised himself gingerly on his elbow, a brief sensation of dizziness sent him falling deeply, endlessly back into his pillow.

He shook himself to find his balance; looked around him.

It was a moment before he knew where he was.

The clock said ten a.m. He was alone in his bedroom at home.

By the side of the bed he reached for the telephone and rang Sonya Mair's mobile number.

'Sonya — Sonya, is that you? Are you all right? You're still there, aren't you? Still at Knox's? Yes, I think I'm OK. I'm at home. I've no idea how I got here. Joanie's gone out to work already and the kids are at school. Listen, I wasn't joking when I said I was going up to Exxington. I need to find out the truth about what happened there. You want me to do it as well, don't you? I'll make the calls today. We're going up to my mother's for Christmas next week. I'll see what I can find out while I'm there. But don't you do anything precipitate, Sonya. Don't tell him you're leaving him. Wait at least until I get back. I don't want anything to happen to you — '

★ ★ ★

For the first time in five years Nigel opened the notebook that had lain in his pocket since the death of Clare O'Leary.

For the first time since 2006, he reread his notes and transcripts, his case interviews and his

322

half-written stories. He reread the bewildered sorrow of Eileen O'Leary, Eileen Bates, who had known him in primary school, who had just lost her daughter; he read the unused testimony of Ian Murray, pointing the finger at Knox; and he read the transcript of Knox's own cynical telephone message warning him off the case.

Nigel picked up the telephone and dialled a number in the west of Scotland.

He heard the familiar, cigarette-blackened voice of his first mentor in journalism. He asked George Young for a favour.

'Yes, George, the names of all the children on the trip that day and their current addresses if you can get them. I'm mainly interested in anyone who's still living locally. Most of them would be in their early twenties now. Clare was the youngest and she was twelve back then . . . Yes, I know it's tricky, but you're a journalist, George: that's what we're supposed to be good at, remember? And you're retired now; it'll give you something to do to keep you out of the pub. All right? Thanks, George. I'm coming up next week, I'll see you then.'

★ ★ ★

Nigel did not see Sonya Mair in the two days before his departure. She had called the department to say she was sick and would be back after Christmas.

When he thought about her it was with a mixture of pity and affection, anxiety and desire. He felt the warmth of her arms on his neck and

323

the scent of her breath on his lips.

He felt her absence.

He did not ring her. She did not ring him.

But the day before Nigel was leaving for Exxington, a handwritten note appeared on his desk. He asked his secretary where it had come from, but she said she'd been on lunch break and hadn't seen who brought it.

In a neat, slanting hand, Sonya wrote of her feelings for Nigel, of her gratitude for the kindness he had shown her and of her fears for his safety if he were to cross Selwyn Knox:

I don't need to tell you, Nigel: Selwyn is a force of nature. He fascinates me, he overwhelms me and I enjoy that feeling, but he also scares me. I admire the good things, the benefits his energy can bring the world, but I also fear the damage his power can cause. He is human in his faults and sins, but superhuman in the strength he possesses. He sees you and me as his safety valves. In my case for the sex, certainly, and you because you are the only one who has the power to restrain him if the forces within him run out of control. You have the knowledge and the power to bring it to a halt. You are his executioner, Nigel; an executioner he needs by him for the time when he reaches the irredeemable point of disaster for himself and for those whose lives he controls. He knows he is not strong enough to stop the forces welling up within him; he cannot take the axe to his own neck;

but he knows you can. He needs you to do that, Nigel — and he feels he can push you into wielding that axe at the moment he needs to bring the whole process to an end.

Nigel and Joanie went up to Exxington once or twice a year.

Joanie's parents were dead and the children enjoyed a week being spoiled by their remaining grandmother.

The car journey on the new Toll-Way from London to Glasgow had been remarkably smooth despite the snow. Joanie felt her husband was a little quieter than usual, wrapped up in his own thoughts, but she didn't say anything and Nigel didn't volunteer an explanation.

On the first evening of their stay he said he was going to see George Young in the Exxington Arms; he thought Joanie would find it boring and she said she was happy to look after the children.

Two days later Nigel went out again.

This time it was not the Exxington he was heading for, but a different pub on the rundown south side of town.

Nigel found himself walking through streets he had never seen before, through the industrial estates of Exxington's under class, through lowering canyons of abandoned factories, across a rubble-strewn landscape where workers' houses had been razed under Knox's Clean-Sweep policies.

By the time he arrived at Bratten Street dusk had fallen.

The street was a strange oasis — a single row of terraced houses among the acres of demolished streets. It stood like a lone tooth in a toothless mouth; a random relic of some apocalyptic air raid.

The street lights were beginning to glow.

Outside the Eagle and Child the pub sign swung in the wind. The eagle gently bore the naked child in its claws, soaring, flying, fixed for ever mid wing-flap, suspended in space and time.

He sat at the bar and ordered an orange juice.

The room was empty apart from an elderly man in overalls in the corner, contemplating his pint.

Nigel waited.

He had told Cathy he would be wearing a leather jacket and green scarf; she could not miss him.

She had told him not to expect too much from her: she had been living in a hostel for the homeless since coming out of the young offenders' institution a year earlier; she had blonde hair and was pretty sure to have a ciggie in her mouth.

Nigel spotted her as soon as she came into the bar.

He waved her over and said, 'Cathy? Cathy James? Thanks very much for coming. George said you would. Can I buy you a drink?'

Nigel bought himself a pint and Cathy a vodka.

As they walked across the cigarette-strewn floor to a corner table, Nigel looked at Cathy and felt a pang of pity.

She was not pretty, but she had a fragile, vulnerable look to her. Her bleached hair was straggly and unkempt, her clothes were dirty, she had the glazed eyes of an addict.

Nigel found his imagination rewinding to the putative Cathy of five years earlier: to the young girl magically unwound from the years of trouble that had brought her to where she was today, an unspoilt girl looking with hope to the years ahead, foreseeing love, friendship, a career, unaware of what fate had written for her future; setting out on a trip to Ben Donnan with the Exxington District Council youth scheme.

What fate had decreed such a fall for Cathy James?

What had changed her from the hopeful, trusting girl to the addicted ex-offender before him now?

Nigel recalled the memo Christopher Brody had sent him the night he himself had been led from another pub by Sonya Mair, led away to Knox's lair in Dolphin Square.

He thought of Brody's mysterious, ambivalent exegesis of original sin, his quasi-celebration of this blight man was born to, of sin as an affirmation of humanity, innate imperfection as a token of human defiance in the face of Knox and Sheen's implacable insistence on perfection, the flawed humanity that negates the princely Angelo's strident fanaticism.

And he wondered now if Cathy's fall was the fruit of original sin.

Was Cathy's fate already decided when she set

out for the mountains back in 2006?

Was her destiny already inscribed in the book of life?

Was it written in her DNA?

After a few drinks, which Nigel paid for, Cathy recounted her life: the schoolgirl jobs in the Exxington supermarkets; her liaison with Billy, the dealer; her first experiences with drugs; the abortion; the thieving to pay for her habit; the months inside; and now the hostel for the destitute; the abuse from the warders who used her body and the inmates who used her gear.

Nigel probed gently.

He asked her about the abuse, asked her if she had been abused as a child.

Cathy thought for a moment, then asked him who he meant in particular.

Nigel mentioned the death of Clare O'Leary.

She hesitated, looked at him with a question in her eyes.

Nigel said, 'Do you want to tell me something about that day, Cathy? About the day you and Clare and the councillors went up on Ben Donnan? About what happened to Clare?'

Still Cathy looked at him.

He could see her formulating her thoughts, struggling to tell him the truth she had hidden within her for so many years. At last she asked, 'Who was he? That councillor — what was his name?'

Nigel sighed. 'His name was Knox, Selwyn Knox.'

As he pronounced the name, Nigel saw Cathy's eyes fill with relief.

'Yeah, that's him,' she said. 'He's the one who

abused us. He abused Clare, he abused me and he abused the other girls. He was known for it. We were terrified of him.'

Nigel sensed he was at last nearing the truth; the truth he should have uncovered five years before, but had not had the courage to pursue. He felt a great weight begin to lift from his mind. The conscience that had tormented him for so long slowly began to ease.

'Thank you, Cathy. Thank you for having the courage to tell me that. And can you tell me anything about the way Clare died? Was Knox with her when she went missing?'

Nigel saw Cathy hesitate again, look at him intently, reflect before taking the plunge.

'Yeah. He killed her. Selwyn Knox killed Clare! I've been too scared to say. Too scared he'd come and get me if I grassed him up. But now I've said it. Now I've told you. Is that what you wanted to hear?'

Nigel took Cathy's hand gently in his.

He told her not to get upset, not to worry. He would protect her. She didn't need to fear Selwyn Knox any more.

Now he would deal with Selwyn Knox and Cathy could find some peace; now at last she could overcome the terrible memory that had haunted her for so long.

★   ★   ★

Nigel and Joanie had four days left in Exxington.

He spent another couple of evenings out of the house.

329

He gave Cathy James as much money as he could afford and told her to use it to leave the hostel and get a flat, to make sure she kept away from the dealers and the abusers, to get herself clean, to drag herself out of the blight she had been born to.

Nigel thought a lot about Cathy.

He thought of her as if she were his own daughter.

He prayed she would use the help he had given her to better herself, to rise above the vices she had fallen into.

And he went back to London to expose Selwyn Knox as the perverted threat to humankind that he was.

15

When Nigel returned to London, his first thought was to find Sonya and tell her what he had discovered in Exxington.

In the period between Christmas and New Year most government departments are skeleton staffed and when he went in to the office, the DfS was like the *Mary Celeste*. Sonya was not at her desk.

He was surprised by the wave of disappointment he felt at not seeing her. He called her mobile and got no reply. He called again. Then again. And again.

By the end of the day he found himself strangely desperate to talk to her. He rang her home number, but got only her disgruntled husband, who told him he hadn't seen Sonya for nearly two weeks.

Nigel spent the following days unsuccessfully trying to contact Sonya and preparing for the showdown with Knox.

★ ★ ★

A few days later Knox suddenly appeared in Nigel's office.

The shock of seeing him threw Nigel into a panic.

For all his preparations, he was alarmed that their meeting had been thrust on him so unexpectedly.

Knox's first remark plunged him into turmoil. 'Sonya tells me you saw her before Christmas and that you've got something you want to talk to me about.'

Nigel's eyes went dim, he felt faint.

Had Sonya been deliberately leading him on? Had she been in it with Knox all along? And what about everything she had said to him that evening? Was it all lies and deceit?

Knox fixed him with a probing stare.

Nigel saw triumph and mockery in his face. He saw there was no way back. 'I don't know what you mean about Sonya, Selwyn. But it's true I need to talk to you. And I think you know what it's about.'

'I have no idea, Nigel. Why don't you tell me?'

Knox was worryingly calm. His eyes were blank, the empty eyes of the dead. Behind them, Nigel felt a vacuum sucking him in, pulling him down.

'All right, I will tell you. I'll tell you about the lies and the cheating. The evil you've instilled into the way the government treats people in this country. The evil within yourself. The paedophile pornography. The way you abuse Sonya and God knows who else. The way you abused and murdered Clare O'Leary.'

If Nigel had been expecting his words to shake Knox, to provoke a breakdown, a confession, a catharsis, he was to be disappointed. Knox's expression did not flicker.

'Well, Nigel, that's all very interesting. And what do you propose to do about it?'

'I let you off the hook once before, Selwyn.

I'm not going to do it again. I intend to talk to the Prime Minister and the cabinet secretary. And if they won't do anything to stop you, I'll do it myself. I'll go to the papers, I'll tell them the truth — '

Knox smiled.

'I wouldn't do that, Nigel. Have you forgotten our pact? I have covered for you, covered up your cheating at the civil service board, and in return you've acted in the best interests of the country and the best interests of Nigel Tonbridge. I don't think that's the sort of story you'd like to see in the papers, is it?'

Nigel had been expecting Knox to threaten him. This time, he was ready for it. 'Well, I'll just have to live with that, Selwyn. We all make mistakes. We're all guilty of something, I suppose; and we all have to live with the consequences of what we've done. But it's a question of distinguishing between degrees of guilt, between the sins all men inherit and the evil some of us make for ourselves — '

Knox smiled again. 'And what about your sins, Nigel? What about your misuse of the confidential information you obtained in the course of your official duties? What about the way you misused the Parenting lists for your own material advantage?'

'What? I misused them? It was you who forced me to hand the lists over, Selwyn. It was you who misused them.'

'Well, I'm afraid that's not what Dave Sopwith will be writing in the *Chronicle*. He'll write what I tell him to write.'

'Look, Selwyn, this is nonsense. The game's up. You can't bully your way out of it this time. You do what you like to me — I'm going to tell . . . '

'Whatever I like? Well then, what if I were to tell the Attorney-General about the way you murdered your father? About the inheritance you so desperately needed? About the poison — ?'

Nigel looked at Knox in terror.

'What are you saying? I told you why we did that. It wasn't murder. It was pity. It was mercy.'

'That's not the way your confession sounded to me. I heard you break down and admit everything. I can remember it quite clearly.'

'My God — you liar. You can't do that to me.'

'Just try me, Nigel. I can't let you stand in my way. The work I'm doing is much too important for that.'

'No, Selwyn, it's the work you're doing that I have to stop. It's the evil you're creating at the heart of this government, the way you're subverting everything good and human in our society. I can't stand by and let you — '

'I don't think you have much option, actually. You probably don't know this, but your efforts to destroy the evidence against you were a failure. You may think you wiped the SnVs of you and your mother plotting to murder your poor father, but you didn't think about the back-up copies on the hard drive, did you? Fortunately, I now have them all nice and safe. It won't be pleasant for your mother to stand trial, but it'll be so much worse for you. In this country people treasure respect for a father more than almost anything:

I've made sure of that since I came to the DfS. You *murdered* your father, Nigel, and I can show you no mercy. You'll find yourself in front of a court that has only horror and revulsion for patricides. I'd like you to reflect on that. Take your time. Don't do anything rash. And then come and see me on Monday.'

★ ★ ★

It was not a happy New Year in Downing Street.

Andrew Sheen and Charlie McDonald were beginning to feel like 3-D chess players, fighting off assaults from all directions, forever trying to shore up their beleaguered defences against incoming threats from unpredictable sources.

Their weekly meetings with Selwyn Knox allowed them to keep one danger at least under surveillance.

Fred Trautberg's agreement to step down following the Internet paedophilia allegations had prompted McDonald to observe that he must have had something even more awful in his closet to persuade him to go so quietly. But it had got Knox off the hook and for the moment at least had staved off his threat to blab about Andy Sheen's former Colombian connections.

McDonald felt the stalemate with Knox was fragile, though, and Number Ten were plotting to find ways to secure their hold over him. In recent weeks they'd been pushing him to come forward with a new initiative for the DfS, something big and radical, in the hope it would either keep him occupied and out of trouble or would prove so controversial he would eventually hang himself.

But if the threat from Knox was in abeyance, the spectre of Cliff Evans at the *Daily Mirror* had risen again with a vengeance.

McDonald suspected Evans had either realized that the Marie Sheen pregnancy scoop had been a charade and was feeling aggrieved, or that he was simply chancing his arm in the way good editors tend to.

Whatever the reason, Evans had resurrected Jim McGee's story about the PM's appearance on possession charges and was threatening to run it on New Year's Day. Geoff Maddle was strongly of the opinion that it was a bit of blackmail by the *Mirror* and that Evans would never risk a libel suit for such a half-baked story.

But McDonald was not inclined to call his bluff.

He had spoken to Evans and asked what it would take to get the *Mirror* to forget completely and for ever about Andy Sheen's disputed past.

Evans had told him it would take something big, certainly much bigger than a phantom pregnancy; and McDonald was now wondering if he could kill two birds with one stone.

In Charlie's office he and Geoff Maddle were weighing Dewi Jones in the balance. It had happened on Boxing Day, and Charlie and Geoff both knew Dewi had been full of festive spirit. But still, Clapham Common — ! The two spin doctors burst into laughter. The image of a tipsy Dewi Jones caught with a strange man on Clapham Common on a snowy Boxing Day at three in the morning seemed so incongruous that they momentarily forgot about the repercussions and gave way to a bout of nervous hilarity.

It was McDonald who cut it short.

'Look, Geoff, the bottom line is we need to kill this drugs thing once and for all. We tried with the pregnancy story but that was a washout. This time we need to give the *Mirror* something big to shut them up. And the only thing I can think of is Dewi Jones. It'd mean the end of Dewi's career, his marriage for sure, and — you know the state he's in — it could drive him over the edge. It's not a call we can make on our own. We'll need to ask Andy; and that means we'll have to tell him how close he's been to seeing his Colombian drugs story in the press. I'll go and tell him. He'll have to make the decision.'

An hour later McDonald reappeared.

'Andy says we give them Dewi.'

★　★　★

A very different Selwyn Knox ushered Nigel into his office on Monday morning. Nigel was struck by the change in him over the space of just one weekend. The belligerent, bullying self-confidence had disappeared: he now appeared diminished, deflated. Instead of fighting for his life, he seemed resigned to his fate, almost willing the axe to fall.

He sat silent, immobile at his desk, his lassitude was all-enveloping.

For his part, Nigel had returned in fighting mood. He was determined to act, but first he wanted answers from Knox.

'So you saw Sonya, Selwyn. Where is she?'

'No I didn't. I have no idea where she is.'

'But you said you saw her, Selwyn. You said you saw her and she told you I wanted to talk to you.'

'You're wrong. I haven't seen Sonya for weeks. Not since before I went away for Christmas.'

Knox's lie filled Nigel with a presentiment of horror. Suddenly he thought he knew why Sonya had not answered her mobile, why she had not returned his calls, why her husband had not seen her . . .

But now Knox was beginning to talk. After the silence, his words were spilling out in a torrent. Nigel listened, fascinated, horrified.

'I've been bearing a burden, Nigel. The burden of the extraordinary man. The weight of responsibility lies heavy on my shoulders. You know I am responsible for the downtrodden and the neglected, for the disinherited and the insulted. I am responsible for their well-being and their salvation. I am responsible for them, Nigel, like a father for his children. But there's one thing you and I both know, something we've learned from our work together in this department: fathers can stumble, they can be weak, they can fail their children. My burden is that at times I have betrayed the faith they had in me, I have let them down.'

Nigel looked at Knox and saw a broken man, a man who had recognized his accuser and now wanted him to hear his confession.

'You know the way children expect so much

338

from their father? They invest so much faith in him. He's an infallible guide, a man with no weaknesses, no failings. They see him as a god. So the father feels the burden of expectation, he cannot slip from the ideal of perfection his children have made him — it would destroy them. But reflect, Nigel: a father is a man and no man is free of weakness, free of inadequacies. So the faith placed in him is an expectation he can never satisfy. And when the father slips from the ideal, the pain is immense. His children are devastated; the depth of his self-reproach, his torment and self-loathing can never be described. He's in hell, Nigel. He feels cast out by men. His loneliness is profound.'

Knox spoke and Nigel listened in silence, waiting to hear the confirmation of what he feared to hear, the confirmation of what Knox had done with Sonya, why she had disappeared.

'Yes, there is evil within me, Nigel. Evil alongside all the forces for good. I know that. I recall the harm I have done and I am ashamed. I shudder when I think of it. I picture the man who did this harm, but I cannot recognize him. It is not me, Nigel; it is another. I know it was my hand that inflicted the pain, but I cannot connect that hand with the hand you see before you now. I did harm. I am capable of evil. But the evil is not me. I am not responsible for its presence. So am I to be damned for something which is not me? For the sin that was visited on me, for what was written?'

As Nigel listened, Christopher Brody's memo came to mind, with its unanswered questions.

339

Can Knox be pardoned? Can the devil be redeemed?

But Knox was pressing on, carried forward on a torrent of words.

'I am saying this to you, Nigel, because I know you too have failed; you understand what I am going through. You too have been bearing the burden of inadequacies and omissions. You feel what I feel. That is why we understand each other, even though you may not wish to admit it.'

Now, at last, Nigel was beginning to understand: Sonya had been right — he *was* asking Nigel to be his executioner.

'And how can the father be saved from his agony? How can he be redeemed? The only person who can understand his torment is the man who has shared his path of sorrow, who shares his past. Only that man can know the horror he is suffering. But not even that man can save him, Nigel. It is too late for that. The best he can hope for now is that a fellow sufferer will take pity on him and bring an end to his suffering — '

Knox rose to his feet and began walking to the door.

Nigel made to call him back, but Knox raised his finger to his lips to forestall him. 'I am going now, Nigel. If you want answers, come and see me tonight at my flat. You know where it is. You have slept in my bed. Come and see me there.'

★　★　★

Nigel spent the rest of the day in the agony that stems from doubt and fear; from an overwhelming feeling that a terrible task lay ahead of him, a task he could no longer avoid but dreaded even to contemplate. His calls to Sonya's mobile still brought no response and he had several times picked up the phone to report her disappearance to the police before thinking better of it. He had enough self-awareness to recognize the complex tricks his mind was playing to postpone that first dreadful step into the pitiless territory of denunciation and public confrontation.

★ ★ ★

Nigel rang the bell by Selwyn Knox's door on the third floor of Dolphin Square and heard the sound of shuffling feet.

The door opened and he walked into the apartment he had visited two weeks earlier. Now it seemed changed, unkempt, unsettled in the way a rumpled bed speaks of the passions and exertions that helped unmake it. Looking uneasily round the darkened room, he saw a picture on the wall off balance, books open on the floor, a chair leaning queasily against the table. Knox had walked ahead of Nigel towards the single table lamp. As he turned and faced him, Nigel saw his face was scratched and bloody.

Nigel feared the horrors ahead of him.

Knox passed his hand over his face and said, 'Do it, do it now. You see what it is. I'm sinking under this. I can't bear it. I can't stop myself. It's

341

an addiction, Nigel. An addiction. Like the poor addicts we berate and punish, I can no more free myself from this drug than they can from theirs. Free me. Please free me from this — '

Panicking, Nigel advanced into the dark room and tripped over an upturned coffee table. He cursed then yelled at Knox. 'Where's Sonya, Selwyn? What have you done with her? Have you done the same to her as you did to poor Clare O'Leary?'

'You should have stopped me. I told you I can't control the forces in me. I can't be responsible for what I might do. You'd be helping me, Nigel. The burden of sin isn't easy. Take it off me. Put an end to this.'

'Where's Sonya? Tell me where Sonya is — '

'It'd be an act of mercy, Nigel. You did it for your father. We spend our lives trying to perfect others, trying to save them from themselves, but who will save me?'

A low moan came from the bedroom. Nigel pushed Knox aside and rushed through the door. On the double bed, Sonya lay gagged and bound, her face was bloody, her eyes black and swollen, stained with mascara and tears.

⋆ ⋆ ⋆

Three days later in Downing Street Andrew Sheen and Charlie McDonald were still trying to bring some order to the chaos that threatened to engulf them. McDonald was rallying his boss, attempting to banish the air of defeatism that had recently crept into Sheen's manner.

342

'Look, Andy, the main thing is Sonya doesn't want to press charges. She doesn't want to hurt Selwyn. I don't know why after what he did to her, but she's devoted to the guy. Selwyn's up against it, though: Nigel Tonbridge has got it in for him. Knox says Tonbridge has been threatening him. Knox won't admit it, but I reckon Tonbridge has discovered something pretty dirty about old Selwyn; something more than just kiddy porn and the way he treats Sonya. But Tonbridge is weak, Andy. He hasn't blown the whistle and I don't think he'll ever have the balls to. He's under Sonya's spell — I reckon he'll listen to what Sonya tells him. Knox is tricky, though. We'd dump the guy if we could, but we've hitched ourselves to him so tightly that if he goes down we go down too. Knox knows too much about us, Andy. He knows too much about you. Sonya's been his eyes and ears; without her, he wouldn't last long and that's for sure. Anyway, we're going to have to stand up for Knox and screw poor old Nigel Tonbridge. We'll have to do the dirty on him — smear campaign, the usual stuff. We need to stitch him up before he starts to blab.'

16

It was messy. It was painful.

Nigel had seen the cabinet secretary.

Sir Thomas had told him he was not responsible for this sort of thing, but would pass the information on to the Prime Minister.

Nigel had asked for a meeting with the Prime Minister.

He had been told to talk instead to Charlie McDonald, who questioned him at length about what he knew, about what documents he had, and about the names of his sources and informants.

Nigel had gone to the police, who told him they had already been made aware of his allegations and that the matter was being dealt with at the highest levels of government.

Then there was silence.

Knox had told his Private Office he would be in his constituency and out of touch until parliament reassembled.

Sonya was back at her husband's, who was answering the phone with a curt refusal to pass on any message.

And Nigel's repeated calls to Charlie McDonald were fielded by a secretary who made increasingly less convincing excuses for why he could not come to the phone.

Nigel and Joanie's agonized discussions about what to do next went round in endless circles.

They knew the acute sensitivity surrounding the allegations about Knox, they knew the dangers involved in going public, and they knew the machinations that were certainly going on in Downing Street to make sure Nigel kept quiet.

He had had enough experience of the ruthless cynicism of McDonald and the Number Ten spin doctors to know they would make his life very uncomfortable if he stuck to his guns.

In the end, his decision was based on a dawning certainty that Downing Street had no intention of dealing with Knox and were even now preparing their cover-up operation. The longer he waited, Nigel realized, the more time he was giving them to find ways to discredit him and rubbish his revelations.

★   ★   ★

The moment Nigel called Rob Tyler at the *Sunday Telegraph* late on Tuesday evening, things started to move with breathtaking speed.

Tyler listened briefly to Nigel's story and told him to wait at home — he would be round in half an hour.

When he arrived he had another journalist with him, whom Nigel also knew, and a staff photographer.

The four of them sat with Joanie over cups of coffee for the next six hours telling and retelling the stories of Selwyn Knox's misdeeds, checking dates and places, listing the documentary evidence for each episode in the litany of lies, firming up the sequence of events for the

345

Exxington story, exchanging exclamations of recognition as they independently recalled more examples of the minister's duplicity, and shaking their heads in shared bewilderment at Sonya's role.

By the time the clock of St Luke's next door struck three o'clock on Wednesday morning, Tyler and his associate were satisfied they had enough for a Sunday splash in the review section and a front-page write-off in the main paper.

They asked Nigel to make himself available in the intervening days to answer any further questions; and as they walked out of the front door into the frost-tinged early morning, Tyler turned and said, 'I don't want to sound melodramatic, Nigel, but I think you should stay away from work for the rest of the week. I know what Downing Street are capable of when they're in a corner and this is going to put them in a tighter corner than they've ever been in. I think you need to protect yourself and your family.'

★ ★ ★

From that sleepless Tuesday night to the eve of publication, Nigel and Joanie lived in the breathless anticipation that often precedes great turning points in people's lives.

Every moment together now seemed charged with significance; they lived like condemned prisoners, treasuring the smallest things others take for granted.

Joanie never referred to the warning Tyler had

346

given; she never questioned Nigel's decision to speak out.

She knew that what he was doing was right — following his conscience, where others had washed their hands and made excuses — but she also knew his actions would unleash the wrath of a powerful and angry government.

And she feared the coming of the storm.

At nine o'clock on Saturday evening it came.

The first phone call was from Jennie Bennett of the *Independent on Sunday*, chirping her amazement at the *Telegraph* splash and asking Nigel if it was all true. He said it was. Jennie checked a few details and said she had to dash to write the story for the *Indie*'s late editions.

After that the phone never stopped ringing.

Next on the line was Joe Clancy at the *Sunday Express*, doing his 'Gorr-blimey, guvnor' turn and telling Nigel the *Telegraph* had written up the story 'like bloody *War and Peace*'. Clancy wanted something fresh for his follow-up, more juicy bits about Selwyn the Perv to titillate his readers, but Nigel replied wearily that he'd revealed everything in the original story. Clancy said OK and told Nigel he would get it onto the front page of the second edition.

Then came Dave Sopwith. His tone was reproachful and wheedling.

'Read your stuff in the *Telegraph*, Nigel. Looks a bit dodgy to me. Just been talking to Charlie. Government says it's a pack of lies. Seems you've got yourself in a bit of bother. We all know you've been plotting against Selwyn — you don't like him, do you? Looks like you've set out to stitch the poor bloke up, doesn't it — inventing all that nonsense about him.'

'Look, Dave. Everything I said to the *Telegraph* is true. It's up to you whether you believe it or not — there's enough evidence. You shouldn't believe what your master's voice tells you every time — '

'Oh, I see, Nigel. Are you accusing the *Chronicle* of telling lies for Charlie McDonald? I'll quote you on that.'

'Don't be juvenile, Dave. This is important — '

'And I suppose you got paid for talking to the *Telegraph*, didn't you? How much did you get for your Judas act? Fifty thousand, sixty thousand?'

'Look, Dave, stop right there. I'm doing this as a matter of principle, in the public interest. I took no money for it.'

'Oh, well, you may say that, but it's not what my sources tell me and I'll be going with them when I write my story for Monday.'

Nigel gave up in despair.

He knew the lengths to which some journalists would go in order to curry favour with Downing Street, and Dave Sopwith was the worst.

At least, he told Joanie, they had now had a taste of what McDonald and Sheen were going to throw at them.

By one a.m. the papers had all got their stories for the late editions and Nigel had turned down interview requests from myriad radio and television producers, who had rung to say they were leading on the Knox story and would he

348

appear live on their programmes. Nigel recognized most of them; many were former colleagues. But he told all of them that he didn't want this to turn into a media circus, that he had said what he had to say and now it was up to the government to put its house in order.

Joanie was already in bed when the phone rang again at two a.m. Nigel picked it up and heard the grim voice of Charlie McDonald.

'Tonbridge? I know that's you. Well, let me tell you something. You've had it, mate; you're dead meat.'

The line went dead before Nigel could collect his wits to reply.

⋆ ⋆ ⋆

The next morning, Sunday, Nigel and Joanie were woken by their twelve-year-old daughter telling them to look out of the window.

When Nigel sleepily opened the curtains, he was amazed to see thirty or forty journalists, photographers and television crews besieging the house.

His heart sank and his stomach cramped in knots of fear.

At that moment he realized exactly what he had unleashed by speaking out, how great was the public interest in anyone who had the courage to blow the whistle on this overbearing government, but also how much anxiety, unhappiness and — possibly — danger his actions were destined to cause himself, his wife and his children.

Cut adrift by the civil service, cold-shouldered by Downing Street, about to be locked out of his department and cursed by Charlie McDonald, Nigel was shocked by the sense of isolation that seized him in its icy fingers.

He closed the bedroom curtains and fought back a pang of regret that he had ever agreed to speak to the *Sunday Telegraph*.

★ ★ ★

Nigel had enough knowledge of the mass media to recognize that the almost universal unanimity in the coverage of his revelations about Selwyn Knox that Sunday morning was a startlingly rare phenomenon.

The tone in all the papers, on the radio and television was one of approval for what he had done and condemnation of the deceitfulness that most of the commentators agreed now charac-terized this government.

Only on the events in Exxington did they show a certain reticence: there seemed to be a certain wariness about a story implicating a cabinet minister in murder.

The press pack outside Nigel's house turned out to be jovial and friendly. He found he knew many of them from his time in the BBC Political Unit and he soon got to know the others as he went in and out of the house to a chorus of banter.

They weren't slow to let him know what they thought about Selwyn Knox and about the Downing Street spin machine, sentiments they repeated in more restrained language in their published articles.

Messages of support rained down on Nigel from his neighbours and, since his photograph was in most of the Sunday papers, from complete strangers who approved of what he had done.

★ ★ ★

Downing Street's fightback began on Monday morning.

Dave Sopwith's article in the *Chronicle* was headlined 'Greedy Civil Servant Took Money to Frame Boss' and claimed Nigel had deliberately lied to seek revenge on a minister who had passed him over for promotion.

Ominously, the article quoted 'government sources', who said Tonbridge was reportedly being investigated for tax evasion and could soon be facing prosecution.

On the *Today* programme, the Education Secretary, Ron 'Fatty' Clegg, huffed and puffed about despicable civil servants who abused the information they received from their work in government to pursue personal vendettas against ministers. He called for legislation to introduce prison terms for any who made unauthorized statements in future.

Of Knox himself, however, there was no sign.

Reporters despatched to his constituency failed to find any trace of him; his apartment in Dolphin Square and Ruth Leeming's house in Scotland were fruitlessly staked out round the

351

clock; of necessity the TV news bulletins continued to use library pictures of the vanishing minister; and the DfS refused to answer any questions about his whereabouts.

Reading between the lines, Nigel suspected Downing Street were hesitating over how to play the story. They could either concentrate their efforts on discrediting Nigel without actively defending Selwyn, in which case Knox would probably be kept out of sight and quietly allowed to resign when the fuss had died down. Or they could go the whole hog and mount a concerted defence of their man. This would mean pushing Knox into the spotlight, attempting to trash Nigel's allegations one by one and staging a public confrontation between the minister and his accuser.

Three days into the story and with the controversy showing no sign of abating, it became abundantly clear they were going for the second, nuclear, option.

On Wednesday morning Downing Street offered Selwyn Knox to every radio and television outlet, and they all leapt gratefully at the chance to enflame the controversy further.

The questioning was hostile, but Knox had been coached well by the spin doctors and had clearly been given the green light to tell any untruth he needed to defend himself.

In response to every suggestion of wrongdoing, he simply issued a categorical denial. Listening to him, Nigel was amazed at the implacable, bare-faced temerity of his lying. In some TV interviews his top lip seemed to sweat a little and his eyes swivelled nervously, but otherwise it was a Rolls-Royce performance; impressive in its chutzpah, ominous in the way it upped the stakes.

★　★　★

Downing Street's transition from defence to aggression was not slow in coming.

It was ferocious in its intensity.

In a slickly co-ordinated campaign, statement followed statement.

First Sonya Mair, her face now healed or covered over with make-up, was thrust in front of the cameras to choke back tears and deny Knox had ever laid a finger on her.

Nigel watched her praise 'Selwyn's goodness and Christian idealism' and thought of those videos released by the terrorist captors of Allied servicemen in the MEWs: it was impossible to tell if she was speaking of her own free will or reading from a prepared script at knife-point.

The following day the police issued a statement ruling Knox out of their Internet paedophilia investigations and specifically denying he had ever been a suspect in the death of Clare O'Leary.

As for Knox's 'alleged lying and political misconduct', a series of cabinet ministers leapt to defend his integrity, culminating in a statement from Andy Sheen giving him his 'full backing and support' and concluding, 'Selwyn Knox will continue to be an important and trusted member of the cabinet.'

The point was underlined by a highly publicized photocall on the steps of Number Ten, where the smiles and backslapping between the two men concluded with a slightly surprised-looking Andy Sheen being given a kiss on the cheek by his triumphantly vindicated minister.

Nigel could not help marvelling at the confidence that had returned to Knox's manner: after the humbled, broken man he had last seen in Dolphin Square, this was another bewildering peripeteia. He could not fathom the way Knox swung from one extreme to another in such short order: it was as though he were two completely different people.

Meanwhile the government's strident support for Knox and Charlie Mcdonald's shameless smear campaign against Nigel had muddied the waters in the media coverage. Several journalists rang Nigel to check Downing Street's allegations against him and most refused to run them, but others didn't bother and simply went into print.

Pro-Downing Street stalwarts like Dave Sopwith had concluded long ago that Nigel was the villain of the story and Knox the maligned hero. Most of the rest of the papers and the BBC continued to favour Nigel's version of events, but Charlie McDonald's clever campaign of allegations and innuendo meant that the unanimity of support and trust Nigel had initially and rightfully enjoyed had been undermined.

Not content with denouncing Nigel's claims about Knox, Charlie McDonald was pressing ahead with a character-assassination campaign.

Nigel was pilloried as an embittered traitor who had tried to vilify a decent, honest minister. He was 'exposed' as a secret NewLib sympathizer who had 'deliberately infiltrated the civil service to sabotage the government's vital policies of moral salvation'.

After another week of unrelenting vilification, Downing Street issued a statement saying that the Minister for Society, Selwyn Knox, would be bringing an action for libel against the disgraced former civil servant, Nigel Tonbridge, and would be demanding punitive damages.

At the same time the Attorney-General announced with a flourish that a case was to be brought in the public interest against Nigel George Tonbridge and his mother Elizabeth Jane Tonbridge, née Dalziel, that they did knowingly conspire to cause the death of Percival Tonbridge by the administration of a mortal dose of a harmful substance.

To remove any doubt, the announcement pointed out that Nigel Tonbridge would be facing a charge of patricide.

★　★　★

The government's attacks and the hail of announcements hit Nigel like hammer blows.

His life fell apart.

From being a heroic whistle-blower, respected and congratulated, he had suddenly become an outcast, a pariah: he had killed his father; he had libelled a minister.

And he didn't have the means or the will to fight back.

He didn't have the stomach to slug it out in radio and television interviews.

He refused all requests for a response to Downing Street's smears and closeted himself with Joanie and the children in their house, which remained besieged by journalists and photographers.

Friends had started to regard him with mistrust, neighbours turned against him, strangers talked about him with contempt.

Downing Street had set out to destroy Nigel and they were succeeding.

He was under intense psychological pressure, close to collapse.

★ ★ ★

It was in this frame of mind that Chris Brody found Nigel when he knocked on his door, called his name through a tentatively opened letterbox and slipped inside to the flashes of news cameras and shouted questions from the throng on the pavement outside.

Nigel and Joanie both said how grateful they were to see a friendly face.

Brody then told them that the DfS had instructed its staff to avoid contact with the Tonbridges, but he had never let the department run his life and he wasn't going to start now.

He said the first few days after Nigel's revelations had been pandemonium.

Those who knew what Knox was capable of

expressed their admiration for Nigel's courage in speaking out against him, but few were willing to add their names to the roll of Knox's accusers.

Most of them feared Knox would be back in avenging-angel mode, and when Downing Street launched their campaign of vilification against Nigel they were proved right.

On his return from his extended Christmas break, the Secretary of State had at first kept a low profile. And apart from her brief stage-managed statement to a gaggle of carefully vetted TV crews, Sonya Mair had not been seen at all.

Now though, Brody said, Knox was starting to get back into his stride.

He had circulated an internal SnV to all in the department, which showed him sitting confidently at his desk, poring over new legislative proposals and looking up to the camera to smile and say, 'The work goes on. Now it is time to draw a line and put recent events behind us. Some individuals in this department have shown they were not committed to the work we are doing here and, indeed, were determined to sabotage it and undermine their minister. That episode is over. Now it is time to move on.'

When Nigel expressed his amazement at the way Knox seemed able to gloss over such damning revelations and carry on as though nothing had happened, Brody laughed. 'What can I say? Knox is not a man, he's a political machine. Knox-the-image is flawless, unfeeling, infallible. The mask doesn't slip, Nigel — '

Nigel disagreed. 'You might be right, Chris,

except that I have seen two Selwyn Knoxes: there's Knox the psychopath, the lunatic social engineer; and there's Knox the idealist seeking the best for society — Sonya recognized that in him. There's the fanatical, unbending dictator, and there's the broken wreck looking for support from me and Sonya and anyone who'll offer it. How can he be two such extremes? How can he be such different people?'

Again Brody smiled. 'Didn't you read my memo? Knox has evil in him, but he says he's not responsible for it. He says he fights against it, but he knows it's a fight he can't win. He's suffering in himself. His sins torment him. He may have tried to excise his conscience, but like the nerve at the root of a tooth it's still there and it puts him in agony.

'The problem for him is that his policies are selling people an invitation to a perfect world — a world without sin; but he knows he himself has no place in that world. He's like the suicide bombers, Nigel: he knows there's no Nirvana for him, but his reward will be here on earth after he's gone. The perfect earthly paradise he's created will be his vindication, his legacy and — perhaps — his vengeance.'

⋆　⋆　⋆

Selwyn Knox arrived for his weekly meeting at Downing Street in a state of some excitement.

He knew the idea he was bringing with him would impress Andrew Sheen and Charlie McDonald; he knew it was a big idea, an idea

358

that could outstrip even the Parenting Licence in the impact it would have.

'Andy, Charlie, listen to this. You remember Jack Willans and Tim Stilwell? You remember they threw all DRE's billions into those bio-engineering firms in the States? And then it all began to fall apart and it looked like they were going bust? Well, they may not have thrown it away after all! They came to see me a month ago — before all that nonsense with Nigel Tonbridge — and I've been talking to them ever since about an idea that could revolutionize our social policy!

'It seems their work on gene therapy has turned up trumps after all. One of their outfits has found something that could rescue them and us with them! It's a fantastic breakthrough, Andy. DRE have identified the gene markers for antisocial and deviant behaviour, and in the last three weeks they've successfully taken out UK and world patents on the technology that does it. The possibilities are endless! DRE can now identify which individuals have a propensity for crime and social disruption. And we can use that technology. Last month I reached an agreement with Willans and Stilwell that they would make their research available to us so we could test it against a selection of known criminals. We used it on petty crooks in the prisons — without telling them what we were doing, of course — and we compared that to tests on a control group of ordinary, decent people. The results were amazing! The accuracy of the gene predictor was ninety-eight per cent among those with criminal pasts. Among the control group of decent citizens, only four per cent had the criminal gene. Think about it! We have in our hands the ability to separate the population into sheep and goats! We can identify those who are tainted with original sin, if you like, and those who are not. And we have the means to wipe out original sin. It's the chance of a lifetime! We have the power to completely transform society, to create a new world, a better world — dare I say it? — a perfect world! We remove those who are tainted with sin and we preserve those who are free from it, those who are innocent.

'And it's easy, Andy.

'If we incorporate this technology into our Parenting Licence programme, we can take DNA samples of the whole population: we can identify those with the gene and we can stop them reproducing. It's a panacea. We stop crime and antisocial activity at one blow. We wipe out deviant behaviour. And, don't forget, the legislation we got through parliament last year gives us the right to enforce abortions in extreme cases. The beauty is that the legislation does not define an 'extreme case': we can make that definition ourselves. We can define it as those who carry the criminal gene! Couples who might produce criminals can be stopped. And in the future we might want to take it even further: those parts of the population with the strongest gene markers for criminality could be confined in preventive detention. We could take them out of circulation; we could stop them breeding. If we apply all these measures rigorously, we could wipe out crime for ever in the space of just one generation. There would be protests, of course — there were protests over the PL — but it would be easy to face the liberals down. All we have to say is that we need to put up with a short period of restrictions (they would call it repression, I suppose) to achieve an eternity of bliss: an eternity without crime, without social disruption, without discontent, without unhappiness. It's paradise on earth and we can achieve it, Andy.'

When Knox had left the room, Andrew Sheen turned to Charlie McDonald with a quizzical look. 'What to do you think, Charlie? It sounds a bit radical, but then people said the same about his Parenting Licence. Do you think Selwyn may have come up with another winner?'

Charlie McDonald winced. 'No, I don't, Andy. I think Selwyn's lost it. I think he's in danger of getting himself consigned to the loony bin of history — and us with him. I think we need to do something about it.'

17

Selwyn Knox's suicide note was typewritten.

The police said this was unusual, but not unknown.

A long, exultant passage about his political career ended with an impassioned encomium on his proposals for compulsory DNA tests to identify the crime gene and remove potential future criminals from society.

The forensic experts suggested that Knox had broken off at this point and resumed typing some time later when the document switched from the political to the personal and the tone became despondent.

It gave voice to his doubts about the morality of the policies he was advocating. It suggested he was haunted by the thought that his legislation was destroying the cohesive bonds of human solidarity and human warmth. He talked at length about original sin.

A message for his political adviser, Sonya Mair, suggested there might have been a disagreement in the days before his death, and concluded by saying he could not live without her. He thanked his director of communications, Nigel Tonbridge, 'for understanding me and what I needed from you'. Perhaps surprisingly, there was no message for his long-time partner and common-law wife, Ruth Leeming.

The news of Selwyn Knox's suicide was broken by a BBC presenter on *Breakfast* news.

The announcement interrupted a live follow-up on the. Corporation's latest reality television series, *Big Sister*, in which the BBC invited attractive, large-bosomed young women to spend a week in a hermetically sealed house with a team of teenage boys, whose task it was to persuade the female contestants to reveal their breasts to the many cameras which covered every corner of the house, including the toilets. The rules specified that the boys must not use physical force and that live sex was not permitted between the participants. The latest controversy had been about young Mark, who had allegedly broken both these rules — and in fact had broken rule one to help him break rule two.

The *Breakfast* news audience was being polled to determine whether Mark should suffer any sanctions — possibly a prison term — on leaving the *Big Sister* house and returning to the real world.

The voting was getting tense, and the BBC audience did not take kindly to the announcer interrupting with a boring announcement about an old geezer who had topped himself.

★ ★ ★

For Nigel Tonbridge, the relief was intense.

In practical terms, Knox's death meant that he no longer had a libel case to answer. Despite

Andy Sheen's recent revisions, the law still held that the dead could not be libelled.

With Knox unable to testify about the alleged confession on the patricide charge, Nigel's lawyer seized the opportunity to request immediate dismissal of the case. After some hurried discussions with Number Ten, the Attorney-General wrote back to say the charge would be left to lie on file, but no further action would be taken.

And, most importantly, Knox's suicide restored Nigel's reputation at a stroke.

In the eyes of the media and of the world, the decision to take his own life confirmed that Knox was guilty and that all Nigel's allegations about him must have been true.

By extension, it confirmed Nigel's innocence.

It confirmed he had been right to denounce Knox. It confirmed he was, after all, a jolly good fellow.

Once again, the weathercock of public sentiment swung in his favour.

No longer was he an outcast, a reviled and lonely man suspected of the worst imaginable crimes.

He was restored to his status of hero; he was respected and admired by one and all.

He was vindicated, fêted by the media as a man of principle, a courageous whistle-blower.

Such was its violence and speed that Nigel found himself almost amused by the cartoon-like ferocity of the reversal that shook his life and threw him from one extreme of emotion to another.

It reminded him of the moment towards the end of *The Duchess of Malfi* when Webster has his mass murderer explain a particularly acute plot swing as 'a contrivance such as I have oft observed in plays'.

It was hard to believe, but for Nigel these successive and alarming reverses of fortune were happening in real life.

★　★　★

In Downing Street the panic was boundless.

For one thing, Knox's suicide had brought the wrath of the media down on all their heads. The widespread acceptance that Knox was guilty as charged had pointed up the extent of the lies Number Ten had told to defend him and to vilify Nigel Tonbridge.

For journalists who had been on the receiving end of the New Project spin doctors' mendacity, it was payback time. Accumulated resentment at all their insults, deceit and double-dealing was being thrown back at Sheen and McDonald with considerable interest.

The pressure on the Prime Minister to explain why he had protected a known paedophile and suspected murderer and kept him in his cabinet was becoming intense. Even Dave Sopwith ventured a veiled criticism, not exactly biting the hand that fed him, but certainly giving it a good flick with the edge of his tongue.

The siege mentality that had begun to grip Downing Street even before Christmas was now reaching its apogee.

The anti-terror cordon around Number Ten, with its razor wire, police security emplacements and two-and-a-half-ton concrete blocks to keep out the car bombers was a reminder to the gloomier minded among them of the minefields, tank-traps, and blockhouses round the Hitler bunker in 1945.

Its occupants were protected from the outside world, but also effectively cut off from it — cut off from the people they claimed to rule, to save and to cherish; cut off from reality.

For privacy from the flapping ears of junior staff, the PM and his closest aides were now holding most of their meetings in the complex of fortified rooms underneath Downing Street, which had originally been intended for use in a terrorist emergency. It was rumoured that many of them were sleeping there as well. But now, like the Soviet troops in Berlin in 1945, the real world was pouring in.

★ ★ ★

And, like Eva Braun, Sonya Mair had refused the offer of a safe flight out of the bunker to putative safety in exile.

After her televised statement supporting Selwyn Knox, she had refused to return Nigel's calls. She had not talked to him since the night he had discovered her gagged and bound on Knox's bed in Dolphin Square, and she would not talk to him now.

Instead, she had rallied to the defence of the besieged Prime Minister and his entourage.

366

When the massed ranks of political journalists and reporters signed a resolution condemning the lies and deceit which Charlie McDonald and Geoff Maddle had been responsible for during their years in power and refused to attend Downing Street briefings 'unless and until these individuals are removed from their posts', Sonya was offered and eventually accepted the poisoned chalice of taking over their duties. On the day she officially took on the thankless task of official Downing Street spokesperson, Sonya sent Nigel a one-line email, which read:

I'm sorry. I couldn't climb out of the well. SM

One of Sonya's first jobs was to deal with her old friend Cliff Evans.

Emboldened by the media frenzy, the editor of the *Daily Mirror* had spotted his chance.

The opportunity to bring down not just a cabinet minister, but the Prime Minister himself, was too much for him to resist.

He ran the story under the headline: 'Cabinet of Perverts Led by Drug Dealer?'

The question mark had been inserted at the insistence of the paper's lawyers, but within hours of the story hitting the streets it was clear this precaution had been unnecessary.

The *Mirror*'s news desk received more than a dozen phone calls from former Cambridge students, contemporaries of Andrew Sheen in the 1970s, who remembered the Sheen-Parks partnership and each of whom brought important new details to fill out Jim McGee's initially tentative story.

The following morning, as the other nationals wrote follow-ups to the *Mirror*'s first-day lead, Cliff Evans was able to print the triumphant banner: '*Mirror* Proved Right: Sheen was Drug Fiend'.

Under a shared byline, McGee and Evans revealed the full extent of Andrew Sheen's drug-related profiteering; his 'student links with Colombian racketeers and murderers' and the narcotics-funded purchase of the New York flat, 'still owned by Sheen and used regularly by Marie and his unwitting children'.

The story was the number-one lead in every newspaper; the number-one topic of discussion on every TV bulletin and current affairs programme.

Perhaps to deflect the public's attention, Downing Street launched a new offensive in the MEWs, throwing hundreds of troops into a suicide mission against al-Qaeda's fortified mountain strongholds. But this did nothing to lessen the intensity of the drugs coverage, and it led several commentators to reflect on Andrew Sheen's 'despicable, ruthless sacrifice of innocent lives in his twisted attempt to save his own skin'.

Sonya Mair rang Cliff Evans in a foul temper.

She reminded him of the deal they had agreed, first over Marie's pregnancy and then again over the late Dewi Jones. She cursed Evans for his duplicity and dishonesty, for breaking his promise to kill the story, for betraying her personally.

But Evans replied, 'I'm sorry, love. You should know better than anyone: if you think you can sin and get away with it unpunished, you're fooling yourself. You know our sins always come back.'

★　★　★

And Cliff Evans was quickly proved right.

The combination of the revelations about Selwyn Knox and the bombshell of Andrew Sheen's student transgressions was always going to be too much for a government which had built its politics on the premise of moral perfection; which had anchored its self-proclaimed right to impose demanding standards on the whole nation to the firm ground of its own irreproachable, saintly wisdom.

The growing perception that the cabinet really was the preserve of perverts and criminals did not take long to bring the government down.

As the invading wave of public disgust and anger rose higher and higher over the Downing Street bunker, Andrew Sheen reached for the political cyanide.

His resignation was announced on the same day the general election was called.

The pundits were united in predicting that the resurgent NewLib party would sweep the board.

18

Galling as it might have been for Downing Street, Andrew Sheen's misfortune was Nigel Tonbridge's silver lining.

Taking their lead from the *Daily Mail*, whose banner headline had proclaimed him 'The Honest Man Who Brought Down Cabinet of Crooks', the media were busy turning Nigel into a popular hero.

He was invited to appear on radio and television discussion programmes, chat shows and panel games; he was profiled in newspapers and magazines; he received lucrative job offers in journalism and public relations; he was promised silly money if he would write his memoirs or reveal his 'true story' to *Hi There!* magazine.

Despite his frequently repeated protestation that he had only been following his conscience when he blew the whistle on Selwyn Knox and that any honest man would have done the same, Nigel could not help feeling secret satisfaction at the respect and vindication he was enjoying.

While he was sometimes embarrassed by the fuss being made of him, he now woke every morning to a deep wave of relief that the nightmare weeks of persecution were over, that he could walk down the street without fearing the disapproving glances of passing strangers, that he could answer the telephone without wondering if it would be news of more vilification by Downing Street.

Nigel and Joanie knew that the trials of the past months had brought them closer than ever. Now the only thing troubling Nigel's idyll of vindicated contentment was a message on his answering machine.

He had discovered it late one night when he and Joanie returned from the cinema.

He had played it once, played it again, listened to it six or seven times.

The words were clear: what he was trying to divine was the meaning, the hidden intention behind the woman's voice asking him to call her as soon as possible.

'You know who this is,' said the voice and Nigel did know.

'You know how to reach me,' said the voice and Nigel did know.

'You know what this is about,' said the voice, but Nigel did not know, or at least he told himself he did not know, did not want to know.

He erased the message before Joanie could hear it and went to bed.

★ ★ ★

Three days passed before Nigel mustered enough resolve to pick up the telephone and return the call. Three days of foreboding, in which the redoubled efforts he felt himself making to enjoy the life he and Joanie were sharing signalled the fragility he sensed within the idyll.

His delay had been the product of fear, he

371

knew. Fear of reopening the nightmare of the past months, fear of talking again to the woman who was forever linked to the world of Selwyn Knox.

His call was answered by a man's voice. It sounded rude, uncaring; the tone was brusque.

Nigel waited.

He heard footsteps on a stone floor, then whispered conversation.

He heard someone pick up the receiver.

He recognized the voice immediately, the voice of a young woman.

'Nigel? Is that you? Yeah, it's Cathy here. Thanks for ringing. I didn't know if you would. Anyway, the thing is I need to see you. No, I can't speak on the phone. I need to see you. Can you come up here to the Eagle and Child? Well, as soon as you can. It's urgent.'

★　★　★

On Bratten Street the eagle was still flying; the child still cradled improbably, eternally, in its claws.

Nigel was convinced of the truth of all he had believed about Knox, everything he had accused him of.

Of course he was.

The man's suicide had blown away any lingering doubts.

But coming back here to Exxington seemed wrong.

It seemed like treading on someone's grave,

revisiting something that should not be reopened.

Cathy was already in the bar when Nigel entered. He had the impression she might have been drinking for some time. She seemed upset.

As he saw her, Nigel felt again a pang of pity; the involuntary sensation that she could easily have been his daughter.

He saw her clothes were still ragged and thought to himself she had not done much with the money he had given her.

He saw the telltale, distant look still in her eyes.

Cathy offered to buy Nigel a drink. He said he would get the round and she asked for a double.

Their conversation was awkward.

Cathy talked about her life and the hardships she was enduring. She said she had been thrown out of the hostel a few days after Nigel had phoned her.

She had already lived as a street person in the past and she was starting to get used to it again.

Nigel felt oppressed by the dirt and gloom of the pub. He sensed Cathy was going to ask him for more money and was making his mind up how he would respond.

In the meantime, he went to the bar and brought back two more vodkas.

Cathy asked him how he was feeling after the controversy over Selwyn Knox. She asked him why Knox had killed himself. He said he didn't know.

Cathy talked about Clare O'Leary. Nigel was beginning to feel uncomfortable about where the conversation was leading.

He asked her why she had needed to see him so urgently.

She asked him for another drink.

Nigel came back with two more vodkas and Cathy gulped hers down.

'I needed to see you, Nigel. I needed to tell you something — I needed to tell you he didn't kill her.'

Nigel looked at her intently.

She was waiting for him to respond.

Nigel drained his vodka.

'Cathy, you told me he killed Clare. You told me — '

'Yeah, I know I did. I told you a lot of things.'

'What do you mean? You mean you told me — ?'

'I mean he didn't kill her and he didn't abuse her. He didn't abuse me.'

Nigel felt his hands turn to ice.

'But you told me, Cathy. You said Selwyn Knox abused you and Clare and the other girls. You said he was a child molester.'

'I know I did. I said it because I wanted to please you. I knew that was what you wanted me to say. I could tell. And I wanted you to give me money, Nigel. That's why I said it.'

Nigel felt the vodka kick in. His head was feeling dangerously light.

'OK, so you didn't see him abuse Clare up in the mountains. You didn't see him kill her. But that doesn't mean — '

Cathy burst into tears.

'I said he didn't molest her, I said he didn't

374

kill her. I know he didn't.'

'But how can you know? That's the point. We can't know what — '

'Yes we can. That's what I'm trying to tell you. I *saw* Clare O'Leary fall off the cliff. I was there. I saw her. And I ran away. I ran away because I thought they'd say it was my fault. I never told anyone. I was scared. I was fourteen — '

Nigel gulped down his vodka and went to order another.

Terror seized him as he walked to the bar, panic that he had hounded Knox, driven him to his death.

Nigel returned with the drinks, tried a last time.

'Cathy, this is very important. Are you sure what you're telling me is true? I believed you last time and now you say you were lying.'

Cathy wiped her eyes.

'I was lying then. I told you, I needed the money off you. But now the guy's killed himself, Nigel. He killed himself — '

Nigel looked at Cathy; he knew she was telling the truth.

He thought of the last time they had sat here.

He remembered how she had hesitated over the story of abuse and murder.

He kicked himself that he hadn't realized, had allowed himself to believe her. Kicked himself that he had let her push him into denouncing Knox, into locking horns with such dangerous opponents, initiating such a frightening process with such a catastrophic outcome.

Nigel's stomach cramped with fear: fear of the

ramifications of what he had just heard.

His thoughts in turmoil, he barely heard what Cathy was saying. He registered the word money and looked up at her.

'I'm an addict, Nigel. I can't give it up. I spent the money you gave me on more gear. But I need more. I need money to feed my habit. I'm already on the street. It means going on the game or going back to Billy and thieving. It'll be the death of me, Nigel, unless you give me more.'

Nigel looked at her in astonishment.

'But, you've just told me you lied to me. You've put me in trouble up to my neck, Cathy. Why should I give you more money? You can't be serious — '

'I think you should give it me, Nigel. I need it. You're my only hope. And there's something else, don't forget: if I go to the police and say that Knox didn't kill Clare, say you were telling lies, what'll that do for you? It won't be good for you, will it? I need the money, Nigel. Give it me and I'll keep quiet. Give it me and I'll never tell anyone what I've just told you.'

Nigel gulped his vodka.

His thoughts were scrambling. He knew the trap he was in.

This time Cathy was telling the truth, there could be no doubt. He knew that danger lay ahead.

In his fuddled state, the anger and disgust he felt with himself turned on the girl beside him.

How could she have deceived him? He had trusted her like his own daughter.

He had tried to help her, given her money and advice.

He had tried to redeem her from the sin she had fallen into.

And she could have responded, she could have improved herself, saved herself.

She could have joined the better society the government was building.

But she had refused to change, refused to pull herself up out of the trough, out of the blight she was born to.

She had been too attached to her faults, too addicted to the imperfections of her type.

Now Nigel's faith was shaken — if Cathy was false, who could he trust?

Was the whole of humankind tainted with deceit? With original sin? Was it written?

Preordained?

Was it in our DNA?

Nigel was getting more drunk.

He had no plan.

Clarity gone.

No fixed idea.

The juggernaut of vengeance was stalking him.

The juggernaut wore the face of Selwyn Knox, Andy Sheen, Charlie McDonald.

He knew he had to play for time.

But how?

'Come on, Cathy. I've got no money on me. Let's find a cash machine.'

They left the pub's smoky warmth.

Out into the street.

End of Bratten Street.

End of the last remaining terrace of houses.

Beyond the last terrace.
Onto the plains of rubble.
Here houses had been bulldozed.
Here lives and memories had been swept away.
Swept under the rubble.
The end of the terrace.
The end of civilization.
Where the wasteland began.
Now Nigel was walking.
With Cathy.
Slowly crossing the waste ground.
Thinking of Knox.
Turning it all over in his mind.
Knox was dead.
Thoughts in turmoil.
He was to blame.
Despair gripped.
But through swirling emotion, rational thought began.
Cling to it.
Like a drowning man to a branch in the river.
'Keep straight . . . think it through . . . what it means . . . for you, for Joanie . . . for the kids.
'If this gets out, you're finished . . . more vilification . . . more trashing in the media . . . can you cope? Dead meat . . . persecuted the Minister for Salvation . . . killed the man who would redeem our sins and save our souls.'
Nigel shuddered.
Get a grip.
'Wait, wait. Get it straight! Knox was dangerous . . . the child pornography . . . the paedophilia . . . and his policies . . . they were

the source of the poison, the lies . . . he needed to die . . . his death brought renewal . . . elections . . . maybe the NewLibs . . . some integrity again?'

In his confusion, Nigel saw himself as the slayer of the hydra; but hydra-like, new danger was springing from the decapitated head of Selwyn Knox.

'As long as McDonald isn't allowed to reinvent Knox . . . to trade on his memory. If Cathy clears him of the murder, it'll be Knox the martyr! Knox the saint! Knox of blessed memory. They'll use it to re-ignite his political legacy . . . they'll raise themselves from his funeral pyre.'

The vodka filled Nigel's bloodstream.

He was walking unsteadily.

Thinking unsteadily.

The thought that Knox could be resurrected even now buzzed in his head.

He glanced at Cathy.

Could she be kept quiet?

Not by paying her blackmail demands. That was for sure.

Then how?

What if she were to die here?

Now.

On this waste ground.

Nigel found himself thinking:

'She'd be just one more vagrant.

'Left for dead in the wasteland.

'No one would miss her.

'And the good that would come from it.

'The good for the country.

'Immeasurable — '

Now they were approaching the centre of the waste ground, stumbling over the levelled ruins of former streets and houses — streets and houses razed under Knox's Clean-Sweep; razed to wipe out Britain's sink estates, the nests of crime and evil tainting society.

Without looking, Nigel whispered, 'Cathy, have you got any family — parents still alive?'

'Nah. They're dead. I'm all on my own.'

Nigel glanced at her.

Ragged clothes.

Glazed expression.

Needle-tortured arms . . .

. . . and he felt such sympathy that tears pricked his eyes.

'These are the people Knox was destroying,' he thought. 'These are the poor, the disinherited. He was 'phasing them out' . . . in the name of social cleansing! Get rid of people like Cathy and you get rid of the procreators of crime, the source of discontent that troubles decent society . . . that's what the New Project wanted. That's what it'll do if it gets back in again now.'

Nigel felt his head throb, lightning flashed behind his eyes.

The months of pressure, the battering his psyche had taken, the strain of the burden that lay upon his shoulders . . .

He looked around as they stumbled forward across the rubble.

This was no ordinary waste ground.

It stretched for miles, no one to be seen.

It was a graveyard and here they were alone

. . . at the very centre of the wasteland.

Nigel glanced again at Cathy.

He pitied her. He loved her.

People like her died every day on waste grounds like this.

The fruits of sins past, the seeds of sins to come.

Nigel felt the vodka kicking in, warming his body against the bitter cold.

He took hold of Cathy's hand with tenderness and compassion.

He led her forward . . .

★   ★   ★

Nigel remembered little more after that.

He had no idea how he had walked back to his hotel.

No idea how he had walked through the lobby, climbed the stairs, fallen into bed.

He vaguely remembered the night — the ominous dreams of blood, Britain washed by a sea of blood.

The people were drowning in the blood, but was it blood that was killing them? Or was it blood that was washing away their sins? Washing away their old life, the imperfections of what had gone before?

Nigel couldn't work it out.

When he came to, he realized the TV had been left burning through the night.

As he surfaced from his subterranean nightmare world, Fiona Thomas was reading the headlines.

'Election countdown, and with five days to go, polls show the NewLibs have an almost unassailable lead. Barring any major upset, any major reverse, the UK will have its first NewLib government in less than a week from now.'

Nigel heard the news, heard it with joy — and with pain.

Why was he not rejoicing?

What veiled memory from the night before was holding him back? Stopping him celebrating? Clouding his thoughts?

Nigel racked his vodka-deadened memory, then remembered Cathy, remembered the secret she held over him.

In a sudden flood, he remembered his own thoughts, his temptation in the wasteland.

The memory convulsed him with shock and horror.

With dawning dread, he realized he could recall nothing after he took her hand.

Why could he not remember?

And how could he have harboured such thoughts?

Contemplated such a deed? To kill Cathy.

These were the thoughts of a Knox, the demonic sophistry Knox would have used to justify his own evil actions.

Had he killed Cathy to save himself?

In a panic of fear and self-revulsion, Nigel strained to remember what had passed between him and Cathy, he berated himself for even thinking of harming her.

'What have I done? What was I thinking? Of course people tell lies. People aren't perfect. She told lies, she has her faults, she's human. Perfection exists only in Knox's empty, sterile projects; perfection means the end of humanity. We may aspire to the angels, but the ancient human law says we end with the beasts. It's not my place to sit in judgement. The Lord said vengeance was His, not mine, not Andy Sheen's, not Charlie McDonald's. Knox had his faults, had his sins, he was human. So if God pardons Cathy, does He also pardon Knox? Will the devil be saved?'

Nigel sat up in horror.

His hotel room was in disarray.

Cups and plates were broken on the floor.

But where was Cathy?

What had become of her after the moment when his memory grew dim?

Nigel looked at the floor beside his bed.

There, covered by a hotel blanket.

Blood on her forehead.

He looked again.

Cathy was there. Breathing lightly. Sleeping. Innocent, like a twelve-year-old child.

His eyes clouded with tears of release.

He felt in his pocket and opened the notebook from Exxington, from all those years before.

He thumbed the pages and turned to the notes of his interview with Eileen O'Leary. He read her lament for the daughter she had lost and now would remember forever fixed in a single moment, the moment of waking from the depths of sleep.

'And when I wake her in the morning,' he read in his faded shorthand, 'she is a child waking from a dream. Her eyes shine; she blinks off the night; all her worldliness is washed away. When she opens her eyes and she's soft with sleep, she's suddenly back to the little one she used to be. And then you can see that inside she's still the same; still full of goodness and simplicity and love.'

After all the spin, Nigel thought, after all the lies, all the deception, all the ambition, all the calculation, all the cruelty, there was only one thing that mattered. Compassion was the only hope.

He smiled at Cathy, stirring by the side of his bed.

THE END

We do hope that you have enjoyed reading this large print book.

Did you know that all of our titles are available for purchase?

We publish a wide range of high quality large print books including:
Romances, Mysteries, Classics
General Fiction
Non Fiction and Westerns

Special interest titles available in large print are:
The Little Oxford Dictionary
Music Book
Song Book
Hymn Book
Service Book

Also available from us courtesy of Oxford University Press:
Young Readers' Dictionary
(large print edition)
Young Readers' Thesaurus
(large print edition)

For further information or a free brochure, please contact us at:
Ulverscroft Large Print Books Ltd.,
The Green, Bradgate Road, Anstey,
Leicester, LE7 7FU, England.
Tel: (00 44) 0116 236 4325
Fax: (00 44) 0116 234 0205

DARK HARBOUR

David Hosp

August 2006. The body of a young woman is fished out of Boston harbour. The mutilations to the corpse bear the hallmarks of the killer they call Little Jack . . . The deceased, Natalie Caldwell, was a high-flying lawyer. Scott Finn, her colleague and ex-lover, inherits the high-profile assignment she was working on. The case involves a terrorist bombing. But as Finn uncovers information about Tannery vs Huron Security, he harbours a dark suspicion. Was Natalie the victim of a psychopath or did the case she was working on have a connection with her death? While the city of Boston is being terrorised by a deranged serial killer, Finn fears for his own survival.

THE REUNION

Sue Walker

Hearing Isabella Velasco's name on her answermachine makes Innes Haldane's blood run cold. It's a name from her past — a past she has tried hard to forget. For in 1977, a fifteen-year-old Innes spent a year in Edinburgh at the Unit, an experimental home for highly intelligent but dysfunctional teenagers. There her fellow patients had included shy Simon Calder, aggressive Alex Baxendale, rapist Danny Rintoul and the beautiful Isabella Velasco. Now, nearly three decades later, Isabella is trying to make contact again. But Innes never finds out why. For only days later she reads a newspaper account of Isabella's suicide. Innes's shock quickly turns to fear when she hears that Danny, too, recently committed suicide. Has some dark event, buried deep in 1977, come back to haunt them all?

KEEP ME ALIVE

Natasha Cooper

Why did investigative journalist Jamie Maxden die? The coroner says it was suicide. Jamie's family agree. The case is closed. Only one man fights to re-open it. Will Applewood is sure Jamie was about to expose a scandal that would shame the British food industry. But Will is notorious for his conspiracy theories. No one listens to him. In despair he turns to his barrister, Trish Maguire, who agrees to help. Will's campaign takes Trish deep into the countryside, revealing a world that seems quite different from the metropolitan life she knows. But cruelty and intimidation can flourish in the ravishing landscape just as they do in the grimmest of inner-city housing estates.

WHEN THE DEAD CRY OUT

Hilary Bonner

One summer's day, twenty-eight years ago, Clara Marshall vanished without trace. A few days later, her two young children also disappeared. Richard Marshall, Clara's heartbroken husband, claimed she had run away with an Australian backpacker, taking the children with her. John Kelly, veteran journalist, covered the case when he was a trainee reporter and he suspected something far more sinister. Police inquiries discovered nothing, and Detective Superintendent Karen Meadows is only too aware that many suspect Marshall of murdering his family. Then extraordinary events reawaken the case and Kelly and Karen become determined to discover what happened to Clara and her children so long ago . . .

THE LONELY DEAD

Michael Marshall

A guilty man walks alone into the cold mountain forests of Washington State, aiming never to return. What he finds there starts a chain of events that will quickly spiral out of control. Meanwhile, in Los Angeles, a woman's body is discovered, sitting bolt upright in a motel bedroom. She is dead, and her killer has left his mark. It soon becomes clear he has something to say, and a lot more work to do. And Ward Hopkins, an ex-CIA agent recovering from the recent shocking death of his parents, is on the trail of his past, tracking down the men who destroyed everything he once held dear, and the murderer whose face he sees every time he looks in the mirror.